PR
FIRE AL

"O
in

"M
bel
the

"Robert Moss is an accomplished
knows how to lay down a firm foundation of fact."
—*Raleigh News & Observer*

"The author of several excellent modern-day thrillers
has turned to pre-revolutionary war America and the
results are wonderful."

—*Rocky Mountain News*

Robert Moss

FIRE
ALONG
THE SKY

Revised and Expanded Edition
containing the newly discovered
love letters of Valerie D'Arcy,
complete and unexpurgated.

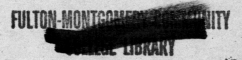

A TOM DOHERTY ASSOCIATES BOOK
NEW YORK

This is a work of historical fiction. Any resemblance to living persons or contemporary events is coincidental.

FIRE ALONG THE SKY

Copyright © 1990; 1995 by Robert Moss

All rights reserved, including the right to reproduce this book, or portions thereof, in any form

Cover art by Larry Selman

A Forge book
Published by Tom Doherty Associates, Inc.
175 Fifth Avenue
New York, N.Y. 10010

Forge® is a registered trademark of Tom Doherty Associates, Inc.

ISBN: 0-812-53536-7

New Forge edition: July 1995

Printed in the United States of America

0 9 8 7 6 5 4 3 2 1

To my beloved wife and daughters,
Our magical friend Wanda,
The memory of my father, a soldier for peace,
And of my mother, who shared
in the dreaming.

I go to my home in the heart of women.

—Iosa, in Fiona Macleod's *The Last Supper*

The heart of woman is deeper than the deepest sea
in the world.

—Breton proverb

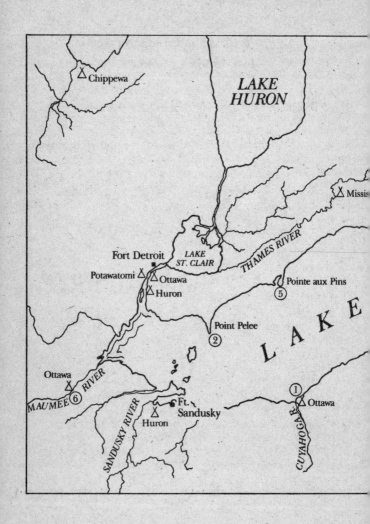

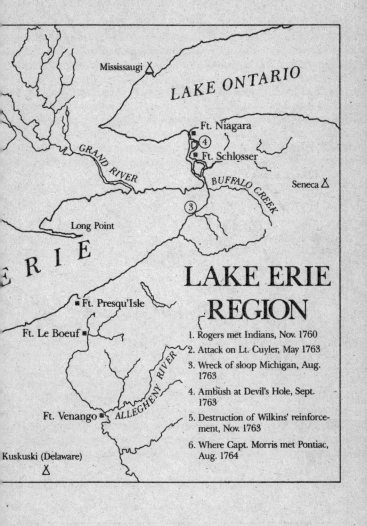

Mississaugi ⚔

LAKE ONTARIO

■ Ft. Niagara
④
● Ft. Schlosser

GRAND RIVER

BUFFALO CREEK

Seneca ⚔

③

Long Point

E R I E

■ Ft. Presqu'Isle

Ft. Le Boeuf ■

ALLEGHENY RIVER

LAKE ERIE REGION

1. Rogers met Indians, Nov. 1760

2. Attack on Lt. Cuyler, May 1763

3. Wreck of sloop Michigan, Aug. 1763

4. Ambush at Devil's Hole, Sept. 1763

5. Destruction of Wilkins' reinforcement, Nov. 1763

6. Where Capt. Morris met Pontiac, Aug. 1764

Ft. Venango ■

Kuskuski (Delaware)
⚔

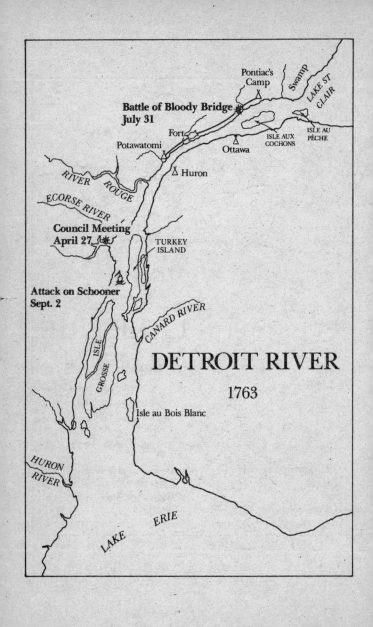

Pontiac's Camp

Swamp

LAKE ST CLAIR

Battle of Bloody Bridge July 31

Fort

ISLE AU PÊCHE

Potawatomi

Ottawa

ISLE AUX COCHONS

△ Huron

RIVER ROUGE

ECORSE RIVER

Council Meeting April 27

TURKEY ISLAND

Attack on Schooner Sept. 2

CANARD RIVER

ISLE

GROSSE

DETROIT RIVER

1763

Isle au Bois Blanc

HURON RIVER

ERIE

LAKE

Contents

Colonel V.H.S. Hardacre
c/o The British Legation
Lisbon, Portugal

Dearest Shane,

I dream you as the leopard. Last night you came to
me in his skin. You frightened me, pressing against my
face. I would have cried out, but for fear of waking Sir
Henry, who is a brute when he is denied his eight-
hour kip.

I knew you by the eyes.

I sat bolt upright, my heart in my throat. You put
your paws on the edge of the bed. I held them to my
lips and kissed them. They were soft as a baby's
hands.

This night vision was entirely real. As I write this, I
feel the places in my body you praised and fed.

I cannot undress in front of Sir Henry tonight, even
if he begs me to do it, because I have bite marks
around the tips of my breasts I cannot explain, and a
spectacular bruise, ovoid and empurpled as an egg-
plant, blooms on my inner thigh.

Do you remember all this?

Do you come to me by night and toy with me fully
sensate, as you were on our last day at Cap Ferrat?

Can you cause a leopard, Shane?

I know the answer because I have been reading your
book. There is much you have tried to conceal. You
write that you lived with native sorcerers in the forests of North America, and witnessed their rituals.
But you grow coy when it comes to sharing their secrets, which is not the case when you choose to indulge

a memory of the bedroom. You say the soul of Indians is more independent of their bodies than ours is, and that their magicians go abroad by night in the shapes of birds and animals. Then you hasten to deny any knowledge of specifics.

I am not deceived.

Who else among your ladies knows you as a shape-shifter?

Did you howl at the moon with your wolf-woman of the Mohawk?

Did you romp like a red setter with Peg Walsingham? (I fancy Peg would have shown the door to any creature more exotic, God love her.)

Do you do this to torment me, or to console me for your absence?

The smell lingers still, rank and feral, about the bedclothes. Sir Henry wished to know if one of our Siamese cats had got in and disgraced himself.

I believe the leopard is truly your familiar. He is quick and sensual and utterly insatiable, a predator who takes more than he can devour.

Write soon. Tell me your dreams.

Ever your

Valerie

Lady Valerie D'Arcy
79 Eaton Square
London

Dearest Valerie,

The natives of America say what happens in dreams
is real, as real as anything in our waking lives and
sometimes more so.

I am delighted to learn that I am able to pleasure
you on four legs as well as two, even when our bodies are separated by salt water. Alas, I have no recollection of my dreams on the night you saw the leopard, so
I can neither confirm nor deny your suspicions about
my mode of nocturnal travel.

Perhaps you will choose to experiment for yourself.
You would love it here. From my stone balustrade, I
look down over mossy paths, winding down the hillside between fountains and tiny waterfalls. Beyond
the broken parapets of the Moorish castle, the sea is
very green today. The olive oil man is laboring up the
hill under his umbrella, bearing a great tin that has
been hammered into the shape of a codfish. Behind
him comes a woman in black, with a pannier of curdled
milk on her head.

If you cannot escape Sir Henry this summer, join
me in your dreams. We will lie among the ferns,
under the glory of the magnolias, and make love to the
rhythms of lapping water.

In this green oasis, my memories of the Indians
and of Sir William Johnson's lost kingdom are
dreams of another man's life. I hardly know this
stranger. Yet I re-enter his world at night, in dreams

from which I struggle to break free like a diver
snagged in a morass of seaweed and strangling vines.
Then I am driven back to my work-table to write by
candle until the dawn breaks and I stumble out red-
eyed to splash about in the pond with the dogs.
There is something that goads me on.

Will I be understood, on either side of the ocean-sea?

I trust only you to tell me the truth. Shall I publish
my book? Tell me only what is in your heart.

Your devoted

Shane

1

The Wager

HAZARD RULES OUR LIVES, or so it has seemed to me. Does the philosopher, sulky and parched from demanding whys and wherefores from Plato and Plotinus, command more of destiny than a common gamester who rides carelessly on a die-roll into the unknown? Are the virtuous, the provident, the industrious, better rewarded than a bold young rake with a well-turned leg who rushes fortune like a dairymaid in a hayloft? Does any plan of life compare with the accident of birth? Is any quality more enviable than luck? When I was rising to manhood, when I bucked like a wild colt among the ladies of Dublin and London, I thought the only men worth knowing were gamesters at heart. I was ready to lay a bet on anything—on the fate of a battle in Germany or the ricochet of a billiard ball, on a cockfight or the color of the vicar's urine, on the longevity of a virgin's maidenhead or the progress of two flies crawling up a windowpane in the smoky games room at White's. In short, I shared the general distemper of my age. Gaming was the ruling passion in our society, and the greatest leveler. The rattle of a dice-

box or the flutter of a deck of cards was a wonderful sol-
vent for snobbery. I have seen a duke sit down to loo with
his footman, and a marchioness to picquet with a two-
guinea doxy from Moll King's bawdy-house. The card
table—and a gathering reputation for staying power that I
labored manfully to earn—assisted my entry into the beds
of more ladies of fashion than it would be prudent to recall
by name. I am generally pretty lucky, even at long odds.
But fortune turned against me with a vengeance soon after
the accession of our new King George, the third of our
German dumplings, and on a dank, drizzly day in London
in the spring of 1761, I was misfortunate enough to accept
a wager that brought all the Furies beating on my head.
The nature of this bet was extraordinary, even among a set
that was voracious for novelty. I laid money on whether a
man would take his own life.

As a result of this wager, I was soon obliged to abandon
all my hopes of an easy life in England and of glory on the
London stage. My fortunes became inextricably entwined
with those of the madman who was the subject of my bet.
Sir Robert Davers had flashes of pure genius, but he was
dangerous to know. He carried an abyss inside him; his
most brilliant insights sucked away reason, as through a
funnel into the Void. Yet, in the sudden wreckage of my
prospects in England, I was mad enough to accept his proposal to cross the seas in a tub like a floating coffin, to try
my luck in the American colonies. I was plunged into the
nightmare of an Indian revolt. I survived to see things I
had never hoped to see in this lifetime. I saw living men
vivisected, flayed and roasted. I was invited to sup the
broth of white men's bones. I would have joined them in
the native cooking-pots, save for my luck with the ladies.
That has seldom failed me.

As a captive among the Indians and later as an agent for
the Indian Department, I came to know the general of the
native revolt as well, I believe, as any white man. His
name once loosened bowels in all our American settlements, and was dinned in street ballads at Covent Garden.
He shook the British Empire worse than any rebel until
George Washington and the Bostonians got up their mu-

tiny. He made a fair bid to drive the white colonists into
the sea and damn-near cost us the whole of America west
of the Alleghenies. Yet who, outside a few frontiersmen in
greasy buckskins, not given to quill-driving, knows anything of Pontiac the man? I knew Pontiac in various
guises—as a sadistic butcher; as a dream-hunter at home
with the unseen; as a military strategist, cool as any mar-
shal of France; as a betrayed, dispossessed wanderer,
crazed and wretched as Lear. I wrote a play about him in
an effort to show the public his true colors. But they
would not touch my script at Drury Lane, or even at
Smock Alley. Garrick told me my depiction was "muddy"
and "insufficiently noble." According to that great ham,
playgoers will only tolerate a principal who is all hero or
all villain—as if there is anyone outside a stage who fits
such a bill. I told Garrick he might keep his opinions and
his ignorance of men.

I am now resolved to suspend my hopes of a stage pro-
duction and to tell my story just as it happened, starting
with that dank day in April when I took a chance on a man
committing self-murder.

I was staying with Peg Walsingham, on the same side of
Leicester Fields as Sir Joshua Reynolds, and there were a
dozen men of sufficient taste to hate me for it. Peg, I suppose, was the wrong side of forty; her glory days on the
stage were behind her. She would sow no more heartache
as the dying Cordelia in teasing disarray. The bucks of my
generation—the sons or younger brothers of the rakes who
beat down the green room door to get at Peg—now flung
their bouquets at Jane Pope, a pert little soubrette twenty
years her inferior. Peg did not smoke herself in nostalgia.
She was grateful for what she was born with—a mind as
quick as a cat on a grounded bird, a red-gold mane that
smelled like burned toast in sunlight, a body that was lithe
and brimming, shaped for the ruin of the ruder sex and
that astonishing, irresistible voice that could whip up the
gentry of the pit into hot frenzy or plunge them down into
white-lipped, trembling despair. She was thankful to London, for all it had given her. When you heard the purity of

her diction or saw her whisked along the Strand in her se-
dan chair between liveried footmen, grand as any duchess,
it was hard to believe she was born and reared in Dublin,
a flower-seller's daughter. I think Peg was also grateful to
me. To a boy of nineteen, as I was then, the wonderful
thing about the love of an older woman is that she gives
you a better education than any university and she thanks
you for it.

Peg was up before noon though we had flourished until
dawn after the masked ball at the Mansion House. The
drab, soggy day, or the prodigious quantities of champagne
and claret we had imbibed the night before, had worked on
her spirits. I tunneled under the covers, but she banged
around so brutally with the tea-equipage that I was forced
to acknowledge the day.

When she saw me wiping the sleep from my eyes, Peg
declared, as brisk as if we had breakfasted on her theme,
"You'll leave me when you've used me up. You'll see me
going to tea with the ladies, fat and sedate as a parson's
widow when you are prancing by in a fancy rig, and your
smart young bride will say, 'Who's that old woman? Do
you know her?' And your eyes will be bright and vacant
as mica, or you'll say, 'That *used* to be Peg Walsingham.
Can you believe men used to buy her champagne?' "

"What abject nonsense!" I was flat on my back like the
king of hearts, in the purple taffeta housecoat she had sent
for from Jermyn Street. "You'll bury me first!"

"Liar!"

She leaned over me, enclosing me in the curtain of her
tawny hair. She smelled of orange-flower water and cinna-
mon toast.

"Liar!" she repeated. "I'll buy you your wedding suit."

She reached to replace her cup on the tea-tray and wriggled her admirable rump closer to me on the wrinkled bedclothes.

"Only if you come on the honeymoon."

This coaxed an evanescent smile. It barely stirred her
features, but it glowed for a moment, behind her skin.

"Liar! I shall order the suit from Maxwell's. You can't

be trusted at a tailor without a woman's guidance. You'll come out looking as if you've been in a sheep dip."

"I don't know any women but you, and you are married already."

"Shameless deceiver! You can't keep your breeches buttoned! I saw you looking at that trollop last night—the one with her chest sticking out like a Christmas goose. You know who I mean. Don't give me sheep's eyes, Shane Hardacre! You'll move on, and on, and on. You'll marry for money when you grow up. Gaius and I will be your counselors. He'll tell you what they're worth, and I'll tell you what they're thinking. Don't you think we would make the most remarkable *entremetteurs*? Perhaps we could advertise."

"My love—"

"I'm not feeling sorry for myself! Don't flatter yourself on that account! It's the one you will marry that is to be pitied. There's no stable door that will hold you. There's the devil in you, Shane Hardacre, red-eyed and poky as a jackrabbit."

> "Sure 'tis the wimmin is worse than the men,
> They was dragged down to hell and was thrown
> out again—"

The old tavern song just bubbled up, like toddy stirred by a hot poker.

Peg snatched a fistful of my hair, which hung loose across my shoulders, and gave it a wrench that made me yelp. Then she softened and drew my drowsy face up to her bosom. The creamy tops of her breasts swelled above her shift. A roguish ringlet vanished into the cleft. I liked her best like this, without artifice, before she was patched and powdered and rouged, the fullness of hips and breasts springing free from hoops and stays.

"Good heavens!" she exclaimed, diverted by a white gleam in the pier glass between the windows that gave onto the balcony. "What am I thinking of! I have no face!"

"You are quite perfect." I kissed her mouth and hung greedily on her lower lip, swollen as if a bee had stung it.

Boldly, I slipped my hand between her knees and slid it upwards, canting back the yellow silk of her shift. She twisted her thighs to refuse me, but when I pouted she laughed and tugged at the sash of my robe. She found me ready for her. She ran her tongue from the root to the hard knob of my sex and indulged me with a thousand little caresses. The yellow silk fluttered away like a blown petal. She mounted her thighs about my hips, taking and giving with the same motions. She floated high above me, chafing the subtle mound inside the mouth of her mysteries. Then slowly, deliberately, she impaled herself, like a dreaming witch on her broomstick. In children's stories, witches treat broomhandles more decorously, but this is not a tale for children. Slowly, slowly, with long, inverted strokes, pestle over mortar, her ripe breasts brushing my face, lover and nurturer. Higher and deeper, into the rich loam. Ravening, feeding. The blood-tides, shining under her skin. The red-yellow bird, beating wings of smoke that burst from above her heart; I could not see it with my eyes open. The scream that carried the lungs and belly with it when she flew above me and set neighbors' dogs yapping and made the milk-seller's dray bolt for Covent Garden. The patter of rain on the tiles. The tears, gleaming like rain on her white skin.

"Bastard. Three words, and you could not find them."

What imp had possessed her?

I said sulkily, "I suppose you wish me to say that I love you."

Her lip trembled. I thought she might hit me.

She spoke very slowly, holding down the pain and anger. "I want you to tell me I am beautiful."

"You are more than that."

"I want you to tell me I'll never be old and ugly."

"Mrs Walsingham, you are immortal."

"You are a child, Shane. A saucy child with a dirty big truncheon. If you weren't excessively pretty, I shouldn't put up with you for an instant! You're almost too pretty for a boy. That's why Gaius likes you. You know Gaius fancies you, don't you?"

"Mmmmph." Our romp had brought on a delicious leth-

argy. I had no desire to talk about Peg's exquisitely dec-
adent husband or to hear any more of her lecture.

She ran her index finger from the roots of my hair to the
hollow of my chin.

"Not a wrinkle, damn you. You'll grow up soon enough,
and then you'll leave me. I won't try to hold you, *chéri.*
I can't abide women who cling. As if we can ever possess
another human soul! But I won't let you leave too easily."

She bit the side of my neck, just deep enough to leave
her brand. She sighed, and covered her limbs with a rose
quilted wrapping gown. Why in blazes was she rattling on
about youth and age and bittersweet regrets? Surely she
was not still angry because I had strutted a cotillion with
a languid slut whose décolletage was a masterwork of sus-
pension engineering. It occurred to me that one of the servants might have tattled about my taking a hasty gallop
with the Reynolds's new parlor maid, a frisky little filly
from Aberdeen. But it was unlike Peg to be jealous, and
beneath her dignity to show it. I don't believe she cared
two pins what pranks I played with domestics, or with the
bouncing betsies along the Strand or in Vauxhall Gardens,
so long as I did not shame her or bring home the clap—or
develop any serious attachment. From her long study of
my sex, Peg had formed the settled opinion that a man will
make love to the hind end of a mule and that a wise
woman makes room for the tendency. Of the pair of us, *I*
was the one who tended to get prickly when Peg spent an
hour or two with an old beau—even over tea and cucumber sandwiches at her sister's—even when the admirer in
question was a sober-shanked old fart, bald as a pumpkin
under his bagwig, who was something high up in a bank
and droned on about shares and bubbles.

Perhaps it was merely the damp of London worming
into the marrow. Perhaps she had detected the mark of an
enemy in the glass, the unwanted trace of a crow's foot at
the corner of one of those dazzling eyes. Who knows the
heart of a woman?

I watched her stealthily from under my lashes as she set
to work with a brush and a battery of paints and powders.
She tied a white cloth around her neck, like a trancherman

warming to his work in an oyster house. She dabbed wistfully at the blue-gray shadows below her eyes. The eyes were very green today, under the dark wings of her lashes. She tilted her head back and made a round O with her mouth. She ran her thumbs under her lower jaw, pushing back the loose flesh that threatened the start of a double chin.

I loved her little imperfections as much as she resented them. They fed my vanity. I was selfish and unformed. I had always been spoiled by women, starting with my mother and my sister Susannah, who first showed me what is under a girl's skirts. I expected to be adored. In a stupid way, the physical reminders of the life that Peg had used up—of her experience and her *need*—reassured me that in our partnership, I was the one who would be constantly pampered and indulged. I suppose you find this objectionable, even repugnant. What's that? Morals of a whore? Come now, I was not Peg's gigolo, at least, not entirely. I had a hundred a year of my own which my father sent me to keep me out of Ireland, since I had rogered the Earl of Eastmeath's daughter Mirabel and run off with her to be married by a couples beggar at a furtive ceremony among the ruins of Monasterboice—an episode I had never confided to Peg. Of course, a hundred a year would barely support my habits for a month in London's fashionable society. I allow that I was a half-kept man, but I gave value for my privileges. You say I should be ashamed of myself? That is uncivil. I was nineteen. I had no more idea of who I was than of heaven and hell.

I spied on Peg as she glued a patch to the rise of her cheekbone and a second near the corner of her mouth. She was very near perfect, even at forty. The little marks of weathering did not diminish her beauty; they made it less daunting. Flawless beauty in a woman makes a sensitive man uneasy and spawns terrors in a jealous one. Women can be trapped by beauty of this sort, as Midas starved among all his gold. They are reduced to surfaces, and presumed to have no more inner life than an Attic sculpture. The most beautiful women I know—apart from Peg—are the property of consummate boors or of hairless old men with more in their pocket than between their legs. They invite the jealousy of Venus, they suffer the ordeals of Psyche whom the goddess compelled to fetch black water from a place of terror at the source of the River Styx, before they are allowed happiness on this earth.

Peg called to me to bestir myself. She expected her hairdresser at any moment. Then she was to call on Mr Beard to discuss a new musical for the Covent Garden Theater. She would take tea with her sister, in South Audley Street.

She gave me a worried look. Her eyebrows made very nearly a straight line. She did not tell me then that her unease came from an obscure presentiment of disaster, that she had roused with a start from a dream imbued with a kind of fatality, one of those dark visions, both fantastic and intensely real, from which the waking mind flinches. She had seen me lost in a thorny wood, trying to bull a passage between spectral trees that wept tears of black blood as I broke their twigs, but would not set me free. She had called to guide me, but I was deaf to her cries. She did not tell me that her foreboding was not for herself, but for me. Had she been more open, no doubt I would have blamed her nightmare on the food at Bedford's. In any event, I think it was beyond her power to alter what came to pass; the dice were already in play.

"Don't forget you are dining with Gaius tonight," she told me. "Wear your new silk. It agrees with your coloring." She fussed about my warm cloak and the need to take a coach, because of the rawness of the season.

"I always do what I'm told."

"Liar!"

It was love of the stage that had brought Peg and me together: that, and the sense that we were exiles even in our native country.

I first opened my lungs to demand liquid refreshment not ten leagues from the storied hill of Tara, in a green valley of Meath. My father traced his bloodline back to the high kings of Ulster, but my mother never permitted any of us to refer to ourselves as Irishmen at home. She reminded us daily that we were English, foaled by happen-

stance on the wrong side of the Irish sea. Home was
somewhere else.

Her insistence that nobody connected with our family
could conceivably be Irish was a puzzle for my father. He
had never set foot in England. The only English blood he
could sniff out in his own pedigree was contributed by a
rough bog-trooper in the reign of Elizabeth of England
who flourished my father's great-great-something without
asking the lady's consent and abstracted himself without
asking her name. My father was raised plain Jimmy
MacShane, and *his* father was Irishman enough to fight for
the last of our Catholic kings in the bloody meadow beside
the River Boyne.

I never blamed my father for denying the ditch where he
was digged. The worst that can be said of him is, he was
no braver than the next man. I have read in the London
magazines, in the accounts of Mr Arthur Young and other
recent English tourists, that the severity of the Penal Laws
has been relaxed of late in Ireland and that an Irishman no
longer faces destitution or violent death for affirming his
racial identity or the faith of his forefathers. It may be that
the loss of our American plantations has taught His Majesty that colonists require temperate handling. But in the
early part of our century, when Jimmy MacShane met
Frances Dempster, conditions were sterner.

They were an improbable match. My mother's relations
in the Home Counties dispose of a minor peerage and a
pocket borough in the Tory interest. My father, after the
confiscation of his family estates, was little better than a
vagabond. Under the laws of Ireland, so long as he remained a papist, he could not own the land under his feet,
or a pair of dueling pistols, or a horse worth above five
guineas. He was unemployable in his native county. His
only recourse was to abandon his home—to go for a
sailor, to join the Wild Geese, or emigrate to the colonies—or else to repair his fortunes by interbreeding with
the new owners of Ireland, or at least their sub-agents.
This would require him to forswear his identity.

I decline to sit in judgement on the choice he made.
Under the same circumstances, I would no doubt have

made the same choice with less hesitation. I have never had difficulty changing my disguises, out of necessity, or for pure sport. I believe a man ought to make it his business to cram several lives into a single span. I have heard many accounts of heaven and hell, and stranger reports from savages who are as conversant with the invisible planes as are you and I, dear reader, with an alehouse or a bawdy-house. But I shall continue to try my luck with what I can see and touch, with what I can get my teeth into, or my leg over. It may be that delectable houris or the smelly pit await me in the great beyond, but I shall go on—while God give me breath—squeezing every last modicum of pleasure from the life I have for certain sure, and in that cause, I shall not hesitate to change my role as often as it suits me, or entertains the ladies.

My father, however, nourished all manner of scruples and was seized, after two or three bottles, with the trembling fear that, in changing his religion, he had consigned his soul to hell-fire. Thus he was never happy. But I suspect he could never have been happy—as Irishman or pretend-Englishman—in the society he knew. Only a cheerful villain could be happy in the Ireland of those times, and my father was ever a reluctant scoundrel. For all the rum-shrub he tossed down his gullet, he could never drown out the ghost of his conscience. He could never forgive himself for being a sold man, though Lord knows there are many who have sold themselves for less.

In brief, my father entered into a business arrangement to relieve the difficulties of the prosperous family of a lady in distress. Frances Dempster was already past her prime, and she was never a great beauty. Those who were kindly disposed called her homely, or horsy. It was no doubt out of quiet desperation that she lay with a Dublin attorney, notorious as a blazer and a womanizer. This decayed rake may have promised her marriage, but I am inclined to doubt it. The man was married already to a lady of fashion who graced the Lord Lieutenant's arm, patched and rouged, with a diamond aigrette in her hair, at Castle balls. No, I believe my mother had simply reached the point where she could no longer contain the roiling passions

compressed within her without forfeiting either health or
sanity. In her matter-of-fact, wholly English way, she dealt
with the situation by presenting her maidenhead to the
most notorious seducer in the small world of the Pale.

This dalliance brought the predictable reward. When her
belly began to swell under her hooped petticoats, her out-
raged family resolved to buy her a husband. My father was
available. The incentives were a dowry, relief from the
bailiffs, the prospect of secure employment as estate manager for my mother's absentee cousins at the Manor of
Waryne and a place among that privileged, rootless gentry,
unique in our age, that clover-boys call West Britons. Thus
my father agreed to drink to the damnation of the Pope
and to celebrate his nuptials in the bosom of the Established Church, which he had formerly described as a public convenience, devised by Henry VIII to solemnize his
leg-over operations. There remained the question of the
family name.

A Dempster could not be demoted to a MacShane. My
father's name was as sooty as a peat fire, though his people heard in its rough syllables the skirl of the way pipes
of their ancient kinsmen, the O'Neills of Tyrone.

An imp of defiance led my father to announce that he
would change his name to Hardacre, the only English
name in his bloodstock, and the one name his people had
always tried to forget, since it belonged to that rude bog-
trooper who ravished one of our women.

The Dempsters sniffed. They did not find the smell of
potatoes, blackened by the fire. But Hardacre was a common, cloddish name, nonetheless. Why not Hardcastle? Or
Johnson, in honor of my father's kinsmen at Smithstown,
who had also turned Englishmen and were connected by
marriage to the illustrious Sir Peter Warren, the victor of
Louisbourg?

Jimmy MacShane held his ground. He would be Jimmy
Hardacre, or he would keep the name he was born with,
and if it did not smell sweet enough to the Dempsters, then
let his tarnished fiancée go hang. He got his way.

After I was delivered—weighing above nine pounds and
raging for a drink—my mother dressed up the rough cog-

nomen by having me christened Vivian, one of those ambiguous, feathery names much in vogue among our debutantes' delights. Vivian sat on Hardacre like a macaroni wig atop a charcoal burner. My father never called me Vivian. He called me Shane. In the shut-up times, when icicles formed inside the windows of the gray stone house at Waryne, he told me stories of Shane O'Neill, the Beast of Ireland, who paid court to Elizabeth of England by marching through her court with his banners flying and his red hair streaming off his shoulders, raising a war cry that carried the heart and the belly with it, until he hurled himself full-length on the flags before her feet.

For as long as I can remember, I wished to be an actor. As a boy, I made a collection of hats. In my father's old beaver, with the brim turned down and a goosefeather stuck in the crown, I was Raleigh, trouncing the Spaniards on a bright blue sea, or Roland spurring to battle against the Moors. In a farrier's leather cap, I was Con-Edda on his hero's quest for the black stallion and the golden apples of the fairy kingdom under the shadowed waters of Lough Erne. In a woolly nightcap, I was dark Othello declaiming love, or Caliban plotting slave revolt. I conscripted the tenants' children to play supporting roles in my productions. But my most lively characters came to me when I was alone, and they came, not from the pages of storybooks, or from Shakespeare, but from wayward fancy. These characters, plucked from the air, inhabited me so fully that, for days at a stretch, I spoke in their accents and walked after their fashion. They traveled with me on my long walks over the meadows and down narrow lanes walled with blackthorn, to the turrets of the nearby Manor of Killeen. They sat with me at the dinner-table and at lessons with Mr Horsfall, my tutor, until my mother waxed fierce and shrill and Mr Horsfall took up his switch and Maureen, the cook, started crossing herself and babbling about Devil's work. There was a pattern to this nonsense. When one of my favorites became too vehement, or too preachy, and began to weary me, together with the rest of the household, the hat that infallibly summoned his presence would

be mysteriously mislaid for a time, while I assumed the
manners of a new-born character. After an interval, I
would retrieve the missing hat, and the banished favorite
would stage a revival, livelier than before. I thought the
lines that frothed from my lips when I played these games
were more fun than any blank verse, and started inscribing
them in a book. I conceived that my vocation was to be
not only a player, but a maker of plays and resolved never
to rest content with a prosy life.

My father was more tolerant of these conceits than my
mother, no doubt because he had accepted a life of play-
acting. On the sabbath, he sat in our family pew, with the
high-backed seats, and the satin cushions, playing at country squire. He would nod off during the sermons, wake
with a start and peer about to see if any of our tenants
were in the same state. If his eye fell on a man who was
dozing, or gossiping, he would stand up and rebuke him
by name in front of the minister. "You there! Patrick
Nolan! Eyes front!" I do not think the tenants held it
against him. He was a fair man to those who belonged on
the estate. But he had little charity for anyone else. He affected not to see the tribes of starving beggars, hollow and
ragged as scarecrows, who spilled out into our lanes in
early summer when the cotters had eaten the last of their
potatoes. I have seen him whip up the horses at the first
glimpse of those ashen, sunless faces and bowl them into
the ditch—even mothers with babes in arms—without the
acknowledgement of an oath or a backward look. His eye
slid away from the sooty burrows and birds' nests of mud
and thatch where the cotters huddled in hollows between
the stone walls of the great estates. I think he turned his
back on the misery of Ireland, not because he was heart-
less, but because he cared too much. He could no more
recognize things as they were, and carry on in his role as
a pretended English gentleman, than the play can go on
when the mob from the pit is allowed to take over the
stage. Instead, he devoted himself to the recreations of his
adopted class, the most irresponsible governing caste that
Europe—and, I warrant, the world—has ever seen. Each
season, he would vie with the neighboring gentry to be

first to carry up a shipment of fresh limes from Cork. Then Mick Dooley or Paddy Nolan would be sent off on a pacer to raise the cry of "Fresh fruit!" and every half-mounted gentleman within earshot would gather at our house to drench himself in rum-shrub until not one was left who could hold a seat. My father kept a pack of indifferent hounds and chased fox-tails—and sometimes a bush priest, which he vowed was better sport—over hedge and stile. He kept no books in his library save the King James Bible and the *Sportsman's Guide*. He knew twenty-seven rhyming toasts, not repeatable before ladies, and he knew how to knock the stem off a wine-glass so a guest has no chance of retiring from a drinking bout until his host, or his supply of claret, is exhausted. He doggedly aped the Tory Fox-Hunter in the *Spectator*. But there was scant merriment in his diversions and certainly little humor. He gnawed and worried and dragged at his pleasures as a beaver works on its dam. He for ever needed to satisfy himself that he had exacted a sufficient reward for a marriage as cozy as Mrs Wright's wax tableau of King Charles under the headsman's axe which gave me the shivers when I saw it in Chudleigh Court.

My father was no born actor. He could neither suspend his own disbelief in his role nor persuade others to believe him in it. Yet I must credit Jimmy Hardacre with one grand performance. He persuaded me to love him as a father, and I have never thought of any other man in that connection. Even in his black dog fits—when he went for me with a leather belt, or an oak staff, until I was big enough to vow to thrash him in return if he tried it again—he never mentioned the name of my mother's seducer. His forbearance was the more remarkable because, in appearance, we were polar opposites. My father was of less than middling height, stubby and thick, with crinkly black hair on his head and black, curling hairs on the back of his white, clumsy hands. By the age of fifteen, when I went down to Trinity, I stood better than a head taller with a quantity of fine-spun, chestnut hair and broad shoulders tapering to a narrow waist that has since been sacrificed in causes that lead, so Dante would have us believe, to the Third Circle of the Inferno.

"O'Neill hair!" my father once cried in his cups when one of my mother's English relations remarked on my coloring. My mother smiled and said distinctly, "It is plain to all eyes that my son was bred to higher things than a sheepfold." My mother used words on my father with the murderous precision of a witch sticking pins in a doll. She used me to needle his most vulnerable spot. If she had ever provoked him into raising a hand against her, or calling me another man's spawn, I believe she would have seized on that as the excuse to leave him and go to her Dempster cousins, which would have surely been best for both of them. But he turned his violence into other channels, including my backside, or let it boil inside until the heat in his brain dropped him like a dead man, and he never denied me my birthright, such as it was.

My mother bore him four more children. My brothers, Evelyn and Beverly, died in infancy, no doubt throttled by the names she had loaded on their necks. My sisters, Susannah—who gave me my first daylight view of what lies beneath a skirt—and Annabel, were hardier, like all the women of my family. I was always my father's favorite, even when my brothers were still of this world. I think the true reason was that my siblings were the issue of blind butting in the dark in a loveless bed, while my father believed, in his fuddled way, that somehow he had *chosen* me.

He taught me to ride, to knock down a fair dinner with a gun, to hold my liquor, and to recognize a shaved ball on a billiard table and a loaded die at hazard. These were more useful skills than I gleaned from my tutor who taught me enough Latin to allow me to puzzle out the naughty bits in Catullus and later, in Mr Gibbon's footnotes. My father's botched attempt to play-act a life taught me something more important yet, by negative example. We are hurled into this world like understudies summoned in the middle of a performance. We are nervous of forgetting our lines; we gabble them under our breath as we wait in the wings. Then we are thrust on stage and receive a greater shock. The play is not the one we prepared for. Worse, the sets and the characters change from one moment to the next, and the critics up in the gods are unfriendly; one false note and they shower us with bottles and sucked-out oranges. We are obliged to live off our wits, to improvise from one moment to the next, to exchange roles as the audience and the ever-changing cast demand. My father was never happy in the part he played. He did not invent it, and it was beyond his wit to change it. I resolved to do better. If I could not choose the play, I would at least choose the part—comic foil over tragic hero, since the hero rarely keeps the lady, or his own hide—and change as quick as the temper of the pit.

Gaius Walsingham maintained that our hearts become more refined as they become more corrupt. I doubt that this statement was original; very little about Peg's husband was that, including his first name. He loved to tell strangers that he had borrowed it from his hero, Gaius Caligula, whose bust commanded the place of honor in the bay window of his library at Twickenham with its back to the river. He was christened Guy Randolph Saint John, and his family had made more money shipping slaves to the sugar islands than he and Peg together had managed to spend. This was no doubt the principal reason she married him. I am not sure why Gaius married at all. He was not, as we say, the marrying kind. Perhaps it amused him to show her off, as it amused him to display portraits of himself by Reynolds and Pompeo Batoni, or his collection of pornographic engravings rescued, so he claimed, from the private hoard of a medieval pope. He may have looked on a beautiful wife as a Venus fly-trap, who would lure an unending procession of good-looking young men into his ambit. It is commonly believed that a man of his type takes a wife to disguise his true inclinations. I do not think that was true of Gaius. He made no secret of his preference and he delighted in shocking other people; he went to a ball at the Mansion House dressed as the Empress Maria Theresa. I suspect that he married Peg because he needed a friend and confessor to supply an element of constancy

in the gaudy flutter of his existence, and perhaps because—prior to that evening—Peg was one person he had
never managed to shock. Whatever the origins of the marriage, the Walsinghams had not shared the same house for
years, and they had not shared the same bed since the day
they came home from their honeymoon in Venice where I
picture them making eyes at the same hairy boatman.

Gaius claimed to know everyone worth knowing in
London. He had undertaken to introduce me to the "right
people." No doubt he had his reasons for patronizing his
wife's lover, as Peg made out. But he had made no advances that would have embarrassed both of us, apart from
a silly episode when he had drunk too deep at the Beefsteak. I made full use of his hospitality, because he had a
wicked sense of humor, and because, in his company,
doors rolled smoothly open that would have been reso-
lutely barred against an Irish interloper.

The rain abated in the late afternoon. The lamp-lighters
were out as I strolled down Piccadilly towards White's;
my shadow walked for half a block behind me. The house
fronts were dark, but from under a sky like fine ash, red
fire licked at my face, so fierce that it hurt my eyes. Its reflection bloodied standing water in puddles and gutters and
brought strangeness into that familiar thoroughfare. I was
glad to round the corner onto St James's Street, and mount
the steps to Gaius's nest of Old Etonians.

Gaius was at his ease in the smoking room, resplendent
in a suit of champagne silk, in the Italian mode, with a
rose-colored waistcoat. He was dosing himself with a mixture of port wine and brandy which he swore by as a sovereign remedy for dyspepsia. He gave me his hand.

"You look well, Gaius."

"My dear, if it were so! One pays for one's pleasures."

Gaius looked as he always did, of indeterminate age and
identity. His skin was completely smooth, without wrinkle
or blemish. His features were soft and malleable. Though
he must have been close on fifty, his face had not been
molded into a definite character. There was something
husklike about it.

I knew some of Gaius's friends—a literary bishop, a

young nobleman with a Guards commission, a retired admiral whose stories were as salty as ammonia. The talk was mostly of politics—of the progress of our war with France and the chances of a peace treaty, a subject that divided every parlor in London. Ordinary people had had enough of it. Wars are damnably expensive; each day brought reports of new taxes. The merchants and manufacturers wanted to return to business as normal. But Pitt, the greatest statesman called up by the war, had blood in his eye. He wanted to go on banging the frogs until they gave up Guadeloupe and Martinique as well as their North American possessions and hang the cost. However, Pitt's star was falling. Our new King George's Tory favorites, headed by his mother's Scottish lover, Lord Bute, had no enthusiasm for a war from which they could expect neither glory nor personal enrichment. Gaius's friends were generally in sympathy with the war-party, but mainly because they hated the Scots and sniffed at the favorite and his crowd as ignorant loblollies.

You might say that I had a personal interest in this war since one of my father's Smithstown relations, William Johnson, had gone out to the American colonies and made a great name for himself leading parties of Mohawk Indians against the French. Romantic legends had sprung up around Johnson. He was said to rule the Indians as a tribal king and to keep a seraglio of dusky beauties worthy of the Great Turk. But Sir William Johnson had done nothing for us, and my ambitions did not run to leaping about behind trees in smelly buckskin in places that fell into the blanks on our maps, and still less to marching up and down in a scarlet coat and a powdered wig to be potted like a woodcock by skulking savages. So I paid only desultory attention to the clubmen's talk of grand strategy. Gaius made one remark that stuck in my mind. If it was not original, then at least it betrayed applied intelligence of no mean order; it might have served George III better than the collective wisdom of two generations of his ministers.

"The conditions for peace are obvious to me," said Gaius, "even if they are a mystery to the government. We ought to return Canada to King Louis. In exchange, we

will take Martinique and Guadeloupe. What is a thousand
miles of snow and ice compared to sugar? Let the frenchies keep their bears and wolves—on two legs or four—
while we take the rum! We will promote trade while
averting intestine conflicts. We need to retain the French
in Canada to keep the colonists in their place. Remove the
French—and their scalping parties—from North America
and it will not be long before the damned colonists imagine they have no use for English soldiers or English
government."

There were snickers of derision at the notion that colonial plowboys and raw frontiersmen could ever present a
challenge to the most powerful empire on earth. But the
admiral agreed that the American colonists were an inso-
lent, unruly lot, not easily governed.

Gaius's attention was deflected by the arrival of a fash-
ionably dressed man in dove-gray. His eyes were as sharp
and quick as a magpie's, looking over a new-turned field.

"Ah, the sage of Strawberry Hill! Come, Shane, here is
your chance to make an impression on our literary lion.
You will forgive us, gentlemen. I owe some service to my
protégé."

Gaius took my arm and whispered, "You know all about
Horace Walpole. He is out of favor at court, but he knows
almost as many people as I do, and his name is still a tal-
isman with booksellers and editors. He'll get you published in the right places if he takes a liking to you."

Gaius gave Walpole a little bow.

"D'you know Mr Hardacre, my wife's lover?"

Walpole received this with aplomb; he was evidently
used to Gaius's eccentricities.

"My compliments, sir," he said to me. "It is far too long
since I had the pleasure of watching the divine Mrs
Walsingham perform. Do I take it you are also connected
with the theater?"

"I hope to be." I told Walpole I had had some modest
success at Smock Alley with a farce about an Irishman
who apes the manners of an English grandee. I did not
think it necessary to tell him that the play's run ended with
a riot on opening night.

"It is my observation that a novice writer begins with autobiography or pornography. With what he knows, or burns to know." Walpole expressed sympathy that I had had no success in bringing my comedy to the London stage, despite Peg's efforts on my behalf. "You must send me your play, if my amateur opinions would be of use to you."

"I would be honored."

"You'll take a bottle with us, Horace." Gaius had already hailed a waiter, and taken possession of a table with a view to the games room.

"I'm expecting a guest."

"Then you'll take two bottles. Do we know him?"

"Oh, I hardly think so." For a moment, Walpole seemed quite embarrassed. "He's only a boy," his eye fell on me, "in a manner of speaking. It's a deuced difficult business."

Gaius put on his hungry look.

There was a great deal of noise coming from the games room. One of the men at the billiard table landed a pair of jennies, tipped back his head and let out a harsh whinnying laugh, *heynheynheyn.*

"That man!" Walpole moaned, and sat down on the chair Gaius had pulled out for him. The waiter came with a bottle of claret, and—perhaps to avoid further discussion of his guest—Walpole fell into the role of literary adviser, directing his whole conversation to me.

"Have you made the Tour, Mr Hardacre? No? Well of course, you're young. An enviable vice. The only one that is abolished by time. I hesitate to say that you have not experienced enough to write, not if you are acquainted with Mrs Walsingham. But you must enlarge your observation to capture the fancy of this fickle town. You must make mankind your study. You must engross all the tempers and humors of our society."

Crack! went the billiard balls.

Heynheynheyn came that screech of triumph.

Walpole wagged his plump little finger—the one with the signet—at the scene inside the games room.

"Consider my noble Lord Sandwich." I identified the source of the whinnies in a long, ungainly figure flourish-

ing a billiard cue. The features were bony and narrow. The
bully-jaw flew out from above a high, tight stock.

"That head belongs on the stage," said Walpole, in a
stage whisper, "to give the mob a worthy target for a pip-
pin! See how the earl twitches, now he has botched his
cannon. He resembles a man who was hanged and cut
down by mistake when the job was only half done."

"Naughty, naughty," giggled Gaius.

"Saturnine! Do you hear me, Hardacre! The Earl of
Sandwich is the very model of the humor. Sour and dog-
ged even in the frenzy of his debaucheries. Ruins unripe
girls—" he quivered with excitement, and dropped his
voice even lower "—it was sheep at Eton. Don't expect an
honest Irishman would know about that. Ask Gaius if you
don't believe me."

"Oh I say, Horace. That's going a bit far."

"Sheep!" Walpole insisted. "Rams, for preference. It
was a rite of passage for some of our sporting bullies. John
Montagu, now—as he was before he got the title—he
liked to have 'em hamstrung so they could not run away
while he was beating them to death with a club. Ram-
clubbing, we called it. Gaius, I believe you are blushing!
You *do* remember!"

Gaius was not exactly blushing, but something strange
had happened to his mouth. It was closed, forming a perfectly straight line. It had moved to one side of his nose
and made a sharp angle like an errant exclamation mark.
It might have been inked onto his pale, smooth skin.

"Study the earl closely, Mr Hardacre! You won't see the
like very often. Can you believe that the king, in his wisdom, has made him First Lord of the Admiralty? God preserve the Navy! Would you not agree that the earl has a
fine, manly, sheep-biter's look about the gills?"

I gave Sandwich a closer look, and tried to picture him
at the head of a howling tribe of young Etonians in pursuit
of a sacrificial sheep. The earl swiveled his skull in our direction; it turned as stiffly as a toffee-apple on a stick.

"Oh Gawd," moaned Walpole.

The Earl of Sandwich had concluded his game and was
advancing in our direction. He moved at a singular, wide-

legged clip, as if he were stepping around the body of a
dead sheep.

Gaius leaped up to meet him and mumbled something
that brought a smile to the earl's thin lips.

"Your friend Mr Walsingham," Walpole remarked to
me, as we watched this display, "has the courtier's gift, to
be never in the way, but never out of it. He is always neu-
tral, except in his own interest. You should watch your
back with him. Sometimes life requires us to take a stand."

He rose without haste to greet the Earl of Sandwich.

"Demmed infernal buzz of wasps in here tonight, eh,
Walpole?"

"I believe that only the female of that species has a
stinger, my lord."

"I defer to your larger acquaintance with pests."

"May I introduce Mr Hardacre?" Gaius intervened. "He
has written a play for the Irish stage."

The earl gave me a narrow look; it suggested that he
considered neither comedy nor my native country a suitable topic for conversation.

"Another demmed scribbler, eh, Hardacre? You keep a
weather eye on Mr Walpole. All sail and no ballast. Do I
know your family?"

I mentioned my mother's Dempster relations. This
produced no sign of recognition.

Gaius surprised me by invoking the name of Sir William Johnson. As I have told you, the King's Superintendent of Indians in North America was my father's
kinsman; after he knocked the frenchies on the head at
Lake George and was made a baron-knight, my father
posted a print of him in the library between a pair of deerhorns and a fox's brush. I often looked at it as a boy. Billy
Johnson was represented the way the London engraver
thought a defender of empire ought to look—confident,
well-fed, with a quantity of powdered hair that was not his
own and a bright cuirass from a different time. I preferred
the portrait of a younger Johnson that hung in the stone
house at Smithstown. It presented a daredevil in a bro-
caded waistcoat of turquoise silk and a flared orange coat,
whose full lips and dimpled chin betrayed sensuality with-

out inhibition. It was a face that intrigued me. I felt that I
might get along with the spark behind it. But in truth, I
knew less about Sir William Johnson than about the Marquise de Pompadour and my father had barely mentioned
his name since a falling-out with John Johnson, the slow,
surly elder brother, who managed the Smithstown estate.

This did not deter Gaius.

"Mr Hardacre," he announced, "is an intimate kinsman
of Sir William Johnson who has contributed so greatly to
licking the French in North America."

This summoned a glean of interest under the earl's
whitish-blond lashes.

"Johnson? Johnson? By gad, I've heard things about
him! Likes dark meat, does he? Keeps a native harem?
I've never tasted an Indian woman but, God's pistols, I
have had Turkey meat. What are Sir William's sultanas
like? Smoky, like gammon, what?"

"I am really no expert, my lord. I have not been to
America." The earl's reference to Turkey meat left me
somewhat fuddled. Gaius advised me later that Sandwich
had cruised the eastern Mediterranean in his youth and had
been much impressed by the sexual delicacies available at
the court of the Great Ottoman. The earl had founded a
very selective club whose members dressed up in turbans
and baggy silk pants.

"Sink me!" Sandwich goggled at me. "Can't think
what's stopping you. War's nearly over—great hulking
brute like you—a useful connection and all that dark meat
going spare, what? You Irish rub along well with natives.
One savage tribe knows another, no? Too many Irish here
for any man's comfort. Go to the colonies! Go to the—
what do Johnson's darkies call themselves?"

"Mohawks," I volunteered.

"Mohocks. Quite so. They'll give you something to
write about. Haw! Walpole wouldn't know. He's a hothouse plant—no games, no girls, no air, eh, Walpole? Just
rattle and scribble, fribble and fleer. *Heyn!*"

"If the thought of exercise overcomes me," said
Walpole, "I generally lie down until it passes. You'll for-

give me, gentlemen. There is someone I have to meet. Your servant, my lord."

The earl sat down in Walpole's seat, and insisted on addressing me as an authority on the natives of North America. He was keenly interested in native methods of scalping and torture. His breathing quickened and his facial tic worked harder as I endeavored to slake his curiosity with a mishmash of wild stories that I drew from the adventure yarns of my boyhood and an article I had seen in the *Gentleman's Magazine*. I was as much astonished by the earl's ignorance as his prurience. True, he had been restored only lately to the penetralia of our government. Yet it seemed to me that Sandwich must have seen something from Johnson's Indian Department and listened to soldiers' club talk about the exquisite butchery of British regulars by Montcalm's savages. I soon realized that this elderly rake was as excited by repetition as by novelty, and that bare-bum flogging and ram-clubbing at the most famous of England's public schools send forth curious men to rule the Empire.

When I invented a particularly lurid tale about naked squaws chewing bits off a missionary, his lordship whinnied and slapped his thigh.

"We must tell that one to Abbot Francis!" he exclaimed mysteriously.

"Capital, capital!" Gaius beamed at me when the earl left us for a few moments to relieve himself. "Keep it up, and he'll give you a place at the Admiralty."

"What would I do at the Admiralty? I don't know one end of a boat from the other."

Gaius gave me a pitying look. He explained to me that I was the only man in White's, if not in London, who imagined that government posts were reserved for people who were in any way qualified to exercise them. He further explained that a sinecure at the Admiralty might be worth a couple of hundred a year—no fortune, but a nice, steady income, more reliable than scribbling for magazines. I resolved to do my best to keep the earl amused, though I found his tastes almost as alarming as his suggestion that I ought to remove myself to the colonies.

"Aha! So that's Horace's little secret!"

Gaius was staring quite shamelessly at Horace Walpole who had returned arm in arm with a slender young man a few years older than myself and a good four inches taller, though I stand above six feet in my stockings.

"Good God! That's one face I never thought I'd see in here."

"Who is it?"

"Tell you later. Have to speak—"

Gaius was on his feet, clearly bent on interrupting Walpole's progress toward the dining room with his guest. Walpole surrendered with good grace. His guest looked at his feet and at the ceiling. He appeared painfully shy. Gaius shepherded them back to our table.

Walpole made the introductions. "Mr Hardacre. Sir Robert Davers."

Sir Robert? The title of baronetcy on such a young man already spoke of tragedy.

Davers was remarkably good-looking. His face was a soft oval, his skin very white, hardly touched by sun or wind. His features were very fine and regular; his nose turned up just a touch at the bottom. He wore his own hair, which was the color of wet hay, tied back in a queue. His clothes were dark and unassuming. He seemed entirely oblivious of the effect his appearance had on others. He was receiving some longing looks not only from Gaius, but from our literary bishop, who was evidently no stranger to what is reputedly the pre-eminent vice in our Established Church.

Walpole explained that Davers had given him valuable help in what he described vaguely as his "gothic researches." The rest of us knew nothing, at that time, about Walpole's bizarre medieval romance, *The Castle of Otranto*, which saw daylight a few years later. I defy any grown man to read it with a straight face. Its spirit was utterly at odds with the school of realism that had come to prevail in the novel, as in the theater, and with the rule of reason that guided our philosophy and tempered our religion. I knew Walpole as the mannerly arbiter of our indiscretions, who could make a memoir out of a casual snub and hold a dinner-table captive to the wrinkle of a neckcloth. I was surprised by the Walpole who took to scaring serving girls with clanking spooks and chambers of horrors and malevolent ancestors who walk out of their portrait-frames in the middle of the night. I would have been more surprised had I not known Walpole's assistant. I suspect that Robert Davers's obsessions claimed a part of Walpole's soul and he wrote *Otranto* to drive them out. Walpole, of course, was a clever fellow, much too clever to bare his inner turmoil to other people. So he peopled his gothic romance with preposterous bugaboos, to conceal from anyone but a dunce—or someone who knew Davers as I did—that, behind the rented costumes, the terrors were real. Once again, Robert Davers casts a shadow before him.

I could not see his eyes, to begin with.

Then the Earl of Sandwich reappeared. He made a face at Walpole's back and set his course for the games room. But he paused in the doorway and said, "I am most interested in your views about native customs in North America, Mr Hardacre. It would please me to talk further on the matter. Gaius, we must fetch Mr Hardacre up to the Abbey. Nothing wrong with new blood, what?"

"As your lordship says," piped Gaius, giving my knee a squeeze under the table.

At the mention of native customs, Davers looked up, and I saw the eyes. Their color was indeterminate. I suppose, if I had to make a report of a missing person, I would put down that they were gray. The fact is, they changed with the light, with the play of colors in a room, with whatever was going on behind that high, pale forehead. They appeared to be out of focus; or rather, they were never focused on anything *I* could see. When Davers looked up at the man who was supposed to know about Indians, his gaze seemed to fasten on a spot just behind my right ear. I put this down to shyness, at the beginning. I came to know better. It was not so much that Davers avoided contact, but that he was for ever looking for something else. I flatter myself that I can generally read something of a man's character—and bend a woman's— when I look in the eyes. I could not accomplish this with

Robert Davers. There was no stillness in those eyes, no
fixed identity, not even the hollowness I sensed in Gaius.
There was something that went spinning back inside
Davers's head. It gave me a faintly giddy sensation for no
reason I could explain. I knew I did not want to go in
there.

"I am very interested in the Indians," Davers said quietly. "I have been told that they are without fear of death.
Is it true?"

"They have a reputation as bold fighters and cruel enemies."

Gaius volunteered the opinion that the sorriest cur will
fight if he is backed into a corner. He could not resist the
opportunity to drop a titled name. "Lord Ligonier says the
savages generally wage a skulking, cowardly sort of war.
You can only count on them to shoot a man in the back,
like banditti."

"That is not what I am asking," said Davers in the same
low tone, staring past my right ear. "I have read in certain
Jesuit writings that the natives of América go to meet
death as if to a marriage feast. Surely this can only be because they believe that they know—that they have actually
experienced—what lies on the other side. I am asking if it
is true that the Indians have discovered the destination of
the soul."

A little shiver ran up my back. These were damnably
deep, difficult questions with which to tax a man over a
bottle of claret in St James's! I was bound to ask myself
whether Walpole's young friend was altogether sane.

I could only mumble that I was no authority on the Indian doctrine of the afterlife. I saw Gaius smirking at my
discomfiture.

This curious exchange struck a damp into my evening,
and I was not sorry when Walpole carried his guest away
for what he described as a "farewell dinner."

"Well?" Gaius demanded, when we were alone. "What
do you make of that?"

"Sir Robert seems somewhat loosely attached."

"Loosely attached! He has no attachments! None! He's
a walking ghost! D'you know what he's gone and done?

He's put his whole estate in trust for seven years. I know the lawyer. Davers came to him and said he needed to find out if he and the world can agree with each other. Agree with each other! Did you ever hear such a notion?"

"I take it he means to travel."

"He's been knocking around the world since he finished school. Venice, Nice, Lausanne, all the usual haunts. Damned little good they did him. Doesn't seem to have any appetites, healthy or otherwise. Doesn't like girls, or boys neither. You saw how he looked. Pale and moony as a nun. I can't imagine what Horace sees in him."

"He must be ill."

Gaius tapped his forehead. "It's all in here. Morbid delusions. They run in the family. Bad bloodstock. The father used to come in here. He drank himself to death and died howling about demons when the son was six or seven. The mother mopes around in black weeds, talking to phantoms. There were some younger brothers. One of them drowned himself. The other took laudanum or hung himself up with a garter-noose, I forget what. Their place is at Rushbrook, up Bury way. D'you know that side of Suffolk?"

"Not really."

"Good pheasant shooting, but damnably flat and foggy. Then there's the boom of the bittern over the fens. Nasty graveyard thing. I expect it sticks in the head. Young Davers says he will travel. I say you can change the scenery, but you don't change the blood. I'll bet you a dinner at the Beefsteak he'll do himself in by Christmas."

I took this as a jest and let it pass. We dined at the common table, where the conversation turned to more agreeable topics. Afterwards, we took a turn at the billiard table. Gaius's hand was off. I had taken ten guineas off him before he missed an easy pocket and threw down his cue and vowed he would play no more. The money could have meant little to Gaius, but his steady infusions of port and brandy had brought out a mean, nagging streak.

"I'll give you a proper wager. I'll lay you a hundred to ten that Davers kills himself before the year is out."

His small black pupils climbed the whites of his eyes

like water-beetles. His mouth had slipped off-side, to make that odd, diagonal sneer.

I had drunk more brandy than I was used to, and the drink, or his proposal, gave me a queasy, unpleasant sensation.

I said that I thought it was in abominably poor taste to wager on a man's suicide.

"I find you have balls enough to amuse a lady past her prime," Gaius said nastily, "but not to risk like a man."

I should have struck him, or simply turned on my heel or walked out.

But when he stuck out his hand and repeated, "A hundred to ten," the gamester in me reached out and sealed the bet.

I consoled myself with the reflection that I had taken the positive side of the wager—that and a few quarts of claret and brandy. I was to need stronger fortification before the term of the wager had expired as I came to understand that a stupid bet in a London club room, over the fate of a man who was a stranger to me, had made me responsible for him.

We walk in the shadows of other people, so my Galway nanny used to say. I had never dreamed of walking in the shadow of a lunatic English baronet. Yet the pact I made with Gaius Walsingham—as much a madman as Davers but in a more predictable way—changed my life irretrievably, for light and dark.

Dearest Shane,

You say that luck rules our destinies. You present
your life as a string of accidents, bereft of meaning. I
wonder.

I had my fortune read on Tuesday by a Gypsy
woman with violet eyes. Sir Henry would not speak
to me when he discovered I had let her into the house
until I had cook make his dreadful bread-and-butter pudding for dessert. Henry insisted on counting the silver, and persuaded himself his favorite snuffbox is
missing. I am reluctant to hold the Gypsy woman responsible. She has an air of exiled majesty. She made
me feel I was in the presence of a queen who was
traveling in disguise.

She put her cards and talismans on a square of silk as
purple as a cardinal's socks. She took my pulse while
she chanted and hummed, calling up her familiar
spirits. Her cards were hand-painted, greasy and
scuffed from hard use, but still quite beautiful.

Have you ever entrusted your future to the Tarot,
Shane? As a devotee of Dame Fortuna, you must be
familiar with its laws. My Gypsy lady says the Tarot
descends to us from the Egyptian diviners who taught
Moses his craft.

"This is you," she told me, giving me a card to inspect. It was La Reine des Batons, the Queen of
Wands. I laughed when I saw the image. The queen in
the picture card has flaming-red hair, streaming across
her shoulders, which are wrapped in a gauze designed
to provoke rather than conceal. She is sprawled, more
than seated, on her throne, legs spread as if to receive
an unseen lover.

And there at her side, having his ears scratched, is

her guardian beast—a handsome, sleepy-eyed leopard who looks very much as if he has spent the whole night tomcatting.

I may have blushed. I must have given some sign, for the Gypsy woman leaped to the attack.

"A man like that can never be tamed," she told me, pointing to the Prince of Cups. A cruel image stood between us—the clashing of swords.

The Gypsy saw many things I knew to be true, and some that I fear may become so. She saw my mother's death. She saw Henry fall from a horse. She saw things from my childhood. She spoke as if she could hear the drone of the insects outside the netting of the hammock Papa had slung for me on our broad verandah at the plantation in Ste Domingue. As if she could see and smell, with my borrowed senses, the rivulets of sweat running between the corded muscles of the field hand working on my mother's garden.

I do not believe she found all these things in the fall of the cards. The spill of the deck must help her in some way to bring into clear focus what comes to her from intangible sources, from her inner senses or the spirits of the air.

Even so, it was the agency of chance that enabled her to see true.

You say that hazard rules our lives.

I will allow it may be so, but only if you will admit that in seeming chance may lie a deeper order than our little everyday minds can fathom. This is not the logic of Aristotle, or the mechanical causation beloved of Mr Newton's devotees. It is a code of relationships that joins the flight of a butterfly to the fall of a king, a secret script well understood by the ancients.

I read its signatures in your account of the seeming accidents that led you to America. When you pretend this string of incidents is without meaning, I think you are sporting with us.

Heraclitus says Time is ruled by a boy who is playing a board game. When things happen unexpect-

edly, when coincidence abounds, I see the hand of this
divine gamester. He loves to thwart our best-laid
plans, to prevent us becoming dull and predictable.
He delights in overthrowing our notions of cause and effect.

You do not show us his face. But you know the
boy-king who sports with our fortunes better than
you confess. His trickster energy moves in you, lithe
and wild as the leopard.

Toujours,

Valerie

2

The Hell-Fire Club

SIR FRANCIS DASHWOOD AND his gang put it about that they were the last word in wickedness. Society gossips believed them, and hayseeds in the neighborhood of Dashwood's travesty of an Abbey at Medmenham up the Thames magnified their tall tales. But when they invited me to their Hell-Fire Club, I thought they did not live up to their legend. They were mostly a bunch of grown-up schoolboys who had trouble getting it up. There was the usual percentage of bum-lovers; you know what English public schools do for the gentry. But the favorite prank was to dress up as a monk and bang away at make-believe nuns or pretend-choirboys, according to your preference. I am told that, to liven things up from time to time, they kidnapped virgins from nearby villages and picked their cherries over a mocked-up altar. I did attend an entertainment that purported to be a Black Mass, and it did involve a lady, but if she was an amateur—let alone a maiden—then I am the Great Manchu. It was all in frightful taste, and I never cared for the sour, inside-out theological kink in Dashwood's copulations, and I would not recommend a session at Medmenham Abbey to anyone with a queasy stomach. But I did not personally witness anything that would consign a fellow to the infernal regions, unless Higher Authority lacks all sense of humor. Sir Robert Davers may have felt differently.

Peg Walsingham says that men have been bragging about their cocks in public architecture since half-apes learned to heap one rock on top of another. She may have a point: what are the minarets of the Turks, the campanile of San Marco at Venice, the steeple of Rochester Cathedral, pinched and narrow as a dog's pizzle, and all those stone truncheons put up in Viking days about the seacoasts of Ireland if not monuments to Captain Standish? Be that as it may, the high point of the garden at Medmenham is an unambiguous stone prick that would make Don Juan weep. It is swollen eight feet tall. The ballocks would fit a thirty-two-pounder. The head stares rigidly at the gulley-hole between two moist, ferny hillocks. This will give you some idea of Dashwood's subtlety.

Coming up from his boathouse, near where the little Wye squirts its water into the speckle-brown Thames, the first thing you see is a pair of lions with human heads. The one on the left, with the round, beatific, dimpled phiz, belongs to Sir Francis. Above the gate is an incised injunction from Rabelais—*Fay ce que voudras*—which is calculated to get you in the mood for Dashwood's triumphal dick and associated erotic statuary that has more to please back-holers and snake-charmers than sturdy horizontalists. There is a bas-relief depicting the orgies in the cave of Trophonius; all the fornicators looked down in the mouth except for a prancing rooster and a giggling Carmelite monk.

"Bit gamy," I suggested to Davers, while Gaius Walsingham gave Priapus a friendly pat.

Davers inspected the scenery with an abstract curiosity, the way a man left waiting for the stagecoach might make a mental inventory of the sights and sounds in the street. He appeared neither attracted nor repelled; he was passing time. He liked the Latin tag under the bas-relief, and repeated it out loud: *"Omne animal post coitum triste."* Ev-

ery beast is melancholy after sex. I told him it wasn't true.
His eyes slid over me as if I were one of the carvings. He
strolled at an easy, regular gait, hands clasped over the
tails of his ink-blue coat, into the shady passage that
opened between the colossal legs of a sculpted Venus
sprawled flat on her back with her knees above my ears.
I rather liked that one.

I realize now that it was a mad idea to bring Davers to
the Hell-Fire Club, quite as mad as accepting Gaius's wager, and I do not know how I let Peg's husband persuade
me to do either. I was told by innumerable Indians later on
that, in their view, a man in liquor is *literally* not himself
and therefore is not accountable for his actions. I plead
this as my excuse. If we had not gone to Medmenham Abbey together, I would never have found myself looking
into Davers's private Abyss; I would never have met Daniel the Wild Man; I might never have gone to America, to
find Johnson and his tribal kingdom. Life is constructed by
chance encounters, reckless whims, random throws of the
dice-box. Look back on them, and you own a destiny.

There really was an Abbey on the Dashwood estate, the
property of Cistercians until Henry VIII invented our Established Church, and the place was abandoned to rot and
ruin. Sir Francis had rebuilt the chapel, the refectory and
the dormitories, leaving enough damp and rubble to feed
the gothic imagination, and raised up a stocky tower—a
bulge in the cassock, you might say—that wasn't there in
the age of Faith. Over a passable claret in the refectory, we
were required to take an oath to keep mum about what we
witnessed at the Abbey on penalty of the direst retribution
from an Egyptian god with a tongue-twister of a name. His
hairless countenance stared down at us from the wall. He
had a forefinger raised to his lip in the universal gesture
for silence. The muralist had achieved a *trompe-l'œil* effect; the gippo seemed to be walking towards us. He had
one foot planted directly in front of the other so the heel
brushed the toes. He reminded me of a drunk trying to
show he could hold to a straight line.

Davers seemed to know something of him.

He mumbled a word that bubbled like an acid attack.

I cocked an eyebrow at him and he whispered, "The Greeks know him as Harpocrates. The Assumption of Harpocrates is the key to the Mysteries."

This was all Greek to me; and all I remember of that language is the swish of the birch against my bald backside when I confused the Golden Fleece with the thatch of a lady's privates.

But I saw Sir Francis prick up his ears.

"Brother Robert. What do you know of Harpocrates?"

"From the depths of the mire, he is unfolded into the light. He is seated above the lotus. He precedes the worlds and comprehends all things in the deep of his being. He is in me and I am in him. When the initiate assumes the godform, after long trials, he is shrouded in the Veil of Mystery. He is invisible to those who see only with their eyes."

As you can hear, Sir Robert's tone was far from conversational. His words came fast, too fast for me to catch all of his drift—not that it would have left me any the wiser. He was intense, but dreamy at the same time. He seemed to be plucking something from the ether; or rather, it was plucking at him. I had the odd sensation that a power was speaking through him, for *his* benefit, not for ours. It struck a chill into me.

The Earl of Sandwich proved more robust. "Invisible!" he roared, tearing a pheasant's wing out of his teeth. "Invisible! 'Od rot me, that's a good 'un! What do you mean to do, Sir Robert? Walk into the wall? Go on with you then! Let's see it! Do your vanishing act!"

Sandwich neighed. *Heynheynheyn.*

Jowly, smutty Charles Churchill shook his wattles and let out a noise that seemed to emanate from his nether orifice.

John Wilkes gave a bestial leer.

Gaius trilled in a high falsetto.

Sir Robert Davers seemed impervious to this uncharitable claque. His mind was somewhere else. Don't ask me where. I am no soul-doctor, nor a mind-healer neither. I don't have a fancy handle to describe Davers's condition, and I suspect there is none that would contain it.

Our host did not join in the raillery. He was tensed like

a cat about to pounce on a wounded bird. I should have explained that we were obliged to call Sir Francis our Lord Abbot for the evening. He sported a fantastic costume that reminded me, simultaneously, of a depraved cardinal from the time of the Borgias and a jolly sailor on shore-leave in bell-bottoms. The rest of us were hardly more presentable. The veteran roués, like Sandwich and Churchill, who called themselves Monks, wore cowls and cassocks the color of young burgundy or elderly black pudding; we Novices wore white.

Abbot Francis leaned into the table.

He said, "I find Brother Robert has knowledge that is deep for a novice. What books do you know? Iamblichus? Hermes the Thrice-Blessed? Are you versed in the spell-books of Abra-Merlin the Mage?"

I do not know whether these quiddities meant something to Davers. I saw a little vertical line appear, like an exclamation mark, between his eyebrows. He blinked and brushed his forearm across his face like a man who has walked through a cobweb.

Davers said, "I beg your indulgence. I have no idea why I spoke as I did. I do not think I read it in a book. I just— remembered it."

Sandwich whinnied.

Charles Churchill declared he had just remembered some antique wisdom too, and gave us a booming rendition of a dirty ditty with the chorus, "Drive it home!"

We were joined, in short order, by the ladies, which vastly revived my spirits; jawing about a gippo divinity is not my conception of a jolly night out. Some of the girls were doughy farmers' daughters, but I think the greater number were recruited from Moll King's bagnio and less salubrious bawdy-houses in town. Most of them were got up as nuns, but there was a slut who impersonated Mary Magdalen and another, as God is my judge, who played the Holy Mother. She was bare-arsed under a robe of cerulean blue.

I may not be much of a churchman, but it has never given me pleasure to see a company of grown men defecating on the altars of others. I have certainly never had

wet dreams about ravishing nuns. When the king made
him Chancellor of the Exchequer and the goings-on at the
Abbey came in for some degree of public scrutiny, Sir
Francis maintained that he meant no offense to the Christian religion, but only to the iniquities of the Church of
Rome. I leave you to form your own judgement of that.
What intrigued me was how Abbot Francis acquired his
cowled fantasies to begin with. He told me that he had visited the Vatican on the Grand Tour. He claimed to have
swiped his choicest pornographic prints and a manual for
the Black Mass from a secret vault behind a false book-
case in the library of Saint Peter's delegate on earth. He
also claimed to have walked among flagellants, giving
them six of the best with a horsewhip. More fantasy, I suspect. I think he was secretly drawn to the Roman Church
and reviled it to conceal his inner leanings; it was a bad
social move, in my time, to show any tolerance for Catholics.

In any event, the high point of our evening was a travesty of a Roman Mass. The chalice was a chamber-pot
adorned with the design of a Stone Age Venus with dragging udders. The splayed body of a naked girl served the
office of the high altar. She was supposed, as I said, to be
a virgin. But her yellow hair had the burned smell that
comes from the dye-bottle, and her hole was as plump and
ready as a pitcher-plant.

I can leave the details of the ceremony to your imagination. Upside-down crosses and pentacles, prayers in pig-
Latin to a goat-footed god: they did not do much for me,
and do nothing for me now. To be perfectly frank, the solemnity of Abbot Francis and his crew made it hard for me
to check myself from laughing out loud.

But Davers turned green about the gills about halfway
through.

He muttered, *"Miserere nobis."* I believe he was actually weeping. "Forgive us."

He got to his feet.

"Sir Robert. Are you ill?"

"Air—must have air."

He stumbled out of the chapel. I suppose I should have

followed, but I didn't, and I am glad of it, because I was
present to observe the incident that resulted in the most
notorious defamation suit of our day.

The ceremonies continued, minus Davers.

Brother Sandwich, the Lord of the King's Navy, was invited to stand in for the Great Goat and try the sally-port
of our pristine prize. Abbot Francis babbled on in his demotic Latin, inviting the Dark One to join our deviltry in
person.

Wilkes, the biggest prankster of us all, in his way, had
disappeared. I wondered if he had gone in pursuit of Davers or merely found our entertainments thirsty business.

The noble earl was having some technical difficulty
with his prong. Mary Magdalen came to his assistance. I
observed her manual and labial dexterity with some interest, since I thought she was the likeliest of our nunnery
fodder.

Abbot Francis intoned, "He is come. He is among us,"
or something to that effect. The next instant, a door
banged open, a wind whipped up and a huge, hairy, panting beast burst from nowhere and came bowling towards
the mocked-up altar. Whatever the thing was, it was most
definitely inhuman. Even Twisted-Mouth Wilkes was pret-
tier than that. It was not very tall—maybe only four feet—
but it was as wide again, and its thick, furry arms hung
down to the floor.

It gave me a turn, and I reached for my hanger before
I realized I had left it with my clothes when they made me
put on my novice garb.

My fears were nothing to those of the Earl of Sandwich.
He let out a scream, let down his ramrod, and tried to
crowd his long bones into the narrow cavity under the altar on which our naked offering was splayed.

Abbot Francis, to do him credit, held his ground, though
he was shaking like a leaf.

He recited formulas of welcome, hailing the demon by
a legion of names that sounded Hebrew or Arabic. Our
visitor hunched over the altar, sniffing the girl, paying
close attention to her mustard pot.

She cried, "Gerroff, yer filthy cunny-catching beast!"

I started laughing, and could not stop until my ribs ached and I had a stitch in both sides. You see, the girl was right—our emissary from the Powers of Darkness was a beast indeed. To be exact, he was a baboon, rented by John Wilkes from the sideshow at the Sun Tavern in town and smuggled to the Abbey for a lark. In my opinion, this was a more brilliant stroke than any of the political sallies for which Wilkes is more generally celebrated, and it displayed, most vividly, the character of some of the most influential men in our kingdom. When you reflect that the same Earl of Sandwich I saw cowering, bare-bottomed, from the onslaught of a monkey is the very same Sea Lord who controlled the destiny of our fleets at the time of the American Mutiny, you will know why I had my doubts about whether Britain would be able to win the latter engagement. The only other thing worthy of note about the earl is that he created a momentary vogue for the nasty habit of putting meat between two slices of bread; it will never last.

The baboon howled and graced Abbot Francis with a stiff right uppercut that laid him out on his back and made a dramatic exit through the stained-glass window at the north end of the chapel. I kept one of the shards for a souvenir.

Inquiries were made. Sir Francis soon discovered that the ape had been concealed in the big closet behind the altar where he kept his satanic paraphernalia and released at the climactic moment with the aid of a string secured to the knob. Our Abbot's suspicions fastened on Wilkes immediately, and were confirmed by the discovery that the rude distiller's son had absconded without the courtesy of a good-bye. The Earl of Sandwich was stroked and petted and assured that Wilkes would not be tolerated at Medmenham again, and sent to bed with Mary Magdalen, which put my nose out of joint, I can tell you.

It was agreed that a baboon-hunt would be the first order of business in the morning. This was the origin, I believe, of the famous feud between Wilkes and the Earl of Sandwich that resulted in the publication of the deliciously dirty "Essay on Woman" and in "that devil Wilkes" being driven out of England, though I am unclear about all of the circumstances because by that time I was wholly preoccupied with trying to avoid being roasted on a spit on the frontier of North America.

Having lost the favors of Mary Magdalen, I decided to forgo the nuns and go in search of Davers, which gave me a closer knowledge of the geography of the estate, and of Sir Robert's mind.

He was not to be found at the main house, but a squint-eyed butler told me he had been seen drifting off towards the church.

Now, you can easily conceive what kind of stories they told about the Medmenham Monks in the neighboring villages—tales of devil-riders and vampires and suchlike rot. To persuade ordinary folk that he was a decent fellow, Sir Francis Dashwood had put up a handsome church on a high hill on his family acres at West Wycombe Park bordering the Abbey demesne. It had six bells and was fronted with elegant, unfluted Corinthian columns and floored with hexagonal slabs of travertine marble. But, because Sir Francis could never resist a giggle at the expense of true believers, he had installed a gilded ball atop the belfry, seven yards wide with benches inside where his comrades could climb up—if they were sober enough to negotiate a dangling iron ladder—and swallow a bumper or two at any hour of day or night. This exalted ball was familiarly known as the Globe Tavern.

The chalk for the roads on the Dashwood estate had been quarried from the hill on which the church stood. The mineshafts, winding deep into the earth, formed one of the varied attractions of the place—principally for those of a dank or necrophiliac cast of mind, for the diggers had turned up ancient bones and the area was believed by the credulous to be haunted by the spirits of the unquiet dead. I fancied this was where I might find Davers, and I was right.

I flatter myself that I generally keep my feet on the ground. I suppose that, what with Black Masses, and hairy baboons, and talk of Egyptian gods and invisible men, well-watered with claret and Nantes brandy, my fancy had

become disordered that night, and that this accounts for
what I thought I encountered in the chalk mine. I will not
tell you all of it for fear that you would doubt my judgement on graver matters. I will say that, as I followed that
mineshaft down into the bowels of the earth, with a flickering candle to light my way, I experienced a crawling
dread. When a bat flew across my face and the candle
went out, I was on the edge of panic. I called to Davers.
My voice cannoned back to me, off the soft, crumbling
walls. I crossed a shallow underground river, black within
black. I stumbled down false turnings and dead-end shafts.
I decided to leave Davers to rot, but could not find my
way back. Each way I turned, I came out on a path that led
downward, deeper into the earth.

"Davers! Are you there?"

My own voice returned, mocking me.

I slipped in a wet gulley and clutched at the wall of the
tunnel. Something scuttled away from my hand.

The tunnel debouched in a larger space, like a cavern. It
was warmer down there than near the entry. There was a
dull light that did not emanate from any source I could
see. As I say, my fancy must have been turned. In its pale
glow, I saw Davers, squatting like some oriental fakir. He
was talking, but not to me. There were others with him,
but their forms were indistinct. As I watched, Davers's
own shape seemed to flicker. For an instant, he vanished
into an egg-shaped cloud, dark as indigo.

"Davers!" There was a catch in my throat. The word
came out feeble and indistinct. I swallowed and tried once
more. "Davers! Sir Robert!"

He wasn't there.

I was ready to take a temperance vow, though of course
I could never have kept it. I searched that cavern thoroughly. I could not find him.

Hallucination? What else could it be? I found my way
out in the end. With fresh night air in my lungs, I was
ready to shrug off these drunken maunderings.

Then I saw Davers again. He was up on the steeple of
the church, hanging on the iron ladder that led up to the
gilded ball. At that instant, the content of my appalling bet

with Gaius came home to me. I was convinced that Robert Davers was about to do away with himself. I launched myself at the hill, bawling, "Davers! Don't do it, man!"

I do not enjoy reviving the memory of that climb. The stairs of the church tower lead up through the bell-pullers' room. From the top of the steeple, you have to crawl on that ladder, swinging with the wind over a giddying perspective, to the east, of the whole valley of the Wye. I made it, of course. I found Davers sprawled on a bench inside the Globe, sipping at a tankard of small beer. Candles sputtered in tin sconces.

"You worry about me too much," he told me. "You are not cut out for a duenna."

I don't know what came over me. I was ready to make a confession of my wager with Gaius. He saved me from doing it by saying, "Did you imagine I was going to hurl myself off the steeple? I would not choose to disappoint your confidence in a person you hardly know."

He smiled at my evident discomfiture.

He said, "How I envy you! Your lust for life, your raw simplicity! You have never once felt homesick, have you?"

I begged to disagree, recalling childhood haunts—the high hill of Tara, the ruined chapel of Waryne, the black waters of the Boyne with the trout leaping.

"You don't have the faintest conception of what I'm talking about, do you?" he said gently. "I was born homesick—homesick for somewhere else. Another world, so to speak. Born with the sense that everything in this reality is gross and insignificant compared with the home of the soul. Own up to me, Shane. Do you have any idea what I'm saying?"

I had to confess I did not.

"We have to serve our time," he said heavily. Now his words weighed like stones. "Like a sentry in an outpost the Empire has forgotten. I will not go before my time, like my brothers who are doomed to walk with the restless dead. Yet they fasten on me, they call me to join them in their loneliness. Day and night, they hover close to me. The unquiet dead feed on the force of the living. They tempt me. Oh, yes. But I am stronger."

I wanted to know where he had found his beer. I could not take much more of this without refreshment. A liquor cabinet. Thanks to God. I poured myself five fingers of brandy.

"It is strange how we came together," he was saying. "You, who live with your nose in the earth. I, who live for the sky. We are like twins who live utterly apart, yet are incomplete without each other."

The brandy burned a passage to my belly. I rubbed it and exhaled a deep gust of pleasure.

He was laughing at me. At least I had accomplished that. I believe it was the first time I had seen Davers laugh.

"We should knock about this world together," he said. "I have found little enough in it to detain me, but perhaps we will be guides for each other. We should not live as if there were no God or as if there were no men."

He told me something of his travels, of the Kingdom of Sardinia, and the philosophers' lair at Lausanne, and of a subterranean basilica at Rome full of the bones of dead monks—because his humor, as you know, was of a saturnine hue. I can no longer recollect all the things that he said. His discourse was freighted with book learning, from Plato and Plotinus, from Dante and Donne. He was steeped in the demented pedantry of Robert Burton, and I looked up one passage that pleased me better than the rest, because it held more of the bittersweetness of life: "Every man is the greatest enemy unto himself. We arm ourselves to our own overthrow; and use reason, wit, judgement, all that should help us, as so many instruments to undo us."

Davers said, "The only obstacle to self-slaughter is knowledge of the afterlife."

I applied myself with grim resolution to the brandy because I was totally at sea. You must have encountered someone like Davers. I suspect that each of us harbors a little of Davers inside us, manageable if we are rooted deeply enough in the life of the senses. But failing that— God help us! You will see what became of Sir Robert soon enough.

Was he mad?

I do not profess to fathom him fully to this day. He was no Tom O'Bedlam, ranting behind a wicket. But he walked up and down the earth as a stranger. He might have dropped from the moon. He was a being without needs or desires—at least any that pertain to the senses. He was deeply homesick, as he told me, not for his hereditary fens in Suffolk, but for something beyond place and time. I could understand the pull of those dead brothers. Suicides run in families; I could sense the cold weight of those dead boys, sapping his strength, dragging him down. But this was not the root of it.

Bad blood, Suffolk weather, easy money: none of this accounts for the mystery of Robert Davers, his nostalgia for the unseen, his infinite detachment. A shadow fell between him and the natural diversions in which you and I can find, or lose, our selves. He paused too much; he agonized over things not worthy of a moment's reflection. When he finally committed himself to a course of action, he did so with a frenzy as total and as terrifying as his previous indifference. I saw him do that on horseback, hurling himself over the edge of a ravine. I saw him do it on a mountain, daring the sheer rock-face to cast him off. He did it most completely with the Indians. That was when life got hold of him with a vengeance.

Again, was he mad?

A man who goes among one of the most savage nations on earth—among women who crack lice in their teeth and men who eat the flesh of their enemies and wear their reeking scalps on their belts—because he cannot find the meaning of life and death among his own kind is something other than sane. I do not say that Davers was *less* than sane.

He was absurd. He was Quixote without the dignity of a windmill. He was one of the bravest men I knew, and possibly the closest to God.

The baboon brought us to Daniel the Wild Man, who called us to America. If you see the hand of Providence in this, you belong with Davers.

We snagged the ape in the morning, with nets and

rods—not before he had caused mass hysteria in the nearest village, by breaking into kitchens—and formed a party to return him to his place of origin—the Sun Tavern in London. Davers and I both volunteered for the escort. We must have made a rum sight on the Thames, with the boatmen beating oars, while we stuffed the monkey with nuts and marrows.

A Mr Grossinger, a Jew from Antwerp, was the master of spectacles at the inn, whose circus offered a better display than the mangy lions in the Tower—a bearded lady and a learned mule and a dwarfish card-sharp who could rook any whist table in London were he only tall enough to see over the top. The star attraction, apart from the baboon, was a squat, pock-fretten, shaven-headed savage with a hide the color of a tangerine gone off who was billed as the Wild Man of North America.

Grossinger was so pleased by the safe return of his baboon, after we gave him some account of our travails, that he allowed us a private viewing free of charge.

The Wild Man shambled out, pounded his chest, raised a fearful whoop—"Ayyeeee-oooOOH!"—and set to macerating a chunk of raw rabbit's flesh, with the fur still on, between his impressive molars.

He was very near naked, apart from an Adam's apron and a set of blue-black gunpowder tattoos. But he was not very big and pretty sloppy about the waist, and I thought he would be less of a contest in an alley of a dark night than the baboon who had scared the Earl of Sandwich near to death.

"What nation is he?" asked Davers.

The Wild Man answered for himself. "I am Daniel Muskrat. I am Caniengehaga. Mohawk in white man's tongue. You come look at me like this, it hurts me little bit everywheres insides."

"Mohawk?" I simply could not believe it. All I knew of the Mohawks, the Flesh-Eaters, was hearsay, of course, at that time. But I could not credit that a circus freak was a member of the tribe that my illustrious kinsman, Sir William Johnson, swore by as the pivot of British influence

among the savage nations of America, a people whose
very name struck terror into other natives.

Daniel the Wild Man did his war whoop again. It pained
my eardrums.

"Do you know Sir William Johnson?" I demanded.

"All Mohawks know Warragiyaguey."

I was glad to see he had not actually consumed that foul
piece of rabbit. He extracted it from between his teeth as
daintily as a gold toothpick and tossed it into a spittoon.

"Warra—" I could not manage the rest. "What in blazes
do you mean?"

"Warragiyaguey," he repeated. He gave us to understand
that this was Sir William's Mohawk name. After repeated
questioning, I learned that it means something like, They
Chop Down The Forests For Him, which suggested that
my kinsman did not lack competence as a land developer.

I could not resist the urge to show off, so I have myself
to blame for what followed.

I told the circus Indian that Sir William Johnson was my
cousin.

He gave me a damp-eyed look and said, "You take me
home. Warragiyaguey no want Mohawks in whiteskin
country."

"I say," said Davers, "what a brilliant idea!"

I was in no mind to humor him, since I had no intention
of making myself accountable for a circus Indian.

"How did you get here?" I demanded of the Mohawk.

He mimed the actions of pouring a jug of liquor down
his gullet, produced a very creditable belch, and said, "I
am very clever man little bit with my own people, but a
hog when I drink white man's milk."

"Shane, we must do something for him." This, of
course, was Davers.

Grossinger was hovering about, nervous about the drift
of our conversation. Under pressure from Davers, I arranged to hire the Wild Man for the evening, so we could
question him more closely about his circumstances. We
went to the Swan With Two Necks and I took care that
Daniel drank nothing stouter than ale. He told us a jumbled story about getting drunk at the tippling-shop of some

German named Klock who shipped him off to a showman at Antwerp, to titillate the European appetite for curiosities from the colonies. He got into deeper talk with Davers about dreams and flights of the soul, in which the natives of North America believe that they can travel to other worlds. I was ready to carry him back to the sideshow, because I had had my fill of this in the exalted ball at the Abbey.

But Davers said, "Nothing is coincidence. We are Daniel's salvation, and he is our direction. We must take him to America. He will do us more of a favor than we will perform for him."

Sir Robert volunteered on the spot to pay for the passage of all three of us to New York.

I rejected the offer. I was not enamored of the notion of exchanging a soft life in London for greasy buckskins and smelly squaws.

And I doubt that I would have changed my mind but for Peg Walsingham and the roll of the dice in the form of an unexpected letter from Guy Johnson which arrived at the same time. Guy was Sir William's jolly, roly-poly nephew with whom I had killed a few bowls of shrub in Ireland before he hared off to the colonies.

Peg, as I probably told you, had given me a hard time since she had heard about my wager with Gaius.

She now said, "Poor Robert Davers. Of course you'll go with him, Shane."

I accused her on the spot of entertaining another lover. My jealousy had already been whetted by her evident fondness for a new actor at Drury Lane, a pretty boy in ringlets of about my own age and dark as a Sicilian.

"Sweet, sweet." She drew my face to her bosom. "How you flatter a girl! But there are plenty more in the bush, and the bush, my love, is where you belong."

I won't detain you with what ensued except to state that the letter was brought to me on a silver salver by Peg's little negro footman.

Guy Johnson opened his missive formally.

"Sir William desires you to know," he wrote, "that he wishes to be of service to all his Irish relations and feels a special affinity for you. He will exert his influence to secure a place for you on His Majesty's Service should you determine to risk the crossing."

I pictured Guy sitting po-faced, taking dictation with a decanter at his wrist.

He added a personal note: "The native girls aren't half bad. You'll get used to the beargrease and fish oil. The madeira is better than we ever tasted in Ireland. For God's sake, Shane, conscript your hindquarters and put 'em on a boat. I need a friend stout enough to get me in the right bed, and the Mohawks too."

What would you have done?

My mistress was holding the door ajar. The promise of fun and profit beckoned from Johnson country on the other side of the ocean. And though I rejected Davers's strange talk of separated twins, I acknowledged that our fortunes were somehow joined. I braved the gales of the Atlantic crossing in the company of a lunatic and a Wild Man.

Dearest Shane,

I am out of sorts today, and your account of the vile
goings-on at the Hell-Fire Club has not improved my
spirits. You cannot have forgotten what anniversary this
is. It is Bastille day, when the voices of my dead are
as strident as at All Souls'. The Revolution, and the
slave revolt in the islands that was its bastard progeny,
swept away the world in which I was reared. It killed
my father, and his closest friends. It broke my
mother, and reduced her to a thumb-sucking defective.

The foul wind that diseased France blew from America. Lafayette, drunk on glory and talk of liberty, gave
us the cutthroats who made the Terror, and where
Sun Kings reigned we must now make obeisance to
a band of Corsican banditti. I blame you and your kinsman William Johnson as much as poor deluded Lafayette. In your forest wars, you lit the powder train that
led all the way to the Bastille, by way of the rout of
two monarchies in North America. Do you see that
now?

Your

Valerie

Dearest Valerie,

I have been blamed for many things, but never before for the French Revolution. I cannot say if your charges have meat to them, because though I may revisit the past, I do not make a practice of walking through life looking behind me.

Hindsight is a useless, unhappy fellow. In the Greek story, he is married to Pandora. What good could it do him or anyone else to know what was in the box after it was opened?

Your

Shane

3

Manhattan Island

"NEW YORK!"

I ran to the bow, eager for my first glimpse of an American town. Bluebill ducks and wild pigeons flocked thick overhead under a powder-blue sky that faded at the edges like a watercolor wash over the sloping cornfields on the Jersey shore. Porpoises sported on the broad surface of the bay. I saw the dun and white canvas of a military encampment on Staten Island. Directly ahead, rearing up from the cleft of two rivers, was the rock of Manhattan. Davers, who had been reading up during our passage, informed me that the name is a garbled version of an Indian word meaning "the place where they got us drunk," which sounded likely enough.

The little settlement on the tip of the island is dwarfed by the splendor of its natural setting. The town is less than a mile long, and half as wide. It has twenty-five hundred houses and one in ten is a grog-shop. From the foredeck of the *Chance*, I saw a turf-built battery projecting in a crescent under the ramparts of Fort George; a line of high-built, steep-roofed brick houses; the jut of steeples and cupolas; the forest of spars at the opening of the East River where square-riggers and fishing smacks contended for room along the wharves with merchant vessels and His Majesty's transports. On the Long Island side, below the little village of Jamaica, a distant blur on the edge of Hempstead Plain, scores of oyster-boats were out. As we drew nearer, I watched the fishermen trawl with long rakes with iron prongs bent inward, for fat oysters and white-shelled clams that curled like the human ear.

When we tied up at Coeyman's Wharf, the piny tang that had welcomed us long before we set eyes on the coast of America was displaced by the sharper smells of industry—the stink of tarpits and skinners' yards, of uncured hides and hatters' dies, of starch-makers and the slaughterhouse, of boiling molasses and burning oystershells heaped in great mounds along the river to make lime. From the slips, the skyline was composed of warehouses, sugarhouses and distilleries.

These sights and smells conveyed the business of the town, for New York's sole manufactures are rum and felt hats, a little cloth and wampum beads for the Indians. The city lives as a go-between, shipping out furs and skins, flour and lumber and pig-iron from the backlands, and bringing in sugar and rum from the islands and manufactures from Sheffield and Manchester.

The stamp of Holland is everywhere visible—in the glazed tiles on the houses, and the way they sit gable-end to the streets, in the names and the manners of those who affect the airs of Old Money, in the public parsimony of the town. The wealth of New York turns its back on the public thoroughfares. It is concealed, rather than trumpeted, by the modest façade of the houses, with the exception of the De Lancey mansion and Captain Kennedy's new residence at the foot of the Broad Way and the fine country villas out along Bowery Lane and the Greenwich Road. The public buildings are shabby. City Hall has felons in the basement and a leaking roof. The Exchange is an elderly wooden pile at the head of a dilapidated pier; both will fall down if they are not soon pulled down. Trinity Church is large and pompous with a clumsy Gothic steeple, but the new church for the English congregation, St George's Chapel, has barely room enough for a billiard game. There are a dozen other meeting houses, for Dutch and Moravians, Quakers and Lutherans, and a synagogue for the Jews, but none are notable for their appointments; the hardy Methodists gospel together in a sail loft.

Yorkers disdain public show, but open the door of a merchant's house and you will find a setting for Marco Polo. We dined with John Watts, a prominent trader allied with Johnson. His rooms were filled with mahogany and teakwood, African ivories and Venetian glass, silks and punchbowls from China. Watts explained to us the principle that rules this society and on which all distinctions are based. "A man who has money here, no matter how he came by it, is everything. Without money, he is nothing. At New York, money is the true fuller's earth for reputation. There is no stain or spot it cannot rub out." The greatest fortunes of the city were made by stealing land from the Indians, by smuggling illegal peltries from the French at Montreal, by privateering off Hispaniola and by filching and fiddling government contracts. The greatest families trace their descent from penniless, half-literate immigrants whose buccaneering spirits made up for their lack of assets or eduction. The ones that preen themselves as aristocrats—Bayards and Philipses, Van Dams and Morrises—are those whose founders did their looting a generation earlier than the parvenus.

In short, New York is a bustling, broiling marketplace made for a cheerful rogue with his eye on the main chance. I thought it might suit me very well. The girls are pleasing and robust, tearing around in Italian chaises or showing themselves off under silk umbrellas in the shade of the locusts and water-beeches that screen the more fashionable streets. They come in engaging variety, in all shapes and colorings, because New York is neither an Englishman's nor a Dutchman's town, but a sort of crossroads. Walk through the Meal Market and you will rub shoulders with Germans and Ulstermen, Swedes and Antwerp Jews, Scots and negroes from the Bight of Benin, all jabbering in their own dialects. In its jumble of races and

cultures, New York is different from Boston or Philadelphia, which of course I came to know only later. Even in
my first week, I sensed that something different was going
on here, that a new kind of society was borning and turning its back on the Old World.

For all that, an English title, especially on a personable
young bachelor, was a wonderful social *entrée*. Davers and
I were invited everywhere. We went to balls at the De
Lanceys' and the Morrises', to turtle-feasts on the East
River, to ring-races on the Greenwich Road, and to serious
nights of backgammon and bumpering at the gentlemen's
club that convened at the Masons' Arms where we drank
the health of the king and Queen Charlotte and General
Amherst and so many others that I cannot complete the
register without giving myself and my reader a headache.
We acquired a certain following among the ladies, although I am afraid that Davers disappointed them. He preferred to talk Indian lore and scientific experiments with
Cadwallader Colden than to hunt petticoats. Colden, then
the lieutenant-governor, was a dried-up, prickly Scots sa-
vant who collected botanical specimens and had written
The History of the Five Indian Nations. Davers shut himself up for a whole day with the book at our lodgings at
Widow Crewe's, near the Green, where Daniel was accom-
modated in a kennel in the slave quarters, much to his dis-
gust.

I will pass briefly over the details of our stay in New
York since the better part of my time, as you might expect,
was occupied in wenching and carousing that has no bearing on the material parts of my story. I would caution a
new visitor to Manhattan not to loiter about the Half-
Moon Battery after dusk. He will find a whole flotilla of
full-rigged trollops, both English and Dutch, at sail among
the thirty-two-pounders. They are mostly fire-ships. I
know what I am talking about. Fortunately, Billy Johnson—no innocent in such matters—knew a native remedy.

The most important event of our stay in Manhattan was
our meeting with General Amherst. I wish I had understood just *how* important it was. We were both disappointed in the general, at that time the most famous British

soldier in North America. Davers thought he was prejudiced and opinionated; I thought him vain and fatigued. Had we realized where Amherst's stubborn folly would lead, then *both* of us might be alive today.

We were invited to a ceremonial in his honor. It was conducted in front of the monument to General Wolfe, the martyr of Quebec, that the civic corporation had put up on the Greenwich Road, on a plot of land donated by Oliver De Lancey. On a large obelisk, below the image of Fame, the sculptor had carved a corpse on a couch with Minerva weeping over him. Mars stood by the dead warrior's head, pointing at a bas-relief of General Amherst in knightly armor.

"Behold the living hero!" Any fool could have gleaned the message, but the orator for the corporation had to say it out loud in front of the live Amherst, who had the decency to look embarrassed.

This was not the end of the embarrassment. The speaker, a tallow-faced man in dark silk, sweating profusely, wrestled with an interminable text.

"We give thanks for your paternal care—Now the peasant may return in security to his fields—May the God of Armies continued to furnish your head with wisdom, your breast with fortitude and your arm with strength—"

This set some of the onlookers to shuffling and spitting. A couple of upcountry farmboys, raw-boned and lanky, in coarse osnaburg shirts, turned surly at the mention of "peasants."

It took the speaker twenty minutes to come to the point—we were gathered to celebrate the arrival of despatches from London, confirming that the best of all possible kings had decided, in his wisdom, to make General Amherst a Knight of the Order of the Bath.

There were ragged cheers, the fusiliers fired a volley and the musicians struck up a tune. Sir Jeffrey, as I may now call him, looked thoroughly bad-tempered. He was a long, lean, elegant man, with a mane of red hair and a sandy complexion. When he tucked his chin into his neckband, the bold line of his nose, sweeping straight down from his forehead, made him look like a ram getting ready to butt.

Colden made the introductions.

"Yes, quite. Heard about both of you. Been remiss. Dine with me tonight?"

I had been hoping to lay close siege to a frisky young lady of provincial fashion named Suky Van Horn, but one does not stand up a commander-in-chief. We repaired to the old stone house inside the fort at seven.

Amherst was spitting mad about his medal, and did not mind who heard about it.

"Didn't want it. Told 'em not to do it. Knighthoods are two a penny. They gave one to an admiral for holing a fishing smack. Johnson got a baronetcy for sitting in his tent sipping punch."

I thought this was a quaint way to describe Sir William's defeat of a French army at Lake George, and this must have showed in my face, since Amherst reined himself in enough to say, "No offense to your cousin, Hardacre. I have the highest regard for Sir William."

"Quite."

But Amherst could not leave off the subject of the knighthood. To add injury to insult—so he complained—he had received a bill for five hundred and twenty-two pounds to cover the expenses of induction.

Steady infusions of claret over the veal and baked sturgeon did not mellow his humor. The general was plainly homesick for the meadows and beechwoods of his English estate at Riverhead and for the lovely Jinny whose portrait hung over the fireplace. The war in North America was over. He was a fighting general. Had he not performed the unheard-of feat of marching three British armies over half a continent, by separate routes, to rendezvous at Montreal and wrest Canada from the French? Why should he be obliged to languish at New York, in a house not worthy of the captain of a whaler, to wrangle with ill-mannered provincial politicians over revenues and recruits?

He was eager for gossip from London about the fortunes of Pitt, our war minister and his personal patron. We told him what we could: that Pitt was out of favor, with a powerful cabal of overripe and underripe Tories levied against him, that his resolve to go on banging the French until they were driven from the high seas was making him unpopular.

"I expect he will fall," the general sighed. "Perhaps then they will let me go home."

He explained that the redcoats we had seen encamped on Staten Island were being assembled for a seaborne expedition against Guadeloupe and Martinique under General Monckton. There was talk of a further expedition, against Havana, if war with Spain were declared. Of the great army of British regulars assembled for the reduction of Canada, there would soon remain only a handful of companies and the sick and wounded under hospital tents. The defense of the province—and of all the mainland colonies—would rest with the local militias.

"And God help them if the frenchies come back," said Amherst.

He treated us to tales of wanton chicanery among provincial recruiters and contractors. A militia commander would present a bill for pay and equipment for, say, a hundred men. It would then come to light that half his volunteers were either dead or "absent." To prevent this abuse, Amherst had ordered that all militia companies were subject to sudden roll-calls, at which one of his officers would count the men present.

"The buggers line up, two deep. As my officer moves to the end of the line, those he has already counted slip round the back to have themselves counted twice. The deeper you dig into the affairs of this colony, the stronger the stench of raw sewage. I wish you good fortune in your expedition, gentlemen. I do not say that I envy you."

I asked the general if he was personally acquainted with Sir William Johnson.

"He came with me to Montreal. He was of some service in restraining his Indians from tomahawking our French captives—those that did not get drunk or run away at the first whiff of powder. Sir William is a remarkable man. Can't think how a man of his quality can abide to live in the woods with those infernal savages."

Davers said quietly, "Mr Colden believes that Sir William knows the Indians better than any white man in North America, and that it was only his influence with the forest tribes that stopped the French from coming down the Hudson and attacking this city."

"God's breeches! If Mr Colden says that, then he does disservice to the memory of a good many honest British regulars!"

The general had evidently been stung to the quick. He pulled in his chin and made little forward motions with his sheep's nose.

"There has been a tendency in certain quarters," he said, "to exaggerate the necessity of keeping the goodwill of the natives. This goodwill costs His Majesty a pretty penny, I may tell you! You should see the bills I am sent by the Indian Department! Thousands of pounds, swallowed down the gullet and pissed away against a bush! I do not know how much of this money we squander on Indian gifts vanishes into the pockets of our Indian agents—I mean no slur on Sir William, gentlemen, but the probity of his associates is another matter altogether. There's an Irish blackguard called Croghan—but I'll leave you to form your own view of individuals. There are larger matters at issue, matters that touch the honor and the safety of the Empire.

"We have an Indian Superintendent and an Indian Department. Sir William is a fine man, no doubt he has a fine department. But the core of his policy is subsumed in one word—bribery. He has turned the Mohawk nation into his hired retainers, at Crown expense. He spends enough on presents for the allied Indians to outfit our expedition to Guadeloupe."

"But surely the Five Nations were invaluable allies during the war," Davers interjected. I let Sir Robert carry the burden of the argument, since he had been acquainting himself with the subject with Cadwallader Colden who evidently took a very different line from General Amherst.

"That was not my observation," Amherst said drily. "They were damn little good to me when I marched on Montreal. My main concern about Johnson's hairdressers," here he let the depth of his hatred show, "was that they would start carving up unarmed Canadians until the French decided to fight us to the last man. I have heard a lot of tall tales about Indian bravery, the noble savage, the covenant chain and so forth. It is romantic hogwash. I have never known Indians who will stand and fight like men in open battle. Butchering women and children and unarmed plowboys is more their speed. Sir William showed off some of his natives to me when I was in the Valley. I had dinner with a pack of them at the Oneida Castle. I brought pork with me, since they give nothing without demanding more in exchange, and I had the satisfaction of watching the squaws grease themselves with the potlickings that were left over. Then their men became intoxicated and stole one of my packhorses. They hacked the poor beast to pieces and ate it raw."

Davers said something about the Indians having no natural resistance to alcohol, and how they were strangers to fermented beverages before the white man came.

"Then how do you explain the Irish, Sir Robert?" Amherst gave me a wink that almost pardoned the insult, not that it truly offended me. An Irishman is inured to jokes about drinking habits, and it is a sad fact that most jokes about the failings of national types contain an element of truth.

The general replenished our glasses—we had graduated to port which was circulating in a ship's decanter—and returned to his larger theme.

"*Ubi dolor, ibi digitus.* We must scratch where it itches. There, in a nutshell, is the policy of our Indian Department. The Indians are itchy for presents, so we oblige them, and send His Majesty the bill. Presents! What a lying euphemism! We feed the wretches, we clothe them, we give 'em guns and powder and kettles and gewgaws and God knows what, so they become too lazy to hunt and lie about all day drunk, as close as they can get to the next supply. What does it profit us? I am told that by these means, we secure their loyalty. What is the value of a man whose loyalty is to be bought and sold?

"If it were merely a matter of pampering Sir William's

neighbors, the cost in money and in dignity would be ruinous enough. But see where we have come to! We have beaten the French, and the French had ten times as many savages in their service as the Indian Department ever had in the war. Ten times! Think on it, gentlemen. The French were always abler at Indian diplomacy than we are. Sir William says it is because the French are kinder to the savages and treat their customs with more respect. I say it is because the frenchies are willing to wallow in the mud and turn savage themselves in ways no true-born Englishman would do, and because King Louis also paid bribes. Now Sir William and his partisans maintain we should give presents to the French Indians as well—to the butchers who were scalping our settlers until yesterday—to make them sweet and silky. I say it is time to cease pandering to the brutes. Let them earn their living like honest men and respect the king's authority. If they turn sulky, by God, we shall teach them more with punishment than with presents!"

I was surprised by the length and the fervor of this speech. If the general expressed himself this frankly to us about his disagreement with Sir William Johnson, it was not hard to imagine the language he might use with his officers—or in his letters to London.

I enquired, as judiciously as I was able, whether Amherst was persuaded that there was no danger of renewed fighting along our Indian frontiers. After all, British and provincial troops were still campaigning against Cherokees in the Carolinas.

The general had already risen to his feet, indicating that our evening was over.

He gave me a steady look. Holding my hand a little more tightly than was comfortable, he said, "The Indians are incapable of anything serious. Please convey that to Sir William Johnson. He has lived so long amongst them that I fear he has lost his moorings."

They have a pleasant habit at New York of cart-whipping their felons. I watched a man who had stolen some stockings off a stage-boat tied to a cart's tail and dragged about the town to receive his punishment on his bare back: five lashes at Furman's Corner, five at the Meal Market, five at the old Slip Market, five at Coenties Market, five at John Livingston's Corner, five at Dealls Corner and four at City Hall. In this way the whole settlement is kept amused. Public floggings, however, are not sufficient to keep a man and his purse together if a newcomer is rash enough to venture out alone and unarmed after dark. The watch is idle and drunken; the streets, for the most part, are unlit, and being very narrow and irregular in their courses, offer many lurking-places for gangs of footpads who lie in wait. I was assaulted by a pack of ruffians armed with knives and cudgels on my way home to Widow Crewe's from cocking at the Sign of the Bull's Head, and had to nip two of them with my hanger before they would leave off.

Davers seemed in good spirits. He now spent most of his days gathering information and supplies for our trip upcountry. In the afternoons, he haunted the Albany coffee-house, which kept the newspapers from Boston and Philadelphia as well as the London papers, two months old, and James Rivington's new bookshop on Hanover Square. In the evenings, before dinner, he pored over maps of the territories beyond the Allegheny Mountains. He rattled on about meeting native tribes that had never beheld a white man before and discovering a water road to China, that chimerical North-West Passage that so fascinated projectors in my time, and brought the celebrated Major Rogers of the Rangers to his ruin. Davers was keen to put cities behind him. I shared something of his keenness. On all sides, I heard rumors and reports of my kinsman Sir William Johnson. He was plainly one of those mythopoeic personalities that generate endless stories and legends. I was eager to form my own judgement. Then, too, in every fine house that I entered, there was a buzz about the fantastic profits to be made in land speculation in the Ohio country and the territory newly annexed to the British Crown now the French had been driven out. I had a mind to find a way to share in the riches, and go back to England as wealthy as an East India nabob.

Even General Amherst felt the itch to get his hands on

some Indian land. I learned that Amherst had floated a
scheme to reward himself and his officers for their efforts
in His Majesty's service by sharing out some huge parcels
of fertile land, nicely situated near the fort and trading-post
at Niagara. Sir William had made it his business to block
this project on the grounds that it would violate treaties
with "his" Indians. Johnson's stake in the hedge—that is
to say, his influence with our political masters—had
proved greater, on this occasion, than that of our commander-in-chief. Here, perhaps, was a more intimate reason for
Amherst's animosity towards the King's Superintendent of
Indian Affairs.

Amherst's feelings were shared by his staff, as I discovered when I had a contretemps with his aide-de-camp,
Captain James Dalyell, as a result of my petticoat-chasing.
The episode may strike you as of no greater consequence
than two cocks disputing a henwalk. But I should not
leave Manhattan Island without some account of Captain
Dalyell, because the bad blood created between us had
larger consequences than any of us could possibly have
foreseen.

James Dalyell was what, at home, we would call a prize
woodentop. He came out of a fancy family and a fancy
regiment—the First Foot Guards, Lord Ligonier's own
(and Amherst's, too). He was well-knit, with smooth, regular features, somewhat high in coloring. His face was full
of blood and animal oil, the glossy skin stretched tight,
like sausage-skin or that useful device the French call a
pardessus anglais. He fancied himself as a womanizer.
With gold lace on his scarlet regimentals and the luster of
having served beside the Hero of Montreal, not to mention
a well-born name and an accent that would ripen plums,
no doubt Captain Dalyell cut a broad swathe through the
ladies of Manhattan. I thought he was a chocolate soldier
which was probably unfair—everyone said he had done
the "right thing" in the Canada campaign. But I was dis-
inclined to be fair to a gentleman who was my rival for a
lady's favor. He pronounced his surname "Deal;" thus I
dubbed him "No Deal," to my own amusement, if no one
else's.

The lady at issue was Miss Suky Van Horn. She was one of the shining stars in our social firmament. Her father was the heir to an old, landed Dutch family whose women all had nasal appendages that hung down like doorknockers, but her mother was English, and Suky had inherited her pert little button of a nose as well as her fine, clear skin and her wonderful auburn hair. Her family had adopted the English style, which is to say, they attended Sunday worship at Trinity instead of the Dutch church, supported the court party and maintained a handsome country house on the Bowery Lane beyond Mr Watts's Rose Hill Farm, where there was good shooting and fishing to be had. Suky was not half as intelligent or well-read as Peg Walsingham, but she was half Peg's age, she stood to inherit twenty times Peg's money and she was *here*. Her life was a round of tea-parties and fashionable routs and visits to the mantua-maker and the hairdresser. At New York, as at London, it is not considered seemly for a respectable woman to employ her time in any more useful way than to capture and keep a husband. If anything, the Americans try to keep their women in closer subjugation than we do in Europe; I am informed that Benjamin Franklin, that herald of enlightenment, sent his own sister a spinning-wheel for her wedding gift. In either society, a woman like Peg is a rarity, and she is rarely considered respectable.

I would not have you think of Suky Van Horn as meek or vapid. She was quick; she was lively, she could talk very wittily about people she knew. She had very beddable eyes, but I recognized her as a flirt and a teaser, who will lead a man on without surrendering out of wedlock—unless he finds the opportunity to put it to her without asking permission. I nearly had her in the river-garden of their country estate, screened from the house by a hedge of box-wood. She had allowed me to forage under her petticoats. I found her deliciously warm and moist. From her little moans and shivers, I think I gave her some satisfaction with my caresses. But when I proposed to go into the affair more deeply, and showed her my jumper, she pulled away and gathered up her skirts and said, "La! Mr

Hardacre! You great unmannerly thing! What kind of girl
do you take me for?"

"I took you, my dear, for a woman of spirit. You are a
girl that is made for loving."

"And I think you, Mr Hardacre, are capable of giving a
woman anything but love."

Not a bad riposte, and it shows that Suky was not without discernment. I was not for a moment in love with her,
though I think I am capable of love. It was a lazy, languid
summer infatuation, there by the East River, with the tree-
frogs shrilling louder than the birds and the lightning bugs
exploding like phosphorous flares in the powdery dusk. I
do not know what my intentions were, other than to enjoy
myself with a pretty, frisky young animal. I suppose it
crossed my mind that I ought to mount a serious campaign
to breach her affections—even if the other thing had to
wait—and marry her, thus securing myself a good measure
of fortune in the New World without having to exert myself further. But I had known the joy of intimacy with a
strong woman who owned her own opinions; I was not
ready to settle into a life with a girl who took her attitudes
from other people and would never dream of expressing an
idea that had not already been presented, rounded and
shaped like a cake from a baking dish, over a polite
dinner-table.

Still, I laid desultory ambushes for Suky, and this is
what brought me up against Captain Dalyell. Suky kept a
whole retinue of gallants and loved to play them off
against each other. Her only intellectual nourishment was
flighty novels, and I believe her highest notion of romance
was to drive two intended lovers to fight a duel over her
handkerchief. She had a taste for theatrical entertainments
which were thought quite *risqué* at New York, where the
Calvinist mynheers groused that Mr Douglass's plans to
open a theater in Chapel Street would turn the town into
a new Gomorrah, and threatened to burn the building
down. So I ingratiated myself by offering to arrange a
light dramatic medley, to be staged at the villa on the East
River. I called it a *mischianza*, because the Italian style
was then all the rage. It would include fragments from the

opera and several scenes from *A Midsummer Night's Dream*. Suky was ecstatic, and rewarded me with another bout of hot groping and burrowing that drove me back in urgent frustration to dice with the pox along the Half-Moon Battery. But Suky's father hemmed and hawed and grumbled about the heat and the expense.

Then my *deus ex machina* appeared in the unlikely personage of Sir Robert Davers.

While I was courting Miss Van Horn, Davers had arranged our passage on an Albany sloop; we were to leave on the third Monday in July. Advised by Daniel, he had also laid in a private store of Indian goods, including several fathoms of porcelain beads, a gross of jew's harps, looking-glasses and prodigious quantities of rum. The purchase I liked best was a brace of neat little shooting-irons manufactured in Pennsylvania, where they call them jaeger rifles.

Davers presented me with one.

I suppose we both fancied ourselves woodsmen when we tried them out later on the ducks in Turtle Bay. With its rifled, octagonal barrel, the jaeger is accurate above two hundred yards. It is short and light. It weighs less than eight pounds and is easily slung by its leather strap over the back of a man threading deep woods. Mine had a prettily turned walnut stock and a brass serpent sideplate. I was delighted with the gift and impressed by Davers's apparent knowledge of firearms.

"Oh, I bagged a few pheasants in Suffolk," said he, with his usual modesty.

I told him about Suky Van Horn and the theatrical evening I had been trying to arrange.

Davers had an inspiration. "Why don't you include a tribute to the Conqueror of Canada? That way, Old Man Van Horn will not be able to refuse you. The general will come, and then the De Lanceys and everyone else cannot fail to accept. It will be the social event of the season."

"Do you really think Sir Jeffrey will accept?" I had a number of misgivings about our commander-in-chief since our evening at the fort.

"What else does he have to do, except swat confounded

mosquitoes?" The glasses on the table clinked as Davers brought a furled magazine crashing down, in pursuit of one of these persistent insects, the bane of summers in the colony.

I was not overly enthused about Davers's idea. A tribute to the Conqueror of Canada sounded like crawling to me, and that is an exercise I have never cared for since I first managed to stand on my hind legs. Furthermore, Amherst had insulted my kinsman Johnson, not to mention the whole Indian race, which made me wonder why Davers, who had come here to find out about Indians, should wish to pay him this compliment.

"It does no harm to keep friends in high places," Davers told me, which made eminent sense but sounded so unlike him that I guessed he must be playing a deeper game.

I began to warm to the proposal as I pictured Suky, in gauzy disarray, as the Spirit of Canada, falling on the neck of her manly liberator. There would be a mock battle, of course, with white-livered frenchies and sinister black-robes falling about the stage as thick as wheatsheaves under the scythe.

"Daniel," said Davers, "will represent His Majesty's Indian allies."

I began to see his game.

I worked up a script, shamelessly cribbing from Addison's *Cato*, from Virgil and a number of lesser rhymesters. Old Van Horn stopped pleading the excessive heat, Oliver De Lancey donated a wooden Doric arch, painted to resemble marble, from one of his own entertainments and Suky mooned over me as if I were the Immortal Bard.

Van Horn warned me, "You shall have to secure the general's permission."

I wrote Sir Jeffrey a note. He responded by inviting me to send him the script.

Captain Dalyell came to call on me after I had break-fasted on Widow Crewe's small beer and cold mutton, bearing the general's comments.

"Sir Jeffrey suggests some minor revisions. We do not profess to be professional scribblers in the military, Mr

Hardacre, but we do have a notion of what *taste* demands."

No Deal inspected me like something he had squashed under his gleaming boot on his way through the market.

"Naturally, I welcome Sir Jeffrey's views."

"The general thinks it imperative that the Hero of Montreal should be represented by a British officer."

This was a major disappointment. I had looked forward to sweeping the Spirit of Canada into my own lusty arms. It came as no great surprise to me that No Deal had cast himself in the leading role.

"Moreover," Dalyell sniffed, "this stuff about the Indians in the van of our conquering army lacks realism."

I pointed out that realism was hardly a prerequisite for a pageant of the kind we were preparing.

"Sir Jeffrey thinks that, if we must have an Indian, it would be a more convincing portrayal to show the savage attempting to ravish the Spirit of Canada, whose honor is preserved by paternal British care."

"From what I have heard, the lady is in more danger from our soldiery than from any number of red men."

"You are impertinent, Mr Hardacre. It is damned easy for a civilian to cavil. You must defer to experience. You will do it the general's way, or not at all."

I nearly told Dalyell to go to hell, but it seemed preposterous to blather about artistic integrity on behalf of a silly little farce that I had crafted for the sole purpose of getting inside Suky's skirts. A romp in Van Horn's river-garden was not exactly opening night at Drury Lane. Thus I submitted to the general's suggestions without further fuss.

I was uneasy about explaining to Daniel the changes that were made in his own part. There was no need for extensive rewriting. He only had two lines, about brightening the silver covenant chain between the Indians and their Great White Father in England. I told him that he would be expected to leap about and terrify the Spirit of Canada with his war whoops until the Hero of Montreal laid a restraining hand on his shoulder and presented him with a small keg of rum.

"You are a professional," I encouraged him. "You know how to work an audience."

Daniel looked quite cheerful when I mentioned the rum. He offered no comment, which I took for assent. When I came to know Indians better, I learned that they think it rude to express open disagreement. Instead of arguing, they wait the moment to make their case in their own way.

We made a brilliant assembly at the Van Horns' the following week—the flambeaux glowing along the river under an indigo sky full of stars; the ladies plumed and painted, beating their fans, comparing the rise of their soaring headdresses under the great lavender awnings striped with rose; the prancing grenadiers; the general sharing his silver snuff-box with Mr De Lancey and Mr Van Horn; the musicians at their fiddles and German flutes. We were all amateurs—though I may have been vain enough to think myself something more—but I got through my rhyming prologue without flubbing more than one line, and the excerpt from *Midsummer Night's Dream* was flawless.

We came to the high point of the evening. I had resigned myself to representing the villainous Vaudreuil, the last viceroy of New France. But I thought I cut a mighty fine figure in my white coat faced with lilac, with the sash and star of a chevalier of France, and I made sure that I found occasion to maul the Spirit of Canada rather more than was called for in the script. Suky was dressed in a filmy robe of vaguely Grecian design that made few demands on the imagination of the males in our audience. It bared most of her bosom and swirled as she moved, to hint at prettily rounded calves. I would have liked to reveal more, but a scandalized Mrs Van Horn had revolted during our rehearsals, crying, "You can't send my Suky on half-naked!" I had endeavored to explain that Suky's costume was meant to give the idea of a beautiful soul held in captivity. "It is a metaphorical design," I insisted. "I am sure Yorkers are too educated to see any lewdness in it." Mrs Van Horn had told me, rather bluntly, that she would leave metaphors for the proprietors of bagnios and would have her daughter decently clothed. The hem came down and the décolletage went up by a lesser margin; we are far more prudish about ankles than bosoms.

We approached the climactic moment. There was a drumroll. Then, to the music of the Grenadiers' March, the Hero of Montreal, in knightly armor with his plumed helmet tucked elegantly under his arm, strutted across the stage.

"May the Lord of Hosts cover you as a shield and make you terrible to our enemies on the day of battle."

This, and similar fine sentiments, were delivered by the Spirit of the Colonies, played by one of the De Lancey boys, who unfortunately developed a stammer.

The Hero and his followers started hacking away at us perfidious frenchies.

Daniel came out, striped red and black, with eagle feathers in his hair and bright bursts of turkey-down about his ears, brandishing a wicked-looking ball-headed war club with a spike on top.

He let out a dreadful howl that so astonished one of Dalyell's stage followers standing just ahead of him that he dropped his spontoon.

Davers, lolling on a wicker chair, started clapping. A few others joined in. Even General Amherst, if I read his expression correctly in the half-light, betrayed faint amusement.

The script called for the cowardly Vaudreuil to surrender his sword and the Spirit of Canada as his supporters fled before the fury of the British onslaught. I shied from playing the poltroon in front of Suky and decided to improvise. I gave her a hot embrace, then drew my sword and flourished it under No Deal's nose. He flushed a dangerous shade of purple and called on me to deliver up the Spirit of Canada. He showed his own powers of dramatic invention by calling me a blackguard, a villain, and several other names that drew a new snap of applause from our viewers. I made a little feint with my hanger, then carried away his lace collar with the point of the blade.

Dalyell bellowed nearly as loud as the Mohawk. "By God! I'll have your blood, you treacherous pimp!"

He lunged at me with his iron in a way that suggested

he was not play-acting. Our costumes were a fraud—his armor was tin—but our weapons were entirely real.

He put me on my mettle. Here I found my Dublin education of some advantage. I was no stranger to dueling and blazing with swords, pistols, cudgels or fighting irons.

Dalyell was good, but heavy on his feet, and slowed by his mock-armor.

I skipped around him, pricking him through the slits in the tin plates.

"Come on! Come on! You dancing master! You *petit maître!*" howled the Hero of Montreal. "I'll spit you like a toasting fork!"

The crowd roared its pleasure. A few sporting men were offering odds for and against the Hero, though I expect that most of the spectators thought we were still following the script.

Suky, of course, knew better. I grazed Dalyell, very lightly, along the side of his neck, drawing a single bead of blood. A lesser girl might have swooned. But the blood rose in Suky's cheeks and her eyes glinted hard and bright. Her lips were very red. She was feasting on the spectacle.

By a lucky chance, I slipped under Dalyell's guard, hooked the tip of my hanger under the quillons of his clamshell hilt and twisted his weapon out of his fist.

There was a considerable stir among the audience. The general was on his feet. Our hosts flapped about him, begging his indulgence.

"Unforgivable—bloody insult—stain on His Majesty's colors—"

I made haste to conclude the performance. I presented my own sword to Daniel, the Mohawk, who gave a scalp-yell and exited, stage right, with the promised keg of rum. I gave the audience a leg and a bow and hurried to follow him.

Dalyell blundered after me and laid a meaty hand on my shoulder.

"I won't forget this," he said thickly. "You planned it, didn't you? To humiliate me—and Sir Jeffrey."

"I have no idea what you are talking about."

"Yes, you planned it! You and that clover-boy cousin of yours. Johnson, the squaw-man!"

"If you wish a return engagement," I said coolly, "you know where your second may call on me."

"Have you both taken leave of your senses?" Old Van Horn interposed. "Mr Hardacre, I think you have behaved disgracefully. To abuse a man's home, and his friends! You are no longer welcome here."

We rode back to town in Mr Watts's coach; he, at least, seemed to have enjoyed the affair. Davers, too, was in rare good humor. After three miles of bouncing and rattling down unpaved roads, I felt chastened. No Deal's blustering, of course, did not move me a bit. But it appeared that by showing off in front of a girl, I had lost the girl and earned the severe displeasure of our commander-in-chief, a bad man to cross. How could I have been so foolish?

"You were magnificent," said Davers in our rooms at the Widow's.

"It's all very well for you to say. What have you lost? I have the feeling *you* put me up to the whole thing."

"You're the one who always demands common sense, Shane. Where is the sense in that statement?"

No sense at all. I could not deny it.

"I will call on Sir Jeffrey and explain to him that what happened was a silly misunderstanding over a woman, not a deliberate insult. He's a man of the world. He'll accept an apology."

"I didn't know that you and Sir Jeffrey were such great friends," I said, remembering how Davers had goaded him on the subject of Indians.

"A title has some uses, dear boy. What about you, Daniel?" The Mohawk was squatting on the floor on his heels, making serious inroads into the rum. "What do the Mohawks say?"

"Mohawks say *niawen*."

This word, I am told, means both more and less than "thank you." It means "that's it."

I last saw Suky and No Deal in Trinity Church the Sunday before we sailed upriver. I had sent Suky a note, but had it returned unopened, and decided that I had gone to quite enough trouble over the little tickler. Besides, I had found some consolation in the arms of a buxom young soldier's widow named Meg O'Cumming. She was a good-hearted, moderately discriminating bawd who told me she had a mind to go upcountry herself, in the expectation that the gentlemen there were more hungry—and more generous— than in the city.

Sunday service at Trinity, I should recall, is one of the great social rituals of New York. As many as a thousand people fill the pews, showing their money on their backs. The silks and satins, and the confident, well-upholstered interior, announce quite distinctly that our Established Church does not disdain worldly treasures. The altar stands at the east end, in a large semi-circular area, painted and gilded in the grand manner. The galleries are borne up by wooden columns in the Ionic style, set off with carved foliage; cherubs blow kisses from between the capitals. We were entertained by a huge gilded organ on the west side of the church and a boys' choir in white surplices.

The rector, Henry Barclay, would have looked as much at home in a colonel's regimentals or a merchant's suit of broadcloth as in his minister's robes. He was large and portly, with a port-drinker's complexion. Davers had come along to hear one of his sermons, because we had been told that Barclay, as a younger man, had been a missionary among the Mohawks. When Davers asked him about his experiences, he looked startled and a little frightened, like a man who has walked into an unseen spiderweb. Johnson told me later that Barclay had fled from his mission at the start of King George's war, not because he was scared of the French but because he was scared of the Mohawks. There was mystery and tragedy in the minister's family. Barclay's father Thomas before him had preached to the Mohawks and tried to root out pagan superstitions. Thomas Barclay died insane, confined in a windowless room in Albany by his friends after he ran through his house, trying to set it on fire with live coals. Davers may have guessed some of this. He had a sixth sense about people who, like himself, were familiar with shadowlands.

That may be another reason why Barclay, politely but stubbornly, turned his questions away. After that, Davers declined to attend service at Trinity. He went foraging about instead among the meeting-houses of other persuasions. He even went to the synagogue. He told me he liked the Quaker meetings best, because the Quakers accept that revelation can flow through any member of the congregation; they do not stand a priest between a man and his God. He was tolerant of all creeds, holding to none of them himself. My father would have endorsed his view of Henry Barclay's church. Davers, who was a nominal Anglican as I was, said our Established Church was a necessary public convenience that had as much to do with the soul as a customs office.

I listened to Customs Officer Barclay read the text for his sermon. He had chosen Proverbs 31, on how "the virtuous woman looketh well to the ways of her household and eateth not the bread of idleness." How I wished Peg Walsingham had been with me, to give her view of that mandate for male tyranny!

I scanned the congregation, and found Suky Van Horn sitting with her family across the aisle. Captain Dalyell was with them. I stared at Suky until she turned to look at me. I drew a blush which consorted charmingly with her honey-colored silk. No Deal turned too. Under his glare, I tipped Suky a lingering, lecherous wink. Dear Suky. You may be no rebel, and no Peg Walsingham, but if James Dalyell leads you down the aisle he will find that neither are you made to be a servant of Proverbs 31. We shall see each other again.

We boarded the Albany sloop at Coenties Quay on the East River. Our vessel was no beauty. She was broad-beamed, bottomed with sturdy white oak, strong enough and shallow enough to lug five hundred barrels of flour and survive frequent hits on the sandbars. We left with the tide. As it ebbed, our pipe-chewing Dutch skipper spread canvas to catch the breeze. When tide and wind both ran against us, we were obliged to anchor and wait for the elements to change.

We were slowed by sudden squalls and grounded for
half a day on a treacherous bar called the Overslaugh, just
below Albany. We made use of the halts to paddle onshore
by canoe. It took us six days to reach the Dutchman's
town on the upper Hudson, instead of the usual three, but
I loved every minute of the journey. Some of Johnson's
German neighbors have told me that the Hudson Valley reminds them of the Rhineland. I have never seen the Rhine,
but I have never clapped eyes on a valley more varied or
more picturesque than that of the river highway between
Albany and New York.

Ten miles or so above Manhattan, the western side of
the river changes dramatically. In place of rolling wood-
lands, sloping gently down to a shoreline the color of pale
brick with little clumps of gray sandstone, great palisades
of stone rear up like the walls of a giant's fortress. Twenty
miles farther upriver, you might be in the Scottish Highlands. Between the wavy crests of fir-clad ranges, the river
flows in a dark, narrow gorge, straight for a time, as if its
passage through the mountains was cut by sappers, then
curving through a deliberate S-shaped bend and running
on straight again. Wild, solitary peaks and windy balconies
of stone overhanging the river have bred fanciful stories.
We heard some of them from our skipper, others from
Daniel who became more talkative—and seemingly more
fluent in his mixture of Dutch-English—the nearer we approached to his native territory. That rock platform, now,
where the fireflies dart in the gathering dark, is the Devil's
Danzkammer—the Devil's Dance-Hall—where a Dutchman's skull was cracked like a quail's egg because he had
spied on a secret ritual of the River Indians. That island
there, covered with cedars, has a ghost that calls to men
who sail on the river alone. That petroglyph rising out of
the water contains the spirit of an Indian sachem, confined
there by sorcery.

There was a great deal more nonsense of this sort. I
would listen for a time, then go to try to hook myself a
sturgeon. They jumped high in the river, displaying their
short, blunt noses. They were too smart—or too well-
fed—to take my line, though I caught some lesser fish.

Davers gobbled up all the stories, the ones that must have been spun in an idle hour by a campfire, as well as the ones that carried the resonance of genuine terrors. I wondered how he sorted it all out in his head, or if he even tried.

I paid closer attention to Daniel as we neared Albany.

"Hoe kom je aan?" he greeted me in his frontier Dutch on our last morning, though he could say it just as well in English. "How is it going?"

"Skenegowa," I replied in Mohawk, to show him that I'd picked up something from the language tutoring he had been giving Davers. "Very good."

"You know Albany?"

"No. I don't know Albany."

"You know how we say that?"

"Albany?"

"Hen. Yes. We say De Fouck."

"I beg your pardon?"

"We say De Fouck."

It took a few moments, and the help of our skipper, before I got this right. De Fouck in Dutch means the Net. It is the name the Mohawks gave to what is now the city of Albany when the first Dutch traders arrived early in the past century. The Dutchman's town has had many names—Fort Orange, Beverwyck, Albany—but to the Mohawks, it remains De Fouck—a net spread to catch their furs and their lands and maybe their souls.

Whetstones
Somerset

26th July

Dearest Shane,

Do you know the value of a pearl?

It maddens me to picture you chasing after an empty-headed gadabout like Suky Van Horn. Her very name makes me think of a fat and stupid Persian cat, primping herself on satin cushions.

I hope you do not intent to go on and on about your previous women. This kind of thing raises the gravest questions about your taste. We will not go into your morals, since the subject is altogether foreign to you.

Your

Valerie

Villa dos Mouros
Sintra

4th August

My dear Lady D'Arcy,

I fear you are becoming jealous. The sentiment is unworthy of you, and quite misplaced. The incidents you protest took place before you were born, and Suky—I am told—is a stuffy old widow living on the Loyalist grants in Upper Canada. Do not judge me by what I was. A riper understanding, and a seasoned palate, have made me more discriminate in love. You will have my undivided devotions if only you can rid yourself of the old warthog.

In haste, Your

Shane

Dearest Shane,

I am not persuaded that love is possible without jealousy. Molière tells us that to be without jealousy is to love coldly. My love for you is fiery and devouring. I am unwilling to share you, even with your ghosts.

You came to me again in my dreams last night and I bit you on the chest. Do you bear the wound?

My bones remember you, Shane, my blood stirs to your rhythms. My skin remembers you as fire and ash, silk and water.

Your loving

Valerie

4

A Tavern Fight

A HAIRY FELLOW IN a dugout canoe took us from the sloop, deposited us on a mudbank where we slid up to our calves in the mire and charged us a shilling a head for the favor. We were informed by Van Schaik, Johnson's factor, that the reason Albany has no wharves or jetties is that when the river ice breaks up in the thaw, it carries everything before it. Davers and I were to share a bed in a filthy garret above the Dutchman's truck room. Van Schaik grumbled about *de Wilde*, but at last consented to let Daniel sleep on the floor of our room, like a dog, on condition that he would hold us strictly accountable for any goods found missing from his stores. The family dined unconscionably early, nearer to five than six, and swallowed prodigious quantities of cucumbers doused in vinegar. I caught a glimpse of a rosy, dimpled, flaxen-haired daughter in bright homespun stockings, but she was kept well out of reach. As soon as it was seemly—when Van Schaik settled himself in his rocker and began filling the room with pipe-fumes and the wind of cucumbers—I proposed to Davers that we should inspect the town. Daniel, who had been fed at the kitchen door, loped along beside us, quite the beau in his London clothes.

Halfway up the hillside, the cross of Saint George hung limp from a flagstaff above Fort Frederick. The town of Albany falls down the slope between the fort and the river, inside a shabby stockade that forms the outline of a warden pear. There was a yeasty smell in the streets from the numerous bakehouses, and a sickly sweet odor of chocolate from Wendell's factory, but these were overruled by the all-pervasive tang of fresh manure. In the gathering dusk, we saw droves of cows, and a few pigs and sheep as well, being fetched in from the pastures below the walls to spend the night inside the safety of the stockade. Horses stood tethered by their masters' doors. They were scrawny, thin-shanked beasts, for the greater part; either the Albany Dutch are no judges of horseflesh or they skimp on winter feed. You would not mistake Albany for anything but a Dutchman's town. The better houses stand gable-end to the street, with tiles on the roofs and porch-seats where the mynheers sit sucking their pipes and long gutters running out over the middle of the thoroughfare so that an innocent passer-by cannot help but be drenched in wet weather. A century of British rule had left little stamp on the city, except for the Anglican Church, which tries to look down its steeple at the Dutch Reformed—without success, because the Dutch meeting-house stands higher up the hill—and a sprinkling of taverns with patriotic names like the King's Arms.

Davers tapped my arm as we neared a tippling-shop at the grimier end of Beaver Street. The shingle bore a very fair likeness of Sir Jeffrey, all butting nose and powdered curls. The words "Hero of Montreal" were picked out in gold leaf that had weathered greenish. I thought the "Concupiscent Sheep" would have been a much better title, but forbore from saying so, because there were a few redcoats loitering by the door with pots in their hands, and you can never tell whether a soldier well-steeped in liquor will stand you a drink for insulting his general or poke you in the eye.

"I say," said Davers. "That's rich. I wonder if Sir Jeffrey knows. Shall we give it a try?"

Daniel put on his thirsty look.

"You've sworn off," I reminded him. "Do you want to go back to the circus?"

He stared at me as if I had told him his mother was rogered by a hog.

I peeped through the door. The place reminded me of a hostelry on Essex Street in Dublin—dark wood well scuffed, sawdust on the floor, a jolly, red-faced jilt in cap and apron. There were a few fellows dicing and a couple puffing away at a backgammon table.

"Just one now," I told Daniel. "I'll be watching."

"Evenin', guvnor," one of our stout defenders greeted me.

"Good evening."

"Blimey, sir. You're not thinking of bringing 'im in 'ere?" This was accompanied by a jerk of the thumb towards Daniel's round face.

"Do you have some objection?"

"Rule one, sir. No bleedin' niggers."

" 'Less he's got a sister," contributed a barrackroom wit.

"You got no smellers, Charlie. Christ though, take a look at this one, dressed up like a bleedin' dog's dinner."

I could not let this pass. Davers's lips had disappeared and Daniel had put on his serene face, which meant that each of them was capable of almost anything.

"Look here. Our friend is a Mohawk, and one of His Majesty's Indian allies."

"Rule two," said the wit. "No niggers."

A swag-bellied fellow whom I took for the proprietor came to the door, all smiles and apologies. His soft brogue and his clever, sidelong look announced him as an Irishman and, indeed, he told us his name was Feeny.

"You do not mean to tell me, Mr Feeny, that it is the policy of the house to bar any drinking man?"

He pleaded regulations—nasty incidents—public feeling. Perhaps he could offer us a private room?

"Damn your private room!" cried Davers. "This Indian

is entitled to sit where he chooses, and he has a better right to be here than any man among you."

Things were getting out of hand. The soldiers had taken to inspecting Daniel's clothing, lifting up his coattails and fingering the lining.

I hate to pull rank but I told our landlord, confidentially, that we were traveling under military orders to visit my kinsman Sir William Johnson, and that I was sure that Sir William would remember a fellow-Irishman who did a good turn for his family. I said more loudly that I proposed to buy everyone a drink, to toast all His Majesty's friends. Daniel's skin whitened by magic. In no time, we were seated at the best table in the house around a bowl of shrub.

Davers was on his high horse, ranting about how we must tell Johnson, and how he must lodge a formal complaint about the behavior of His Majesty's finest regiment.

"There is no profit in complaining about common soldiers," I reminded him, "when they borrow their prejudice from their commanding general."

If Daniel shared Sir Robert's outrage, he did not display it. He applied himself remorselessly to the rum-shrub.

To provide Davers with a diversion, I suggested that he should propose the toast. He made a little speech about the brotherhood of man that I fear was rather over the heads of our company.

So I chipped in with, "May I roger whom I please, and please whom I roger," which cheered up both our fusiliers and our landlord, who was busy chalking up mysterious figures on the blackboard at the back of his hutch.

"To days of sport and nights of transport!"

And then Daniel came alive. He banged his fist on the table and roared, *"Snakiren!"*

I expect that is the first word of Mohawk I ever learned. It has a snaky look to it, and a snaky sound, which is as it should be, because Mohawks say that a serpent lives inside every bottle of booze that was ever distilled.

Daniel picked up the punchbowl, tossed what was left down his gullet, and howled again, *"Snakiren!* Drink 'em down!"

Then he started singing. I don't know where he got the words, but it was not in a gin-mill. I suspect it was the Bible-bashers over at Wheelock's school in Connecticut. Anyway, he came out with:

> "Hobgoblin nor foul fiend
> Shall daunt his spirit
> He knows he at the end
> Shall life inherit."

His lips rarely met when he spoke—there are no labials in the Mohawk language—so "hobgoblin" sounded like "oh golly" and "spirit" like "syrup" (he remembered the *p* in time to insert it at the end). The whole performance reminded me of a man trying to make himself throw up by tickling his tonsils.

Daniel carried on for two or three verses. Davers looked mildly depressed. The soldiers spat and rumbled. A loose-boned, surly, lantern-jawed brute who had been squatting silent by the fireplace with his bottle started up from his place.

"As God is my strength," he cried, "I willna endure more from this murdering spawn of Satan!"

His voice was much disguised in liquor, but its origin was surely north of Hadrian's Wall. I will not weary you by reproducing all the idiosyncrasies of that dialect.

He leaned over our table. His eyes were hidden far back, in cavernous sockets under the bony overhang of his forehead.

"Come away with you, Ian," said a fellow-Scot, plucking at his sleeve.

The man was boiling with rage. I believe he was ready to kill, though I had no idea why. Daniel's singing was pretty awful, but surely not *that* awful.

"You—you—"

There was something fighting to get out. He could not find the words, but Daniel knew. The Mohawk was crouched on his heels, on top of his seat, ready to take flight—or to spring on his adversary.

"I don't believe we've been introduced," said Davers. Breeding will always tell.

Our visitor did not acknowledge Sir Robert.

"Is this curious fellow known to you?" Davers asked the Mohawk.

"*Iah.*" Daniel grunted the negative.

We waited. The stranger gripped the edge of the table until his knuckles gleamed white. His hands were enormous.

His neckcloth was loose and none too fresh. His Adam's apple bobbed wildly above it as he gasped, "You will pay. Lord hear me, you will pay."

He threw up his right arm as if he meant to strike Daniel. I reached out instinctively and prisoned his wrist.

"Explain yourself, sir!" I demanded. "Do you have some complaint of this Indian?"

"Complaint? Aye, that I have. But no complaint of the dead!" This came with a ghastly, hollow laugh. He tried to wrench his hand free. "Leave go, you miserable vaguing Teague."

He was strong, and got away from me.

He brandished something in front of our faces. It appeared to be his tobacco pouch. It was neatly sewn together from human skin, a shade or two darker than Daniel's.

"See that?" The same hollow laugh, as merry as a death-rattle. "Got that off a Mingo, in the Ohio country. Skinned him myself. That's a good Indian. Do you want to make something of that, Indian-lover?"

Daniel was ominously quiet.

I marveled at the depth of this drunken fool's hatred. A few of the redcoats egged him on, but most of the patrons turned their backs in embarrassment or contempt. Albany was a traders' town, built on the soft gold of Indian peltries. Indians came to De Fouck to be skinned metaphorically, not in the flesh.

"Come away with you, McDonner," the ruffian's companion tried again. Davers was on his feet, deathly pale, his hand twitching towards the hilt of his hanger.

"Sure it's only the liquor talking, gentlemen," said our

landlord, who busied himself removing candles and empty
glasses from the long center table.

"When the Prince of Darkness and all his minions were
chased out of Europe, they took up residence here, with
their own kind," McDonner said wildly. "No God-fearing
man is safe while one of them lives."

I concluded that the man was deranged.

"You tell 'im, Mac!" cried one of the fusiliers. "Rule
One. No niggers."

"Damn your insolence!" I called McDonner a sottish
loblolly, a raw haggis and a few choicer names.

He pulled away from his friend and laid hands on a
thick-bottomed firing-glass. I ducked down, and it missed
me by an inch. McDonner grabbed a poker from the hearth
and flung himself at me. I snatched up a stool and put it
up as a shield.

The Mohawk was faster. He must have slid under the
table. He brought our assailant down with a flying tackle
and squatted on his backbone, wrenching his head back by
the hair until he was bawling loud enough to bring the
roof down. The soldiers made a bid to join in the fun, but
Davers blocked their path, sword in hand, and swore he
would spit the first man that interfered like a game-hen.

I got hold of McDonner's tobacco pouch which had
fallen on the floor and threw it into the fire.

This concluded the livelier part of our proceedings at
the Hero of Montreal. Daniel must have inflicted serious
damage, because McDonner was carried out insensate with
a slime of blood on his chin. I have been in rougher slopshop brawls, but it was the first time I had seen a man
ready to do murder because of the color of another man's
skin.

I asked Feeny what he knew about our attacker.

"He's a Belfast man," said the publican, polishing his
thumbs on his greasy waistcoat, as if this explained everything.

When I pressed for more information, I was told that
McDonner had had a bad time in the war. He had tried
farming down Pennsylvania way where it seemed there
were a large number of Scots-Irish. His place was burned

out in an Indian raid, his whole family murdered and scalped. He had tried to make a new life in the Mohawk Valley and had fallen in with some crooked land-sharks who were trying to enforce a suspect deed to Indian land. The Mohawks burned his barn and threatened his life and Sir William refused him protection. He had lost everything twice over and blamed the Indians—*all* Indians—for all of his misfortunes. You might have thought that a man like that would have turned his back on the frontier. But McDonner came from a stubborn, stiff-necked people. And hatred can possess a man as completely as love.

We followed the trail of the Dutchmen's thick wooden-wheeled wagons for sixteen miles, through the pine barrens to Schenectady, a brawling traders' town on the Mohawk River. I found I had been rooked by the mynheer who sold me my horse at Albany. He looked like a fine roan pacer, high in spirit, but I neglected to search under the saddle which came with the bargain we struck. When he shied in the woods and tried to buck me off, I made closer inspection, and discovered that his back was infested with botflies, nasty hooked creatures that are the very devil to extract without leaving bloody craters in a horse's flesh. I traded him for a tired old mare at Schenectady, and fell into an evil sulk.

My humor revived as we trotted along the king's highway, which is only a rutted trail, studded with potholes and boulders. The air was sweet and clean; the sunlight danced on the river; the scent of wild balm and young cedar carried from the woods. Wild pigeons hung in the evergreens, thick as blossom. Northward, I saw the blue tips of the Adirondacks. The sky above me was immense.

In Johnson country men breathe a larger air.

Dearest Shane,

I hope you no longer haunt taverns and that your hand
on the bottle is lighter than Henry's. He disgraced himself at table last night, nodding off before the soufflé.
I left him snoring into the gravy.

I would leave him and fly to your arms tonight, except that I am a coward about poverty. I remember the
ache of hunger when my father lost everything.
Henry is generous only so long as I spend what he
gives me in his sight. He allows me to hoard nothing,
so I have no means of accumulating my own money.

We would not enjoy being poor together. Eloise
told Abelard she would rather be his whore than the
empress of Rome, but think how badly all of that
ended! You and I are sensualists, more than romantics.
We cleave to our comforts. I envy you not one minute of your time in the forest, slathered in bear
grease.

Even if money were not at issue, Sir Henry will
never give up the children, and no English magistrate
would award them to a woman whose native language is French. I could not bear to be separated
from them.

This reminds me of a singular omission I have noticed in your narrative. Glancing ahead, I find one
woman after another yielding to your advances.
Where are the consequences? Where are the children?

If you discovered some native method for preventing
childbirth, do let us know. I hope someone will bring
us a method more satisfactory than the wretched *pardessus anglais*, which I am required to call a French letter on this side of the Channel. It is no wonder neither

the French nor the English wish to assume responsibility. Wearing the thing must be like getting into the bath in a sack dress.

Your

Valerie

5

Johnson Country

"**I** ROSE, AND THE SUN rose with me," Sir William greeted me. "Is that not what King Louis used to say?"

It was barely day. The first rays of the sun sparkled on the brown-green river and threw long shadows from the willows and the locust grove.

Johnson sat on a wooden bench with a light shawl over his knees despite the warmth in the air, nursing a cup of brandy and surveying his world.

"Sit with me, Shane."

His handsome face was puffy and pale from pain and lack of sleep. His broad shoulders slumped forward. His alert, quizzical eyes seemed pinched. Under his strong jaw with its sensualist's cleft, loose flesh threatened to sag into wattles. He was no longer master of his body but his fierce will refused to allow his sickness to master him.

I sat beside him looking at the sun on the water, at the green islands in the stream.

The dark woman came from the house, not that I heard her steps or saw her coming. She might have risen out of the ground or out of the spray of the willows. She did not

come and go, as you or I come and go. She materialized
and then vanished.

Her tawny hand on his wrist, questioning his veins.
Wordless, she takes the brandy from him. He does not resist. She raises a china mug to his lips, as if she were feeding an infant. The tea smells bitter. What is it? Sassafras,
spicewood, rudbeckia?

I asked her.

"Ononkwa." She has eyes only for her patient. She slips
her fingers under his queue. She is kneading the small of
his neck. She goes deep, deep as the brain-stem, deep as
the limbic memory of our ancestors who crawled out of
the primal swamp in the time when there was no time.
Johnson sighs and sits upright. His chest swells under the
loose morning gown. His mouth softens into a smile. His
delicate hand—long tapering fingers, an artist's hand—is a
white shadow against her skin. She is gone. The breath of
sweetgrass lingers in the air.

Ononkwa. Medicine. Medicine woman, guarding her secrets, ranging the deep woods and the creekbeds at dusk
and at dawn, talking the language of plants, asking permission to use the gifts of herbs and roots, returning thanks
with native tobacco. Spirit woman, in white men's cloth of
midnight blue hung with silver.

Johnson said, "She gives me back my life."

He laid his hand on his thigh where the poisoned ball a
Frenchman shot into him at the battle of Lake George fes-
tered beyond the reach of any surgeon.

He tossed the dregs of his tea across the lawn and
laughed to lighten his confession. "But I'll wager arsenic
or water hemlock would taste sweeter than this filthy
muck."

He referred to her as Mary, or less frequently, Molly, in
white company. But mostly he called her by an Indian
nickname, Chicha, which means Flower. She was a Mohawk of the Wolf Clan, but her mother's people were Hurons, brought back as prisoners from the Bay of Quinte by
a Mohawk war-party and adopted into the Longhouse. I
suppose she was in her late twenties when I met her,
though she looked older. She must have been quite fetch-

ing before the smallpox left its marks on her face, but I
think she could never have been described as beautiful.
Her face was flattish and the slant of the eyes, her best
feature, wide as a doe's, the deep brown flecked with
golden lights, and her tawny-yellow complexion gave her
something of an oriental appearance. She wore her glossy
black hair in braids. Her body was straight and sinewy, a
little too scrawny for my taste, and she walked in that
pigeon-toed way that native women have that saves them
from tripping over loose rocks and protruding roots on the
narrow forest trails.

It was not her looks that had induced Johnson to install
this native woman as the mistress of his house. He had his
pick of beautiful women of all shapes and colors, and I
never noticed that Chicha's presence prevented him from
indulging his grosser appetites whenever he found relief
from the gravel and the flux and that old wound in his
thigh. He needed more than a bedmate. He needed Chicha's medicine, and he needed her to screen him from the
constant demands of the Indians who surrounded him.

We sat together, watching the first stir of activity along
the river—the gang of negro slaves under the eye of an
Irish overseer, lugging sacks of flour from Johnson's mill
down to his wharf; the cloud of dust thrown up by a Pal-
atine farmer's wagon creaking along the King's Road from
Stone Arabia; the Mohawk boy standing up in the stern of
a canoe, his spear poised to take a fish. General Amherst
had found it incomprehensible that a man of rank and
money, a baron-knight, could live among woodland Indians. I now knew why Johnson had remained in his Valley.
He had built a whole world around him. How many men
have accomplished that in this lifetime except in airy
imaginings?

I will try to call back this world Johnson made with
stone and iron and men.

The house was built with raw fieldstone, quarried from
the great gray limestone bluffs that pinch the Valley between the two Mohawk castles. The two-story building,
with its five bays, its hipped roof and its center portico on
a platform of tooled limestone, recalled the stone house at

Smithstown where Johnson was born. But it reminded me even more of an ancient stronghouse that I climbed as a boy, set among weeping beeches off a fierce back road in West Meath. The place was raised by a bog captain in the times of the Shadow Lords, when death was an arm's length away; there were slits in the rude stonework for archers and arquebuses and portholes for hurling down boulders and pitchers of boiling oil. In place of loopholes, Johnson had set five dormers in the roof. Behind them, inside the high attic, he kept wall-pieces and musquetoons ready for use by snipers if his home came under attack. The stone house was flanked by three blockhouses, one at either corner in front, commanding the road in both directions, the last, with portholes and room enough for a garrison of twenty fusiliers, standing off on a little hill on the north side looking towards Canada across the blue Adirondacks. Three sides of the compound were enclosed by a wooden palisade, with a walkway where a redcoat sentry was prowling, with a shallow moat and a drawbridge on the west side and a cold, fast-running creek to the east.

Citified people might think the interior of Fort Johnson modest, but it was a palace by the standards of Johnson's neighbors, white and red. The stone and the timber were local, but every item of hardware, every latch and hinge and bolt, every screw and sash, every pane of Crown glass, even the brushes and dry white lead for painting, had to be fetched from England, calculated down to the last nail and ordered months in advance. Two big rooms and two narrow ones opened off the center hall on each floor. The staircase was of oak with slender mahogany balusters. The withdrawing room was paneled from floor to ceiling with beveled walnut, painted a deep Prussian blue matching the blue of the enormous closets on either side of the fireplace. The dining room was papered with scenes of Fontainebleau—fountains and fawns and ladies with capes and parasols. One of the smaller rooms at the back was called the Cherry Room because the cherrywood wainscot was left unpainted. This was reserved for the family, and was the only place, apart from the master's bedroom, where they could enjoy any privacy, because the house was always full of strangers and as busy as an inn. Chicha and Johnson's Indian children shared one of the smaller bedrooms upstairs. His white daughters shared another. Davers and I slept in the room reserved for guests which John Johnson, Sir William's son and heir by a German housekeeper he had bought for five guineas, had occupied before he married Polly Watts and moved to his own establishment.

Only Sir William had a room to himself, and he was rarely alone in it. His bedroom was also his office and his private council-chamber. It looked like a cross between a library and a game hunter's trophy room. Foxed and watermarked books from London—Hume's *History*, Newton's *Principia*, Smollett and Fielding—lined the wall nearest the high-posted bed which was draped with a smelly black buffalo robe; the eyeless head lolled over the end. The other walls were filled with native curiosities—skins of white deer, ermine and a prized white wolf, wampum belts and feathered pipes, war clubs and fetishes, drums and a huge rattle fashioned from the shell of a snapping turtle, the head stretched on splints to make a handle. There were a couple of racing prints of Newmarket, a reminder of the world Johnson had turned his back on.

The stone house lorded it over a community of tributary buildings, as populous and as varied as a good-sized village. Immediately behind the house, in a Palladian arrangement that formed a courtyard, were the slave barracks—Johnson owned thirty negroes, which made him the greatest slave-holder in the province—and the servants' quarters; a stone stable with eight stalls for his beloved Arabians; a large barn and a bakehouse with a pigeon-loft in its cupola. Johnson's miller ground his wheat in the gristhouse by the creek; his baker made his bread; his boatmen carried his sacks of flour to Schenectady on his own fleet of bateaux. His lumberjacks hauled hardwoods for building and white pines for the masts of His Majesty's men-of-war to his sawmill. Two blacksmiths labored with bellows and tongs, mending barrels and locks, forging bullets and springs around the charcoal fire of his smithy. Near the river, under close guard, were silos for his grain and peas, and warehouses crammed with Indian goods. Across the creek, on a gentle rise, was the huge bark lodge where he sat around the council fire with the Indian chiefs; nearby, the ruins of bark shanties and huts that had housed a thousand of his native guests in the critical moment of the war, when he had held the Confederacy of the Longhouse to the English cause with paltry bribes and infinite blarney.

He employed sixty people, not counting his slaves, but he controlled the lives of thousands more. He imported tenants from Ireland and the Scottish Highlands—wild, hairy, kilted men who spoke only Gaelic and were as fiercely devoted to Billy Johnson as if he were the Young Pretender born again—and sent them to hack down forests and sow wheat for the West Indies. The Mohawks supplied him with spies and couriers and bodyguards and with women to entertain visiting grandees. The Dutch and German freeholders who shared the Valley with them may have resented Johnson, but they generally bent according to his will. The cheerful John Ogilvie, the vicar at Fort Hunter, lived on his largesse and served as his household chaplain. Johnson ran the Indian Department and used it like an estate office. His lieutenants were kinsmen and old drinking cronies. They were all Irish and good bottle-men, with the exception of Daniel Claus, an earnest and humorless German who naturally got to do much of the work. I felt very much at home, sharing a dozen of wine with fat, jolly Guy Johnson, Sir William's nephew, and with the hard-drinking, hard-swearing Butler boys, the spawn of some old horse artillery barracks in Meinster. Through gusting clouds of claret and rum-shrub, they presided over the affairs of the Indian nations from Fort Johnson as far towards the setting sun as any white man had traveled.

The Kingsland Patent had added eighty square miles to Sir William's domains, and he had already cleared a great expanse of meadow, ten miles back from the river, with the aim of building a grander manor house and of founding a market town that would be a magnet for new colonists and open the whole interior to development.

He was the greatest landowner in the Province of New

York, and probably its wealthiest resident. He was judge and merchant prince, imperial agent and Superintendent of Indian Affairs, a major-general of the provincial troops and an adopted headman of the Mohawk nation, the only white man who has ever been permitted to wear the living bones—the ceremonial deerhorns of a *royaner*, a traditional Indian chief. The sum of the parts is less than the whole.

Sir William Johnson—Warragiyaguey to the Mohawks— was a feudal king. We have seen nothing like him in the civilized parts of Europe since the great O'Neill lay roaring drunk on a hilltop in Ulster surrounded by clansmen of high and low degree. When Johnson paid a visit to one of the Indian castles, he was preceded by kilted warriors skirling on the bagpipes. At home, by his fire, he would call in the blind harpist he had shipped from Castlebar to soothe him with Carolan's receipt. He was as absolute, in his way, as Kubla Khan or the Tsar of All the Russias and could afford to be as whimsical, though he acknowledged a distant king as his master and enforced his laws in more subtle ways. Like a warlord in savage times, he could say what no modern king can boast: "My dynasty begins with me."

The Americans I have encountered in this new, Republican age do not know what to make of him. His world seems alien and inexplicable to them; they can hardly believe that he lived in the same continent, in the same time, as Sam Adams and the Sons of Liberty. His world, it appears, has died with the Revolution. Yet, for a time, it seemed to me the one place in America where white men and red men could make a life together. There was even a time when I thought that Johnson's world was the only place worth living.

I was young. I had been knocking around like a billiard ball, with no higher purpose than finding a lodging in a soft pocket. I was ready for a hero and a cause. Johnson gave them to me.

He did not cut a very heroic figure that morning, with his belly hanging out under his sick-robe and bags under his eyes the size of portmanteaux, looking at least a decade older than his forty-six years. In fact, he looked seedy, and perhaps a little crooked. He was those things too. As I tried to explain to Garrick, there are no heroes without shadows anywhere but on a stage. The greater the man, the greater, potentially, is this dark side. The same energy that fuels his achievements, misused or misplaced, will turn on him, or on those around him. If love fails him, if he loses his lust for life, it will coil into suicidal despair. Johnson knew something of this; it was why he worried about Davers.

Doyle, Sir William's bodyservant, came around the side of the house with a shaving bowl and began whipping up a lather.

Johnson asked him what he thought of Sir Robert Davers who appeared to be sleeping late.

Doyle thwacked his straight razor against the leather strop, thinking about it. He was a nubby, knobby, good-natured little man in a green waistcoat and buff-colored breeches.

"I don't know rightly how as to say it, your honor. Sir Robert sure ain't no child from the ashes."

"No indeed."

"Don't see a whole heap of English noblemen hobnobbing with injuns, your honor. Might I ask if he got a lady in trouble?"

"Not to my knowledge."

"Must have been something worse then, to leave home and all. Not as if he would have been hungry. Faith, he's a puzzlement to me, sorr. He puts the poor mouth on life."

"I think that sums it rather well, eh, Shane? Puts the poor mouth on life. In England, Doyle, they call it melancholia. It runs through the better families like the measles."

"Can't say I've heard tell of it, your honor."

"It comes of not having enough to do. *Non est cura melior quam labor.*"

The Latin tag was for my benefit. It means roughly, "There's no better cure than work." Doyle was scraping away at Johnson's stubble.

"You've knocked about the world, Doyle," his master

went on. "Sir Robert means to go up the lakes and find Indians no white man has interviewed. How do you suppose he will do?"

Doyle's blade made an elegant dip into the cleft of Johnson's chin. He wiped the scum off and said, "Seems to me it's an experiment, sorr. Like them hothouse plants you get from Mr Colden. Some of them take over the garden. There's some that is throttled by crabgrass and such. Then there's them that just gives up the ghost as soon as they get a good look at where they are. There's no ways of knowing till you've put them in."

When he had shaved and dressed, Johnson felt stout enough to take me for a ride up onto the plateau where he had measured out the plot for the mansion he intended to dub Johnson Hall.

He said to me, "I am of Doyle's persuasion. It's a risky business, taking a fellow like Davers into Indian country. Here, at least, they won't eat him alive. Out west, anything can happen. Your friend Sir Jeffrey Amherst is quite deluded about the state of Indian affairs. We may have beaten the French in Canada, but we have not taken possession of their territories. Generals look at maps and draw lines across them. Land-sharks peer over their shoulders, laying out tracts. The real world is not on the maps, Shane."

He pointed to the charred stumps of a stand of elms, and the fireweed and sumac that had sprung up among them.

"Do you know how long it takes to clear a few acres from this wilderness? These forests had never heard the sound of a steel axe before we came. Three days' journey from here, the forests are untouched. They have swallowed up British armies. White men get lost in them. They lose their heads, like a castaway drunk on salt water. The men who own the forests are no friends to us. Oh yes, you see what I have made of the Valley. But it is a damned treacherous, slippery business, holding on to the Mohawks, even though other Indians call them Englishmen. I wait on them night and day. I am their slave as much as their master. Their kinsmen have no love for us, and I cannot say that I blame them. Our soldiers rape their women who will give themselves freely to a man who asks nicely. Our fur-traders cheat them blind and grab the whole fruits of a winter hunt for a keg of watered rum. I know a Dutchman who boasts that he waters his grog with his own product. Our officials are haughty and mock native customs. Everywhere, the natives fear the coming of settlers and speculators who will drive away the game and steal the land from under their bark huts and reduce them to vagrant broomsellers and shabby drunks, like the Indians of New England. And on top of all this, our commander-in-chief now wants to deprive them of the guns they hunt with and the kettles they cook with and the very clothing off their backs!"

Johnson had already lectured us on the subject of these Indian gifts that General Amherst found so disgraceful. Of course Sir William had an interested view; who among us does not? What he said made a good deal of sense to me, and made me less rueful that I had offended our commander-in-chief. Johnson explained that the natives are a Stone Age people who had been exposed, almost overnight, to the latest improvements of our eighteenth-century technologies. The clever ones had perceived the need to adapt in order to survive. In their haste to make the change, they had forgotten all their traditional crafts. They no longer hunted with bow and arrow; they no longer cooked in bark vessels or hand-pressed pots of clay. Even those who lived a semi-nomadic life, on the edge of subsistence, required guns and powder and copper kettles and steel hatchets and knives—things they could not manufacture, or even repair, for themselves. Unless we supplied these things to the Indians in sufficient quantity, they would starve. Hungry men are thieves and rebels of necessity, and Johnson read the signs of a great native revolt brewing all along the frontier.

He was planning to voyage to the outpost at Detroit, which had been in British hands for only a year, to meet with the chiefs of all the western tribes in the effort to sow his peace among them. He had offered to take me with him, and had already floated the idea that I should serve under him, in the Indian Department. I think he saw in me

something of himself as a younger man, with an appetite
for life that had yet to be shaped by experience. I flatter
myself that there was more of Billy Johnson in me than in
John, his son and heir, a conceited, indolent prig who
lounged about putting on airs, dainty and slow as a cater-
pillar on a cabbage. Johnson had included Robert Davers
in his invitation to Detroit. It would have been unmannerly
not to, and I learned that Sir William would countenance
almost anything except a lapse from good manners. He
told me also—after I confessed to my wager with Gaius
Walsingham—that he meant to help me win my bet. But
he had deep misgivings about Davers, and I think that they
sprang from his recognition that Davers represented a part
of that dark side in himself that he had always sought to
beat back. There is, after all, a Davers in every man, a
creature that, in Doyle's phrase, "puts a poor mouth on
life."

Johnson's comprehension of Davers did not come all at
once. When we first arrived, he was suspicious that the
baronet, consciously or otherwise, was the tool of his enemies, especially after Sir Robert mentioned that he was
carrying despatches from General Amherst to Captain
Rutherford and to Captain Campbell, the commanding
officer at Detroit.

Johnson quizzed me privately about these letters.

"Have you read them?"

"Good Lord, I hope you think me enough of a gentleman not to open another man's letters."

"Do you know what's in them?"

"Not the faintest idea. I presume they are routine instructions of a military nature. We gave Sir Jeffrey no
cause to entrust us with sensitive intelligence."

Johnson grumbled about land speculations and people
going around his back. I would not be surprised if he had
Doyle, or one of his other retainers, rummage through
Davers's bags when he was out in his canoe—he proved a
handy lad with a paddle—or jawing with the Mohawks at
their castle at Fort Hunter where the Schoharie Creek
rushes into the river. If Johnson found what he wanted to
know, he did not tell me.

I watched him try to strike a damp into Sir Robert's enthusiasm for his quest by telling him horror stories about Indian atrocities. They struck a chill into me, but Davers seemed wholly unmoved.

He said that he wanted to study with native medicine men, to find out what they knew of the human soul.

Johnson doused himself with punch—he ordered limes by the thousand—and got out a word that sounded like the onset of a rash.

"Ratetshents."

This received blank stares.

"I see your Mohawk lessons have not taken you very far," Johnson said to Davers. "That is the Mohawk name for a medicine man, or a witchdoctor. *Ratetshents.* It means, He Who Dreams."

"Do you know one? I mean, is there one near here?"

"The Mohawks are mostly Anglicans. The vicar does not think very highly of dreams." Johnson's smile faded as quickly as it had blossomed. "I knew a Mohawk dream-hunter once. I would rather not talk about him."

His eyes became very gray and intent, and he issued the closest thing to a direct warning that I ever heard him express to Davers.

Johnson said, "If you go looking for the spirit world of the Indians, you will find you are already inside it."

"I know," said Davers.

"If you truly know that, you had best be warned that if you journey beyond a certain line—a line you may not recognize until you have left it far behind—then you may never be able to live in the ordinary world again. That would mean that, in the terms of our society, you would be insane. Trust me, Sir Robert, *Wa gaderion dare.* I know that whereof I speak."

Davers, the holy fool, said, "I know."

Dearest Shane,

We came up from the country for the races. I looked
for you last night, in the manner of one of your native
shape-shifters. I flew to you like a seagull.

I believe I saw you clearly, ranging your terrace
above the green cliffs, gulping demitasse after demitasse of your savage Brazilian coffee. I saw the olive-
skinned, black-haired woman who tends and comforts
you there. I watched her walk, slump-shouldered, to
a little hut or chapel, where she made fire and prayed
before a wooden statue. I saw her weeping. I sensed she
fears for you.

Are you ill, Shane? Or have you returned to breaking hearts?

Or was it your hero Johnson that I glimpsed?

I confess that your first portrait of Sir William is cap-
tivating. I felt the thrill of the high kings returning.
Here, of course, it is a self-made king, but a king out
of Ireland nonetheless, building his armed house stone
on stone among the forest-seas of the New World, treating all who live under his aegis as family, heedless
of color and creed.

Truly, you walked with giants who made thunder in
the earth. Johnson's shadow is with me now, as I write.

Then my eye falls to the start of your next chapter.
It seems we must endure another ode to your cock.

What is it, in man, that obliges him to vest so much
of self-value in this item of anatomy?

My mother cautioned me that a man will make
love to the hind end of a donkey. You make yourself
her proof and vindication. You report yourself galloping
at women like a mad stallion. You take your pleasure
and rush on. You dare to boast that you gave satis-

faction because you elicited grunts and whinnies in your wild career.

You owe my sex better than this.

Your

Valerie

Villa dos Mouros

15th September

Beloved,

You never complained when we were together. Come to me quickly and I will remind you.

In the meantime, do not pass judgement on my narrative until you have been where it leads.

Your

Shane

P.S. I found a seagull trapped in the chimney of the room I use both to write and to sleep. I was gentle with her.

6

Apples and Flints

THE SMELL OF AN apple orchard always makes me as lustful as a jackrabbit. My sniffers take me back to the time when I first discovered what a man's equipment is good for, and got rid of my virginity in a frothy gallop with Nancy Nolan, the complaisant daughter of one of my father's tenants. Dear Nancy! What has become of you? She had freckles on her tits, and she rutted like a rattlesnake. We did it for the first time in the apple-loft behind the tack room. I was twelve years old; Nancy was sixteen or seventeen. Ever since, the smell of ripening pippins brings back the musky, feral tang of a woman in heat. When Nancy's father found out she had a bun in the oven, there was the devil to pay and no pitch hot, as we used to say in our section of Meath. I suppose my father paid them off—Nancy removed to her grandmother's in a dull, sodden corner of Leitrim. I got a good taste of my father's riding crop. The pain of the welts is forgotten, but not the sweetness of green apples.

There was a fine, high smell of apples around the Indian house on the rise above the rich black bottomlands where the Mohawk River curves in a majestic crescent between the Upper Castle and the Nowadaga Creek. Before we came upcountry, both Davers and I had expected to find Indians living as wild animals, under flimsy wigwams and drafty bark huts that rotted back into the earth and left no trace of the passage of men. We had certainly never expected to find Indians who lived better than white men. I was amazed and delighted by our discovery. Davers—or the febrile, over-educated caveman that was loosed inside him—was disappointed; he wanted savages, not entrepreneurs with red hides. He found what he had come for soon enough. But let me first describe what we encountered at the house among the apple trees that set me to calculating how many nights it had been since I had flourished a lady, and to testing whether it is true that native girls give themselves freely to a man who knows how to ask politely.

The house was the property of a well-timbered Mohawk sachem who was generally known as Brant, or Nickus Brant, though Davers insisted on using his Indian name, which was Canagaradunckwa, and means something like Flying Antlers. The names of Indian men are full of the machinery of clouds and winds and thunderstorms, or peopled with birds and animals; I shall say more about this at the proper time. The Brant ménage resembles the popular conception of how Indians live—the image promoted by scribblers who have never laid eyes on a Mohawk—about as closely as Sir William conforms to the general idea of a white frontiersman in a coonskin cap, picking his teeth with a ten-inch blade.

Brant and his family lived in a good-sized frame house, with the door in the gable end in the Dutch style, and a big Dutch barn at the back. While the German farmers across the river at Stone Arabia had oilpaper in their windows, these Mohawks had Crown glass. They had plank floors, a luxury beyond the reach of many of their white neighbors. No digging sticks for the Brants; they had horses to drag their plows, and they planted wheat as well as corn. They even kept a one-horse cariole. Margaret, Brant's wife, rode it down to Fort Hunter, sitting up switch in hand, nose in the air, in a bright taffeta dress as fine as anything you might see along Rotten Row.

They sat Johnson in the place of honor, in a walnut chair at the head of an oak table covered with a linen cloth. They served us tea in Jackfield cups and gave us bone-handled forks to use on our apple pie. The only concession to native cuisine was a fat slab of cornbread studded with blueberries. Davers tucked into this with relish. I found it lay heavy in the stomach, like a dab of cement.

Margaret smiled and said in clipped, careful English, "Cornbread is for fighting men, and for hunters. It will give a warrior the strength to run for two days. I give it to my boys when they are going to play lacrosse, and to my husband when he is going to kill Frenchmen. It puts a larder in your belly. Then you have to work it off."

She was a strong, handsome woman, light-skinned, with soft, humorous brown eyes. She was unusually animated, for an Indian. Her face was full of life and expression. Even when her features were still, her moods stirred there like a current beneath calm water. She was dressed in European fashion, in a sack dress of deep scarlet. She wore a number of those silver luckenbooth brooches—twined hearts that the Indians seem to favor—and half a dozen silver bangles on each wrist. Her black hair was rolled up in a tight bun. Looking at her, listening to that educated accent that put our white frontier riffraff to shame, I guessed I need seek no further for the secret of the Brant family's prosperity.

Her husband wore a blue coat trimmed with gold galloon and a ruffled shirt over an Indian breechclout and leggings embroidered with dyed moosehair and porcupine quills. Three gorgets hung from his neck; one bore Sir William's personal cypher, another the emblem of the Turtle Clan. Brant was much darker than his wife and looked more like my untutored notion of an Indian. His head was shaved to a few greasy locks above the fontanel, festooned with feathers and porcelain beads. His eyes were sharp flints, close set around a cruel beak of a nose. When he was silent, his mouth set in a perfectly straight line, turning down at the corners. His chest was immense. His affluence had won him a ball-belly, that sat on him like a pregnancy. But his hips and his buttocks were narrow, and the corded muscles that showed through his borrowed finery suggested he was a man to be avoided when he had blood in his eye.

Anger was in him now.

His son had brought Sir William a message, couched in the metaphors of native conversation: "We have caught bad birds that have been pecking at us. Come and see who they are."

Indian etiquette, as punctilious as that of the Great Manchu, on the dirt floor of the Longhouse or around the Brants' tea-equipage, required that guests must be fed and watered before business is discussed.

While we made casual conversation about food and weather, my eyes kept sliding back to Christina, the Brants' younger daughter. She was dressed in a Mohawk girl's traditional Sunday best, a fringed white doeskin, worked to a buttery softness that left her arms bare to the shoulders and exposed her supple, coppery legs and her lower thighs to my admiring gaze. She might have been fifteen. She moved with such fluid, natural grace that it was hard for me to know whether a local buck or one of the transient river rats who came with the spring migration of traders and trappers had already picked her cherry. I tried one of my bedroom looks across the table. She dropped her eyes modestly. But when I was talking to her mother, I sensed Christina searching my face. She looked intelligent and self-possessed beyond her years. I tried to engage her in chitchat, but she responded in monosyllables or left it for her mother to answer. I thought she might be uncomfortable in English, but Margaret Brant remarked that all her children had gone to the church school at Queen Anne's chapel at Fort Hunter, and that Christina had won the prize hymnal.

"Perhaps Christina could help me with my Mohawk," I suggested.

Sir William raised an eyebrow.

"That is," I added hastily, "when we come back from Detroit."

"You are not married, Mr Hardacre?" said the mother.

"Why, no."

"Then perhaps, at the proper time, you will tell us something of your intentions."

You could have knocked me down with one of the feathers from old Brant's topknot. I might have been dealing with Mrs Van Horn or Lady Eastmeath! I saw Johnson put his hand over his mouth to stop himself from laughing out loud.

The women gathered up the tea things. Christina had a trim, high saddle and a nice swing to her hips, and she knew it.

A fresh, clean scent—white cedar and the juice of wild-flowers. Something wilder and ranker underneath.

Now if I could only get her to myself, under the apple trees, and put it to her nicely.

Brant brought out a redstone pipe and a pouch of sun-cured native tobacco, which is green and harsh on the tongue even when sweetened with dried sumac leaves. This was evidently the signal that serious matters were about to be discussed. The women did not leave the room, as they would be expected to do in New York or London. Margaret got out a little pipe of her own, with a carved face on the wooden bowl, and added mightily to the smoke that began to fill the room.

Brant did most of the talking for a while, and he spoke mostly in Mohawk. His English, though serviceable, was of the trading-post kind that sounds comical to you and me and is littered with a lot of trash picked up from grog-peddlers and vagabonds that has no equivalent in their own language. Natives can't see why white men think it is bold or dirty to talk about fucking and shitting. Indians who live in the old style—as even the Brants must have done, until recently—are accustomed to performing both of these natural and necessary functions in a sociable en-vironment surrounded by ten or twenty of their family and friends under a flapping bark roof. If they want to shock the stockings off you, then they might call you a witch, or a rattlesnake or a man-with-a-woman-inside-him—now, *those* are dirty words—but they won't try to impress you with a dozen words for emptying the bowels, or rogering. At least, that is how Johnson explained it to me. So, knowing that his English belonged to the slopshop more than the council-house, Brant put his case in his own tongue. I cannot translate what he said word for word. It took me a full year to master his lingo which contains noises no English-speaker makes, except perhaps when gargling or throwing up—glottal stops and pulsing glottal stops, and things philologists may have names for but probably can't perform. I will try to give you a sense of what Brant was steamed about, because it involves the biggest rogue in the Valley, the brute that packed Daniel off to a circus and worked as hard as any man in America to pull down what Johnson was trying to build. A doctor from Albany told me the black-livered hellion is still going strong. If these lines fall into his hands, I hope they make his hippo-bone dentures fall out and stick in his throat.

Brant was talking about Uri Klock, grog-seller, gristmill owner, out-and-out sharper and author of the biggest land fraud in the memory of Valley people. Klock's square lime-stone house stood on a steep hillside on the north side of the river, above the Lutheran church. I could see it from Brant's window, beyond the point of an island thick with cedars.

"This snake is wriggling nearer and nearer to our fires," said Brant—or words to this effect. "We hear he has offered lands of ours for sale, although we are ignorant of any right he has to do so. We hear he has forbidden the white men who live on our lands to pay us the rents they have paid these many winters past. We see our ruin approaching quickly unless our brother Warragiyaguey takes a great stick and breaks the back of this serpent. He haunts the Upper Castle as an evil spirit. He steals the minds and hearts of our young men and makes them mad. When the owl hunts, his people come stealthily, with chains, to measure out our destruction. He disturbs the bones of our ancestors. He raises them from their sleep. Our grandfathers are angry. Their eyes are upon us. We feel their breath on our necks. Soon they will drive us to send his soul from his body. Then war will return to the Valley.

"My brother, I hold other white men only by the fingers. But you I hold next to my heart. We have risked together. We are joined by a silver cord that never rusts. I ask you to free us from this night walker and set our hearts at peace."

Johnson responded in Mohawk, in a similar style. Only a few names and technical expressions came out in English: Klock, Livingston, Pickard; patents and surveys and affidavits. I admired Sir William's coolness, even more than his fluency. He spoke softly and calmly, in the same lilting rhythms as the sachem. The long periods rippled over each other like waves. Yet he was plainly angry. The blood rose hot in his cheeks, and at the back of his neck above the white border of his stock. It is rare for a fighting Irishman to hold his voice and his body in check when rage is in him. But Johnson had learned from the Indians that a man who betrays the violence of his emotions, when sober, is despised.

The origin of Brant's complaint, I discovered eventually, was a piece of paper known as the Canajoharie Patent. It had been hatched during the famous Albany Congress of 1754, when delegates from the English colonies gathered to debate Ben Franklin's scheme for a unified defense against the French. The plan foundered on sectional jealousies, but some pundits find in it the origins of the confederation that now styles itself the United States. I leave this bone for historians to gnaw at. The lasting product of the Albany convention was a number of swindles perpetrated on the Indian ambassadors by various swag-bellied speculators in back rooms, using the time-honored technique—oil the natives with rum, then get them to put their thumb on a paper they cannot read. All the deeds that were signed around a bottle in Albany that summer produced hatred and bloodshed. The notorious Wyoming massacre was one result. The dirtiest rogue in all that bunch—so Johnson and Brant agreed—was Uri Klock.

In partnership with Philip Livingston and some other gentlemen with fancy handles and pull with governors, Klock got some Indians to put their marks on a deed to a prodigious quantity of land on the southern bank of Mohawk River in return for a few kegs of grog and a miserable fistful of dollars. The partners then bribed some crooked Crown officials at New York to authorize their transaction and issue letters patent. Their purchase became known as the Canajoharie Patent. There were white men living on the lands included in the tract. Some were tenants of the Mohawks. Others had paid for their farms and thought that they owned the freehold. This was cause for scandal enough. But the true scandal is that the Patent included not only many square miles of virgin forest and native hunting-grounds, but even the lands where the Mohawks of the Upper Castle had built their lodges and tilled their cornfields. Klock's swindle threatened to deprive the Mohawks of the very ground beneath their feet. With the French wars behind us, and America lost to the Empire, it is difficult to convey the enormity of Klock's fraud. We were on the eve of a war on three continents, the first *world* war. British victory in North America depended, above all else, on control of the Hudson and Mohawk valleys, which in turn depended, whatever Sir Jeffrey Amherst may think, on the friendship of the Mohawks. On the eve of this titanic struggle, in the midst of it, and afterwards, Klock pursued a claim that would dispossess the Mohawks and turn them into rebels and enemies.

I knew none of this, of course, on my first afternoon at the Brant house, and my attention was fixed on Christina's brown legs more than on a dialogue in an alien tongue. Davers, however, was listening hard, frowning, trying to put his tutoring with Daniel to some use.

He must have gleaned something of what passed between Johnson and Brant because, when they came to a long pause, he sat up and addressed himself to the Mohawk.

"It is my understanding," said Davers, "that the Indians were taught by their forefathers that Mother Earth cannot be bought and sold, that her body must be revered and that her fruits belong to a whole people, not to individuals."

Brant said nothing. His eyes flicked towards Sir William.

Christina's mouth opened. Her lower lip was moist and full.

Johnson said, "You cannot generalize about natives, Sir Robert. The Mohawks are far more advanced than most of our Indians."

"Then why did some of your people sign a deed for this fellow Klock?" Davers was staring at Brant. "How is it possible? Which of you signed? How have you punished them?"

Brant gave Davers a long hard look. His expression was impenetrable. Then he stood up. He picked up a cocked hat trimmed with lace and put it on his head. Then he strode, with some dignity, to his front door which had a tobacco box on a shelf above, as in one of the mynheers' residences at Albany, opened it and vanished into the sunlight.

"Good Lord," said Davers. "I hope I have not offended him."

"You have a way of going in at the deep end, Sir Robert," said Johnson. Sir William rose from his place and stood by Margaret. He spoke to her gently, his hand on her upper arm. He called her *Istenha*, the Mohawk name for mother. "It is all right, *Istenha*. We will see this through. God knows we have been through worse together."

"Yes." The ghost of a smile flitted across her handsome face.

She spoke to Davers. "You must not judge us too quickly, Sir Robert. You will see many things among my people—among all the *Onkwehonwe*, the Real People—that will be strange to you. You should not be in a hurry to tell us who we are."

Davers blushed bright red, like a schoolboy.

She stared at him intently. "My husband signed a deed for Uri Klock. The deed says that Klock and his partners own the land from the ridge to the two bald rocks we call the Twins. It does not explain that he gave Klock the earth underneath my house, the garden I planted with my own hands, the cornfield my daughters and I dug and weeded and harvested so we could live through the Starving Time."

"It's all right, *Istenha*," Johnson repeated, lightly massaging her shoulder. "If Klock tries to touch you, I will shoot him like the thieving possum that he is. I am going to get you your freehold. I have already spoken to Colden. He understands. Nothing like this will come on you again."

Indians with freehold title! It may give you some notion

of the vastness of the transformation Sir William was bringing about in the Mohawk world.

"But why?" Davers persisted. He could see so far, yet he could never see the bald stump right in front of him until he tripped over it.

Margaret Brant hesitated. She looked at Johnson, as if seeking his counsel, and he nodded, as if he knew what she would say.

"I cannot say this in front of my people. I have never said it to anyone of the Tiorhensaka—the People from the Sunrise—except Warragiyaguey, who belongs to us as much as to the English. You are his brothers. He makes me know I may talk to you as I do to him.

"Warragiyaguey—Sir William—carried my family with him when he went to Connecticut to inspect the Indian school and to take the sea air at New London, for his health. I saw men catching crabs along the beach. Have you seen what crabs do when they are taken and thrown in a barrel? One tries to escape. He climbs up, higher and higher. His pincers are waving over the top—he is almost free. Then his brothers pounce on him and drag him back down.

"This is what my people do to one who rises above the rest. And they do it in invisible ways, because we are joined by common instincts, like a flight of birds. Do you know how long it took me to persuade my husband to build this house? And when the last slate was on the roof, do you know what he did? He set fire to it. And while we were putting out the flames, he made a hole in the ice and tried to drown himself in the river. Does that answer your question?"

Davers's lip trembled. He said, "Perhaps—perhaps—he is afraid of losing his soul." He added, in a voice no louder than the breeze through the open door, "As white men have done."

The Mohawk women, mother and daughter, looked at him as if he had dropped from the moon.

Johnson wiped his mouth and said, "Sir Robert is what we call a philosopher."

We paused, because Brant had reappeared in the doorway, followed closely by a negro slave—it seemed these Indians even owned slaves!—carrying a sack.

"Your brother," he addressed himself to Sir William in English, but indicated Davers by the jut of his jaw, "want to know why my brothers give land to rattlesnake. I come show you. Here, Pomp!"

The slave named Pomp, a lithe, well-made young fellow with a brilliant set of ivories, deposited the sack in the middle of the floor and held the top open.

Brant reached in and retrieved an empty liquor bottle.

He slammed it down on the table in front of Davers.

"That—mark of Cobus on white man's deed!"

He grabbed another bottle.

"That—mark of Paulus!"

And another.

"Mark of great warrior, Araghiadecka!"

Then three bottles together.

"Mark of Nickus Brant. Great war chief, great word-carrier. He sees many looks away. Brant Canagaradunck-wa. *Yo-hay!*"

Davers looked ready to burst into tears.

I could not help myself. I snickered, I spluttered, I rocked back and forth. I laughed until my sides ached.

Sir William said, solemn as a judge, "I apologize for my friends. They have much to learn. I shall personally attend to their education."

Johnson warned that you cannot generalize about Indians, and of course he was right. But Mohawk society was very small—as a result of constant war, white men's plagues, emigration to the mission settlements in Canada and, not least, the demon rum, there were only four hundred and twenty Mohawks still living in the Valley at the time I knew it, according to the census the Reverend Mr Ogilvie conducted for Johnson. At the risk of offending some of my former native friends, I will report that these Valley Mohawks formed three camps. The most influential was composed of the Anglican Apples, red on the outside, white on the inside. Margaret Brant and her children and Mary Hill and her three huge, bearlike sons at Fort Hunter were prize Apples; each of them was worth a thousand sterling or more by the time of the Revolution.

The Flints made up the second camp. In their own language, the Mohawks call themselves the Caniengehaga, or People of the Flint. There are big flint mines in Mohawk country which must have been valuable as a source of arrowheads and knives before white men came with metal. Then, too, if you believe that we are what we eat, you might say that the Mohawks have flint inside them, because they grow their corn, beans and squash in flinty soil. The Flints were the ones who clung to the traditional ideas of chiefly government by the *rotiyaner*, or Men of Good Minds, under the watchful eye of the clanmothers and the Longhouse religion of a race of primitive farmers, whose ritual year revolves around the death and rebirth of the corn. They looked to Onondaga, the ancient capital of the Confederacy of the Longhouse. They were having a hard time upholding the old notions of communal life against the lure of white men's riches and the obvious need—with settlers pressing closer and closer to the villages—to adapt in order to survive. The old religion was dying under the booming voice of the God of the Big Battalions who seemed to be so generous to his followers.

Then there were the Wild Men who did not obey either the grayhaired chiefs or Johnson's war captains, or even the clanmothers, who were the scariest of the bunch, unless they felt like it. They would carve up an army packhorse or pillage a trader's flatboat because they were in the mood for a feast or a bit of random deviltry. In the same spirit, a band of them would team up together and head off to tomahawk Flatheads or Cherokees, sometimes in defiance of both Johnson and the chiefs, because they wanted to swagger in front of the girls with warm, reeking scalps in their belts. A fair proportion of the Wild Ones were half-breeds, adrift without moorings in either culture, like William of Canajoharie, one of the few of Johnson's bastard sons that he acknowledged. His Indian nickname was Tekawironte, which means Twin Children Fighting Each Other, and nicely sums up the conflict that raged within him. He was a born firebrand, usually drunk and always in trouble.

The boundaries between these three camps were never fixed. The principal reason, I suppose, was that just about every Mohawk—every Mohawk man at any rate—signed on, from time to time, in the Bottle Brigade. If you think you know an Indian, wait until you see him drunk; you will find you are dealing with a different man. Indians don't hold a man responsible for his actions when he is in liquor. In their view, a fellow who drinks himself silly has delivered his body into the possession of wild spirits. Since he is not himself, he cannot be blamed for anything nasty that ensues.

You begin to see the measure of what Johnson had to contend with. He commanded the Mohawks, but he also had to carry them. I think he felt, at times, that he was being eaten alive.

I wanted to know what Sir William proposed to do about Uri Klock, and asked him about it as soon as we had taken our leave of the Brants.

"The devil sweep that treacherous, litigious rogue!" Johnson swore. "I would give my best horse to see him grace a halter."

I asked him why the Mohawks did not simply drive Klock out of the Valley. I was reckless enough to volunteer to undertake the job myself, with the Butler boys and a few of the tenants.

"By Jove, Shane Hardacre, aren't you the blazer? A very Mohawk in tenderness! I can see why little Christina took to you."

I protested that Margaret's daughter had not even indulged me with a favorable glance.

"But that's it, don't you see? They are bred to public modesty. If they like a fellow, they'll take him without preliminaries. They do not go in for romantic courtships. She likes you well enough. You must have seen that from the way she used her body in front of you."

I remembered that appetizing hip-roll, and began to feel hungry again.

Johnson laughed and feinted a punch at my midriff.

"Keep it down, boy! For all that, Christina will not be easy. She will make you run the gauntlet, one way or another. She will do nothing without her mother's consent, and Margaret knows how to set a price. I have seen that one outwit the meanest mynheer in an Albany beaver house. They will try to own you, and a good part of whatever you have."

"God's breeches! You don't mean marriage?"

Johnson's expression was as hard to read as old Brant's. One of the oddities about him was that one of his eyes was set slightly higher than the other. This imperfection, rarely noticed for what it was, produced an air of mystery, the sense that nothing about Sir William was what it first appeared.

"There are relationships that can be quite as binding as marriage," he said after a time. "And no less galling. Never underestimate the willpower and the ruthlessness of a Mohawk woman."

He saw our surprise.

"Oh yes," he pursued, "you will have heard that the Mohawks are a warrior people, the terror of all others."

Actually, most of the white men I had encountered in New York, before I got to the Valley, jumbled all Indians together as "niggers" or "savages." I forbore from quoting their opinions.

"It is true," Johnson went on, "that the Mohawks are a race of warriors. The other tribes hung the name of Man-Eaters on them for a reason. At Boston, I saw New England Indians take flight at the sight of a lone Mohawk in the street with his war club. But Mohawk women are stronger than their men. They rule here. The bloodline runs through the mothers who have sole authority over the children. The matrons choose the chiefs, and dehorn them if they are not up to snuff. The women are the business managers, the farmers, the successful traders. They are tough, and they are wily, and your Christina is the daughter of the cleverest and toughest of them all. If you wish to take that one on, you had best be prepared for the consequences, if you mean to stay in the Valley."

I said, rather sniffily, that I didn't know about any of that. I had come out with Davers to try the air. Johnson, the old fox, could see I was peeved because, as the Earl of Sandwich would have put it, I had not had my dark meat served up on a platter.

"I think you will stay," Johnson said quietly. "I hope we will find reasons to make you wish to remain with us. You've got fire in your belly, Shane Hardacre, and you are a joiner, and those are two things that Indians love. Those and stamina—that is where you have yet to be tested. There's very few Englishmen who can deal with natives. The English, for the most part, are too haughty. There's a few odd ones, of course, who go native with a vengeance and forget who they are. They generally end up badly."

Davers was not around to hear this. He had gone off in his own canoe. He said he was going to look for Daniel who had dropped out of sight almost as soon as he got home. We had been up at Canajoharie to ask about him, and found that his wife had taken a new husband while he was away in England. He had promptly got drunk again and tried to bite her nose off. I thought that Daniel was a lost cause, myself—as did Johnson—but Davers had formed an attachment, no doubt because our circus friend was the first Indian he ever clapped eyes on. In the few days we had left in the Valley before we headed upriver on the first leg of our journey to Detroit, I did not notice that Sir Robert formed any other Mohawk attachments. As for the Mohawks—well, frankly, I don't believe they quite saw the point of Davers. I watched him trying to question some old harridan in a filthy bark hut with lice and vermin crawling about on the floor about dreams and the meaning of life. When he was leaving, she tapped her skull and cackled, *"Rotkon."* Now this can mean a spiritual person; but it also means someone who's just plain crazy.

"You make rogering a squaw sound like a matter of state," I said to Johnson.

He laughed, but said, "For you and me and the Indian Department, boyo, it could very well be. By the way, you'd best not say that word to a Mohawk lady."

"You mean squaw?"

He nodded.

"But *everyone* calls native women squaws."

"Not natives, they don't. Do you know what *squaw*, that is to say, *otitskwa*, means in Mohawk?"

I shook my head.

"Well, it's the first word a ladies' man like you needs to get into his skull. It means cunt. I imagine that if you addressed Suky Van Horn by that name, you'd expect her to poke your eye out with the ferrule of her umbrella."

"Quite."

"I imagine some Jesuit, trying to pick up the native language, was jabbing his finger at people and things and asking some Indians to tell him their names. He points at a woman, rather low, and they tell him that's a *squaw*.

"Now, the next thing I will say to you is this. A temporary wife is a necessity for a man traveling in Indian country. But we shall have to see that you choose right."

He really was making it all sound as complicated as arranging a state wedding between Habsburg and Bourbon.

I must have looked irritated—which I was—because he quickly went on. "The itch, now. I will never deny the itch. You won't need to go running off to the trade squaws over at Eve Pickard's—those sluts you *may* call squaws—and get yourself poxed again to satisfy it. I know a good few Indians something less *advanced*, shall we say, than the Brants, who will loan out their miss curly-locks for a night or two. But I have a mind to let you taste something as sweet and homely as twelfth-night cake before we go to Detroit."

He kept a beautiful boat on he Sacandaga River, which winds through vast marshlands and the foothills of the Adirondacks behind the site of the village Sir William founded a decade later and named, without false modesty, Johnstown. Davers was not invited on this expedition, and I doubt that he could have enjoyed it the way I did.

The wetlands—called the Vlaie by the Dutch and the Drowned Lands by the Indians—were teeming with ducks and wild geese. Cranberries grew everywhere; there must have been enough of them to accompany every turkey ever roasted in America. It was muggy and hot, but we cooled ourselves with shrub and kept off the insects with the smoke of a brown fungus burning in a cast-iron pot on a pole, while two of Sir William's slaves worked the oars.

After a couple of hours on the river, a log house came in sight, on a little knoll covered with blue-joint grass.

Sir William fired off his two-barreled gun, and we heard

an answering shout. To my surprise, we sailed on, around
the bend, where Johnson ordered his slaves to rest their
oars while we tested our luck at hooking fish. I caught
three or four trout and a sunfish. Sir William hooked some
lovely fat perch.

He left me to wonder about the signal shot.

I discovered its meaning when we waded ashore at his
camp which was actually an unfinished lodge. The frame
of a largish house stood on a promontory of hard ground
between the river and the Vlaie, but only the west wing
was completed. The boards were unpainted, but I saw a
curl of smoke rising from the fieldstone chimney.

"Fish!" bawled Johnson. "Strong, fresh, jumping fish!
Come and get it, girls!"

The door flew open. To a man of my propensities, who
had been starved of female company for two weeks—while
Johnson and Doctor Daly administered blue lobelia and
keyser's pills for my Half-Moon complaint—and a few days
since, what was then revealed was verily the gate of Paradise. Two smiling ladies, neither of them above twenty,
rushed to greet us. They were in alluring *déshabillé*. They
wore loose shifts, without jumps or stays, so that their more
notable charms vibrated in the most delightful way as they
hastened to endow Johnson with hugs and kisses.

I admit to a momentary pang of envy. It seemed the
London rumors were well-founded; the beast had the
whole Valley for his harem!

"Shane, my bucko," said he with a leer. "It is my privilege to present to you the Wormwood girls."

I thought the name must be a pleasantry in obnoxious
taste, in view of my recent malady, but was soon assured
that the girls' cognomen was, in truth, Wormwood. Their
father Henry was a modest farmer for whom Sir William
had done many favors. If he knew what went on at Fish
House, as Johnson called his half-built lodge on the Vlaie,
then he turned a blind eye.

Susannah was the elder of the sisters, and evidently
Johnson's favorite. He gave her a lingering kiss on the
mouth and, holding out a string bag of dripping fish with
one hand, set to foraging into the folds of her shift with

the other. I was impressed by this promptitude in a man who had been writhing in the grip of the gravel and the quatern ague only a day or two before.

Susannah was no ordinary farmer's daughter. Her skin was as fair as a water lily. It made a striking contrast with her raven hair and melting dark eyes.

The younger one, Elizabeth, was a little more sallow and more boldly curved. The dark of her nipples and of the curving hairs about the delta of Venus made it difficult for me to restrain myself from greeting her as manfully as Billy Johnson had greeted Susannah.

I was not obliged to restrain myself for long.

"Susannah, Lizzie," said Johnson, with an arm around each of their necks, "Shane and I was digged in the same ditch and must needs plow the same furrow. He's an Irishman and a gentleman, and a good deal more and less, and because I love him I invite you to love him as you love me. I'll wager he knows what will please a woman for, by God, you'll not see the likes of either of us again."

Do you wonder that I became devoted to Billy Johnson?

The punchbowl was brimming, the fire was ready for our fish to be broiled and the bed was turned back. The bed was wide—for two, but not for four—and it was the sole item of furniture in that single room. Since Johnson seemed fully bent on having at it without delay, and the girls seemed entirely accommodating, I volunteered to lie with Lizzie on the floor.

"Don't play the fool," said Johnson. "We have Davers for that. You'll pain yourself, or bruise Lizzie who is too soft and sweet to roll on planks, and then one or t'other will curse me for it. I will show how it is to be done. Ladies, if you please."

He made a sweep and a bow, and soon had the girls tastefully deployed in the center of the bed.

"Now, Mr Hardacre, if you will, sir," with another flourish, he indicated Lizzie's side, "you will mount yourself there and please Lizzie, while I get in over here," he clambered, in his ruffled shirt, onto the other side of the down mattress, "and do what an old bull may to please my Susannah."

Of the remainder of our entertainments on that glorious afternoon, I will say only that the Wormwood girls were woefully misnamed.

Davers found Daniel, our missing Mohawk. He found him at Klock's, sprawled dead drunk on a heap of cow-manure. It seemed Uri Klock and his son Jacob each kept a tap in that square stone house by the gristmill, and would all but abduct any passing Indian, if such treatment were required, to fetch them to liquid refreshment. I could hardly believe that a man who had been abused as Daniel had could return to the place of his punishment for any reason other than to thrash the man responsible. I might have been new to Indians, but I knew that they have long memories and will do almost anything to get revenge. I was reminded of Margaret Brant's tale of crabs in a barrel, and wondered whether it offered any key to Daniel, or whether our circus performer was born a hopeless case.

Robert Davers got him cleaned up and announced that he intended to take Daniel with him to Detroit, as his personal servant.

Johnson did not object openly. He said languidly, within the papered scenes of Fontainebleau in his dining room, "I wonder whether Daniel is actually a Mohawk. I seem to remember that his mother—or father—or both—were brought home captive from among the Flatheads. Or was it the Hurons?"

"Hurons," said Davers. "Surely you would not deny him his Mohawk identity, nonetheless. From what I have gleaned, the Mohawks have adopted captives from all the neighboring tribes. Not to mention the fact that almost all of them *obviously* have European blood in them. I am not surprised they trace their descent through the mother. Who can say who the father was, for certain? Is there such a thing as a pure-bred Mohawk?"

Some of this was rather baldly stated, and might have even been calculated to give offense to Sir William, who had a score of little sepia copies of himself running loose up and down the Valley. But our Superintendent had clearly decided to take a relaxed view of all Sir Robert's eccentricities since the young Englishman seemed impervious to both caution and common sense.

"I should think Mohawks are somewhat like Jews," said Johnson. "If your mother is a Jew, then you are a Jew, too. Tell me if I have it wrong, Shane."

"That is my understanding." I knew as much about Jews as about Mohawks at that time—which is to say, very little—though I was to learn something more from Isaac Chapman, the Jewish trader taken captive during the revolt, who gave all of us a lesson in grace under pressure.

"But in practice," Johnson went on, "you are a Jew if you think you are, and if others believe you are."

I think he must have been fatigued, or full of port. The rest of his conversation made even less sense to me. Well, great men must have their *longeurs*, their dips, as well as their shadows.

There is one question that was nagging at me beyond all the rest. Why had Johnson failed to give Uri Klock a lift out of his stirrups? Sir William had explained to me that he was bound by the laws, and that Klock had powerful friends in Albany and New York, that the master of Fort Johnson was by no means as absolute as it might appear to a new guest. To be candid, I began to wonder whether this Klock had something on Billy Johnson. I caught only a brief glimpse of that sour phiz before we left for Detroit—a carbuncle of a nose on a bullet-head, the cheeks caving in about the gums where Klock's own teeth had fallen out and been replaced by those hippopotamus-bones that were all the rage in America. I have a great deal to tell you about Uri Klock and his villainies, as about my misadventures with Christina Brant, and a bitch-squaw called She Drags Down The Boats.

But all this must wait until I have described our mission to Detroit, and Davers's final departure from ordinary reality and my first encounter with the most beautiful and wickedest creature I ever knew, a lady with the soul of a male debauchee, cold and cynical and Cartesian as only a Frenchman could be, inside the body of an odalisque.

Dearest Shane,

You could at least omit the Wormwood sisters. I
am sure they smelled like Smithfield market on a hot
day.

Your book does nothing for women. I see you have
set out to build yourself a trophy room, festooned
with the scalps of your lovers.

You do an injustice to yourself, as well as my sex.
Perhaps you do this to conceal yourself. But I know
your secret; you cannot hide from me.

You have a woman inside you. How else could you
please us so well?

Men are taught not to reveal the colors of their
feelings. I have observed Sir Henry closely. He af-
fects to have no more inner life than his favorite beagle.
He has consigned his soul to a reserved pew in a fashionable church, and visits it on occasional Sundays.
The sight of a grown man in tears would drive him
to apoplexy. Poor Henry.

But I have seen you cry. Not for yourself but for the
rage and pain you have sensed in another. That is the
wisdom of the woman inside you. Let her speak!

I can hear you protest that your booksellers and sub-
scribers are bound to be men, and you cannot risk the
derision of your clubmates—if you still dare show
your face at White's.

But I must tell you the Shane Hardacre who exposes
himself in these pages would never have prospered with
me. He is so offensively cocky I would have kicked
him in the teeth, or perhaps somewhere lower.

Your

Valerie

P.S. I am disappointed to find Sir William Johnson, though weighted with years and honors, also suffered from *nostalgie de la boue* and could not keep his pants on.

7

Passage to Detroit

OUR VOYAGE TO DETROIT was no pleasure trip. The water was low which made hard work for the boatmen, straining at their setting poles, blinded by sweat, and for frequent portages. The first carry was at the Little Falls, where the cataract makes a wild leap between horny ridges down to a rounded basin where granite spikes rise up like the spires of drowned cathedrals to scrape the face of the river. Beyond the falls, the valley opens out into fat, loamy bottomlands, the preserve of stiff-necked German farmers. We tied up beyond their stone church—more of a blockhouse than a house of worship, with a swivel gun poking its nose out of the belfry—so that Johnson could hold a council with the Oneidas, the Mohawks' western neighbors.

I shall give a brief account of this interview, because it was the first time I saw Sir William "perform" in front of Indians other than Mohawks, and because it will give some idea of what was going on among the natives, even the ones our officialdom took for granted.

The Indians lounged about on the ground, airing their

backsides and puffing away at their pipes. The Oneida speaker, stroking a wampum belt the way you or I might caress a woman's thigh, went through the rigmaroles of welcome which are tedious beyond belief once you have heard them a few times. Even iron-bottomed Johnson was in the habit of excusing himself from time to time to steal a nip of brandy to give himself patience to go on.

"Brother Warragiyaguey, we are come to wipe away your tears, and open your ears, and unblock the passage from your heart to your mouth."

I don't know what a medical practitioner would make of this. Johnson told me that these are ancient formulas borrowed from the ceremony of condolence for a dead chief which orators of the Six Nations—that is, the Mohawks and their allies—use to begin every powwow.

"We are come to take the axe out of your head and to wipe the blood off your seat and to cover the grave of your brother who has gone the long trail."

This sounded quite nasty, but I had an idea what it was about. Guy Johnson, who was scribbling minutes for Sir William—Guy has a nice copperplate, when sober—had told me that an Oneida had pulled a German farmer off his cart and carved him up like an ox-roast.

The sachem explained that the killer was drunk and, therefore, could not be held accountable. Furthermore, the Germans themselves had killed two of his tribe and had not been compelled to make redress.

"We dig up the great tree whose branches touch the clouds. We bury this matter in the clear stream that flows beneath its white roots."

This seemed to me a cavalier way to dispose of a murder, and I wondered if Sir William would rest content with an allegorical apology. He did reprimand the Oneidas, but first we had to listen to a litany of Indian complaints. The traders were rooks and swindlers; the soldiers raped their women; the British officers were arrogant and had Indians beaten for hanging around the posts roaring drunk; they could not get powder for hunting; since peace had broken out, the price of beaver plews had plummeted. There was a good deal of whining about the land question, which I took seriously after what I had heard and seen at Brant's house.

"Our land was given to us by a great spirit," said the sachem. "We ask you to forbid your people to settle any higher up the Valley. If the Germans come any nearer to our castles, we will give them a kick that will fling them back into the sea. If my brother comes to kick us in return, we cannot say to what we might be driven."

The Oneida even asked for an undertaking that the forts that had been constructed in Indian country during the war should be pulled down, now we had beaten the French. And this was a "friendly" talking!

Sir William delivered a measured response. He gravely thanked the Oneidas for taking the tomahawk out of his head. He observed that British officials could not comprehend how one man could murder another without being punished by death for the offense.

"My uncle, the commander-in-chief, insists that you deliver the murderer into our hands. As your friend, I strongly advise your speedy compliance."

Johnson observed that the dead Indians had been killed by a farmer who discovered them pillaging his house.

On the land matter, he reported that His Majesty was graciously pleased to send orders to the colonial governors instructing them not to grant lands to any white man without the permission of the tribes, which sounded a bit thin to me, given what Uri Klock and his cronies were trying to get away with.

The Indians went into a hubbub. The sachem came back and said they could not do anything about the murderer because he had gone off to see distant parts. They deigned to accept a few trinkets and strouds that Johnson had for them. We were rather short of presents throughout the journey. General Amherst had declined to supply the goods Sir William requested from His Majesty's stores, so Johnson had been obliged to order them from merchants at Albany and New York on his own account; there was no telling when the shipment would overtake us.

Our meeting with the Oneidas set Sir William to grumbling about grog-sellers like Klock and the need to define a clear boundary to white settlement, and to enforce it. I suppose that, in his youth, he peddled liquor as merrily as any of the traders. Now he was Superintendent and responsible for the Indians, he wanted to put the cork back in the bottle. He recognized that this was a hopeless ambition. We had given the natives a taste for liquor. They would do anything for it, and precious little without it. If we banned it all along the frontier, they would paddle down to Albany or Montreal, from as far west as the Illinois, to bring it back.

The land business might appear equally intractable, given the flood of new immigrants from all over Europe hungry for freehold property, that was rolling into the colonies, and the greed of sharp-eyed men in company offices. It did not seem so to Sir William. I have heard his critics berate him as the biggest swindler of them all who, having swallowed more Indian land than he could ever hope to digest, applied himself to denying other men lesser morsels. There may be an element of truth in the charge; the man on top can afford to sit pretty. But Johnson claimed that he bought most of his land from white men, not natives, who had honest deeds, and acquired the rest from tribes who wanted to return the favors he had done them. I am not going into the ethics of Johnson's land deals, not at this time anyway; ethics was a word you hardly heard on the frontier, or in a London withdrawing room, for that matter. I do know that Johnson felt passionately that, if Indians and colonists were to live together after the war, a boundary line would have to be drawn, with markers that told every white man, hunters and grogpeddlers as well as farmers and surveyors: Keep Off. This Is Indian Land. He could not yet see how to do it. But the idea was scratching and nagging at him all the way to Detroit as we listened to one pack of Indians after another complaining about new encroachments on their territory.

General Amherst was nagging at him too. At each of our major stops, we received a new express from Sir Jeffrey offering Johnson his "advice" on how to treat the natives. Amherst did not actually say "spare the rod and spoil the child" or call Johnson a "squaw-man" who was soft on the Indians—he was too much of a stylist, in the epistolary vein—but you could read these sentiments between the lines.

"I know the proper use for this," cried Sir William, snatching up the first letter from the general as he went into the bushes to evacuate his bowels.

The next express came close behind. It caught up with us at the mouth of West Canada Creek. With its arrival, Johnson lost his sense of humor, not because of Amherst's letter, but because of one he enclosed. It was from Captain Donald Campbell of the Royal Americans, the commanding officer at Detroit. It contained the details of a full-fledged Indian conspiracy.

"Damned treacherous villains!" Johnson swore as he read it. His breathing came fast and shallow. He balled his fists. He was ready for a fight and he didn't mind who knew it. "I've warned Amherst that this was coming. I sent Croghan to tell him. The opinionated prig refuses to credit that Indians are capable of killing anything more lively than a packhorse. But to think that some of our Six Nations are behind it! As God is my judge, I will make an end of this, and if there's to be killing, then killing there will be."

He showed us the letter.

Captain Campbell reported that two Seneca envoys had made a secret visit to Detroit and circulated a red war belt amongst the Indians of the nearby villages. The Senecas had spoken at a secret council of the western Indians, urging them to send their chiefs to Sandusky, a point on the south shore of Lake Erie, to concert the plan for a general uprising. Similar messages had been sent to tribes as far east as the Gaspe, and as far west as the Illinois country. The Senecas proposed to surprise and seize all the English forts beyond the Allegheny Mountains, starting at the end of the month.

I had yet to meet my first Seneca, but I knew that this tribe was the largest and one of the most warlike of the Six Nations, the owner of the great bulge of land, like a buffalo head, made by the Province of New York below Lake Ontario. Within the Confederacy of the Longhouse, the

Senecas are formally addressed as the Keepers of the Western Door, as the Mohawks are known as the Keepers of the Eastern Door. If Campbell's intelligence was true—it seemed to come from French interpreters—then it could spell ruin for Johnson and his policy of accommodation between the races. The far tribes who had served the French until a few months before might be assumed to be disloyal and disaffected. But the Six Nations, thanks to Johnson, had fought with the British. The defection of the Senecas would overthrow all his years of patient coaxing and cajoling. At the very moment that regular British troops were being withdrawn from North America, it threatened war, a war to be waged with that ferocity that is unique to Indians and, perhaps, to the Assyrians of old.

Hot on the heels of Amherst's rider came three Mohawks from Canajoharie in an elmbark canoe. I recognized Brant's son Joseph, a fleshy young man with his mother's pale skin and mobile, intelligent face. They brought another tale of conspiracy. One of their kinsmen who had been living among the Chenussio Senecas had fled for his life when he overheard Seneca warriors discussing a plan to attack our forts around Lake Oneida and to strike into the Mohawk country.

"Brother Warragiyaguey," they told Johnson, "you must listen to the wind and take counsel with foxes. You are traveling towards people we no longer know. Your name is written on the edge of their hatchets. They have promised to eat your liver and drink the blood of your companions. We ask you to return home quickly. We will go before you to clear your path of all obstructions. We will go behind you to watch where you cannot see."

This put the fear of God into me. We were a small party—a dozen fusiliers, the boatmen, the Johnsons, Sir William, John and Guy, Davers and me, with a couple of Mohawks and the Superintendent's servants—bobbing about at the edge of a vast sea of untamed wilderness. However, the prospect of imminent danger seemed to revive our leader's spirits. He took a pinch of snuff and informed the Indians that he was meant to pursue his mission and devour any man who stood in his path "as the

ox licketh up the grass," a metaphor that mightily pleased
the Mohawks. A passing acquaintance with the Old Testament is of some advantage in talking to Indians. Sir William instructed Joseph to tell old Brant to meet with him
at Niagara, and gave a string of beads to another Mohawk
to carry along the Iroquois Trail to Onondaga. Indian runners are fast, considerably faster than we were in our
clumsy flatboats, moving along shadowy paths invisible to
a white man's eye. I knew Mohawks who thought nothing
of running a hundred miles in a day. The Iroquois Trail
was the Indians' nearest approach to a highway. It was a
strip no wider than a woman's hips, beaten down into a
groove six or eight inches deeper than the earth around by
numberless trotting feet.

I kept my jaeger rifle primed after this, and stayed close
to camp at night. Our water-road ended at Fort Stanwix, a
strong log fort with bomb-proof bastions commanding the
mile-long carry to Wood Creek, the main inlet into Lake
Oneida. Our passage down the creek was the most
wretched part of the whole journey. The stream is clogged
with fallen trees, heaped up into great barriers we had to
hack through with axes, wading chest-deep in brackish,
stinking water ahead of the flatboats, attended by stinging
clouds of blackflies and gnats and mosquitoes. This stage
of the expedition taught me the virtue of tallow. Many of
the natives smear themselves with bear grease or raccoon
fat from one end of the year to the next, to keep off the insects in summer and the cold in winter; it gives them
much the same odor as a rabbit left hanging for the month
of July. I expect I smelled much the same by the time we
came out at Oswego at the mouth of a rushing river that
drains all the Finger Lakes.

"Bit high, aren't we, Shane?" Johnson ribbed me, as we
received the salute from Major Duncan and his little garrison. Sir William had made do with a flat-brimmed hat
with a patch of gauze hanging below. It was all very well
for him. He was on his boat, swilling shrub and writing his
endless letters, while I was up to my chin in the muck. I
suppose I should have realized then that he meant me to

earn my keep, not that it would have made any difference. I was already smitten, you see.

Oswego straddles the river, overlooking the blue of Lake Ontario, where a full-rigged schooner, the *Anson*, lay in wait for us. There is an old stone fort on the west side and a newer log one, Fort Ontario, on a higher bluff to the east, which the French dismantled after they captured it during the war; Major Duncan's carpenters were still banging and sawing to make good the damage. The major was a mild, easygoing sort who gave us a tour of his gardens and won two bottles off me in a game of bowls on his private bowling green which he kept clipped and silky as a five-guinea courtesan's legs. We lingered for two or three days at Oswego because Johnson was expecting the chiefs from Onondaga in response to his message. They arrived on cue, which impressed me, because I had heard Sir William say that gathering Indians together for a conference is like trying to fill a rain barrel in a dry season.

The Onondagas were led by a big-chested man with the profile of a Roman senator and a storm of white hair blowing about his head. Johnson called him the Bunt, and greeted him with more than usual warmth. The Onondagas professed ignorance of the Senecas' intrigues. The Bunt referred to one of the trouble-makers who had gone to Detroit as *onato*, which means a water snake. This was reassuring. The Onondagas, in their green valley set in dreaming hills in the heart of the province, are the Firekeepers of the Six Nations. If the Bunt was telling the truth, it meant that the Seneca plotters were acting on their own initiative, without the approval of the Confederacy. The Bunt, like all the Indians we met along our way, had an inventory of complaints to set before Johnson. We heard tales of tribesmen robbed and beaten and shot at by traders and soldiers; a hunter named Kanadacta had his camp looted of thirty buckskins by sutlers or fur-traders heading for Fort William Augustus. The Bunt also objected to our voyage to Detroit.

"We acknowledge only two council fires where all the *Onkwehonwe*—the Real People—may assemble," said the Bunt. "There is our central fire at Onondaga and there is

my brother's fireplace, where the Real People and the Sunrise People may speak from the heart."

He insisted that if Sir William wished to confer with the
western Indians, who until yesterday had been bent on eating our livers without salt, then he should make them
come to Fort Johnson and meet him on his own ground
where he would be surrounded by friends who could protect him against treachery. I believe that the Bunt's concern was less for our safety than for the fading role of the
Six Nations as buffers and middlemen between the English
and the Indians—and the Indian peltries—of the interior of
North America. The Bunt saw our soldiers and traders
pushing west, going around the Six Nations or going
through them. He feared the day when a stampede of
white men would trample on the Six Nations in pursuit of
an ever shifting frontier. He could neither read nor write,
but he was more subtle and far-sighted than half a dozen
of His Majesty's ministers that I could name.

Johnson said the obvious things, that the tremendous extent of the British conquests made it necessary to hold
conferences outside the territory of the Confederacy, and
that these would be good for business and for peace. I
could see the Onondagas were far from happy, even
though Johnson distributed most of the blankets and ruffled shirts we had left and instructed Major Duncan to give
them two barrels of powder.

"Without careful management," Johnson observed after
we boarded the *Anson* for the voyage along the southern
shore of Lake Ontario to Niagara, "we could lose them
all."

Driving north-west winds kicked whitecaps towards us
across the wide surface of the lake. The schooner tilted
and rolled and my belly heaved with its motions. I was as
seasick as I had been on the Atlantic passage.

The weather lifted in time for me to get a good view of
the mouth of Four-Mile Creek, where Johnson and
Prideaux had landed their men for the assault on the
French fort at Niagara, almost two years before to the day.
Thick woods pressed down to the edge of the stream

which was blocked by a humpbacked sandbar and choked by the debris of fallen timber.

Johnson indulged in old war stories. He got the command of the Niagara expedition—and the credit for our victory—when Prideaux, a straitlaced soldier of the old school, positioned himself an inch too close to a coehorn mortar and was killed by a bit of shrapnel when it burst. Johnson had many unusual qualities, but more important than any was his luck.

Sir William pointed out the thickets where his Indians had concealed their canoes, the place where the engineers had sweated to clear a channel through the sandbars for the soldiers' transports.

"General Amherst says that Indians can't fight and are not to be relied on," Johnson concluded. "I may tell you that without the Indians, our guns and our sappers might not have delivered Niagara into our hands. It was our Indians who brought us intelligence of the French relief column and enabled me to ambush it in the woods at La Belle Famille."

At last I saw the crosses of Saint George and Saint Andrew—no place, I'm afraid, for Saint Pat—coupling on the flagstaff above Fort Niagara.

The Frenchmen who built the place were students of Vauban; on the land side of the fort they constructed ravelins and bastions, curtains and counter-scarps, ditches and pickets, according to the book. The keep was a big stone house with dormers in the roof for cannon-ports, as at Fort Johnson. Sir William told me that, in the early part of the century, a brilliant French agent named Joncaire tricked the Senecas who owned the land about the falls. The frenchies asked permission to put up an innocent trading-house and built it with bomb-proof walls and cannons in the attic. Within a few years, the stone house had become the hub of a permanent military encampment that covered about eight acres, with barracks and raking batteries and dungeons with equipment for stretching captives to make them talk and for garrotting those that were done talking. Niagara matters, then and now: it commands the water highway of Canada and New York to Lake Erie, the Ohio

country and the western posts. Cut off Niagara, and you
separate the seaboard provinces from the heartlands of
North America.

The fort stands on a ridge above the lower landing and
the jumble of grog-shops, bawdy-shops, truck stores, warehouses and Indian shanties that the French called La
Platon and the English called the Bottoms. When he was
in one of his metaphysical sulks, Davers liked to say that
each man creates his own hell, and that there is nothing
more real. I would add that those of a more convivial disposition create offshoots of hell, in a manner of speaking,
that can be seen and wallowed in by others. The Bottoms
was one of these out-stations. I have rarely seen such a
choice collection of rooks, sharpers, cutthroats, fireships
and lost souls.

From inside the fort, we could hear the dull boom of the
falls. I went to inspect them with Davers and Normand
Macleod, Johnson's commissary at Niagara and a man after my own heart—a man who knows how to take a bottle
by the neck and a woman by the waist—while Sir William
sat in council with delegations of Chippewas and Mississaugas. We peered down over a plume of mist. When
Macleod remarked that the view of the Horseshoe Falls
could not be seen adequately from our side of the river,
Davers must needs go climbing down rickety wooden lad-
ders hanging off a precipitous cliff with a drop of two or
three hundred feet to the rocks below. I followed him
down, cursing his intemperance. Davers could never do
anything without plunging himself into it heart and soul.
There was no middle way for him; he was either barren
and indifferent to the swirl of life around him, or a zealot.
I did not care for the climb down. It was an Indian
ladder—young treetrunks stripped of their foliage, with the
stubs of the branches left protruding to supply footholds,
lashed one above the other and secured to boulders and evergreens that grew out from the face of the cliff. The ap-
paratus wobbled nastily under our weight and swayed back
and forth with the gusting winds along the gorge. But I
must concede the descent was worth the pain. I will not
bore you with a lengthy description of the falls. Many Eu-

ropean travelers have strained their vocabularies to describe them, from the blackrobe missionaries onwards. Normand Macleod said to me that he can conceive a day when some venturesome projector will arrange excursions for citified people to view this natural wonder. I am sure this will not come to pass in my lifetime, not with the bloody nightmare of frontier massacres fresh in living memory, and the way from civilized settlements so long and so fraught with dangers. I remember two things with peculiar vividness. The first was the host of butterflies fluttering above the spray. The other was Davers, wading and swimming, falling and floundering, out into the river to hurl himself into the space between the cataract and the rock wall behind it. He vanished for such a long time that I began to think I had lost him. He came back dripping from head to foot, his face flushed livid pink.

"It is indescribable!" he replied to my questions. "It is like being reborn."

Johnson invited me to attend his audiences with the Senecas. They were held in the commandant's room in the stone house. It was a large chamber with a fine mahogany table and windows overlooking the lake. The panes were colored; they broke the daylight that filtered through into narrow beams of amethyst and beech-green. The high chiefs whom Johnson had summoned from Seneca country had avoided compliance, on one pretext or another. They had gone hunting, or trading, or were condoling on the death of a relative, or were naming their children in the Festival of the Green Corn.

These and similar excuses were presented to Johnson by an old rogue called Sonajoana, who had fought with Sir William about this place in the war, but had gone home as soon as he laid hands on suitable booty. He came with thirty or forty warriors, most of whom vanished into the slopshops along the Bottoms. These Senecas were sturdy, well-made brawlers; their skins were old cordovan, much darker than the Mohawks. In their company, Johnson abandoned the oriental *politesse* I had seen him keep up in earlier Indian councils. He knew they were trying to deceive him. His voice carried the thunder of distant cannons.

They had real grievances to present to him—one Seneca killed by a soldier near Fort Pitt, another near Venango, five Delawares cut down by some of our frontier riffraff near Shamokin. Broken guns, no powder, high prices—the usual complaints. They said also that the belief was growing throughout their country, as the natives watched British convoys marching and sailing west with sixteen-pounders and coehorns, that the English designed to fall on the Indians and slaughter them to the last man.

Sir William was not deaf to these complaints. He knew their force; he could feel the revolt stirring in his very marrow and he blamed General Amherst for it more than any Indian. While we were at Niagara, he tried to tackle the endless complaints about crooked traders. He issued an official table of prices for the barter with the Indians, minute in its detail, down to the value of a fathom of small wire (one small raccoon or two muskrats) or a pair of horn combs (three muskrats). The commandants of the forts were empowered to police it by stripping traders of their licenses and, if necessary, by shipping them out in irons. When Sir William's supply boats, loaded with goods, finally caught up with us late at night on August 9th, he was able to answer Indian grievances with things more tangible than oratory and paper regulations.

But he was angry with the Senecas. He suspected that the Joncaires, those remarkable Indian agents for the French who had been his most dangerous rivals since he had first set foot in the Valley, were active behind the scenes, together with other embittered Frenchmen who refused to believe that the war in North America was over. He had received more detailed accounts from Campbell at Detroit about the subversive activities of a Seneca named Tahaiadoris and a second Seneca ambassador.

He wanted straight answers from the Senecas at Niagara, and he wanted to leave them in no doubt that, even if Sir Jeffrey and some of our coarser frontiersmen regarded him as a squaw-man who was shockingly soft on the natives, he was capable of exacting terrible revenge on those who crossed him.

"You have shamed the Six Nations," he rebuked the Senecas at the fort. "Your deceits had astonished even the tribes that were at war with us before last winter. You come to me with frivolous excuses and with stories for children. I require you to tell me whether the Seneca nation authorized the embassy to Detroit."

The Indians said they would have to think about this heavy matter, and went away. When they reassembled, they pleaded ignorance; they had no knowledge of the affair at Detroit.

At this point, Sir William called up his reinforcements.

Nickus Brant arrived in response to Johnson's message. He came with Araghiadecka—Burning Sky—and other chiefs of the Mohawks at Canajoharie. He came painted red as slaughter, black as mourning. In place of his cocked hat, he wore the *gustoweh*, a plumed headdress with deer-horn antlers set at either side of the chased silver headband and eagle feathers revolving in little sockets at the top. He carried his war club incised with little figures recalling the scalps he had taken among the French and their allies. His eyes boiled like tarpits inside the paint. I called his family Anglican Apples before. That is not an adequate description for a Brant on the warpath.

The Mohawks called the Senecas to a council. We were invited as observers. Sir William was in splendid good spirits.

"*Now* you will see what the Mohawks are worth," he told me. "I allow that they are small in numbers, a dwindling people, who have melted in contact with our nation as the snow before the sun. They err and stumble and bruise themselves on the bridge they have made between our two worlds. Yet I would trust my life to them. I would not barter their friendship for that of all the natives between here and the realms of the Great Manchu."

Brant took his stand under the rude bark cover of the Indian meeting-house down on the Bottoms. Johnson had soldiers posted to shoo away curious boatmen and grog-peddlers.

"We have always listened to the voice of our brother Warragiyaguey," said Brant. "Now we have learned that our brothers the Hill People," this was the Indian name for the Senecas, "have been listening to the twitterings of evil birds, and that the western door of our Longhouse lies open before our enemies. Open your eyes and look at the sun. We Mohawks are come as the mouth of our Six Nations to recall you to your duty. Though we are one great family, if you stir a finger against our brothers the English, we shall rise up as one man and cut you off. Do not flatter yourselves that our warning is empty because we have fewer warriors than we had before. What does the wolf care how many are the sheep?"

There was a lot more in the same vein and the Senecas responded with every sign of meekness and respect, promising to polish up the covenant chain and bury all hatreds under the great tree of peace, though it was hard to tell what these assurances were worth, because Indians do not air their differences in front of white men and an Indian has no equal at concealing his private thoughts. Moreover, a spy for the Indian Department slipped into the fort with news more alarming than anything we had heard from Captain Campbell.

The spy's name was Sunfish and, like the man who employed him, he was an original. He was a free mulatto of middling height with tight curly hair and honey-colored skin, the child of a runaway Yoruba slave and a native woman. He wore a crimson ruffled shirt over a breechclout embroidered with quills and a circlet of bear claws around his neck. A curious blue stone, suspended by a wire through his septum, bobbed above his upper lip. I learned that for many years past, he had lived among the Senecas in the fertile valley of the Genesee, and kept a Seneca wife at a village whose Indian name means the Place Where The Earth Meets The Sky. I do not know whether the Indians called him Sunfish after its many colors or its shining leap; *kentson*—fish—is a pet name for the male organ among the Six Nations.

Sunfish sat with us in the mottled light of the commandant's room, chewing a plug of Virginia tobacco, talking of a Frenchman who lived for revenge and an Indian dream-hunter who walked with the Master of Life.

"Santang come in Seneca villages," the spy reported. "He be coming in white, like soldier of France. Santang say the king across the water, he is always very much father and protector to his children. He say Roi Soleil—Sun King—was taking long nap with his wives when soldiers were fighting. But now he comes with floating castles and warriors and thunder-sticks as many as the leaves of the forest. He be coming with his armies down the Rapid River and up the Great Lazy to kill all the English, man, woman and child."

"Lies!" Johnson exclaimed. "The French are defeated! How can the Senecas vest their faith in these deceptions?"

"Santang is well-loved. He knows the tongues of many nations. He has wintered in their camps. He has led braves on many warpaths. Now he come with gifts of powder and steel. He say the English will not give these things because they wish the death of all Indians. He carries a great black belt with a red hatchet in the middle. He asks the Nations to clear a path for the Sun King by cutting off the soldiers at the forts."

"I knew the French were at the bottom of this affair." Johnson stood up and walked to the window, clasping his hands behind his back. He was puzzled by the strange name, Santang. He asked Major Walter of the Royal Americans, the commandant at Niagara, to send for de Couagne, the sleek young French interpreter at the fort.

De Couagne smiled at the mulatto's pronunciation.

"The Chevalier Louis de Saint Ange," he translated. "But surely you have heard of him?"

"I have," Johnson agreed. "I was informed Saint Ange was dead."

"The savages say Saint Ange walks under the hand of a powerful spirit."

"They say that of me, too," Johnson said, without humor. "We shall see whose spirit is stronger."

The shadow of Louis Saint Ange traveled with us from Niagara to Detroit, magnified by rumor, omnipresent yet elusive and insubstantial. He was one of the veterans of

New France. He had fought Foxes about the Great Lakes
and Chickasaws in the Louisiana territories. He had led
native warriors into battle against our regulars along the
Monongahela and the shores of Lake Ontario. Johnson
said he was one of that peculiar breed of Frenchmen who
had acquired the habits and prejudices of the Indians, including a cold, inexhaustible appetite for revenge. It was
said he had private scores to settle—a brother shot down
like a game-hen by Virginia militiamen when Major Washington ambushed Jumonville's party near Fort Pitt and
started the war in this continent; an Indian wife raped and
scalped by frontier marauders. I do not know if these rumors were true. I think that Saint Ange was one of those
lost soldiers for whom there is no peace on earth because
war lives in them.

Johnson was eager to lay hands on him, and to hear
from his lips whether the revolt was being actively supported by the French at New Orleans and at the posts they
still held in the Illinois country.

But Sunfish reported that Saint Ange had left the Seneca
territory and moved west. Some Indians had seen him near
Presqu'Isle, a narrow promontory crooked like a finger on
the southern shore of Lake Erie, where General Amherst
had sent carpenters to raise a fort.

"We must see if we can beat the devil from cover," said
Johnson.

Sunfish had another item of news, and it seemed to
weigh on Johnson quite as heavily as the report about the
Frenchman.

In a wild corner of the Indian country, a man had blackened his face and gone up onto a mountain of white quartz
to seek a vision from the spirit world. Before he kept this
solitary vigil, this native was of no consequence among his
people, who may have been the Delawares, though Sunfish
was uncertain on this point. He was an idler, a drunk and
a wifebeater, good only for stealing blankets and horses
from the traders' camps. But he came down from the
mountain a new man. His family no longer knew him.
Now he ranged the forests, from the headwaters of the Allegheny to the farther shore of Lake Michigan, with an as-

tonishing tale of a spiritual journey in which, after countless hardships, he had sat with the being the Indians describe in hushed voices as the Master of Life. This powerful spirit had given him detailed marching orders. He was to go among the natives and command them in the name of this Master, to give up all the bad habits they had acquired from the white men; to forswear liquor, the devil's blood, and to drive the "red dogs," meaning us, back across the salt water to the lands where they belonged. The former reprobate walked barefoot through the Indian castles, all but naked, his white hair gusting about a face like polished basswood, leaning on his staff, shaking and wailing and crying uncontrollably as he recounted the contents of his dream. They called him the Prophet.

This was the first time I heard mention of the Prophet, and I admit that I did not take his revelations very seriously, especially when I heard about his shaking and blubbering. I have seen curious things when I have punished my liver overmuch, and have made solemn resolutions about turning over a new leaf when I found my hands trembling too violently to strike a flint for my morning pipe. I have never confused *delirium tremens* with a visitation from the spirit realm.

But Johnson listened intently to the spy's account of the Prophet, pressing for details until he had gleaned all that were to be had.

"This goes deeper than I thought," he said pensively when he had dismissed Sunfish with the gift of a few dollars in specie. "The only divinity of these natives is the dream. This dream touches on all their fears and their hopes. If this Prophet is convincing enough, he may defeat all our policy."

Robert Davers followed all of this closely, motionless and intent.

He announced, "I will find the Prophet."

Johnson narrowed his eyes until the pupils were hidden beneath the folded lids. He said, "The Prophet will be expecting you. If he exists."

* * *

The rain came down in buckets, turning the portage road
up the cliffs above the lower landing into slippery, stinking
mud. Our native porters crawled on all fours under the
burden of their heavy packs. It took us five days to cover
six miles along a narrow, sloppy terrace, with dense woods
at one hand and a vertiginous drop over vertical cliffs on
the other, to the wooden blockhouse at Little Niagara, opposite Navy Island. One of our mules shied and tumbled
over. I watched its clumsy carcass cannon between the
limbs of hardy evergreens that projected over the watery
void.

A flotilla of whaleboats and bateaux waited for us off
Navy Island. We boarded Johnson's launch with an Indian
pilot and led the convoy. We showed the white ensign at
our stern by day, a lanthorn by night. The Royal Americans of our escort rowed to our right, the Provincials to the
left, as we crept like water-beetles through the passage to
the west of the island towards the wide waters of Lake
Erie.

When we pulled opposite the high, rocky bluffs about
the swampy mouth of the Cuyahoga, Johnson told off a
party under Lieutenant Maxwell of the Royal Americans
to hunt up some fresh meat and to put out feelers after
Saint Ange, the French agent. Davers and I volunteered to
go along. Daniel the Mohawk accompanied us; on the
journey he stayed as close to Sir Robert as his shadow, except when in liquor.

The soldiers made a great slaughter of ducks and wild
turkeys among the sedge, but Daniel had an idea he could
find us some deer, so Davers and I went off with him by
ourselves. If I have given the impression that Daniel was
a comedian, I owe this Mohawk an apology. In the woods
he became a different animal. He ran along the tops of
fallen treetrunks, light as a squirrel. He could smell day-
old deerscat half a league away. All his outward senses became sharper and keener. But what made him a better
hunter than any white man I know was an inner sense. He
seemed to know where the game was to be found before
he looked for the tracks. He even appeared to call the
game to him. He made us sit in the shade of a clump of

young firs while he sang a little dirge. When I asked what
he was doing, he said, "Talking to *oskenenten*. Talking to
the Master of Deer. You got to ask permission." I had had
my fill of this, and was just getting up to see what I could
beat up without aid of mumbo-jumbo, when a fine ten-
point stag trotted out of the brush and stood, not ten yards
away, calmly inspecting us. I took him with a ball just below the neck. Daniel jabbered some more words and gutted and skinned the beast with amazing speed, slipping his
knife from the back of the belly up to the throat. He offered us a piece of raw liver. I wasn't hungry enough for
that, but Davers had a mouthful. Daniel quartered the carcass and hung it up for the soldiers to collect.

Our trail snaked by an Indian summer camp. A twist of
smoke rose up from a scattering of hillocky bark huts. A
naked child sat up in a butternut above the tassels of a little field of green corn, tossing stones at crows and blue-
jays. He hooted and flapped his arms when he saw us, and
there was a stir amongst the women drying their laundry
on flat stones beside the creek.

Daniel did not wish to go near them.

"Short Ears," he hissed. "Bad people. Love French, not
English."

But I thought we might learn something about Saint
Ange and insisted on paying them a visit. A grayhaired old
man came out to receive us with a firelock in his hands,
followed by a swarm of boys with miniature bows and
spears. I cocked my rifle, but he gave me to understand by
his gestures that he meant us no harm. He was showing us
that the lock of his gun was broken. He patted his flat
belly to indicate that he was hungry because he could not
go hunting.

He had a few words of French. This and sign-language
were our sole means of communication. I learned later that
Short Ears is the name other tribes give to the nation we
know as the Ottawas, a word that means Traders in their
own tongue. I thought the term Short Ears must be a pleasantry, given this old boy's appearance. His earlobes were
slit in several places and so weighted by bones and beads
and articles of trade silver that they hung down to the root

of his neck. He sported a curious necklace of eagle bone whistles which seemed to increase Daniel's nervousness.

"Rataenneras," Daniel muttered, fingering the grimy deerskin pouch that hung about his neck. "Witchman."

I thought it suspicious that the village seemed deserted of young men.

"Vos hommes. Où sont-ils?"

The old man mimed the action of throwing out a fishing-line.

He was anxious to communicate something more to us. He pointed at Davers and at me, and then towards the west, repeating, *"Blancs mauvais. Blancs mauvais."*

A dark, pock-fretten woman, round as a keg, advanced and started shrilling something at us. Impatient at our frowns, she pointed at her genitals and commenced rubbing her palms briskly up and down on her plump thighs.

"Do you suppose that is an invitation?" I said to Davers.

Sir Robert was quicker than I was on this occasion.

"I think they are trying to tell us that white men attacked their women. Daniel?"

Reluctantly, Daniel bestirred himself and engaged in some brisk hand-signing with the woman.

"She say English took woman from here."

"When?"

"Maybe one, two hours."

"Good Lord," said Davers. "We must do something."

I did not much care for the idea.

I pointed out that it was highly likely that this was a trap. "Their warriors may be waiting in ambush for us."

Another woman came up with a howling baby squirming inside a cradle-board, with its umbilical cord hanging from the frame in a little embroidered pouch as an amulet.

"She say," Daniel interpreted the urgent fluttering of hands, "this baby need milk. This baby's mother go with hairy-faces."

This was enough for Davers. He vowed he would give pursuit alone if I declined to go with him. I considered sending Daniel back to alert Maxwell and the fusiliers, but realized we would need him to find the spoor of our quarry. I scribbled a note and gave it to the old man. I

asked Daniel to explain to him that he must take it to our
men at the river. He made signs of assent, but I did not
trust him. His eyes were almost frightening. They seemed
to reach out inside you and measure the intestines.

We set off westward. The Mohawk loped ahead, noise-
less in the moccasins that fitted his high-arched feet like a
second sole and through which he could read the furrow of
an old trail, the pattern of bent grass. At the ford of a sluggish creek where our quarry had entered the water and
waded upstream to evade pursuers, Daniel told us there
were five white men and that they had been forced to carry
their captive. This gave us hope that they were not too far
away, unless they had reached their boats. It also made me
worry about the odds we were facing.

Daniel set us a hard pace, making loops and zigzags
around great heaps of fallen timber and brambles that tore
the skin. We passed through dank, sunless places where
ghost flowers, pearly white, curling into a bowl like an Indian pipe, blossomed from the mold of rotting vegetation.
My mouth was dry. My heart thrashed against my ribs. I
swore that we were wasting our energies on a fool's errand. The sun was halfway down the sky. It glinted on the
treetops, but we were running between wells of shadow.

Then Daniel dropped down behind a wrinkled ash and
signaled for us to be still. I crept up to him, trying to avoid
the dry twigs.

I could hear nothing for a time above the roar of my
own blood.

Then I heard snuffling, chuckling noises. Through them
came a ghastly, hissing sound. I do not have a morbid
fancy, but it sounded to me like something issuing from a
crypt. The hiss came again, stronger and more vicious, and
I thought of a raccoon cornered by snapping dogs.

Daniel flitted from tree to tree, working his way nearer.
We aped him, I with my little jaeger gun, Davers with his
long smoothbore loaded and cocked.

They had made camp on a rise above a sluggish brown
creek choked with driftwood. They had horses tethered
under a stand of cedars. A slab of deermeat was broiling

on a spit over the fire. One of them lolled near it swilling
from a jug. The others were enjoying the girl.

They had her stretched out like a blood-offering to the
sun. Her wrists and ankles were lashed to stakes hammered into the damp earth. The wind sawed through the
treetops. The last rays of the sun striped the high grass
with tawny light between long, swaying shadows. A great
bird of prey sailed on straight wings high overhead.

They had forced her body open, but she fought them
still, with every nerve, with every breath, with the feral
hiss that escaped from the filthy rag they had stuffed in
her mouth. I saw the coppery gleam of her haunches, of
the high, small, uptilted breasts. Her captors were naked
below the waist. One of them laughed and thrust his
weight down on her. His buttocks shook like a custard.
One of his companions crouched down beside him, chafing his own member.

I knew that Davers was right to make us come. We had
heard Indians complain of incidents like this at every stop
on our journey to Niagara. Those were only stories; this
was real. I had cared nothing for this girl before. She was
still anonymous to me; I could not see her face, only the
muscles straining, the lean, hard body twisting and rolling
under her assailant. There was beauty in her defiance
under that sordid evil. I felt ready to kill every man that
had touched her.

I found myself giving orders.

"Daniel." I pointed to the sentry swilling his rum by the
fire.

With only the briefest of glances at Davers, the Mohawk
slipped between the trees and vanished into the shadows.

I told Davers to cross the stream lower down and circle
round to their left, while I took the right.

The water was cold and deeper than I had anticipated. I
had to hold my gun and my powder horn above my head.

When I came out and tunneled my way up through the
rushes, I saw that the sentry was still lounging by the fire
with his jug in his hand and a blanket roll under his head
which was turned towards me. I froze. He did not raise the

alarm. I saw the blood pumping from the hole in his neck
where the Mohawk had slid in his knife.

What a fool I was! I should have instructed Daniel to
stun the sentry or hold him captive. My anger had dulled
my reason.

"Go again, Jake!" roared one of the scum with the girl.
"She's dying for it!"

And the anger came back.

I ran across the clearing. One of them turned to me,
open-mouthed. I clubbed him full in the face with the
stock of my rifle, hard enough to cost him his front teeth.
I swung at the brute who was trying to mount the girl. He
howled and rolled free. I struck at him with the barrel,
ramming him between the legs until his howls became a
falsetto.

The others hurled themselves on me, wrestling for the
gun. The hammer smacked down on the pan and a ball
flew off into the trees. One of the brutes had his arm round
my neck, forcing my head back, stealing my air.

"Gentlemen, if you please! I don't mind which of you
I kill first."

The chokehold relaxed.

Davers stood under a black walnut, sighting along his
barrel.

"Goddam, you're English!" said the fellow who had got
his paws on me. He was a big, broad-shouldered lout
about my own age, smelling vilely of liquor and bear fat.
"What you want to come interfering for?"

The one I had hammered in the teeth was crawling towards the fire where their guns were stacked.

"I wouldn't do that if I were you," Davers warned him.

"Christ! Look at Tiny!" He had spotted the sentry. Daniel came out of the shadows, caressing his knife. The
wounded man moaned and stumbled back towards us.

The young one kept protesting. "What you want to
come meddling for? It don't gall a squaw to serve a man,
no more than it galls a woodchuck to dig a hole."

"It seems to me you neglected to ask the lady's permission."

I set about cutting the girl's bonds. She was a beauty,

long and supple, her oval face set off by a mass of glossy
black hair that fell to her waist. I am not sure what kind
of thanks I expected, but it was not what I received. When
I removed the gag from her mouth, she spurted a huge gob
of spittle that got me in the right eye.

The young one sniggered. "See! She's a game 'un. You
try asking permission."

While I stood wiping my face, Davers stripped off his
shirt and offered it to her. She stared at him as if she was
contemplating biting off his nose. Then she snatched the
shirt from his hand and draped it about her shoulders.

The young one went on giggling. Perhaps it was the
drink or plain funk.

"We did the squaw a favor. Injuns don't know how to
please a woman."

She moved faster than the eye could follow. She stabbed
into his face, along the ridge of the cheekbones. She
hooked her nails in, and dragged them down, tearing skin
and flesh away in long, bloody strips.

She ran for the shelter of the woods. We did not try to
stop her. She had had enough of white men's company.

"That's the thanks you get for your meddling," said the
one they called Jake, who had a face like a side of beef on
which the nose glistened like a carbuncle. "Now, by God,
you'll answer for Tiny!"

I could see that the dead man posed a problem. A Mohawk had slain a white man, for abetting an offense that
most of our frontiersmen thought no more criminal than
pissing behind a bush. It could cause no end of bother.

I resolved to brazen things out. I demanded to know
their identities and their business. They said they were fur-
traders who had been robbed by the Ottawas at the village
and were merely claiming repayment in services. I asked
to see their licenses, which brought a significant lull in the
conversation.

"I am in the service of His Majesty's Indian Department," I told them, and I suppose that, at that moment, I
crossed my bridge and became Johnson's man. "Sir William Johnson is on the lake, with king's ships and king's
men. You will answer to him."

It struck me that, if Johnson made an example of these ruffians, it might go a long way towards pacifying the Indians who complained of persistent abuse.

Jake did not like my suggestion. He said they were partners of McDonner, and McDonner had a license from Pennsylvania as good as any paper from Sir William.

"McDonner?" The name brought back unpleasant memories of a brawl in an Albany tavern. "Would that be Ian McDonner?"

"And a better man than any Indian-lover what calls himself Sir." This was a new voice, and it belonged to McDonner himself.

I thought we were dead men, because the dour, bony-head loblolly had crept up on us in the dark with two or three attendants. I presume they had been out trading or hunting or preying on Indians in a different quarter. They had the advantage over us. After our last encounter at Albany, there was no need for introductions and little hope of an understanding.

"We'll do it legal-like," said McDonner. "You killed one of mine. I'll kill one of yours. The injun don't count, seeing as injuns ain't human. He swings anyway. You two may draw lots to see who swings with him."

"That won't be necessary," said Davers.

I told the fool to hold his tongue and tried to impress McDonner with the fact that Maxwell and his soldiers were nearby and had already been summoned to our assistance. If McDonner dared to lay hands on us, he and his men would face summary execution.

My words rang hollow in the immensity of the forest night inside that circle of outlaws. I have met very few men whom I regarded as wholly evil, but McDonner was one of them—a little man, yet possessed of a hateful and desolate force.

Daniel was singing his death-song.

"I have explored the four quarters, and the above
   and below.
I have flinched from none of the six directions.
I am going to walk the path of strawberries."

He had his chest puffed out. He may have been showing
off a little, demonstrating that a Mohawk knows how to
die. The effect was wasted on this crude lynch mob.

I did not know the words of any death-song, and felt entirely unready to die as I watched them throwing ropes
over the branches and forming the nooses. To travel so far,
for this! To twist in the wind because of a girl who had already suffered the worst, and whose idea of thanking her
manly rescuer was to use him as a spittoon!

I believed fate was against me that night.

They gave Davers and me straws, and I pulled the short
one.

"I'll take it," said Davers.

I might have let him have it, except that I have always
despised a fellow who cheats in a game, and I thought the
outcome would be the same since it seemed unlikely to me
that McDonner's gang would string up two of us and let
the third man live to tell tales.

I kept looking for a chance to make a break for it, but
they had us securely bound. I was obliged to play the passive spectator while they set Daniel up on a barrel and
threw the cord round his neck.

I suppose I was praying.

Surely Maxwell would come. Surely Sir William would
miss us and send out search parties. The immense silence
of the forest mocked these hopes.

No doubt I gave myself over to self-pity, to thoughts of
Peg and the soft life I could have enjoyed, but for a certain
evening at White's.

I have no definite recollection. I know that I looked
away at the moment when they seemed about to kick the
barrel away from under Daniel, and that when I looked up,
everything was changed. Without war cries, without shots,
a pack of blackened Indians, indistinct as shadows, swirled
around the clearing. They fell on McDonner's men with
war clubs and tomahawks, hacking and gouging. I saw one
of the white men's heads burst open like a melon. Mc-
Donner's men got off a couple of shots. Then they were
fleeing for their lives towards their frightened, whinnying
horses or into the blackness under the trees. I do not know

how many of them escaped. I know that McDonner survived. If he had not, my own story, and perhaps that of the frontier I knew, would have had a happier outcome. It is curious how little events and little men drive the engines of history.

The man who came to free us was not an Indian though his face was streaked with warpaint. He wore a heavy silver cross and an officer's gorget around his neck.

"*Je suis votre valet, monsieur,*" he said to me, dainty as a fop at Fontainebleau.

"May I know to whom I have the honor of expressing gratitude for this timely deliverance?" said I, not to be outdone by a frenchie in *politesse*.

"I am the Chevalier de Saint Ange."

"Saint Ange!"

The face was as sharp and sudden as a hawk's.

"*Oui, monsieur.* You have been of assistance to the daughter of a friend of mine. I am come to return the service. You will find Sir William, the *lion belgique*, in that direction." He pointed out a trail to the lake that was passable for the horses McDonner's crowd would no longer be needing.

"You may tell Sir William," Saint Ange continued, "that he is not wanted in this country."

"I will tell him nothing of the kind."

"*Je le regrette, monsieur.* The slate is clean. If we meet again, it will be as adversaries."

30th September

Chéri,

How misfortunate that your mother tongue is not
French. It is the language of the senses, and the ra-
pier for wit. You can only do justice to your skirmish
with *la belle* Angélique at Detroit in French. What English word gives us the throaty pleasure of *volupté*?
"Voluptuousness" is a poor, plodding literal rendition.
It lacks the giddy gulp of pleasure.

I hope the French cat left scars on you. You deserve
them.

I do not think I can get away this season. Sir
Henry grows daily more watchful, like an old hound
losing his scent that doubles his patrols.

Dream only of me.

Valerie

8

The Pompadour of New France

JOHNSON SENT OUT RANGERS in pursuit of Saint Ange and McDonner. They returned to report that they had discovered the bodies of two white men, scalped and mutilated, but no live ones.

The watch was doubled by night for the remainder of our voyage to Detroit. The only game we took was the gift of the wolves. At dusk, we saw a pack of them sallying out of the woods at the edge of the lake. They had run down a fine buck. He plunged out into the water, bleeding from his flank. Sir William claimed the buck for himself. He shot it cleanly, through the heart, and divided the meat among our party. He kept the hooves, the skin and the sinews for his own use and remarked, "The wolves, at least, are our allies."

On the first Thursday in September, we threaded the islands at the mouth of the Detroit River and came out into a strait of dark blue water a half mile wide, with native settlements on either shore: Potawatomis—Fire People—at our left hand, Hurons at our right. Beyond the sandbluffs, we had our first view of the tall log palisades of the fort rising up from the river's edge. The salute from the cannons of the fort was echoed by the two ships of war riding at anchor in the channel, and by the firelocks of the natives who came trooping down to the shore to companion our passage.

Detroit is a thriving metropolis, by the standards of the frontier. I suppose that, at the time of my first visit, it had above two thousand white inhabitants, surrounded by as many Indians, in the summer villages of the Hurons and Potawatomis, and of the Ottawas, on the south bank higher upstream, and the rough encampments of the Chippewas and the western tribes who had been summoned to sit with Sir William at his council fire.

In spirit, Detroit still belongs to the French. Within the *chemin de ronde* inside the palisades, a hundred houses are laid out along narrow streets bearing the names of Catholic saints, with a stone church at one end and the priest's house at the other. Most of the *habitants* live outside the walls. Their whitewashed houses are mostly built in the steep-roofed Norman style, set close together along the river road for conviviality, like rows of grinning teeth, with narrow strips of orchards and kitchen gardens winding back to the edge of the woods. Every few rods, you see a high wooden cross with a carved bird on top to remind the faithful of how Saint Peter denied his Savior three times before the cock crowed. Why the French in these latitudes choose to remember this act of betrayal is a thing that was never explained to me. But the behavior of Dandy Cuillerier and his compatriots during the revolt made me think that Peter's cock was a fitting emblem for the *habitants* of Detroit.

A carpenter in a red cap, mending a hole in the palisades by the river gate, waved his pipe in our direction and gave a lusty rendition of a canticle in praise of a Parisian brothel.

> "Le couvent le plus doux de Paris
> Est celui de Madame Paris:
> On y voit fourmiller les novices,
> Suivent la règle avec docilité

Au prochain rendant plus de services
Que trois cents soeurs de charité."

The sweetest convent in Paris
Is that of Madame Paris.
You see novices swarming there
Sweetly obeying the rule of their order,
Supplying their guest with more services
Than three hundred sisters of mercy.

This, together with a powerful aroma of ripening pears and apples, and the view of a number of curly-haired mademoiselles teetering about on spindly heels, in charming short petticoats that covered barely half the leg, made me eager to investigate the pleasures of the town.

Under the walls of the fort, a file of redcoats performed a wheel of the quarter circle. I hope they impressed the natives. Our regulars looked like a shabby, miserable lot to me, sweating under their broadcloth, their bobwigs and their pipeclayed belts and bandoliers.

Our commandant at Detroit, Captain Donald Campbell, was a plump, hearty Scot with enough of the moss-trooper in him to make him more at ease with Indians than the majority of our regular officers. He presided over a garrison of a hundred men at the water-bridge between Lake Erie and the upper lakes, ringed by tribes that had been flaying and quartering anything in a red coat until the day before yesterday, and by white men as vain as peacocks, nostalgic for the lilies of France. Sir William's principal business was to make his position, and that of our traders, safe, by binding the western tribes to a lasting treaty, and by stamping out the embers of revolt.

I witnessed more of Johnson's counciling than I might have wished to, because he had made me a formal proposal to sign on with the Indian Department, and I had accepted. Sir William had promised to get me a lieutenant's commission, whatever General Amherst had to say about the matter.

I envied Davers's greater liberty, though not the use he made of it. He went over the river in a canoe with Daniel to visit the Mohawk's Huron relations. Some of the Hurons—a fine, manly people with pretty regular features who shaved their heads to a bristly ridge—were relatively tame, and attended church service with Father Pothier, the Jesuit chaplain. Davers, inevitably, sought out the wild ones who talked with stones and trees and offered white dogs to the rising sun. He was deadly serious about finding the Prophet, or what the Prophet was about.

He came back across the river in high excitement. He announced that the Hurons were going to adopt him at a pagan ceremony. He said he was going to live among them, and travel with them across the upper lakes, to some mystical island where he would sit at the feet of a famous dream-doctor whose name was never said out loud, because it would call him of an instant, in the shape of an owl or a hawk.

"They seemed to know me," Davers announced. "They seemed to be expecting me."

I was sufficiently disturbed to have a word with Father Pothier who was a shrewd old buzzard and a lusty trencherman like most of the Jesuits I have come across. I will say this for the Society of Jesus—it does not harbor many blockheads. Father Pothier conversed as easily about hydrography or horticulture as about parochial business, and he kept an excellent half-breed cook.

We discussed Davers over a very passable ragout, a salad from the Father's own garden, and a bottle of bordeaux from the old country.

"Sir Robert is a God-haunted man," said Father Pothier. "He does not find God in his own church, yet he cannot live without Him."

"Will he find what he is seeking among the Indians?"

"I cannot say. The beginning of wisdom, we are taught, is the fear of the Lord. That he will surely learn. I have talked with him a little. It seems to me he is driven by that boundless spirit of curiosity that leads a man to seek to penetrate into the future, and into the secret of things that God, in His wisdom, keeps hidden from men. If he pursues this quest, he will encounter powers of darkness as well as powers of good."

"He says he means to study with a medicine man."

"A sorcerer. Perhaps it is the One from the Island. Do you know anything of the native sorcerers, the shape-shifters? No? Some of them are remarkable. They would put our circus conjurers to shame. Yet, that is not the end of it. I have seen some of them go into a state of ecstasy that binds all the senses and holds them in suspended animation. I have seen a foreign spirit enter into them in a corporeal manner. It speaks from the depth of their chests and raises them up into the air. I have seen unspeakable things."

Father Pothier's hand was unsteady. I wondered if I had been mistaken in my favorable judgement of the Jesuits. It seemed to me that these fables were as credible as an Irish milkmaid crying witchcraft because the butter in her churn has gone off.

"There is something else," he pursued. "The soul of the Indians is far more independent of their bodies than ours is, or so they believe it to be. They think that in dreams and waking visions, their soul leaves the body to take flight and make excursions. They imagine that, in this way, they can travel to the most inaccessible places, half a world away, and to the upper and lower worlds. Their attachment to this belief would beggar your imagination. I have not been able to extirpate it even among natives who have lived for three generations within the bosom of the Church. It defies the tenets of my own religion, yet I cannot altogether dismiss it.

"Once, when I was teaching my charges the catechism—which we sing to music because that is the only way to hold their enthusiasm—I noticed an old, wrinkled, grayhaired man at the back of my church. I had never seen him before. I knew that he was not among the converted, because he wore charms and fetishes that are banned among my flock. There was an intensity about his gaze which I cannot convey to you in words. When he stared at me, I felt that he had somehow transported himself from one end of the church to the other. I even felt his light touch on my face, like the brush of feathers. Naturally, you will not repeat these things outside my house. I could hardly include them in my reports to my superiors. They would have judged me a victim of the Indian madness, like your reckless young friend.

"At the end of my lessons, my visitor spoke to me in the Huron tongue which I speak adequately enough. He asked me if I had personally visited the heaven and hell described in our holy scripture, and if I had walked with Christ, our Savior. I told him that I put my trust in revelation, as recorded in our Holy Bible. He mocked me. He said I was a fool to vest my faith in a book, when it is the duty of a man to journey, in his own person, to the spirit world and walk with the hidden masters. I had answers for him, of course. We Jesuits are schooled in debating."

Father Pothier took a gulp of wine.

"But he shook me. Between these walls, I will confess that I almost thought myself in the presence of the Tempter. I remembered the dreams of *our* prophets, in the Old Testament of the Hebrews. I thought of Jacob's vision of the slippery ladder to paradise. My life is consecrated to the service of God. Yet, for an instant, I felt bitter envy, that at the end of all my study, and of countless vigils, I have not walked with my Creator as that half-naked savage claimed to do. I recovered myself. *Ça va sans dire.* But part of my flock left with the conjurer. They came back when they were hungry. I do not delude myself about the depth of my conversions.

"So you see, I understand Sir Robert Davers. I do not condone him, but I will pray for him, even though he is not of my faith. In part of myself, I would like to go with him, wherever his journey may take him. He is a holier man than those that worship appearances."

I had hoped for more practical advice from a man of Father Pothier's order. But his words had a practical effect. I decided I had done with chaperoning Davers. Let him go chasing off with the Hurons on their fall hunt in quest of a dream-hunter reputed to kill with a song and a bone. I would apply myself to the ladies of Detroit.

But first, I must give some account of our business at this outpost of the Empire. At the treaty council, and in the more select huddles where the real business was trans-

acted, I saw Sir William Johnson at his high-water mark,
as Indian agent, spymaster, charmer and charlatan. I also
had my first encounter with Black George Croghan, the
only man in the Indian Department, excepting Sir William,
who was truly indispensable, and the only one Johnson
could never rule.

Black George lived with a Seneca wife in the Ohio
country, and had become enough of an Indian that he
would never take a straight path if a crooked one was on
offer. He was a rough, bawdy little stump of a man with
a nose that bulged out like a beet, decked out as a fop in
his Philadelphia silks and ruffled linen, with the tail of his
new bagwig flapping between his shoulderblades.

Black George took me aside after our first meeting, and
said, "Stick by me, boyo. If you treat George right, he will
put a plum or two in your dish. My name is the only pass-
port you need amongst the Indians. That and your own
pretty face, my dear. Sir William will tell you the same. A
sprightly lover is the ablest missioner you will ever see
amongst our natives. He is worth a dozen canting priests,
and the high Archbishop of Canterbury, and two regiments
of fusiliers."

Croghan introduced me to a gathering of Huron and
Mingo women who brought little gifts of maple candy and
stewed berries. We entertained them with rusk and shrub.

"Go on, then," Black George nudged me. "That one's
giving you the eye."

The one in question was a fat, frumpish thing of questionable age. I indicated that I preferred a slim girl who
wore her hair in braids and would not look at me directly.

"You're making a mistake," said Croghan. "The older
one knows a trick or two."

But I persisted, making signs and ferrying drinks to the
girl who had caught my fancy. She exchanged a few words
with her elders and slipped outside, giving me a quick but
significant look. I followed her into the dark and was introduced, without difficulty, onto a sleeping-mat under the
stars. She held me uncomfortably tight, clamping her legs
around the backs of my thighs as if she feared I would
spill my seed. It took me a little while to grow accustomed

to the smell of hung meat that hovered about her and the way she gritted her teeth and rolled her eyes. I cannot say whether I gave her much satisfaction. She lay wordless while I banged away, sucking in her breath. When I spurted my seed, she clutched me tighter and went on clutching me to her hard, lean body for a good time afterwards.

She had wonderful nipples, fleshy and steeply pointed like baby pinecones, but would not let me fondle them. I was horny enough after our tedious voyage to put it to her a second time without delay. I tried to rearrange her limbs into a more interesting position, but it seemed she would have it only the one way, on her back, with her knees raised up to my ears. But this time she worked her muscles more industriously, pumping me as a dairymaid draws milk from a cow's teat. She spoke for the first and only time, when I felt the currents of her body flowing with mine. When I tried to replicate the sound to Croghan, he laughed and told me it meant, "Are we making a baby?" My alarm must have showed in my face because Black George roared and said, "It would not be the first time, boyo! There's a reason they say the kids belong to their mothers."

I considered Croghan a grand fellow after this, as did Sir William, though we came from utterly different sections of Irish society. Johnson and I, of course, were products of the Pale. Croghan was born in a cotter's cottage where no doubt he shared a straw pallet with the household pigs in front of a sooty peat fire before the potato crop failed and he fled the squalor of home to seek fortune in the colonies. Perhaps the insecurity of his boyhood explains why he never clapped eyes on anything—not a tract of Indian land, certainly never a commissary train or a warrant on the treasury—without wanting to make a buck out of it. His Indian nickname was Anagurunda, which means the Buck. I shall go on calling him Black George, because that sobriquet suits his looks and his character. I remember him not only as the man who could always provide a squaw or a bottle for a thirsty traveler, but as the swindler who worked his corruption even in Johnson's great heart, and all but ruined his kingdom.

The girl hung about the fort for a few days, to my discomfiture, since I had no thought of attaching her to my household. One morning, I even found her sitting at the door of Notary Navarre's house, where I had a room to myself since Davers had decamped to live rough among the Hurons. I gathered that her name was Fruitpicker, and that she belonged to the mixed tribe of Mingoes who live about the Ohio. I gave her a silver armband and a pair of combs. You may think me ungenerous in trying to dismiss her so abruptly, but she meant nothing more to me than a doxy at Covent Garden, and my attentions were soon wholly occupied by a lady who fancied herself, not without reason, as the Pompadour of Detroit.

Johnson sat, day and night, with the Indians, bribing and cajoling, currying information. He met all the chiefs separately before he convened them all together in a great open area outside the fort; there was no room for that colorful assemblage under Captain Campbell's roof. In addition to the tribes living around Detroit and the Chippewas from Grand River and Saginaw Bay, there were Kickapoos and Twightees, Delawares and Shawanese, Mahicans and Mingoes, Mohawks, Oneidas and Senecas.

Sir William would have made a good stage manager. He came out in a scarlet cloak, trimmed with gold, in defiance of the heat, over a ruffled shirt of spotless cambric, with his hat on his head, flanked by interpreters bearing countless strings and beads of wampum. Our old friend Nickus Brant followed close behind; he had trailed us from Niagara with a little fleet of canoes. He carried a lighted brand which Johnson took from him and held up in front of the circle of chiefs and warriors. Sir William announced that he had brought this sacred fire from his great council fire in the Mohawk country, to kindle a new flame at Detroit, though I would wager he had set the brand alight with a common flint in Campbell's house not ten minutes before.

"The friendly warmth of my fire," said Johnson in Mohawk, "will be felt by the remotest of the nations, in the lands towards the setting sun."

I was getting the hang of Indian diplomacy by now, and was steeled to listen to the endless succession of rolling periods, wiping blood and tears from the eyes of the native audience, opening the passage from their hearts to their mouths, sweeping their paths clear of all obstructions. Johnson paused frequently, to hand a few strings of beads or a wampum belt across the fire to one or other of the chiefs.

"This belt contains my words."

The natives maintain that no speaker can be trusted unless his words are accompanied by these beads, which were originally tooled from clamshells, although Johnson gave out so many that he had them manufactured from porcelain in England and shipped out by the fathom.

He held up a great white belt of twenty rows wide, with figures of white men and the Indian nations joining hands around the Tree of Peace, and presented it in commemoration of the sealing of the covenant chain between England and the western tribes.

He gave assurances that his father the king would not permit white men to take possession of Indian lands to which they had no lawful claim, that he would oblige the traders to give honest value, and that the natives would not be deprived of powder for hunting and of blacksmiths to mend their guns and tools. In some of this, as in the size of the vast heap of presents he had piled up under the walls of the fort, he was exceeding his instructions. But General Amherst was a long way off.

Johnson demanded a straightforward accounting of the plot that had been hatched by the Seneca ambassadors, warning that the details were already known to him.

"I see many looks away. I hear a leaf fall from the maple in the farthest depths of the forest."

Each of his statements was received with loud shouts and grunts of approbation by sachems sprawled full-length on the dirt or squatting on their heels.

Nickus Brant stood up when he was done and gave the Mohawk view.

"I now clear away and dispel those dark clouds which your late fathers, the French, threw over the earth by plucking the sun out of the firmament so you could not see your true friends, the English, or your own interests. I now put the sun back in its rightful place."

It is hard not to admire the confidence of a man who professes to move the sun around like a rook on a chessboard.

"We Mohawks are the door of the Six Nations as we live next to the English. We are the first who are acquainted with what is stirring among them. You must pay not the least hearing to evil rumors that come to you from other nations. You must ask us. We know the hearts of the English. Our brother Warragiyaguey is come into your country for your own good. His passage makes the lakes smooth. The forest opens like a curtain before his feet."

This, too, was received with outward enthusiasm, though it is hard for me to say whether it was the speeches or the sight of all those folded blankets and strouds and kegs of powder that moved the audience.

The spokesmen for the western tribes promised to be faithful allies of the English and to heed the advice of the Mohawks. As for the small matter of the plotted revolt, they said that one of the Seneca envoys was in their midst, and must answer for himself.

Black George rounded up the Seneca that evening and brought him round to Johnson's quarters in the commandant's house, in company with his half-breed interpreter, Andrew Montour, and some Indians I did not know. The Seneca's name was Kayashuta. He was a man-mountain, taller than me by a head, and weighing perhaps four hundred pounds. He was said to be capable, drunk or sober, of hoisting one of our oak-bottomed flatboats on his back without assistance. He seemed to me as shifty as he was strong. He denied any acquaintance with Saint Ange or the mysterious Prophet. He said he had come to Detroit to buy supplies for his family since the traders at Niagara sold only rum.

Johnson let him off with a caution, though he had orders from the general to treat the ringleaders of the revolt with the utmost severity.

I asked him afterwards why he was so gentle with a man who was patently both a liar and a rebel.

He said, "We will win no friends by making martyrs. The natives believe that they hear the voices of their dead men crying out for revenge. All their wars have the nature of a blood-feud, and I do not propose to give the Senecas cause to start another."

He told me a curious story about the origins of the Confederacy of Six Nations. Once, in a dark time, Onondaga was under the sway of a cannibal tyrant named Tododarho—the Entangled One—who was feared as a powerful sorcerer. He was eventually defeated by the reformer Hiawatha with an army of Mohawks. Instead of killing the defeated tyrant, Hiawatha healed his mind, won him to the Great Law of Peace, and restored him to power as first on the roll-call of traditional chiefs.

"There is a lesson in the fable for any man who purposes to rule Indians," said Johnson. "We will never win them by Sir Jeffrey's way, which is hanging and flogging."

General Amherst was a long way off, but he was breathing down Johnson's neck, even at Detroit. Sir William received a string of despatches by military couriers, quibbling over accounts, offering the general's thoughts on how to deal with natives. There was one, I remember, that drove Johnson to toss down even more brandy than was his wont at the breakfast-table. I dug it out of the records of our Indian Department two years later, when the Lords of Trade at London mounted their inquiry into the causes of the revolt. You have seen something of Sir Jeffrey's character and his prejudices. Here is a specimen of the Indian policy he was attempting to impose on Johnson.

"The more the Indians get, the more they ask. I think it will be much better to avoid all presents in future, since that will oblige them to supply themselves by barter, and of course keep them more constantly employed, by means of which they will have less time to concert or carry into execution any schemes prejudicial to His Majesty's interests. Keeping them scarce of ammunition is not less to be recommended, since nothing can be so impolitic as to furnish them with the means of accomplishing evil."

As for the rumors of revolt, the general professed himself sublimely untroubled. "Their machinations never gave me a moment's concern as I know their incapacity of attempting anything serious. If they were ever rash enough to venture upon ill designs, I have it in my power to punish the delinquents with entire destruction."

This letter set Johnson trembling at the knees like a horse after a steep pull. The views expressed in it got Captain Campbell, and a great many lesser men, killed. I know that General Amherst has his partisans to this day. But his policy, if it prevailed, could lead only to a general war between white men and Indians at a time when there were only a handful of colonists west of the Allegheny and our regular forces had been shipped off to fight frenchies in the Gulf of Mexico. It was a war the Indians could win.

I suppose a majority of the white men in our colonies would have agreed with Sir Jeffrey Amherst that Indians did not rate as human beings and that, if they became troublesome, they should be exterminated like groundhogs in the garden. Nickus Brant's son told me that, when he was at Wheelock's school in Connecticut, he was at Sunday service when the collection plate was passed round to raise money for educating the natives. The plate returned to the front empty, save for a musket-ball.

I know I am in danger of becoming preachy on this subject, which is not my style. But as I came to know the frontier, it seemed to me that the sneering contempt of the Amhersts and the black hatred of the McDonners, if uncurbed, would result in one thing—a line of white men marching abreast across the continent, shooting every native in sight, herding those that were left into Bad Lands beyond the interest of any land company. I never became as attached to the Indians as Johnson; certainly I never wanted to join them, as Davers did, or the way the rough *coureurs des bois*, who came out of the woods reeking of fish-oil and tanned as dark as any redskin, had done. Yet, as I followed Johnson round in a shuffle-dance in the native villages, bawling my lungs out, stripped to an Adam's apron hanging down in front and below, or watched him dazzle the Huron children with the magic of a magnet

from London that picked up iron filings and turned into a
porcupine, it struck me that his was the human way, the
way that allowed room for people of both cultures. My
American friends tell me I am a reactionary, that the
"manifest destiny" of their country is to dispossess the natives and whip 'em if they holler. The march of history
was never that obvious to me. I was twenty years old at
Detroit. I belonged to Johnson's Indian Department, and I
believed in his cause.

The *habitants* of Detroit gave a ball for us at Antoine
Cuillerier's villa up the river. It was a sturdy, high-built,
whitewashed frame house with green shutters, set among
apple orchards on the skirt of a wild ravine, where a clear
stream tinkled like silver bells over rocky falls.

We made a grand entry, punting upstream in army
whaleboats, with pine torches blazing in the prows. Sir
William was in his dress regimentals with a gorget at his
throat and a sash across his chest. I wore Peg's favorite
suit of dove-gray silk with an embroidered waistcoat set
off by the buttons she had presented to me as a going-
away present. They were little paintings on ivory under
glass. The one above the heart bore her portrait in her
great role as Cordelia. The other depicted grinning satyrs
leaping over picnic baskets or gamboling with amorous
nymphs. Peg had urged me not to be ashamed to wear
her portrait at sociable routs. A girls of spirit, she maintained, would take it as a challenge. A woman of experience would take it as evidence I would not disgrace myself
in bed.

The party was already in swing under a canvas mar-
quee. I cast a pioneering glance about the company. It was
evident that the merchants of Detroit had not gone hungry
during the war, and that their ladies had not forgotten the
graces of Paris, living cheek-by-jowl with Indians in the
middle of the forest. The candlelight glinted on brilliants
and diamond aigrettes, on swan's feathers and the heady
plunge of décolletages. I saw what I wanted immediately.
If you could believe me, I would swear that I never had

serious thoughts about another woman, at least for two weeks at Detroit.

Her lips, painted blood-red, enhanced the fullness of her mouth, opening like a wound in the heart-shaped face, whitened with pearl powder, colored as deep as wine-lees by the rouge along the cheekbones. Her hair was tightly curled and powdered, with dark ringlets left free to wanton in front of her ears. Her torso was tightly laced into daffodil silk, her high-slung breasts pushed higher to spill over the lacy border. Her eyes, under the dark wings of her lashes, glowed brighter than the brilliants at her throat and ears.

"Hold it down, boy," said Johnson. "You could be prosecuted for looking at a woman like that."

"Who is she?"

"She is our host's daughter. If bloodstock counts for anything in these parts, I dare say she is the wickedest woman in Detroit."

I noted that Sir William was contemplating the girl with quite as lecherous an eye as I had. The tip of his tongue flicked out between his lips like a lizard's.

He pulled it back in and made a bow to our host. Wherever Angélique Cuillerier got her looks, it was not from her father. He was mud-colored, between his frothy lace and vast quantity of powered hair that was not his own. He had slippery, retreating features and bulging eyes, and his lips were as thick as my earlobes.

He inspected my buttons, as I did his, which were glittering things composed of paste and pearls.

Sir William made the introductions. Antoine Cuillerier shook hands with Guy and John and Captain Campbell, and said to me, "I admire a man who knows buttons."

If there was a Madame Cuillerier, she had been banished from the entertainment. I learned later that "Dandy" Cuillerier kept a harem of native women; rumor had it that the prettiest of them was his own daughter, by a Chippewa squaw.

Sir William exercised his *droit de seigneur* and led the delectable Angélique in a cotillion. I danced with Madame Chapoton, the doctor's wife, and the Widow Gervaise,

who kept a tavern and a truck store in the *faubourg* across
the river, near the Huron village, while Johnson and
Angélique trotted their paces in a string of country dances.
Widow Gervaise laughed at my lack of expertise in these
novel maneuvers and showed me the steps.

"You are not married, Mr Hardacre?"

"No indeed."

"Then how do you amuse yourself?"

"Oh, I generally gallop among the ladies like a wild
colt."

"Then you must pass a little time at my stable."

This was quite promising. As you know, I have a weakness for women of a certain age. But the Widow was a little older and fuller-stuffed than my preference, and my
heart was set on Angélique.

I found a propitious moment to cut in on Sir William,
observing that the punchbowl was all but empty.

Angélique, the cold-hearted tease, pleaded that the heat
of performing with so manly a partner was too much for
her. She must sit with Sir William to recover herself.

She gave me a haughty look over her turkey-feather fan
as they sat close together on a high-backed settee, as if to
say, Whatever you've got under your breeches, it doesn't
match a baronetcy and the Superintendent's commission.
She engaged Sir William in highly animated conversation, and appeared to have no time for any of the younger
men. Several of them—members of our party, and well-
heeled young traders of the settlement—attempted to fill in
her dance-card. They were all turned away. It occurred to
me that the slut was making a real set for Johnson. His circumstances, of course, were generally known. He had an
Indian woman under his roof and no end of other diversions. But that would only heighten the challenge, to follow Peg's line of thought, for a girl of spirit. Sir William
was unmarried in the eyes of the law and the Church, and
what a prize he would make!

I tried to imagine what Chicha, Johnson's Mohawk
châtelaine, would do if he came home with a perfumed
French tickler in his baggage. Would she try to tear her
face off, like the Ottawa girl did to McDonner's man?

It was past three in the morning when I got my chance with Angélique. Johnson had had a few more than his kidneys could deal with and was making frequent visits to the bushes behind the house.

During one of these lapses, I made a bold advance on the lady, gave her a leg and a bow, and told her that if she refused to dance with me, I intended to throw myself into the river.

"Then, monsieur, you would be wetter than you are already."

This stung, because it was damnably close beside the river, and I knew that my fine silks did not bear close examination about the armpits.

Yet there was a sparkle in her eyes, and the pearly shadow between her breasts was deliciously inviting.

I looked deeper into her eyes and gave it my best shot. "Demoiselle, I cannot command my emotions. To see you is to love you."

"Chansons!" Her throaty laughter came in a deeper rush under the tinkle of the water over the falls.

"One dance," I insisted.

She gave a fleeting glance into the shadows. She did not find Johnson. She gave me her hand.

She trotted beautifully, but too precisely, like a mannequin atop a music-box. I tried to engage her in gallant conversation, with little success, until I shifted to a different tack.

"Do you know the Chevalier de Saint Ange?"

I do not know what possessed me to say this, except that Saint Ange had been on my mind since the grim episode near the Cuyahoga and I was amongst his countrymen. My words had a remarkable effect on the girl. Even under her warpaint, I saw the color rush to her face, like watering through moire. She became as stiff as pasteboard in my arms.

She whispered, "What do you know of Saint Ange?"

"Well, nothing very much, except that he saved my life and did not seem awfully happy about it."

"Come with me."

She took me by the hand and led me out into the apple

orchard, an admirable situation, except that I was confused about the exchange that had provoked it.

"Tell me everything."

I took her hand and kissed the inside of her palm. It was warm and dry and carried the scent of sandalwood. She let me hold it on condition of satisfying her inquisition.

I told her about our adventure, not without magnifying my own contribution to the outcome. In fact, I was perfectly shameless. I invented a scene in which Saint Ange was at the point of McDonner's knife before I dashed the ruffian's arm away. This had a brilliant effect. She hugged me. Her lips grazed my cheeks. I felt the rise of her bosom against my chest. I took her by the waist. I pressed my lips against that wickedly red mouth. Her teeth came down like a portcullis. I pushed my lower body against her, contriving to let her know, through the hooped rise of her skirts, that I was more than ready for her.

She broke from me, her chest heaving so deep that I hoped she would burst from her stays.

"You forget yourself!" she reproached me.

"I cannot apologize. You rob me of the power to conceal my affections."

"I would be sorry to occasion the discomfort of any body."

"Then help me."

The stage is in my soul. I got down on my knees and blubbered, "Only you can save me."

"Chansons!"

"Only say you will let me call on you."

"Tais-toi! Coquin!"

"I won't get up until you do."

I had my nose in her petticoats. I was contemplating a deeper plunge when she cupped her hand to her ear theatrically—oh, she was born for the boards, too—and said, *"Ecoutez!* My father is calling me! We cannot be seen like this!"

"Then say you will make me happy. Say I may call on you."

"As you say. But you must tell me all of it. Where is

Saint Ange? How many are with him? How close is he followed?"

As you know, I had no answers for these questions. But it became apparent to me that something curious was at play, and that I could draw advantage from it.

I got up on my hind legs and said, rather huffily, "Your questions are improper. Those are secrets of the Indian Department."

The sauceboat fussed with her bodice, contriving to draw the border out so I could see all the way down her bosom.

She wet her lips and said, "I am not interested in what everyone knows. You will not deprive Angélique of entertainment?"

What would you have said? With her tits bulging out and the moonlight glistening on those red, red lips, she might as well have proposed to me, I'll show you mine if you'll show me yours.

We formed, you may say, an understanding. We would meet at a certain hour, when her father would be out on business, which seemed to consist mostly of selling Indians the means to get drunk and cheating the commissary at the fort.

It occurred to me, from her line of questioning, that Angélique was a spy, or, as the frenchies would say, *une mouche*. But it seemed to me that if she were a spy, she was one of the most amateur sort. What, in any event, could she hope to learn from me? I thought it more probable that the elusive Saint Ange was an old flame of hers or a connection of her family's.

In my haste to get under her skirts, it had not occurred to me that she might be smart and subtle enough to work several layers of deception and overcome a man's caution by making herself the semblance of a clumsy spy when she was as artful as any.

I did not yet know those lines of Tartuffe, which always remind me of Angélique: *"Je l'ai mis au point de voir tout sans rien croire."* "I brought him to the point where he sees everything while believing none of it."

* * *

I still think Angélique had set her cap at Johnson. The first
thing she required of me when I rode up to the Cuillerier
house two days later was that I must swear to say nothing
of our liaison to Sir William.

"Do you wish me to give you a string of wampum to
confirm the promise?"

"*Chansons!* You are a teaser, Shane Hardacre."

"And you, my dear, are what we call at home a cock-
teaser."

I clutched her to me in a fierce embrace. We were in the
parlor of the house, which seemed to be empty of servants.
She was in an inviting state of *déshabillé*, her muslin
gown billowing open over a light shift.

When I reached between her thighs, she slapped me,
hard enough to sting, not hard enough to erase all hope.

"Do you always go at women this way, like a mad
bull?"

"Only those that please me."

"You are like—a wild beast! A force of nature! Beyond
reason, beyond prudence."

I enjoyed being likened to a force of nature and laid
close siege to her ramparts, but her drawbridge was raised
against me.

"Sit with me."

She indicated a clumsy, old-fashioned chair with a nee-
dlework cushion, separated by a table from her own perch.
She offered me a beaker of the local wine pressed from the
grapes that grow wild everywhere in the woods. It was
thin and a little sour, but it improved after a glass or two.

"Your countrymen drink too much," she reproved me.

"It is the effect of the climate here. It drives men to extremes."

"*Pouf!* You drink yourselves *soûl comme une grive*—
full as a thrush—and you teach the savages to copy you.
Even Sir William."

"Sir William can hold his liquor," I defended my patron.
I did not forget that, in this connection, he was also my rival. I added, "His plumbing may be in need of repair."

She plied me with questions about Johnson's health and

habits, about his children and his style of living in the Valley.

She did not ask directly about Johnson's women, but she remarked, strangely, "I do not think Sir William cares anything for women."

"My observation is exactly the opposite."

"Ah, but you are like him! You take women as you take wine. You admire the vintage and the bouquet, but you require to taste many. You do not give your heart."

"Madam, I give it to you readily."

"*Chansons!*" She took to beating her fan. "And who was that lady on your button? The old woman with the dyed hair? Don't tell me she is your mother!"

"Angélique! She is the greatest actress in England."

"I suppose she taught you some tricks. Did she teach you how to please a woman?" Those wicked, velvety red lips.

I rose and took her wrists. "You shall be the judge."

She played with me, touching and avoiding. We were of the same age, more or less, which says everything and nothing. Women are generally wiser than men, or at least, more practical. A young man, as I was, is a charioteer pulled by a strong horse which is always getting away from him, to butt at fillies and chomp on sugar. Angélique knew me better than I knew myself.

She let me take her upstairs, or rather, she took me. She knew positions that would baffle many a professional. She liked it best in a sitting position, on the edge of her high-canopied bed or on a rush-bottomed chair. Her bottom was exactly the shape of a cello. From her moans and her patter, which would have enlarged a sailor's vocabulary, she gave me to understand that I pleased her. But she held me in check. When I was ready to come, she withdrew from me and made me lie full-length on the bed. She flew above me, allowing me only an inch or two of her womanhood, her taut nipples teasing my control.

"You say that you love me." Her voice in my ear.

"*Ma mie*, I do, I do."

"You say you will do anything for me."

The torturer, raking my balls with her nails, from above,
to cut off the flow.

"I will. Only—"

"I must know everything Sir William knows, about
Saint Ange."

I gasped out some made-up story, about Saint Ange and
the Ottawas.

"What does Sir William know of Pontiac?"

It may surprise you that I had never heard this name,
since in this age there is no Indian as celebrated, or as infamous, as the Ottawa war chief Pontiac. I had attended
Johnson at his private councils with the Ottawas inside the
fort. If Pontiac was among them, he was not introduced by
that name. The head chief of the Ottawas at Detroit had
the tongue-tripping name of Macatepilesis and seemed
much of our persuasion, blaming the rebellious mood of
some of his nation on the twittering of bad birds. In fact,
I believe that, at that time, Pontiac was entirely unknown
to the Indian Department. That tireless self-promoter, Major Rogers, claims in his *Concise Account of America* that
he had an encounter with Pontiac on his road to Detroit in
1760, when he claimed possession of the fort from the reluctant Commandant Belêtre. I believe that Rogers was
improving his story. I have also read his *Journals*, which
describe his journey to Detroit in rather more detail;
Pontiac does not figure among the sachems he met along
his way.

Angélique was squeezing me painfully hard.

I croaked. "Sir William is very well informed."

"What am I worth to you?"

Her firm breasts grazing my chin. Her smooth, rounded
belly angled above mine.

"Have mercy on me!"

"I must see his reports. His reports to Amherst," her accent made this sound like Amorist, "and Amherst's letters
to him."

"Can't—do—that."

She was moving again, grinding me very slowly. She let
me enter an inch deeper, than held me suspended.

"I must have this in writing," she said.

I tried to roll her over by main force. She sprang away, agile as a cat. She ran her finger along the lower edge of my jumper, and kissed the swollen head with her lips.

"It is only a little thing that I ask."

"God's triggers! I think you ask more than I can give. Why do you wish these things? For your father?"

Those deep red lips opening to me. She took me in. How much I had to learn!

She spat me out again. Her hand, clamped like a vise around my balls.

"You will do this little thing for me. It is not much. I will show you things none of your women know."

Could I deny her? Of course not. The horse had bolted. The charioteer, tied to his reins, was hanging on for dear life. I did not intend treachery. In the back of my mind was the idea of carrying forgeries to her, or of avoiding my debt altogether, as I have been obliged to avoid the bailiffs on more than one occasion. In the forefront, there was only Angélique and her red lips.

You may see why I called her Frétillon, Little Tickler.

I ran hot and cold about the business afterwards and decided that my best recourse was to make a clean breast of the affair to Sir William. Not that I wasn't keen on a return bout with Angélique, mind you. But it was plain to me that something ominous was afoot. The frenchies outnumbered us on the border, just as the Indians did, and few of us deluded ourselves that the *habitants* had any deep regard for us. The traders would tolerate us as long as we permitted them to make a buck or two. *Il faut marchander* was their motto, as it is the motto of businessmen the world over. But the war was still raging abroad, and at the first signal that King Louis had any serious design to take back North America, they would revert to their original loyalty. I did not know exactly what game Angélique Cuillerier and her father were playing, but she had made it obvious they were no strangers to the schemes of Indian revolt.

"You too!" roared Johnson, when I told him. He slapped his thigh and offered me a drink.

"And she demands paper!" he guffawed. "A lady of her kind generally insists on coin she can get her teeth into!"

I may have blushed. My face felt damnably hot. Johnson reached out and pinched my cheek.

"She was having you on, Shane. 'Trying you out' puts it better. She told me something of it. She said she would prove to me she could turn my best man against me."

"It isn't possible."

"Ah, but it is, my dear."

"But she is a spy!"

"That is not the least of her talents, nor the greatest neither. She is *my* spy."

I suppose I gaped at him, because he said, "You are creating a powerful draft, Mr Hardacre. I don't ask constancy of the French any more than the Indians. I ask them to heed their own interest and ensure that their interest flows in the same channels as mine."

"But Angélique asked for secret documents!"

"Secret! Secret indeed! How many eyes do you suppose examine my correspondence before it reaches me? She wants something to gratify her father—now *he* is no friend of ours—and the ultras about him, Méloche and Mini Chêne and your Chevalier Saint Ange, wherever in blazes he may be. Angélique, now, she has her head screwed on right. She knows where the wind is blowing. She will marry a Britisher with money and prospects. Me, for preference. Oh, yes, she has even made me something approaching a proposal. Billy Johnson and Angélique Cuillerier, a marriage made in heaven, with the world at our feet! On condition I let her kill me off in a year or two and leave her the bulk of my estate. Can you picture it, Shane? Do you think I would trade Chicha for a score of Angéliques?"

I would not have hesitated to make the trade myself, but I mumbled, "I suppose not," so as not to stop the flow.

"She might take *you*," Johnson said to me. "But I imagine she will take James Sterling. If I don't run him out of the colonies first."

I knew Sterling only slightly. He was one of the British traders at the fort, a sandy, well-furnished Scot who had an

in with Amherst and had earned Johnson's displeasure by
claiming possession of Indian lands about Niagara. I had
seen Sir William work himself into a lather as he watched
carpenters banging away at the frame of a house for Sterling along the carry between the upper and the lower land-
ings on the Niagara River. Johnson had the house torn
down, beam by beam.

Johnson chuckled. "I gather Sterling considers her a
lady, and intact. We must do our best to ensure that he is
not disillusioned before he claims occupancy."

These parlor-games were too intricate for me.

"What about the letters she demanded to see?" I asked.

"We will most certainly accommodate her."

Sir William dictated them, then and there, around his
china punchbowl.

Near the end of our stay at Detroit, Johnson returned the
hospitality of the French inhabitants by holding a ball in
their honor, at the commandant's house. We hopped about
until seven in the morning. Angélique, a magnet for all
men's eyes in her scooped silks of quail's-egg blue,
showed me no particular favor, though she had rewarded
me several times for my show of treason. She divided her
dance-card equitably between her many admirers, displaying a dutiful preference for our host, Sir William.

I left Detroit without regrets, and without any fixed desire to see Angélique again. I had not got over her, but I
fully intended to do so. She used men the way we seek to
use women, and that is hard for any self-regarding man to
take. With hindsight, I do not know whether Johnson was
right to be so relaxed about her efforts to gather intelligence. She made the pretense with him, and with Captain
Campbell and his successor, of belonging to our camp. At
the same time, her father, Dandy Cuillerier, was poking his
saurian snout into all kinds of mischief. I think Cuillerier
used his daughter as an insurance policy, to ensure that, if
his intrigues went amiss, he would not be obliged to pay
for them. We did not get to the bottom of the French mischief before leaving Detroit and Saint Ange eluded all of
Sir William's scouts. We left powder in our wake that

eventually exploded Johnson's overt success at the treaty council with the Indians. Yet I question whether any man could have done more than he did to construct a durable peace.

If I felt any sorrow as we trooped down to the landing behind Johnson's calèche, it was for Davers. We spent a night in the Huron village on the south side prior to our departure, as guests of Teata, the Christian chief of the tribe. But Sir Robert had already gone up the lakes with a party of wild men. I hoped he would find what he was looking for, which Father Pothier seemed to understand better than I did. In a curious way, I felt that, in losing Davers, I had lost a part of myself.

Dearest Shane,

I would like to know Angélique better. But once
more, you charge away at full tilt, another scalp in your
belt.

Have you ever tried to put yourself inside a woman's mind, to imagine yourself inside a woman's
skin?

I suppose I am asking the impossible. No man can
know what it is to live as a woman, no more than a
man can know the pain and fierce delight of giving
birth.

I can imagine myself a man. I have dreamed myself
inside a man's body, on more than a single night. I
have seen this face in a mirror. Dreaming, I have
shared in all his intimacies with his partners. Waking, I
have envied this strange alter ego his license, his free-
dom to come and go, to say his mind and dispose of
his chattels.

But I envy no man in the department of sex. You
must flag and fall in the end—yes, even you, my beloved! This is a matter of gravity. But woman—ah!—
woman is tireless as ocean, wave building on wave.

Men would be terrified if they knew how much more
pleasure a woman is capable of knowing. This is why
men put about the lie that good women do not enjoy
sex. Men are terrified of being tested beyond their
endurance. They fear we will devour them.

You know these things. If you wrote the plain truth
about them, grand dames and housemaids would read
you, under their mantillas or aprons, the whole length
and breadth of the country.

I long for your smell, for the rough and smooth of
your touch. I cannot get away. Will you come to En-

gland? If you cannot, you must come again soon in my dreams. My room is filled with your absence.

Your

Valerie

Sintra

11th October

Dearest Valerie,

What you say of women and their supremacy in the arts of love will not be disputed by me. I have studied women too deep to deny your truth. But I leave it to one of your sex to state these things plain, ever mindful of the fate of Tiresias, the blind seer. Do you remember the story? The Greeks say Tiresias angered Hera, the Great Goddess, by insisting that women enjoy physical love more than men. The sacred mountain shook with her fury. She punished the sage for stating what you hold to be obvious by putting out his eyes.

Would women gain or lose if the facts were made known to all? We men would certainly be put on our mettle! As things stand in our society, a "good woman" is presumed to tolerate her husband's copulations for the virtuous purpose of child-bearing, and to relieve her spouse of his grosser appetites. Women who revel in the sport are held to be pompadours or worse.

I have always taken a more generous view, and acted accordingly, stoking the subtle and long-burning fires. Yet you take me to task for celebrating my devotions. Is this fair? Is this just?

Your doting

Shane

9

The Untamed

IT WAS A LONG, weary road back from Detroit, longer by
far for Johnson than for me. His stamina had been tried
to the limit by the long hours of Indian counciling. Now
the raw, blowy weather fired up his old complaints. He
journeyed without sleep for three or four days at a stretch,
racked by fevers and a violent disorder of the bowels that
produced bleeding and delirium. The poisoned musket-ball
in his thigh seemed to be working deeper into the core of
his being. Guy Johnson and I took turns to share Sir William's night watches. By candlelight, among the thwarts of
a whaleboat or under canvas on a rocky bluff, he dictated
his endless letters. I never knew such a man for letter-
writing. From the heart of the wilderness, Johnson hurled
letters in oilskin pouches as a mountaineer throws out a
rope to secure his next foothold. He tailored his style to
his audience. Writing to the general, he was sober and
statesmanlike, delivering assurances that, after his treaty
council, the western Indians would lie quiet so long as
they were treated fairly. To the omnivore Colden, he enclosed observations on the native use of blue lobelia in

healing social diseases and of maidenhair ferns for rheu-
matism along with samples of Indian oratory. To merry
bumperers like Witham Marsh, the colonial secretary, he
retailed saucy intelligence of the "summer cabbage" on offer at Detroit, and the "belly-bumping" accomplishments
of his company of ball-drivers. I received honorable mention in several of these missives.

"Mr Hardacre has entertained several of our ladies with
a brush of the cue. He goes at it so brisk I fear he may tear
up the baize for others." Or so he wrote to Goldsbrow
Banyar, the sleeping partner in some of his land deals.

Through reasoned argument and coarse raillery, through
hints of profit and the tedious heaping-up of council minutes, Johnson fought his case and built his faction at New
York and London. Behind all the incidental details, his
mind was working on a grand solution for the Indian problem, on a boundary line that would break the flood of
white settlers and sharpers and allow the natives time and
space to make their adjustments to the new world that was
crowding in on them, as the Mohawks had done.

"They are a Stone Age people," he told me repeatedly,
during his insomniac nights. "To survive our coming, they
are obliged to make alterations in the space of a few generations that required the leisure of millennia for our ancestors. They did not have the wheel. They had the idea of it,
but they never saw the need, until we came with horses and
made roads wide enough for wagons. They did not have
metal. We gave them guns and tools, but not the secret of
working metal for themselves. They did not have writing,
apart from rude pictures daubed on bark. With the exception
of the cornplanters of the Six Nations, most of them still
lead the wild life of hunters and gatherers. They touch the
earth lightly, Shane. Their abandoned villages rot back into
the earth and the forest reclaims the site. A rude cairn of
stones on a high place is the only mark of their passage.

"They are an untamed people, even the Mohawks,
which is why our countrymen fear and despise them. To
make a peace that will outlive my treaty fires, we must
give them the means to change. We must teach them our
tricks. We must show them how to farm, with plows and

manure. We must send them to school, so they can read a
property deed or a royal proclamation. We will send them
to church, because the tenets of our religion are a shield
against their dreams and their sorceries." He faltered. "Ah,
but none of it is easy, Shane!"

He rubbed his thigh, and I offered him the brandy.

He shook his head. "That," he indicated the flask, "is
our most damnable gift to them. Their metabolism is different, you see. The woodland Indians had no fermented
drinks before we came. You have seen them in liquor.
Their bodies have no resistance to it. Yet the tamer they
become, the more they injure themselves with alcohol.
Even our friend Nickus Brant. He told me once that he
drinks to forget the dreaming."

Johnson sighed. It was about four in the morning, the
hour, Doctor Peters told me, when old people most commonly die and most infants are born, the hour when Sir
William's energy ebbed lowest and he saw the future slipping away from his grasp.

"There are times," he took the brandy after all, "when
I doubt that I can succeed. There are times when I think
it is wrong of me to try. If we make the Indians a tame
people, will we allow them to live? Will we leave them a
reason for living?"

I waited. A screech-owl hooted nearby. A smart white
frost was forming on the sedge along the shore. The waters of Lake Erie were black as ink.

"Do you know the tale of the wolf and the puppy-dog?
No? It is like this. A starving, lean-shanked wolf came
upon a sleek puppy-dog who had just enjoyed the leavings
from his master's table. The dog told him that there was
always food to be had in his master's house and a warm
place near the stove. He invited the wolf to join him. The
wolf was ready to go when he noticed the strip of leather
with metal studs about the dog's neck. He asked what it
was. The dog explained to him what a collar was for. The
wolf said he would rather go hungry than wear his slavery
round his neck and ran back into the woods.

"The Indians are not bred to servitude. It is something
we will never teach them. I do not know if we can even

draw them into a settled life. The rhythms of their world are vastly different from ours. Before we came, the cycle of each year was the same. It turned with the seasons, with the fish-runs and the rutting of the deer, with the planting and harvesting of the corn. What was expected of a man was simple—to walk in balance with nature, to bring meat for his family, to prove himself as a warrior, to live as his grandfathers lived before him. The life of the natives followed a spiral path, endlessly returning on what had passed before. They did not have a history, not as we imagine history, as a relentless forward motion along a straight road into the future. The great events they recall in the ceremonials of the Longhouse took place in a dreamtime in which spirits moved among men. Their own lives have a gusting quality, like that of dreams.

"Our people are different. We make plans. We plot a future that is different from the past, and we hurry along after it. The Indians must learn to do this too, because we have imposed our history upon them, and their lives can never be what they were before. But the change is not easy for them. It is not natural."

"There is Margaret Brant," I reminded him.

This drew the shadow of a smile. "Yes, there is Margaret, God love her. And her daughters. Did you know my Chicha is her eldest?"

I must have registered surprise. I had heard no reference to this family relationship and there seemed to be little in common between the silent, retiring medicine woman at Fort Johnson and her anglicized, outspoken mother.

"There is a jealousy between them," said Johnson. "Margaret took old Nickus away from another woman. He is not Chicha's father. The minister made rather a fuss."

He fell silent. I wanted to hear the rest of the story, but I did not press for it. The best way to elicit confidences, I have generally found, is to allow them to emerge in their own time, preferably oiled by a quantity of drink.

"Chicha tries to live in both worlds," Johnson said at last. "But it isn't easy. That is what I tried to explain to your friend Davers."

He growled his pain and shambled away into the bushes.

It is hard for me to convey the depth of Johnson's heroism. In the years I knew him, he was hardly the stuff of historical romance. Indeed, I am inclined to doubt that he was ever that, for all his amours and his exotic paraphernalia. He had seen battle and his life was often in danger. During those sleepless nights on our homeward voyage, he recounted some of his war stories. He told me how the year before, he had accompanied General Amherst's army on its descent of the St Lawrence to Montreal. Many of the army flatboats were dashed to pieces in the boiling waters of the rapids. Hundreds of our redcoats were drowned. On shore, hanging from the branches of the trees, were French Indians, waiting to snipe at the survivors. Recognizing Johnson's boat, they concentrated all their fire upon it, permitting the general's launch to slip past unscathed—which may give you some notion of the relative value of a British commander and our Irish Superintendent of Indians in the eyes of these hostile natives or their French advisers. There were other stories, of assassins lying in wait for Sir William along the King's Road to Albany, of a night attack on Fort Johnson, of a woman sent by the Joncaires to poison him with the water hemlock which ruptures the stomach and leaves the victim to drown in his own blood. But I think that Johnson was never a warrior in the conventional sense, though he was credited with our victories at Lake George in 1755 and at Niagara four years later, and though he was fond of displaying himself in a major-general's regimentals or the warpaint and feathers of a Mohawk chief. He left it to others to fight with firelocks and tomahawks while he waged his own campaigns with subtler weapons—those of diplomacy and intrigue. His heroism was in his vision and his brute perseverance, tested every day by the afflictions of his body, the jealousy and greed of his countrymen and the behavior of the Indians he was trying to defend. A lesser man would have sold out and gone home to Ireland, to live the sweet life among parklands rolling softly down to the sea through fountains and floral borders. Sir William had the endurance of the long-distance runner. And day by day, his native charges made him run the gauntlet. I saw many specimens of this along our road to the Valley, and during the year I spent learning the Indians before Johnson sent me back to Detroit to spy on Pontiac.

There was no king's ship available at Niagara to ferry us on to Oswego. But Mohawks came to fetch us in birchbark canoes, skimming the blue shadows of the lake. The traders at the Bottoms met them at the landing, waving bottles of grog. Before we got wind of what was happening, they had traded their trophies from Detroit and the king's silver medals for a few stinking kegs of New England rum. Some of them were thirsty enough to run up impressive debts. I saw the entries in Visscher's account book, figured in crude drawings of buckskins and winter beavers, enough to consume the whole produce of a winter hunt. By the time we interrupted the proceedings, the Mohawks were no longer themselves. One of them had chopped a hole in the side of a trader's truck house and was trying to make off with another keg, howling that he had been cheated. Another had bitten off the earlobe of a Seneca in no better condition than himself, and was threatening to start a tribal war under the walls of the fort. These diversions were accompanied by howls and whoops that made our Irish war cry sound like a nursery rhyme.

Nickus Brant was one of the worst offenders. It took three soldiers to restrain him. One of them took a blow from the side of Brant's hatchet that would have killed a man less thick-skulled.

We were delayed two days waiting for our escorts to recover, and Johnson was in an ugly mood.

He went to Major Walters of the Royal Americans, the commandant at Niagara.

He said, "I want you to lock up the rum."

"What, all of it?" said Walters.

"All of it."

"But there must be three thousand gallons of the stuff down at the Bottoms."

"Lock it up or stave in the barrels. Then perhaps our traders will be encouraged to bring goods the Indians can use."

"The traders won't like it."

"Then let them swill their own piss. I will not tolerate them robbing *my* Indians under my nose."

"The natives won't like it any better," said Walters, giving Sir William a doubtful look. "They'll come skulking in here, begging and whining."

Johnson relented to the extent of giving the major permission, at his own discretion, to issue visiting chiefs with a two-gallon keg. He knew, of course, that he was playing Canute. There was no way of stopping the liquor trade, not even by nailing traders caught breaking the regulations up on crosses. Every peddler along the frontier knew he could triple his money in a single season by flogging inferior liquor. And we had given the natives a taste for something they refused to forgo. Still, the need to put a stopper in the liquor trade was one thing that Johnson and General Amherst and the missionaries and the native revivalists all agreed on. Sir Jeffrey issued a blanket order in the spring, with Johnson's approval, forbidding western traders to carry rum, on penalty of losing their licenses. I don't believe it did any more good than Sir William's gesture at Niagara. As they say of Ireland, there are problems that have no solutions.

We fought heavy swells and surf, bailing water along the southern shore of Lake Ontario. At night, I swaddled myself in a beaverskin robe that Nickus Brant gave me against the chill. We ran into a young officer traveling west to our far post at Michilimackinac on the buckle of Lake Huron and Lake Michigan. I asked him to keep an eye out for Davers, and to drop me a line if there was anything to report. He brought news that elated Johnson. In our absence, Chicha had been delivered of a child—a girl.

"Thank God for that," said Johnson. He added, oddly, "Perhaps now I shall be allowed some peace."

I wondered how his white family would greet the arrival of another brown Johnson. John Johnson went off by himself along the pebbly beach, disdaining our toasts. I had not had much to do with Sir William's white daughters. They lived behind a veil, in the keeping of a stiff-backed Scottish governess, screened from the sights and sounds of their father's Mohawk world. I saw them walking together in the grape arbor in the mornings, or sitting at tea in the afternoons, or at their embroidery as the daylight failed. Anne, the elder, seemed intelligent bud stolid and homely. She stuck her nose into difficult books and declined to be drawn from them into idle conversation. I was not surprised when she married Daniel Claus, an equally humorless German who was away at that time trying to manage the affairs of the Indian Department for Johnson at Montreal. The younger sister, Polly, was comely, with more of her father's robustness; she loved to ride and cleared fences and thickets at a breakneck pace. Guy Johnson had warned me off as soon as we got to know each other, telling me they were betrothed and purposed to marry in the summer. I never saw any of Sir William's white family behave with open cruelty towards Chicha and her children, except John, who was a poor excuse for a Johnson. Instead, they put their screen up and generally behaved as if Chicha did not exist, which some would consider a greater cruelty. It was hard for them, because their own identity was never secure. The whole Valley knew the story of how the young Billy Johnson had bullied a neighboring Dutchman into selling him their mother—a runaway from New York, a German indentured servant with a price on her head—for five guineas, on pain of a flogging if he refused. John Johnson lived in mortal terror that the king would refuse him the title of baronet on the grounds that he was a bastard. Family friends put out the story that Sir William had married his serving-girl on her deathbed, which no one believed. So here they were, the white Johnson heirs, unsure of their place, threatened by a growing brood of half-Mohawk siblings living under the same roof. The wonder of it is not that there was tension or sullen avoidance, but that they escaped open warfare.

We were drenched by heavy rains all the way from Oswego to Fort Stanwix, at the end of the Great Carry. The downpour raised the level of the streams and made our boating easier. It also brought on Johnson's hacking cough. He shivered at night under the weight of several blankets and a steaming buffalo robe. At all our halts, the drumbeat of Indian complaints we had heard on our outward journey grew more strident. The most pervasive grievance, and the one that troubled Sir William most, was the lack of gunpowder. Near Oswego, we watched a native trying to buy powder from a trader. After long haggling, he succeeded in bartering four huge salmon, worth a dollar apiece, for a wretched half-pound of the most inferior sort. The commanders of the little garrisons at our forts along the trail apologized that General Amherst had issued stern instructions that they were to dole out no more free gunpowder and ammunition to the Indians and that, even if they had been at liberty to do so, their stocks were so depleted they had nothing to give.

Johnson cursed and dictated letters.

"It is cheaper to buy the favor of Indians than to pay for an army to hold them down," he wrote to the general. "And it will soon come to the latter if we persist in denying them powder. If the Indians lack powder to hunt, they will resort to stealing cattle and horses. The soldiers and farmers will answer them with force, and out of a series of minor incidents, we will make a war. Great events have little causes."

I pictured Sir Jeffrey and Captain Dalyell sitting among the ladies of New York at whist, mocking the idle fears of the "squaw-man."

Huge thunderheads rose up like mighty anvils as we neared the eastern end of Lake Oneida. The storm burst over us as we paddled up Wood Creek, dulling the fires of the sugarbushes. The trees creaked and complained. Then the sky hurled down white spears of lightning. They fell on all sides of us, striking terror into our native boatmen. Some of them drew their canoes up into the doubtful shelter of the trees, refusing to go farther. Another kindled a fire and offered shreds of Indian tobacco to appease the wrath of the Thunderers. Man rides to the heavens, so the natives say, on a cloud of tobacco. There *was* something strangely personal about the pattern of the lightning. The bolts struck close to us, turning in the circle of the four quarters. I had the eerie sensation of a gunner taking aim at us, turning his barrel as he sought our range.

Johnson would not be delayed. He was close to home; he had a girlchild to meet, and a thousand urgent things to attend to. He drove us on. It was full darkness when we reached the carry, but he declined to make camp in that swampy field. He ordered candles lit and placed in the boats to guide our feet as we shouldered them and struggled behind him through black woods where the earth sucked at the ankles. I was muddied from head to foot when we came out near Fort Stanwix.

Captain Ogilvie of the Third New York, the chaplain's brother, revived us with good canary wine and the warmth of a great fire of pine-knots and the heartening report that Sir Jeffrey Amherst was sailing home to England. Had this last report only been true, there might be less horror in the narrative that is to follow. Captain Ogilvie also gave us a tour of his storehouse. He showed us barrels of salt beef and salt pork, rotted to yellow-black slime, the gift of our crooked quartermasters. He showed us kegs of gunpowder mixed with dirt and sand despatched by the same gentry.

He said, "We trust in you to keep a bridle on the Indians, Sir William. For if they escape you, I doubt that we can do much to hold them. It is the most I can do to stop my own lads from deserting since I can neither feed nor clothe them."

On the last Thursday in October, we dined at Conrad Frank's, at the German Flats. The geese honked loud overhead, flying south in arrowhead formations, under a sky like wetted ashes. We slept that night at the Brant house near the Upper Castle. I was so exhausted by our journey I paid little attention to the lissom Christina. I may have hit on the right line of approach without studying the matter since the girl was openly attentive to me.

"Did you learn something about Indians?" she asked in English quite as good as her mother's, while Margaret was talking to Johnson about some new chicanery by that scoundrel Uri Klock.

"I heard a lot of speeches. I did have the chance to converse with some Huron ladies."

"How were they?"

"Very sociable. Not so elegant as Mohawks."

She looked down, but not before I caught a glint in her eye. There was something of the scamp in her after all. The ache in my bones, from lugging things over the portages and lying out in the damp, began to recede. An element of caution remained, however, between Sir William's warnings about Mohawk women and the knowledge that this charmer's big sister was the mistress of Fort Johnson.

"How is your friend Sir Robert Davers?"

"He's run off with some Hurons. He said he wants to learn how to dream, or some rum idea like that."

"I knew he would do that."

She gave me such a knowing look that I wondered whether Davers had had her on the side. No, not Davers. Surely not.

"What will you do now?" she demanded.

I explained that I was joining the Indian Department. I would spend the next year helping out at headquarters, so to speak, and seeing whether we were cut out for each other.

"And learning Indians," I suggested, with an awful grin.

"My brother will take you hunting," she said with such assurance it sounded like a royal command. "That is a beginning."

I can't tell you everything that happened to me in Mohawk country before the first sign of life from Davers in nearly a year had me hastening back to Detroit, and I dare say you wouldn't believe it anyway. But I will tell you about hunting with Christina's brother Joseph, because you don't know an Indian until you have seen him in the woods.

Joseph's Mohawk name was Thayendanegea, which means Woodstacker. He was a big, burly young man, a year or two younger than me, with a yellow-brown skin, like a pear, and a high, intelligent forehead. He spoke very fair English, having spent a season or two at the Indian school in Connecticut. He was quite the bush dandy, in his ruffles and lace, when he showed up for powwows at Fort Johnson or turned out for Sunday service at Queen Anne's chapel. In the woods, he was something different altogether. I considered myself as good a shot as the next man and as quick to bring down a bird or a buck. I realized I knew nothing about hunting when I went into the woods with Joseph.

He made fun of the way I walked.

"You walk like a duck! Can't you keep your feet on the trail? Can't you be quiet? The animals hear you many looks away!"

He teased me relentlessly. "You don't see! You don't smell! You won't be a hunter until you can *hear* the tracks of a bear."

I assumed he was playing me for the awkward greenhorn that I was.

"*Hear* the tracks of a bear? You won't gull me with your mumbo-jumbo."

He made a wet popping sound with his lips. "You can hear the tracks of *Okwari*," he insisted. "A big stickymouth who has put on a nice thick layer of summer fat and lingered for a while, munching on berries. Now, *he* leaves a rumble in the earth that will guide you to him. If you can hear."

Or so Joseph said. I never could tell when he was jesting.

Our expeditions always began the same way. In the late fall, after we returned to the Valley from Detroit, or in early spring, Joseph would turn up without warning. Sometimes he came alone. More often he came with some of his friends from the Upper Castle—Moses, Aaron, and Conrad The Song. If I was squinting over Sir William's papers or checking the inventory in his truck house, the Mohawks would sit and wait, not saying anything. Indians are good at waiting. They do not fret over time, but they are not exactly passive either. Joseph and his friends reminded me of a hawk suspended in air, seemingly motionless but taking everything in, capable at any moment of diving into violent, unpredictable action.

"We might go hunting," Joseph would say when I came out to greet him.

This would launch a leisurely debate among his friends over where the deer and the elk were running. Each of the Indians seemed to carry an intricate map inside his head, crisscrossed by trails that led all the way north to Montreal and west to the headwaters of the Allegheny.

In the woods, rid of his white men's clothes and his borrowed identity, Joseph short-stepped trails invisible to me at a rapid, relentless jog-trot. He seemed to be able to distinguish the stir of a single leaf, the scuttle of a deermouse many musket-shots away.

On the first of these outings, I lagged badly behind, sucking on air, nursing wicked cramps. As I grew in endurance, I found, little by little, that my senses were honed sharper until I could smell deerscat under a glaze of frost and recognize the bend of grass on an overgrown trail. When I stopped trying to work everything out in my head—when I lost track of time and my own identity—I could see the forest breathe and sense the blood rising in its hollows. But I never managed to hear the tracks of a bear.

After the first snowfall, in the time Mohawks call the Moon of Popping Trees, Joseph and his comrades led me north into the wild foothills beyond Sacandaga Lake. I traveled like one of them, with a blanket roll on my back, a copper kettle at my hip and a deerskin sack stuffed with Indian rations—parched cornmeal sweetened with maple sugar and a handful of dried pumpkin flowers to thicken the gravy of our stews and to tide us over when the game eluded us.

We camped under the stars, clearing a space in the snow, cobbling a shelter together with boughs of cedar and spruce. We set snares for rabbits and lines for perch and rainbow trout and cooked up huge, steaming breakfasts.

When we paired up to seek bigger game, Joseph always took me as his partner. He taught me how to travel without a compass, pointing out how the tops of the pines tip towards the rising sun and how the moss clings to the roots on the northern side. He made me *see* the knife-edge incision of a muskrat's tail at the edge of a stream, the double-print pattern of a leaping weasel, the way the opossum's big toe sticks out when its hind feet hit the snow. He taught me to call the deer, puffing into a wooden instrument whose tongue was a single, beating reed that mimicked the cry of a scared fawn begging for its mother.

On a morning of ice-blue shadows, when frosted tufts of grass creaked at our every footfall, we tracked dark pellets of deerscat to a stand of young firs where an old stag and his harem were breakfasting. Before I could prime my jaeger gun, the deer bounded off into the deep woods.

Joseph grunted, shuffled a few paces the other way and

set about heaping spruce boughs into a comfortable nest
for his backside.

"Satien." He patted the ground beside him. "Sit down.
The deer will come back to us."

"How do you know?"

"Why do white men ask foolish questions? When deer
get scared, they run in circles, and they never cross their
own tracks."

Joseph filled a redstone pipe and struck a flint. The
thick smoke that billowed out smelled fouler than usual.

"If the deer are coming back," I teased him, "then
surely you must forgo your smoke. That stink will scare
away anything on two legs let alone four."

He went on puffing away. After a while, he said, "This
is the real tobacco, not that trash you white men smoke. It
brings the deer like the smell of a female in heat."

I did not believe him, of course. I brushed snow off a
fallen log near his perch, settled myself on it and sneaked
a swig of brandy from my flask. The Mohawks don't drink
on the trail.

I took another swallow, and the liquor, together with the
long walk and the harsh glint of sun on snow, must have
made me drowsy. My chin lolled down into my chest.

When I snapped my head back and opened my eyes, the
stag—a twelve-pointer, if memory serves—was in plain
view, sniffing the air.

Joseph met my glance with steady eyes, offering me the
kill. I aimed for the stag's heart. His legs buckled. His
blood beaded the snow like red berries.

I expected Joseph to fire at one of the does which were
bounding away among the firs. The Mohawk laid down
his gun.

"Our grandfathers taught us to take only what we can
use," he said. "Without sleds, two men cannot carry two
deer very far."

"We can call Conrad and the others."

"We could. But do we need more meat? The does are
with young. In the starving time, they will still be here to
feed us. Unless, like white men, we forget what is enough."

This, of course, was the native side of Joseph talking. In

other situations, I observed that he had as keen an eye for a profit as any white man—or any Brant.

He watched me critically as I skinned the deer, making the first incisions at the hooves, working my way up to the belly. I did not much care for the half-digested green stuff that spewed out of the dark belly-bag. We quartered the deer and tied the meat in two packs to haul back to the camp.

At night, with slabs of venison drying on a wooden frame over the fire, I asked Joseph about his pipe. I could not believe that deer were really drawn to the smell of native tobacco.

"So many thoughts rattling round in your head, White-face! That is why it takes you so long to understand anything! Use your nose!"

He opened his pouch and took out a pinch of tobacco. I could see there was something paler mixed in with it. He flourished it under my nose.

"Remind you of something?"

I got it eventually. The smell was reminiscent of the hooves of the stag I had skinned. Johnson told me later that Joseph must have ground up roots of the aster—an old Indian hunting ruse.

"Hunters know all sorts of tricks," said the Mohawk, lounging back with his heels to the fire. "I can teach you plenty that my grandfather taught me. But nobody can teach you the best trick. Even we have forgotten it since we started living next to you."

"What is that?"

"The real trick," he said softly, "is to dream your kill."

I did not understand. "You mean, you dream where to find the game?"

He spoke in a soft, lilting voice—the chief's voice, Mohawks call it. He said, "My grandfather dreamed a kill in the starving time, before Warragiyaguey came to the Valley. He caught a cow-moose in a thicket and shot her behind the shoulder. He made his mark on her hooves with red paint so nobody else could claim that meat. In the daytime he went on the trail. He found that she-moose in the thicket, just as he dreamed. He shot her again, behind the shoulder. And he found that red paint on her hooves."

I snorted. I had no doubt that Joseph was testing my gullibility.

"Have *you* dreamed a kill?" I demanded.

"I can hear the tracks of a bear," he said, not answering.

It snowed again in the night. At dawn, when we strapped on our snowshoes, the snow was layered like a wedding cake, powder over wet mush over ice.

Joseph laughed at me floundering about in my boat-shaped footgear.

"You want to break your ankles? Raise up!"

He showed me how to lift my feet clear of the holes I planted in the snow. This made it easier to avoid falling on my face, but caused violent cramps after a mile or two.

The north wind was biting. I tied the flaps of my rabbitskin hat across my face. The cold still got through. It pricked at my eyes.

"Joseph! What are we hunting today?"

"We might get a bear."

"Bears have got too much sense to go out in this. Or did you hear the tracks?"

"Maybe I dreamed one. The old ones say you cannot kill *Okwari* unless he lets you. Unless he gives permission."

I did not bother to respond to this. It was the native side of young Brant talking again, run a bit wild after being cooped up at a white man's school. But I should mention that the Indians do surround the bear, even the smallest, cuddliest black bear, with all manner of taboos and superstitions. The bear represents medicine power; I suppose this is because they see him rooting among herbs and berries with the air of a connoisseur. The grizzly bear, of course, is also the most dangerous animal in North America and perhaps the only one that will attack a man without provocation.

I trailed along behind Joseph, grumbling a bit, dragging farther and farther behind. He stopped in a clearing, waiting for me to catch up.

Then I saw them, or rather, he lingered, waiting to see if he had taught me anything.

"Joseph!"

"Hen."

I was staring at a set of scratch-marks on the ribbed skin of a giant pine. They were low down near the snowline.

"How old?" he demanded, squatting down on his haunches.

I scraped at the snow, through my moosehide gauntlets. The scratch-marks began several inches down.

"Since he went to bed," I suggested.

"White men don't know how to look."

He let me make my own discoveries. I meant to prove myself. I searched for the tell-tale signs of a winter den among the roots of the tree, for the lumpy shape of branches dragged together beneath the snow, for the tiny hole melted by the breath of a hibernating bear. I did not find them.

"You don't know how to *see*," Joseph taunted me.

My eyes traveled up the trunk which must have been fully three fathoms wide. I saw more scratch-marks, filled with ice, and wounds in the bark where smaller limbs had been torn away. A bear had climbed the great pine, forty or fifty feet above my head. Somewhere up there, concealed among the needles, there must be a hole big enough for a den.

"He's up there," I announced.

Joseph snickered. *"She,"* he corrected me. "He-bears hug the earth. Only a she-bear dens in a tree, squashed in a hollow, shaken by every wind. To keep her cubs safe. Maybe this mama-bear got married in the Blueberry Moon. Maybe she carried the seed of life in her belly through the fat moons till she went up there to give birth and take her nap. If she's got cubs, she'll be dangerous, more dangerous than a he-bear. She'll fight to the death for her little ones."

He watched as I circled the pine, taking backward steps, looking for the hole. I found it. The she-bear had chosen well. Her retreat was a giddying distance above my head and the limbless lower trunk of the tree offered few footholds that I would trust. To go up there after her was to invite a broken neck.

"I think the lady is safe from us," I said to Joseph.

He grunted and reached under his bearskin, worn hairy side in for the warmth. He brought out his hatchet. He aimed a few brisk strokes at the trunk of a young evergreen. When his blade had bitten halfway through, he pushed with the flat of his hand and the tree came down. He motioned for me to help. Soon we had the younger tree propped against the trunk of the great white pine and I realized that Joseph had made us a ladder.

He cut a long staff from a hickory and set me to gathering scraps of dry, rotten wood which he lashed to the top with a strip of rawhide.

Next he kindled a small fire near the base of the pine and I began to see his method. He meant to smoke the bear out.

He offered me the pole. I looked up towards the hide. It seemed higher up than before. I did not like the way our ladder swayed and bumped with the wind.

Joseph showed me his teeth. "I'll go," he said. "*Okwari* takes some killing."

I did not want to disgrace myself in front of the Mohawk. I slung my rifle over my back and took the pole from him. I was about to dip the punkwood into the flame, but he restrained me.

He squatted beside his fire, sprinkling tobacco and crooning one of his hunting songs. He addressed the she-bear as *Aksotha*, which means Grandmother. Indians talk to birds and animals as if they belong to the same family. He told the sleeping bear that we did not have the strength to kill her, but hoped she would give her life willingly, because our relatives were hungry and needed her fat. If I had been the bear, I would have given him a dusty answer.

But small worries have a way of blunting larger fears. I was more scared of the climb at that moment than of what I would find at the end of it.

Joseph dipped again beneath the folds of his bearskin and produced a bone knife, half the length of my forearm. The handle was the jawbone of a bear.

"This belonged to my grandfather. Now I give it to you." He repeated, "*Okwari* takes some killing."

I thought I would rather trust to steel than bone in a scrap with a bear, but I tucked the antique weapon in my belt. I got my torch alight and secured the lower end of the shaft against my hip.

The limbs of the young evergreen groaned and sagged under my weight. My calf-muscles tensed. My throat was uncomfortably dry. I looked down, missed my footing, and hugged the trunk of the pine to save myself from falling.

"Arosen!" Joseph mocked me. "Red Squirrel!"

Mohawks seem oblivious to heights. I have seen them leap through the forest canopy like monkeys or trot along the slippery edge of vertiginous ravines as if they were running down the King's Road. I swallowed and resumed my ascent.

I could see the mouth of the den, sealed with dead branches and scraps of bark. Sparks flew wide as I swung the torch and plunged it into the debris.

For a time, I heard nothing except the hiss of wet needles and the keening of the wind in the boughs and Joseph's high nasal whine reduced to a string of nonsense syllables.

I jabbed my torch into the hollow again.

I heard snuffling and soft, chuffing sounds from deep inside the tree. I had called the bear.

"Kats kanaka!" Joseph shouted. In excitement, he forgot his English. "Come here! Come down now!"

I did not need a second invitation. The chuffing gave way to an ugly coughing noise, a bark that rose from deep inside the belly.

I let the torch fall and started scrambling back down.

At that instant, a fierce gust of wind kicked the ladder away from under me. When darkness exploded from the mouth of the hide, I was hanging from the tree by my fingers, trying to check my downward slither with my knees.

I heard the snap of Joseph's firelock. It did not stop the bear. She was coming for me. Her breathing was fast and shallow. She was lean and fast after the long sleep, wild with anger at the stranger who had invaded her home.

The pine cast me off. A splinter stabbed through my right glove and under the nail of my index finger searing me to the quick. I fell, more than wriggled, to the foot of the tree, losing skin from my nose and cheeks.

Joseph was reloading. I saw him plunging the ramrod home. He could not fire again. When I hit the ground, the bear dropped on top of me. We rolled together in a furious, whirling heap, feathered by snow. I tried to wrestle, but the weight of the animal squeezed the air from my lungs. Joseph was whooping and hollering, but that was somewhere outside my world. My world contained only teeth and claws and round, furious eyes that knew my life. Somewhere, my blood was streaming. I was giddy with the fight. My senses were confused. I was battling for my life, yet my survival instinct was ebbing away. I was prey to bizarre hallucinations. I stared into the eyes of my opponent and thought that I knew her. The eyes held more than rage. They held the desperate, protective fear of the mother for her young. They held weakness as well as strength; they reflected a forest peopled with cunning enemies whose claws were Sheffield steel. I spoke to the bear in a voice I did not know. The words were Mohawk. I was asking permission.

I saw the wicked curve of the bear's great canines, the molars behind, broad and tough as pounding-stones. *Okwari* looked at me. For an instant, she relaxed her embrace. In that single heartbeat, I reached for my knife. My hand closed on the bone weapon Joseph had given me. I found the bear's heart. You may think that my wits were turned, but I believe to this day that she gave me her life.

Joseph came to inspect the damage to both of us. I had a flesh-wound, over my right nipple, nothing to be concerned about. I still carry the claw-marks. The four ragged lines, ridged white and hard, make quite an artistic pattern if you go in for tribal tattoos. They are a novelty that pleases the ladies, and I have often amused them by embellishing the tale of how they were acquired. Women, in my experience, are excited by a whiff of gunpowder.

Joseph offered me no compliments, but I think he was pleased when he saw that it was the bone knife, not his second bullet, that took the bear.

We were in for another snow-storm. A fine powder was being driven into our faces in stinging points by the great bellows of the lakes to the north-west. Joseph set to work skinning and butchering our kill, dividing the meat we could carry into packs, hanging the rest of the carcass up out of the reach of the wolves.

I had the feeling scratching at me that something remained to be done.

I propped up our Indian ladder against the pine and started scaling it.

"You crazy?" Joseph called to me. "Come help. We better get to shelter quick."

"This won't take long."

I groped around inside the soft lining of the den compounded of dried moss and powdery bark and pliant needles of pine until I found it. The cub was a pale, mewling bundle of fur no bigger than a winter squash.

Joseph inspected it and turned down his mouth.

Born blind and deaf in the fall, when it was small enough to lie concealed in the rolled toes of its mother's front paw, the five-month cub was still helpless in the world. It might have weighed ten pounds. It made damp, sucking noises with its rubbery lips, peering about myopically for its mother. If it was lucky, it would starve to death before it met a predator.

"Give it here," said Joseph. He had his skinning knife in his hand.

"No. I think we should keep it."

"You're crazy," he said definitively. "It's going to die on you."

"No it won't. We'll give it cow's milk."

"Bears don't like cow's milk. No more than Mohawks."

"I shall give it to Christina," I announced. "I'm sure she will know what to do."

Joseph narrowed his eyes. He said, "You won't get my sister for a bear-cub."

The cub was the first of many gifts I made to Christina. The Brants farmed it out to a nursing mother at the Upper Castle. They said she had agreed to suckle it at her own teat. She belonged to the Bear Clan, you see. I had to see this prodigy for myself.

Joseph took me over to the Upper Castle which the Mohawks also call Canajoharie or the Pot That Washes Itself.

The name derives from a giant pothole in the bed of the Canajoharie Creek below the rapids in the S-bend of the limestone gorge where the waters foam and swirl. This was the original site of the Upper Castle. As the villagers exhausted their cornfields, they shifted farther and farther east along the bank of the Mohawk River so that today Canajoharie stands twelve or fifteen miles from the creek of the same name. It does not correspond to a white man's notion of a castle, though it stands high up on a rise, defended by a stout cedar palisade with perches for lookouts. Elmbark lodges of varying sizes are scattered like jackstraws inside the walls. The biggest is the council-house where they beat the water-drums and bring out the ancient wampum belts for their ceremonials. When I first set eyes on it, there were twenty or thirty scalps, stretched on hoops and painted red on the hairless side, flapping on poles in front of this Longhouse.

I found my cub's foster-mother in a smoky hut, noisy with children running wild around the fireholes or playing hide-and-seek under the high sleeping-shelves. The place was festooned with braided cornhusks hanging down from the beams like a frenchie's onion-strings. The matron of the house sat on a reed mat in front of the fire with her legs folded to one side, puffing on a pipe. She was bare to the waist and seemingly unembarrassed at our presence. Her dugs hung down like withered gourds. Attached to one was a native baby the color of red pipeclay. My bearcub sucked lustily on the other.

"These people are traditionals," said Joseph in his Anglican Apple manner.

The woman gabbled something in Mohawk.

"She says you bring her good luck," Joseph translated. "She says if the cub lives, it means you own the Bear dreaming. She says you are an Elk dreamer already."

"What the devil does that mean?"

"Traditionals say the Elk dreamer has love power. He makes women fidget. Powerful medicine." He rolled his eyes, mocking the superstitions of the Flints, though I knew from his song in the woods he was by no means a stranger to them.

"How does she know?" I demanded.

"She says she can smell it."

I knew I was in need of a bath, but I thought this pretty impudent, given the stink in the lodge. The children made water and emptied their bowels on the dirt floor without drawing a rebuke from their parent.

The woman spoke some more, and Joseph gave me a wicked grin. "She says she wants to show you her daughter. She says when you return, they will throw a tree in your path."

"Meaning?"

"Meaning whatever you make of it."

The cub lived, which vastly improved my standing among the Flints, and I had my rendezvous with the wetnurse's eldest daughter. You may tell me that I should have rested content with applying my addresses to Christina Brant, or flourishing the Wormwood sisters, or bundling with cheerful, apple-cheeked Dutch farmers' daughters in sweaty petticoats in front of their fires, or languishing for my cold-hearted tickler at Detroit. You would be right. I will not respond, however, to charges of inconstancy or disaffection. I regard love as the most healthy and natural instinct and have made it my policy to indulge it on every occasion that has presented itself. I have always loved with passion. I admit only that I have seldom loved for long and that the angle of my pecker has sometimes proved a defective compass.

By the end of my first winter in North America, I was suffering a violent cabin fever and ready for a new romp. It is hard for those of us who dwell in Northern Europe to imagine the extremities of the climate, at the same latitudes, on the far side of the Atlantic. The lakes and forests north and westward of the Mohawk Valley are the forges and bellows of Arctic storms in winter; they suck in the air and then blow it out with intemperate force. At Fort Johnson, in the same month I went bear-hunting with Joseph, I watched an icy slush form on the punchbowl in front of the fire in Sir William's parlor, while the ink froze in its well on a table by the door. Many nights, when I woke thirsty, I found that the only fluids in the house that were not frozen hard were rum and brandy. Naturally, I applied myself to the refreshments that were available. Beef hung in the storehouse in November was still fresh in March, but we had to cut it with saws. Soldiers on the King's Road were frostbitten within half an hour through leather gloves and boots, and parted with toes and fingers. We had no horseback riding from late November until April, and few visitors from afar, except for Indians, traveling on snowshoes. But there was skating and sledding on the river, and ice-fishing for trout—I took twenty big ones with a single dip of a basket, fashioned like a collier's, through a hole I cut in the ice—and snow-snake games with the Mohawk boys. And there were cards and billiards and parlor-games and story-telling with Johnson and his household. When the neighbors' and tenants' womenfolk came to the stone house to feast Saint Patrick with us, I taught them an old one—"Kiss the one you love best without showing who she is." This was a puzzler for the Valley people until I showed them how it is done. You must know the secret. I made a circle of every woman in the room and bussed every damn one of them.

There was plenty of business to attend to, even in the dead heart of winter. Sir William was preoccupied with calling the Six Nations together for a grand council after the spring thaw, to lay down the law to the Senecas. Native couriers sped back and forth on snowy trails carrying his wampum belts and counting sticks with a notch for each day before the assembly was to convene. Johnson was kept equally busy badgering General Amherst to pay the accounts of the Indian Department, which included my meagerly eighty pounds a year as a humble assistant, and in lobbying the Provincial Council to tear up Uri Klock's land deeds. He had partial success on both fronts. The general, protesting all the way, agreed to pay most of Johnson's bills. But he demanded "retrenchments." How that word dins in my ears from all his mean-spirited, grumbling letters! And he refused point-blank to honor bills from Black George Croghan, Johnson's chief deputy for the western country, on the grounds that George had been fiddling the books. Sir Jeffrey charged that Croghan had put in expense claims for

Indian presents at Detroit that were also listed in Sir William's accounts. I don't doubt that George Croghan was a fiddler. But if the general had treated him in a more generous spirit, and avoided adding to the burden of personal debts that eventually reduced Croghan to hiding from his Philadelphia tailor, Black George might have played a more honorable role in the later part of my story. As for Klock, he was summoned, at Colden's behest, to answer to charges before the council at New York in the spring. Sir William had no confidence that this would resolve the dispute. Klock had powerful, moneyed friends in the Livingston family. But it was a beginning.

I was engaged for several months in working the sluicegates to control this flood of paper in both directions. I was also called out to play fireman on several occasions when Indians ran off with a German farmer's cow or an army packhorse and the scrapping began.

I felt awfully remote from the larger world, and hung on the news that filtered through in aging newspapers and letters from Sir William's friends. The great Pitt had been given the boot, the reward England generally reserves for those that serve the Empire well. But there was no sign of an end to the war. Our fleet had sailed to the Indies. At the end of March, when the ice on the river broke up with the crash of a bombardment and swept all before it, we heard that our troops had taken Martinique. But the war went on. Soon we learned that in distant parts, we were fighting Spaniards as well as frogs. Our troops, riddled with scurvy and malaria, were being despatched against Havana. Our admirals were making their fortunes, carrying off prize ships worth half a million a throw. The king had celebrated his wedding to Charlotte. And from Boston came news that a stallion had been brought to the whipping post and flogged for the shameful offense of covering a mare on the Lord's day, in defiance of all the saints of New England.

I was ready for action. Croghan, in one of his letters, threatened action of a muscular kind. He warned that the Senecas and the Shawanese about Fort Pitt, deprived of powder and ammunition, had turned surly and were ripe for mischief. In his eccentric spelling, he commented that "if an acsedant should happen, the general must take the consequences."

The bear-lady's daughter promised action of a more agreeable sort.

I first set eyes on the girl on the day of my adoption into the Wolf Clan. There was quite a turn-out at the Upper Castle for this event, on a fine spring day with a south wind blowing warm as a fawn's breath, and the smell of rich, deep earth in the air and yellow dandelions poking up through the grass. Joseph was my sponsor, and he organized the whole business with that managerial skill that is characteristic of all Margaret Brant's children. Three elders, announced by their Mohawk names which meant Loftiest Tree, Double Life and Great White Eagle, the chiefly titles of the Wolf Clan, passed on from one *royaner* to his successor, as the Duke of Westminster bequeaths his name to his heir, made speeches in the council-house. A formidable old matron spoke words over my head, stroking a fourteen-row belt of wampum that bore the figures of a wolf and a man and a woman holding hands. The beads had a dull sheen from generations of oiling and rubbing. I was given to understand that this belt symbolized her authority, as *kanistenha*, or Mother of the Clan. The women decide who belongs to the clan and the clan names are their property. No Mohawk may bear the clan name of a living person, but it is customary to "raise up" the name of a dead Indian by conferring it on a live body. The name they had chosen for me had once belonged to a famous orator, or so Joseph said, but I suspect that they made it up. This name was Roteriwajenni, or He Flowers It Up, and I think it was probably a commentary on the way I talk to women. I rarely used it, except to impress white men who know nothing of Indians. Among the Mohawks, I was always Shane or Arosen, Red Squirrel, Joseph's jesting name for me when I fell off the ladder.

I assumed that the adoption would be an idle lark, but Sir William had urged me to take it seriously because it carried both privileges and obligations. Johnson was not present at the ceremonies because his kidneys were clawing him. Amongst all his ailments, he belonged to the infamous Fellowship of the Stone. I never knew the pain of a kidney stone until later years; I would not wish it on my worst enemy. The sensation is that of a dragon's egg starting to hatch inside your belly. It is remarkable how many of our great men in the colonies belonged to this fellowship of exquisite pain. Ben Franklin suffered from the stone even worse than Johnson.

In any event, jolly Guy Johnson, who was already a Wolf, came as my honor guard and joined in the shuffle-dances. To the percussion of water-drums and the turtle-shell rattles, we stomped harder and faster, until the clan warriors broke into the fast, circling gait of a wolf closing on its prey. They snapped and growled and showed their fangs, miming the actions of tearing out the throat of a deer and spilling its guts. I participated in this with some gusto. They had stripped me of my white man's clothes, leaving me only a breechclout. When I had worked up a healthy sweat, they dragged me down to the creek and set me to stew in a little round lodge six or seven feet tall. Round stones, glowing red from the fire, were arranged in the center.

"We'll boil the white man out of you," Joseph promised me, shoving me through the opening.

"Aren't you coming?" I called to Guy.

He graced me with a beatific smile, held up two fingers in a travesty of a blessing and intoned, as heavy as a bishop, *"Felix quem faciunt aliena pericula cautum."* For those of you who were even duller at school than I was, this means, "He is a happy man who learns caution from the dangers of others."

I dropped my breechclout, as Joseph indicated I must do, and crawled inside the sweat-lodge, naked as a worm. With the flaps down, it was the very heart of darkness inside, except for the dull glow of the stones. Joseph dribbled water on the rocks, and the hut filled with dense clouds of hissing steam. The heat very quickly became insufferable. The steam seared my lungs. I felt the blood boiling inside my veins.

The Mohawks rocked on their heels, taking it without complaint. An old man's voice rose in a thin, nasal whine, droning a song of power.

They poured more water on the stones. The heat increased. The fire was inside me. I knew I was going to die if I stayed in there. I began wriggling towards the opening on my backside.

The old man restrained me with a grip like a vise.

"You must become one with the fire," he told me.

I think I blacked out for a while. I was the victim of strange delusions. It seemed to me that natives from an earlier time were skipping around our circle. The living dead, ghastly things of bone and rotted flesh, joined their parade. Yet in the place where the old man was singing, everything was light. It fell in a brilliant cascade. It burst into white particles, into shells of life.

I will say no more about this lest you think me as unhinged as Davers. But I will make one observation. The natives of North America leave little architecture on this earth, but they build palaces and sphinxes on the inner planes, in the realm of the unseen. Any man of the slightest susceptibility—and I believe I am less susceptible in this area than many—will know what I mean.

At last they permitted me to haul my spent body out of that steaming hell-hole. They laughed and pummeled me and yelled, "*Rokwaho!* He is a Wolf." They pushed me down towards the creek. I stumbled out over the pebbles and hurled myself full-length, plunging through warm yellows down into the cool, fern-green depths. What blessed relief! I could have sworn that my ballocks had shriveled up entirely. Now the cool rush of water between my legs pleasured me with teasing caresses.

I broke surface, and saw the girl.

She stood straight as a spear on a high boulder that rose out of the water near the farther shore. She held a fish-hook in her right hand and studied my flounderings with the poised intensity of a fish-eagle hovering over a trout. Oil and water gleamed on her long, coppery body. She was as naked as I was, except for a little leather apron attached to the thong around her middle. She looked utterly wild with the creek foaming below her feet, suspended between flight and attack.

"That's a likely one, Shane!" Guy Johnson called to me. "Why don't you try flowering that one up?"

Some of the Mohawks laughed, which should have
made me cautious, because I had learned from the Brants
and from Johnson that Mohawks don't invite white men to
share their women when sober, except as a matter of courtesy to weary travelers or of fine political calculation.

"Do you know her?" I called to Joseph.

"She's the bear-woman's daughter."

"Kahwenta!" Conrad The Song howled at her.

The girl's great eyes opened wide, so wide I could see
the whites all the way round the dark irises. Her lower lip
turned into a V-shaped spout. Her whole face became a
mask of savage fury. She scared me a little, but she provoked me too; I like a woman of spirit.

"Kahwenta!" Conrad shouted again.

They told me later that this name means She Drags Down
The Boats, and if you cannot puzzle out this metaphor for
yourself, you may be too pure to read the rest of my narrative. I should perhaps say a word about the native attitude to
sex. It is commonly believed by Indian men, even the mod-
erns, the Anglican Apples, that sex weakens a man. In traditional families, a warrior is encouraged to delay marriage and
forgo intercourse as far as he is able until he has reached his
thirtieth year. Hunting and warfare and even games of lacrosse are all surrounded by sexual taboos, requiring weeks
or months of abstinence even between husbands and wives.
After a mother has given birth, her husband is expected to
forgo his connubial rights for two whole years. All these taboos and forfeits are incomprehensible to the *homme moyen
sensuel* of our culture. I expect they have their roots in the
need to prevent excessive breeding in tribes living on the
very margin of existence. But there is something less tangible
involved. Native men seem to believe that in giving a
woman hilt and hair, so to speak, they also part with some
portion of their spiritual essence which should be closely
conserved for hunting and fighting and adventures in the unseen. Joseph told me, in a confidential moment, that he found
the white man's habit of rutting in all seasons quite disgusting. I think that some of the women of his nation, the ones
asked politely, may have found it something of a liberation.
But I risk offending all parties in the matter and will confine

myself to my own experience for the remainder of this chapter. Kahwenta's nickname has told you already that, though native men profess to be strangers to sexual jealousy, they have their own ways of hanging a scarlet letter on a woman of stronger than common appetites.

"Kahwenta!"

Guy and the Mohawks were all urging me on. The only one who stood aloof was Joseph. He waded out into the creek and bobbed away upstream, making wide, deliberate strokes with his powerful arms.

I thought I had nothing to lose by attempting an introduction.

I swam up to the boulder and called up to the girl in my best Mohawk, "Have you caught any fish?"

It was hard to read her expression, but she dropped that evil eye she had been turning on the braves along the bank. She inspected me with hard curiosity, as an ichthyologist or a fly-catcher might scrutinize an unfamiliar bug. Her flanks were taut and slippery. Her breasts curved up like hunting horns.

She raised the shaft of the fish-hook above her head.

"God's breeches! I meant no harm."

The last bit I shared only with the river-trout. I doubled over and dived for the bottom just as the girl released her spear. From Guy's account, I know that it missed my pristine backside as it broke water by no more than an inch.

I felt my temper rise. I broke surface in time to see her shoot off into the stream, smooth and swift as an eel. I splashed along after her. A girl who thinks enough of a man to throw a fish-hook in his face cannot be wholly indifferent.

I know I was right in this case, because I would never have overtaken her without her complicity. Mohawk girls are trained to swim like champions before they can barely toddle. I have seen two-year-olds, tethered to a root or a clump of driftwood by a rope about the middle, kicking back and forth, back and forth, under the mother's stern eye. I am a fairly strong swimmer, but I pound the water too hard so that it resists my progress.

Half a mile down the creek, I saw the gleam of her coppery skin. She was crouched up on a limestone ledge watching me. It was a curious rock formation that supported her. It reminded me vaguely of a gravid animal or one of those Stone Age goddesses. But my intent was not focused on geology.

Dripping and panting a little, I scrambled up after her. She did not avoid me. To my pleasurable surprise, she had stripped off her only article of clothing. She squatted on her haunches like a wolf with her long arms trailing between her knees. She did not address me in words. She sniffed at me and came out with a throaty rumble, something between a growl and a whimper. Then she turned a little handstand and presented me with an agreeably rounded backside.

Now, I flatter myself that I generally know a lady's spot and stand to attention rather promptly on demand. But I do not mind confessing that I was floored by *this* lady's directness. I had encountered nothing quite like it except in the animal kingdom.

However, I did not let the side down. I advanced at slope arms and gave her a few long strokes. She shivered and groaned. Her voice rose in a long tremolo. She bucked hard as if she meant to throw me off. I managed to hold my seat. She led me a brisk gallop, throwing me deliciously over the fence a little sooner than I would have chosen.

I did my share of grunting and slavering. My horse was in charge. The charioteer, tied to the reins, hanging on for dear life, had no recourse but to follow.

She spoke to me only once. When she had finished pumping me, she reached between her legs. She withdrew her hand and smeared love-juice and semen on my chest, above the heart, and then on her own.

She stared at me and uttered a single word. It made me a little uneasy, because it reminded me powerfully of the social disease I had picked up on the Half-Moon Battery.

"Gonnerunkwa."

The next instant, she had snatched up her things and was gone, as if the earth had opened and swallowed her up.

"How was it?" Guy demanded with a nudge and a wink when I swam back up the creek. He loved a bawdy story.

He generally had too much drink inside him to do more than look and listen.

I told him. He clapped me on the shoulder and said, "Next time you make water, salute it! You've joined the clan."

Joseph looked glum.

I asked him if he intended to tell Christina about my dalliance with the wild thing by the creek.

He shrugged and said it made no difference. "Christina is not for you."

I was a trifle annoyed about this since my wooing of his sister had now gone on, in a desultory fashion, for several months. It had cost me five pounds worth of trinkets, and a painful amount of restraint, since I had never been less than a gentleman with her.

I demanded to know whether Joseph meant to stand in my way.

He cheered up a bit. "Not me," he said. "Your clanmother."

This was lost on me.

"You," he poked his finger in my ribs, "Wolf Clan. Christina, Wolf Clan. You cannot have knowledge of her as man and woman. It would be incest."

I thought this was another of his jokes but I learned better. Mohawks—Apples, Flints and Wild Men—take their clan totems very seriously and, though I am Irish by birth, they now considered me a full member of the Clan of *Ohwako*, the Wolf. I felt a little cheated, since I suspected that Margaret Brant and her children had an ulterior motive in inducting me into their own clan. Nothing personal, mind you. As I have related, they handled marriage questions with the political finesse of a Spanish ambassador. The eldest daughter was married to Johnson, the most powerful white man in the Valley. Margaret's plan was to marry the younger daughter to the warrior who would one day be Tekarihoken—Two Minds—the hereditary chief of the Turtle Clan who ranks first among all the *rotiyaner*. Shoving me into the Wolf Clan removed an impolitic diversion.

While I was fretting over all of this, I asked Joseph, with some bitterness, whether they had sent me chasing after Kahwenta to render me *hors de combat* in a more technical sense.

He gave me one of his blank looks.

"She's sick, isn't she?"

He took my meaning and said, "Maybe, maybe not. She sinks many boats."

I tried to repeat the lone word she had spoken. *Gonnerunkwa.*

"Ummnh," Joseph grunted when he understood. "Could be bad, could be good."

"What does it mean?"

"She says she wants your soul."

Mr Addison says, in one of his essays in *The Spectator*, that there are matters about which a civilized man should remain an agnostic, and that one of these is witchcraft. I did not go hunting sorcerers and miracles, like poor Davers. Yet I had a brush with native witchcraft, and it was because of that woman that bayed like a wolf. Sir William took it seriously. So did his Mohawk consort.

They found out about it when I began to sicken in the hot, sultry days when the tree-frogs shrill and the first fireflies come out, before Johnson left for his council with the Delawares at Easton, Pennsylvania.

I was kept working pretty hard, with the conference of the Six Nations—when four hundred thirsty Indians trampled Johnson's flower-beds to mud—and the household disorders that began with the dismissal of Tom Flood, the head overseer, for getting mad drunk and scaring Mrs Butler by prancing naked through her kitchen.

I did not give Kahwenta much thought, no more than I gave the clutching Huron girl at Detroit. Yet I found myself straying back to her, to couple on a filthy cornhusk mat in her mother's lodge, heedless as a mongrel of the curious eyes about us, or to lie with her on soft evenings in a grove of elms behind Tribes Hill. She turned up, uninvited, at Fort Johnson. She made little demands at first— for an awl, or a piece of calico, or a slab of beef. She never said thank you, but she gave me little things in return—strawberry jelly, blueberries and later a tiny amulet, a sandstone carving of a bear, which she hung round my neck. I became strangely attached to this charm. As the season progressed, her demands became more onerous.

Finally, she announced to me. "I had a dream. You gave me a gold ring with a sunburst on it. What do you think it means?"

I told her I had not the faintest notion, but was sufficiently alarmed to inform her that I wished to have no further converse with her. Mohawks call the British the Sunrise People, and we all know what a gold band portends. It was plain to me the wild tramp wanted to possess me, and I was having none of it.

I received a letter from Peg about the same time that was curiously prescient. I had told her something of Angélique, and she cautioned me to be wary of women who make it their vocation "to avenge their sex on yours." She expressed curiosity about "Sir William's dusky princesses," and added the following line: "I hope you have not set the Indian ladies to sticking pins into a doll with an oversized member."

The illness came upon me soon afterwards. I do not doubt that my symptoms all have medical names, but the combination was new to me. Headaches rolled up from the root of my neck in hostile waves. I could no longer concentrate on Sir William's correspondence. My bones ached, my legs turned rubbery and would not support my weight. I broke out in angry sores that vanished as fast as they came. My urine turned dark. My sleep was interrupted by feverish nightmares. I woke many times with obscure memories of a repetitive dream in which I was summoned into a native hut and listened for a seeming eternity to an old woman reciting spells as she deployed beads and fetishes. In one of these dreams, it seemed to me I was inside the body of a younger woman. She was caressing herself, crooning aloud how beautiful she was, how a man who knew her could look at no other woman. I crawled about in the daylight hours, feeling like an oyster that has just been shucked. For the first time in my experience, I seemed unable to pleasure a woman—or myself.

Lizzie Wormwood said sorrowfully, over my wilted manhood, "You are not yourself, Shane."

Chicha took matters in hand. In the process, she taught me more of what she meant in Johnson's world.

I had doused myself in the river at dawn, trying to get my head together. Chicha came down through the meadow and saw the amulet round my neck.

"Who gave you this?" she demanded, not touching it.

I told her.

"Wataenneras," Chicha hissed. It is an ugly thought, in any language. In Mohawk, it is about the worst thing you can say of someone. It means, "She is a witch."

She spoke to Johnson, who spoke to me.

"I am surprised to find you so vulnerable. Our race are not generally susceptible to native sorcery. If it were otherwise—" He shut off the thought, and poured both of us some madeira. He traveled on, at a different tilt. "Witchcraft thrives on the decay of the spirit world. We have taught the natives to desire the things we want. Some of them pursue them in older ways. I know something of this. But for Chicha—" He cut himself off again, and swallowed deep.

"You are in good hands, my dear," he recovered himself. "Chicha will handle this affair. You must learn from the experience, and turn it to good."

I will not tell you the things Chicha did, or the phenomena I believe I witnessed. They are so far outside the ordinary experience of a man in our society that I fear you would disbelieve the remainder of my narrative. I will report only that the amulet was stripped from me and cleansed in a pure waterfall, and that songs were chanted to cast an evil spirit into the form of a snake, and to return intended harm, magnified sevenfold, upon the sender. Kahwenta sickened, and I became well. I can hardly believe that these things happened myself, now I have left the world of the Mohawks behind me. They have no rational explanation, and our age is one that reveres reason, even above gods.

For all my discretion, you may understand why I resolved, after this experience, to avoid native women so far as my grosser instincts allowed. I might have been able to hold to this salutary resolution if I had not rejoined Davers and encountered the rebel called Pontiac.

Dearest Shane,

I wish to know more of the native love medicine. Did
your feral wolf-woman feed you a potion? Did she
make a small friend, with a handsome pecker, and
chant over him in the dark of the moon?

It would take powerful witchcraft indeed to make you
constant. I wish you would give me its secret.

Your enchanted

Valerie

Villa dos Mouros
Sintra

30th October

Enchantress,

I was once witched by a native woman. She employed
a sorcerer who was much feared by all the tribes resid-
ing about the Great Lakes. My friends had remarked
on my loss of appetite in all departments. I was dragging about as if I had been drained of blood. I was in
no mood for frolic of any kind. I preferred to lie in a
darkened room, in all weathers, in a twilight state between sleep and waking.

The cause of my curious malady was revealed to me
in a dream. I say it was a dream, though I was half-
conscious, from beginning to end, of my slack body

on the bed, the clamor of tree-frogs beyond by window.

When I entered this dreamlike state, I thought I was home in Ireland, rooting about in the gorse of the hill above the Boyne where our progenitors raised a passage grave that is older than the Pyramid of Cheops. I came upon a guardian stone, incised with spirals revolving inward and outward. Eyes of the Goddess, Sir William called them, when he was seized by one of his Celtic moods.

I stared into them. Somehow, I fell through them. And was windborne. I was drawn at great speed to a native cabin, on a swale near a spruce-bog. I did not know the place, but I believe I would recognize it if I saw it with normal sight.

I found myself in a room with an earthen floor, where the shadows leaped about a fire that glowed dusky red. An old fellow in a fright-mask, adorned with bones and claws, watched me closely, tilting his head. He was missing part of an arm and a leg. The place stank of blood and meat left hanging for too long.

The dream became stranger.

I looked into a trade mirror, no bigger than the palm of your hand, framed with silver-gilt. A woman's sharp eyes stared back at me, out of a narrow, burnished face.

"I am so beautiful," she crooned. She ran her hands over her naked body, lingering at the mount of Venus and the firm swell of her buttocks. I felt these sensations as if her fingers were stroking my own skin.

"With all other women, you are fallen. You are a cold wet leaf, stripped from the tree. With all others, you are dead. You live only for me."

The woman's chant went on and on. It was hypnotic. It drew me deeper into sleep. But I struggled to preserve my faculties, because of that twisted, masked figure who was craning to inspect me more closely, and because of more extraordinary sensations.

While the woman sang, I could feel her swallow, to moisten her tongue. I could feel the thinness of her blood, the itch of an insect bite, swelling on her outer thigh, a deeper ache in her secret places.

Her body had no secrets from me. I was inside it.

When I realized what had happened to me, I panicked. I had been told that native witches lure the souls of the living out of their bodies, to inflict disease or death, or bind another to their will. I had dismissed these stories as barbarous superstition. I was now convinced that some vile sorcery of this kind had been committed on me.

I fought to get out of that woman's body, out of the dream.

I saw the sorcerer throw some foul-smelling mess into the fire. It hissed and spat a putrid cloud of smoke.

He was whistling and humming, beckoning to me.

I am not ashamed to admit that, in my rank fear, I invoked the name of a saving power.

This helped me to get loose from the dream. But returning to my own place, to the daylight world of familiar forms, was not easy. I felt I was pushing through membranes that stretched and resisted before they let me go. You will know the feel of it if you can imagine having to push through house-size sheets of those clever sheepgut sleeves we call French letters, if you do not think this allusion too disgusting.

I got out of the dream exhausted, but grateful to be back.

I plucked up my courage and reported the dream to Sir William. I am grateful that he took it quite seriously. Johnson discussed it with his Mohawk confidants, who recognized the sorcerer with the missing bits. Then he sent out a party that came back with a medicine bag, made from the skin of a lynx or a wildcat, that was burned over a fire. I recovered quickly after this.

I have no theory to explain this experience. I know only what I saw and felt. If you would know more, dream on it.

But I counsel you not to apply the method I have described to any of your gentleman admirers, not even one so little able to ward off your charms as myself. As the Indians say, there are things without forgiveness. This is one of the few subjects that cause me to lose my sense of humor, at least for the time it takes my servant to fetch a fresh bottle of the excellent porto seco we consume here in the milder seasons.

Your servant

Shane

10

The Mohawk Scare

I WAS IN JOHNSON's bedroom. Through the window, I could
see the fireflies flashing among the branches of the locust trees. Sir William told me there is a predator, an assassination bug, that can mimic the glow of a female
firefly, luring the males to a greedy death. I was taking
dictation. I have a writer's bump on the second finger of
my right hand, just below the nail, that I never earned in
school; I must thank Johnson for that. He was writing to
the governor of Pennsylvania, to complain about the Quakers who had openly insulted him at his Indian council at
Easton. "I will do no business in a mob," he declared, and
fell back against his heaped pillows to reflect on his next
thought.

Chicha sat on a rocker, with Elizabeth, the second of her
children by Sir William, now nine or ten months old, on
her lap. Lizzie Johnson sucked on a native toy, the skin of
a muskrat stuffed with maple sugar, with a hole in the
stitching near the top, so a baby could get a taste of the
sweetness inside. Chicha had been far more open with me
since the incident involving Kahwenta. She crooned baby-

songs to the child, and entertained it with another Indian toy—the leg of a fresh-killed deer, with the muscle left intact so that when Chicha tugged on it, the hoof snapped back and forth in a lifelike way.

Chicha stiffened. She said quietly, "There is trouble. Violence of men and of horses."

Johnson and I listened. Five minutes later, or maybe ten, we heard the pounding of hooves along the King's Road. Then came hoarse cries.

"Murder! Mutiny! The Mohawks have risen!"

"What's this?" Johnson raised himself from the bed. Chicha flung his wrapping-gown over his broad shoulders, and he led us downstairs barefoot, his chestnut hair winged with gray falling in sheaves about his shoulders.

A militiaman reined in his steaming nag at the door.

"There's the devil to pay, your honor!"

"For God's sake, man. What has happened?"

"The Germans is all murthered at the Flats, their houses burned. The Oneidas is up in arms and the Mohawks is with them."

"Mohawks? You haven't the truth of it. It is not possible."

"Hand to God, your honor. The bastes come down and burned them all out."

"Did you see it yourself?"

"Cap'n Herkimer, he said to go for the sojers."

Johnson stared up the King's Road. It was a glorious summer night. The breeze had carried away the day's heat. The river lapped softly in the clear white light of a crescent moon, riding on its back. The Valley was still, apart from the shrill of the frogs and the distant sound of roistering at Fonda's tavern beyond the swell of Tribes Hill.

Sir William spoke to Doyle who ran inside the house and returned with the conch-shell I had seen hanging in the stairhall. Johnson raised it to his lips and blew lightly into its mouth. The wail of that conch must have carried halfway to Albany. It put me in mind of Sunday school readings, in which some ancient general of Judea dinned the armies of the Lord into battle.

The scream of the conch bought streams of people

flooding in towards Johnson—fusiliers of the garrison, who formed up in an orderly line, servants and family members, tenants and slaves.

Johnson spoke crisply and quietly. He knew how to make his voice carry. He told off men to saddle the horses and break out arms and ammunition. He designated messengers to ride post-haste to Fort Hunter, and to carry his orders to the militia captains up and down the Valley, to rendezvous with him at Han Nicholas Herkimer's house upriver. He posted his Irish servants with blunderbusses and fowling-pieces to protect his house. As he made a rapid walking tour of our defenses, he dictated notes to Captain Winepress of the Albany garrison and to General Amherst at New York. Guy took these down as best he could manage under the moon.

Sir William turned back at the western gate.

"It can't be the Mohawks," he declared. "It can't be."

He glared at us, at his son John's pale, nervous face, at Guy, flabby and puffing as if he had run five miles, at Doyle, who offered him his military coat and his long blade of Damascus steel with the clamshell hilt. His eyes rested on me.

"Shane. Will you go to Brant? We must get to the root of this quickly. If the Germans start killing Mohawks, we stand to lose everything. Join me at Frey's house, if you can manage it. If not, come to me at Herkimer's. Take Romancer."

I needed no further incitement. Brutus, the negro ostler, helped me get Sir William's prize stallion out of the stables. He was sired by the Arabian beauty George II presented to Johnson after his victory at Lake George. He stood nearly fifteen hands high. His neck rose up from his withers and turned over in a graceful bow. I could just see the tips of his ears over its upper arch as we trotted out across the drawbridge.

I stood up in the stirrups, and we flew like the wind up the rutted, hard-baked road. My heart banged against my ribs. Every clump of trees might conceal an ambush. The road narrowed to a perilous ledge between the river and the wild bluff we called St Anthony's Nose where the rattlesnakes are as thick as flies on a summer's day.

If it wasn't the Mohawks, I thought, it would be the Oneidas. We had had no end of trouble earlier in July with the scrapping between the Oneidas and the soldiers at Fort Schuyler, the blockhouse near their castle. The Oneidas complained that the redcoats abused their women and drove them away from their fisheries. The soldiers had broken up a fishing weir the Indians had made at the eastern end of Oneida Lake, and poled for perch and trout in the creek that flowed right in front of the Indian village. The friction came to a head when the natives beat up a crooked sutler named Bourke who stole the soldiers' grog rations and salt beef to flog them to Indians at five times the cost. Some Oneida wild men made off with a keg of Bourke's rum, but their own women chased them into the woods and staved it in. We were used to such incidents, of course, but the whole frontier was as dry as tinder; it required only one spark to set it ablaze.

I made out the rise of the Upper Castle on the far side of the river. Above me, to my right, on a shelf of limestone tilting sharply down to the road, was Uri Klock's square-built stone house. I saw men with guns about a bonfire.

Several of them started down the slope towards me.

"Wat wilt ghy hebben?" one of them demanded, in the bastard Dutch of the New York frontier. "What do you want?"

"I ride on Sir William's business."

I recognized old man Klock's bullet-round head. His cheeks were sucked in about the ruins of his teeth and peppered with stubble. In the excitement, he had neglected to insert his dentures, of which he was inordinately proud. They were made of hippopotamus bone; I am told George Washington had a similar set, although Englishmen like to paint him as a country bumpkin who made do with wood.

I reined in Romancer and demanded of Klock, "What do you know of the rising?"

He chewed on his gums and grumbled, *"Ten duecht niet.* It is no good."

I did not know what to make of this.

I saw a woman come out of his house. She stood with her hands on her hips talking to the men around the bonfire. She was huge and shapeless and dark, darker than the Indians. I took her for Eve Pickard, the free mulatto who was Klock's partner in pouring bad liquor into the natives.

"The *wilden* scared my women," Klock complained.

"They were here? Was there any killing?"

"Maybe at the Flats."

Maybe? I was displeased with the man's answers, and his sullenness, and told him I expected straight dealing from him because Sir William had called out the militia and sent for help to Albany and the general.

The dog laughed in my face.

"I don't know what your game is," I told him, "but I can assure you I will return to make further inquiry when I am at leisure. I am ordered to go post-haste to the Upper Castle. Will you lend me one of your boats?"

I have been informed that the rogue pretends to a family motto, in French, if you can credit this. The motto is, *Prends-moi comme je suis:* "Take me as I am." Uri Klock lived up to it. He presumed to deny me the use of a boat. I was obliged to go down to the river and pop my gun into the air until I saw Mohawks on the other side sliding an elmbark canoe into the water.

Klock's behavior was hardly that of a man living in fear that his scalp is about to be lifted, and it prepared me for the discovery I made on the other side of the river.

Joseph came with the Mohawks in the boat.

The first words he said to me were, "I am sorry."

"Upon my soul, Joseph! Will you be good enough to inform me what is abroad? The whole Valley is up in arms! We are told the Germans at the Flats are burned out and your people are run amok!"

"Your friend is ashamed." He would not meet my eyes.

He would not respond to any further questions. I was made to understand that I would see for myself.

Near the Brant house on the Nowadaga Creek, I saw Daniel, Sir Robert's Sancho Panza. He was stripped naked. They had him tied and trussed like a game hen ready for the oven. This had not altogether dampened his spirits. He greeted me with a bawdy song he never learned in a Mohawk village, nor from the frenchies at Detroit neither.

"As I walked out one ev-en-ing up-on my night's
   ca-reer
I spied a pret-ty fire-ship, and to her I did steer,
I hoist-ed up my sig-a-nal which she did quick-ly
   view—
And when I had my bunt-ing up she im-med-iate-ly
   hove to—"

Joseph rocked back and forth gently, chafing one leg against the other.

"We did not know he was back," he said. "He was supposed to go to you at Fort Johnson with despatches. It is a long way from Detroit. Daniel got thirsty."

It dawned on me that I was looking at the Mohawk revolt.

"Daniel. Would you be good enough to tell me what happened?"

Daniel, alas, was not himself.

He threw back his head and bawled:

"So up the stairs and into bed I took that mai-den
   fair
I fir-ed off my can-non into her thatch of hair—"

He stank worse than a Boston distillery.

In the end, Joseph told me what I needed to know. Daniel had returned from Detroit before noon. He repaired at once to Klock's grog-shop. Whether Klock's barkers were lying in wait for him on the road, or whether he deliberately sought out the scene of old humiliations, I do not know, and I doubt that it matters. When Klock's people had fleeced him of whatever booty he was carrying and got him several sheets in the wind, they kicked him out. He still had a powerful thirst and returned in the late afternoon when Klock was taking his nap. He had managed to divest himself of his clothing and gave the women attending the taps an almighty scare, leaping about with his pecker hanging·out. One of the sluts ran out into the road screaming about naked savages on the rampage. How this was translated into a militia report that the Mohawks had razed a whole German settlement, I cannot tell you, except to repeat that the frontier was tinder, waiting for a light.

To paraphrase Sir William, great events do not require great causes. That one drunken Mohawk caused Johnson far more than embarrassment. The Mohawk Scare, as we came to call it, fatally weakened Sir William's position in relation to Sir Jeffrey Amherst and the political masters of the colony, at the precise moment when he needed all his influence to head off the revolt he had *smelled* all along.

I reached Sir William at Frey's stout little freestone box at two in the morning, and saved him from marching all the way to Herkimer's at the head of his ragtag column of militiamen and tenants.

Johnson used some pretty strong language.

He also said, "Amherst is going to use me as a dartboard." He was not mistaken.

He sent out fresh despatches. Military riders thundered back and forth along the roads to Albany. Letters overlapped. From Captain Winepress—what a blessed name for a regular—came an indignant report that Major Switts of the First Battalion of the Albany militia had declined to muster his men to come to the aid of Sir William and the Valley settlers. Mind you, this was before news had reached Albany that the Scare was nothing more than what the word suggests; the mynheers never had much love for Johnson, who had usurped their old monopoly of the Indian trade. A few days later, we received the inevitable, crowing missive from the general. He remarked that he was by no means surprised that the emergency in the Valley had fizzled into a false alarm. "I judged that it would turn out to be no other than it has proved to be." In short, the natives were all clowns, like Daniel, constitutionally incapable of "anything serious."

Against his instinct and his better judgement, Sir William had cried wolf. The general had an excellent pretext not to listen to him when the wolf was at the door.

* * *

When Daniel sobered up enough to remember where he had left them, he produced letters for Johnson, from Captain Campbell and Major Gladwin, who was taking over the command at Detroit. Campbell reported that "a certain mademoiselle" was anxious to know whether there would be any councils at Detroit the next summer requiring the personal attention of Sir William or his "winning apprentice." You may be sure Johnson missed no occasion to bait me over the sobriquet Angélique had awarded me.

The most interesting letter, however, was more personal, and it was addressed to me. It contained the first news from Robert Davers that I had received in almost a year, and I pored over it for hours before I shared its contents with Sir William.

"I have sat at the feet of the Prophet," Davers wrote. "I know that his heart is pure. He has walked with the Master of Life and I ask for nothing better than to follow in his tracks.

"His message is damnably abused by those who traffic in politics and sedition. An Indian of good character visited me this night and told me of a secret council convened at the Ottawa village this summer, and attended by the chiefs and warriors of the Hurons, the Chippewas, the Fire People and various tribes that reside on the shores of Lake Superior, above Michilimackinac and Fort La Baye. This council was kept on a great secret from the English, as from all Indians save those of the greatest renown among their nations. Two Frenchmen came down in native dress; I believe that one of them was our friend Saint Ange. There was much talk of the Prophet, but his words were construed to mean evil against all our countrymen. The speakers called on the Indians to cover the earth with our blood as high as a horse's neck. They have sent deputies among the Twightees and the Illinois and the tribes settled along the Wabash, to inform them of the desperate resolves of this conclave. Their envoys will journey through the Ohio country, but I understand they are prohibited from converse with the Six Nations.

"I implore you to prevail on Sir William Johnson to

send me a man of confidence, to help me to interpret the true words of the Prophet. For I fear that if matters are allowed to run on, the force of hatred that is building against us, with the encouragement of the French, will demolish all restraints, and let loose the dogs of war, until there can be no peace between our races but the quietude of the grave. In the spring, when the frogs begin to croak, there will be a general war unless we move now, with love and bold resolution, to heed the true words of the Prophet.

"Whatever you think of me, Shane, you must trust me in this. I have found what I came to find. I am not what I was before. I have been in the valley of bones. I have died to the old life and risen to something that beggars description. I never belonged to this world, until I knew others. Share as much of this with Sir William as you dare. I think he understands far more deeply than he will confide to a man of our race."

The mix of hard intelligence and fey vaporings puzzled me, as it may puzzle you.

When I showed the letter to Johnson, however, he pounced on it like a robin on a worm.

"He has met the Prophet," said Sir William. "Can you conceive what it means? The opportunity—to turn these damnable prophecies to good!"

His eyes were stormy.

"Did I hear you volunteer?"

"It was on the tip of my tongue," said I, truthfully enough.

"I trust you will not spend your *whole* time in Mistress Cuillerier's bed," said Johnson. "The general is examining every penny of the Department's accounts."

"I would not wish to let the side down."

"If I were your age again—"

Sir William's smile made him look like a schoolboy. He flapped his hand in my face, and said, "You will go in the husking time and you will earn your keep until then."

I will mention only the last of the Indian councils at Fort Johnson that I attended before my return to Detroit, because it shows something more of Sir William's artfulness, and is an ironic foil to the events that ensued.

We played host to the Onondagas, the Firekeepers for the Confederacy of Six Nations, and took inventory of the stock complaints about cheating traders and licentious soldiery.

What interested me was that the Onondaga speaker, a fellow round as a hogshead, blue-black from belly-button to hairline with gunpowder tattoos, laid claim to a prophet among his own nation.

He got up, fondling a fistful of beads, and declared, "One of our people lately, in a vision, was told by the Great Spirit above that when he made the world, he gave this Turtle Island to the Real People for their exclusive use. The Great Spirit told him that the Sunrise People belong in their own islands that he made for them."

Sir William chewed this over and made his formal response the following day.

"Your romantic notions of dreaming and seeing visions, however common among you, can only appear in a very ridiculous light to white people who will consider this language as merely a ruse by certain devising persons to serve their own interests. If divine will is at issue, the triumph of British arms is abundant proof that the Great Spirit is entirely satisfied with the justice of the cause of my father, the best of kings."

The Onondagas swallowed this, which is to say, they did not contest it openly.

That evening, Johnson told me something of his experience of native dreams and visions.

"When I first came to the Valley," he said, "I was imposed on beyond belief. The natives came to me with their dreams and expected me to fulfill them. In their benighted superstition, they maintain that when a man dreams, his soul flies away from his body to visit other places, and returns to confide knowledge of its secret desires. They claim that unless these secret wishes of the soul disclosed in dreams are gratified, then the body will sicken, or even die.

"I was fascinated by all of this, at the beginning, and so

I allowed them to gull me. At last I acquired enough wisdom to know that dreams are not divinities, and may be manufactured to serve grosser intents. A Mohawk called Hendrick—" He smiled at the recollection, and I looked up at the London print of a feathered savage with a tomahawk scar from the corner of his mouth to his cheekbone that hung on the wall of the parlor. "This Hendrick," he repeated, "was my first Mohawk friend and my first enemy. He came to me once and told me that he had dreamed I would give him a coat of scarlet broadcloth, trimmed with gold galloon. I gave him the coat. When I met him again, I told him that, thanks to him, I had learned to dream like a Mohawk. I informed him that I had dreamed a dream in which he gave me the title to a sweet piece of Indian land fronting the river. He put his mark to the deed. Then he said, 'My brother, we will dream together no more.' "

Johnson chuckled, and rubbed his thigh.

But a cloud passed over his face.

"This is not the end of the story, Shane. Not all dreams are alike. There are some that carry a kind of fatality. You must watch Davers closely. He is one of those that allow themselves to be sucked into a spirit world that holds beauties and terrors that few men of our race comprehend. I rely on you to report *everything*. If Sir Robert truly knows this Prophet and has entered his dreaming, then he can be a weapon for us, or the bitterest enemy, to himself and his own kind. You know more of this already than you or I would have wished."

He did not pronounce the name of the bear-woman's daughter, but I caught his drift.

"You must be my eyes and ears," he went on. "There are so few I can trust. Dear God! A madman and an apostate Irishman, to save us from an Indian war!"

15th November

Dearest Shane,

Your patron Sir William is as teasingly oblique as you
on the theme of native dream practices. I wish you
would tell us more.

Your Indians are right. Dreams are the language of
the soul. They come from a source that is deeper and
wiser than our little everyday mind, a source that knows
who we truly are and what we need to be whole.

You met forest people who know these things and
live them. Not only men, but those proud warrior
women of the Iroquois. I would love to learn from
them. Our society would be better regulated if our
women had the power to raise up our princes and
generals, as the natives do, and pull them down when
they fail to please.

I wish you would let these woodland dreamers
speak to us without interruption. They have so much
to teach us.

In dreams,

Valerie

Lady of Dreams,

The woodland Indians say that big dreams happen
because our soul takes leave of our body in sleep and
wanders in the spirit worlds, where gods and demons
converse with it.

They say we dream things before they happen.

When a Mohawk of the Upper Castle gashed himself
with an axe, his father demanded to know if he had
dreamed this. When the boy cried "No!" as he tried
to staunch the flow of blood, the father became
wrathful. "You dreamed but you forgot!" the old man
bellowed. "See what disaster you bring on yourself
when you neglect your dreams!"

I saw stranger things. A war chief dreamed he was
captured by enemies and murdered slowly by being tor-
tured with fire. The grayhairs of the village gathered to
hear this dream and advise on what must be done.
They determined to assist the dreamer by binding him
to a stake in the clearing. They half roasted the poor fellow and seared his flesh with hot knives and hatchets before they cut him down. They sought to avoid the
fulfillment of an evil dream by mimicking it.

This play-acting would surely be comical had it not
been so painful for the victim. The chief died soon after
in any event, not by fire but by breaking his neck when
he climbed on the roof of Klock's grog-shop, drunk.

I could regale my readers with no end of similar
tales, but I doubt there is an audience. Is this not the
age of reason? Do I not recall a certain evening
when you professed yourself a devotee of science?

Your

Shane

Dearest Shane,

The method of science is surely to report the facts,
regardless of whether they run counter to our theology
or opinions. Events in the inner world are facts, not less
than events in the outer, although they may be more
refractory to proof in a conventional sense.

A science that pronounces phenomena impossible because they do not conform to its view of what is possible is only medieval superstition in new dress.

The native beliefs you report are evidently founded
on experience, and must be tested by experience.

You only pretend ignorance. If you did not know better, you could not have come to me again last night,
to torture me with your kisses, while your corporeal
body lay on a bed in Portugal.

Your wakeful

Valerie

11

The Change in Davers

PEG WALSINGHAM ONCE TOLD me there are two sorts of actors—those who give themselves heart and soul to their part and *live* the characters they play, and those who hold themselves at a strict remove, impersonating emotion on stage, without surrendering to it. Peg maintained that all true actors belong to the second category. I think I was a little shocked when she informed me that she was capable of figuring her household accounts in her head while playing Cordelia in transports of grief and tragedy.

By Peg's reckoning, Sir Robert Davers was not much of an actor on the stage of life, because he belonged wholly to the category of those who can only commit themselves to a role if they allow it to possess them beyond all reason. He told me he had found what he was seeking in the Indian country, that he was not what he had been before. This was no exaggeration. Near Detroit, I encountered a man I no longer knew. He had gone questing for the meaning of life and death among savages, and he truly believed he had found it. He had given himself, heart and mind, to the role of the White Indian, but that is a poor euphemism for what he had become.

I counsel you to be wary of dreamy spectators of life, such as Robert Davers. Once they commit themselves to a course of action, they give themselves over to it without guard-rails or inhibitions. But I will allow Sir Robert to tell his tale for himself.

The new commandant at Detroit was Major Henry Gladwin, of the 80th Foot, Gage's Light Infantry. He was a sandy, stubborn, bull-necked soldier of the old school, the one that says you have no business thinking in His Majesty's Army. Give a man like Bulldog Gladwin a position to hold, and he will sit on it like a limpet on a rock, or a hound at his master's front door, but Lord help you if you need him to puzzle out something unexpected.

Gladwin was a Derbyshire man, so when Sergeant Toole, whom you shall meet presently, had a bone to pick, he sauntered near the commandant's house humming the air of an old ballad whose lyrics, if memory serves, went somewhat as follows:

> They brought the baste to Derbytown,
> And drove him with a stock,
> And all the girls in Derby
> Paid to see his c--k.

This generally threw Gladwin into one of his black dog fits. He was phlegmatic by nature, but he had lost his good humor to recurring bouts of malarial fevers, and the bloody flux, and mendicant Indians. I heard him swear he would show Toole the scavenger's daughter—a singularly nasty form of corporal punishment the torturers of the Spanish Inquisition would have enjoyed—but he never did it, because Toole had a Chippewa girlfriend, and was the closest thing to an intelligence officer that the garrison possessed.

Gladwin's idea of intelligence-gathering was to round up Jemmie Sterling and James Rankin and some of the other British traders about the post, and hear them confirm his prejudices about the fecklessness of the natives and the duplicity of the frenchies over rum and toddy. Stout, canny Donald Campbell, who had stayed on as Gladwin's second-in-command, was wiser than this. He gave Sergeant Toole permission to stay overnight in the native villages. He made the major sit down and listen to the French interpreters, Pierre La Butte and Jacques Saint Martin, who were our principal informants on the Seneca intrigues the year before. I fear Bulldog Gladwin's idea of talking to foreigners was to grill them like sheep-stealers.

As you see, I had my work cut out for me. My first thought was of Davers. No, I will not deceive you. My first thought was of Angélique. But I thought I had best behave myself until I had discovered the lie of the land. I inquired after Sir Robert and was informed that he had taken up residence on an island thick with cedars, the Ile au Bois Blanc, in the mouth of the river; we had sailed close by it on our passage upstream. There was snow in the air, and I resolved to call on Davers promptly. Captain Campbell counseled me to quiz Sergeant Toole before leaving the fort. I duly ordered my countryman to report to me at my lodgings in the doctor's house on the Rue St Jacques, and had a rum story out of him over several noggins of the same.

Toole was a comical little fellow, but he had walked a fair portion of the earth's crust and was endowed with greater native cunning, I believe, than his commanding officer.

"I and her," said he, referring to his Chippewa squaw, "got wind of it, see, but Old Derby will only hear what he agrees with. The chiefs held a powwow down the river, near the Potti-Wotti village, and they arranged to come to the forts in the spring when the tree-frogs shrill and unbowel all the English, which includes you and me, your honor, since we all look alike to them beasts. There's no health in it, sir.

"There was a big Ottawa that did most of the talking, and he said that the Prophet had dreamed a dream and that the will of the Great Spirit is that all the red dogs—that's us, see—must be knocked on the head or drowned in the

sea. There was a frenchie there, dolled up like the White
Knight, who said Old Louis is sending an army to help.
The major, now, he says there's nothing in it because we
had a big scare last year and no harm came of it, and he
got a letter from the general that says that Indians aren't
capable of anything serious."

"But you feel different," I said to him. All Toole had
told me so far matched the letter from Davers. "What
makes you believe this isn't just the liquor talking? We
know how the natives lose their good manners when the
drink is in them."

"Ah, that's the way that it is, your honor."

Toole gave me a thirsty eye and I replenished his glass.

"But these natives have got religion, so to speak," he
went on. "See, they had a keg or three at this conventicle,
and this big Ottawa had them all stopped up and sent
away. That is the truth of it, sir. Did you ever see Indians
refuse a drop that was offered them? This lot stopped up
kegs of good rum and brandy that was open. That's why
I know they are serious."

I had to agree with Sergeant Toole. When Indians refuse
a drink, you had better look to your hairline. I rousted out
Joseph and Conrad The Song and told them we were going back down the river to find Davers.

We passed the mouth of the stream where Toole said the
secret Indian council had taken place. Its French name is
Rivière des Ecorces, or River of Bark, which made me
think of a frenchie proverb I may have gleaned from
Angélique. *Entre l'arbre et l'écorce il ne faut pas mettre
le doigt.* Don't put your finger between the bark and the
wood. This drew my thoughts back to Angélique, and to
marveling that I had placed the affairs of the Indian Department above the chance of a return engagement with
the sauciest tickler west of Manhattan. The need to get accurate intelligence to Johnson was urgent. But my desire
to see Davers, I confess, was no less urgent; here was a
man who had pressed the flesh of the Prophet! How had
his year among savages changed him? In my mind's eye,
I endowed Davers with long, unkempt hair and a wispy

beard, floating over a white smock. Then I changed the image and dressed him in native skins and warpaint.

The man who followed a deer-run down through the thickets to hail us at the water's edge matched neither of these images, except, perhaps, for the length of his hair which he wore unbound but neatly brushed. Sir Robert wore a plain check workshirt of coarse osnaburg cloth, deerskin breeches and leggings and the high-topped native moccasins that clothe the ankles. There was nothing exotic about his outward appearance save for a circlet of shells, or bones, about his neck. He seemed bigger and stronger to me. His chest had filled out. He carried his shoulders well. When I jumped out of the canoe, he clasped my hand between both of his, then pulled me to him in a fierce bear-hug. His touch jolted me like an electric shock. I felt the strength of the life force that flowed through him. This was completely novel.

I felt that this man was a stranger. He looked like Davers, but there the resemblance ended.

His eyes shone like mirrors.

"Robert. You are not the same."

He laughed and said, "You are entirely correct. I am not the person you met at White's, nor the person you left at Detroit. You must leave behind whatever expectations you carry with you."

He smiled at my evident confusion and took my arm. "Come. I have a story to tell."

We lay side by side, feet to his campfire, under a pair of smelly beaver robes. The flimsy bark roof of his shelter let in a wintry night blow that aimed for the marrow. From both sides of the river, I heard the freezing sap in the hardwoods snapping like musket-volleys. Sir Robert's chronicle began at the same time of year which the natives call the Moon of Popping Trees, when deer and moose go north to yard in evergreen hollows and the hunters go after them. He left the area of Detroit with a gang of High Hairs, breakaways from Teata's band of Romanized Hurons, heading off beyond the Grand River. I wanted to know what had become of the Huron missies Black

George had rounded up during my last visit, but once Davers got rolling I had no mind to interrupt him.

"With the deep snow," he told me, "we were pinched with hunger and aching from fatigue. At each turning, the game fled from us. Our best hunters returned empty-handed. We were reduced to grubbing for ground-acorns and scraping the inner bark from the trees. Seeing our party in this wretched state, an old woman, the mother of our chief, spent a night in prayer and fasting. In the morning she told us to take our guns and shot-pouches and follow a certain path.

"'Go quickly,' she instructed, 'because the Great Spirit has given us meat. He has heard our tears. I have seen you returning with many elk on your backs. The Great Spirit is sending a wind that will speed you on the trail and conceal your scent from the quarry. You must not take them without returning thanks.'

"We followed the woman's commands. We found a big herd of elk where she had foreseen. But one of our number was hungry, and hasty. He fired too soon, starting the herd. Though we were weakened by fasting, the Indians determined to run them down. The elk, being in fear of their lives, outstripped us by many miles, despite the depth of the snow. But we kept on and on at a steady pace until at last we caught a glimpse of them. They fled from us, a great stag watching their rear, and it was hours before we overtook them again. By such forced marches, as you know, the natives wear down the elk or the deer till they are reduced to a slow trot, or are trapped in deep drifts where they can hardly raise their legs. The hunter drives himself to the outer boundaries of endurance.

"I do not know whether my High Hairs took the elk. My legs gave up as if I had been hamstrung. My friends helped me to clear a hollow in the snow, for a firepit and a shelter from the wind, and told me they would return for me.

"The storm began with a light breeze from the north. It became a low moan, and then a shriek as of all the damned. The snow fell hard and thick, making blackness at noon, extinguishing my fire. I could not see my hand in front of my face. I was too weak to find better shelter. I had no food and nothing to drink except mushy scoops of snow. I knew I was dying, Shane.

"You know I have never feared death. My problem, in this life, has always been that I have been more than a little in love with it. I have always known that death is not extinction but the womb of new life, a higher life, for those who can rise to it.

"I did not fight the blizzard. I welcomed it as deliverance. I do not know how long I lay there. I think I must have died and come back, because I saw a tunnel opening in the darkness. When I traveled along it, I was greeted by a form of dazzling white light. This being was of unearthly beauty. I felt rapture in his presence, but he gently rebuffed me. It was not my time. The trap-door closed, so to speak, and I woke into another dream in which a native woman was calling me to come and heal myself at her fire. I saw the trail to her camp beneath the fresh snow. I do not know how I found the strength to follow it, but an owl flew with me to guide my way."

I don't know whether Davers expected me to believe that he had sprouted wings and feathers. As you know, the natives credit the wildest reports of shape-shifting, and maintain that their conjurers can change themselves into birds and animals in the blink of an eyelid. But as I say, I did not want to cut in on Davers as he came up to speed, and once he was in full spate, I doubt that he would have heard my questions anyway. He spoke very fast, but very precisely, with that same dreamy intensity that had baffled me when I first began to know him, at the Hell-Fire Club. Yet there was something new—a certainty, an authority, the sense that, in a way that it is hard for me to explain, this man was *empowered*.

I believe that the woman who called him in the dream was a member of the Chippewa nation which they call Ojibwa on the Canada side—the People of Puckered Moccasins. Davers's story was short on names and long on marvels, as you might expect. But something about his sheer presence made me hold disbelief in abeyance. He spoke of dream-hunting, and shaking tents, and a duel with an evil sorcerer, and of his own induction into a native medicine lodge. With rough lines on a page from my account-book, he sketched the path of initiation, the malevolent spirits and tempters lying in ambush at each turning, the immense powers over the unseen that belong to the soul-doctor who survives all trials and graduates from the highest circle of knowledge.

"The greater the power, the greater the danger, because, if it slips away, if it is abused, it will turn on others, and finally on the adept himself, with the force of a lightning bolt. Beyond the highest house of initiation," he scribbled more lines, "the road of the adept follows a zigzag course, as that of the lightning, charged with power, freighted with peril, never free of conflict because it is through friction and self-questioning that we are brought to add to the creation."

Don't expect *me* to give you a paraphrase. All I fathomed was that Davers fancied himself some kind of medicine man, and not of the common variety either. He said things that would sound fantastically boastful to you, if you could follow what he was talking about in the first place. He said that he had learned to dissolve time and to travel outside the body from one side of the continent to the other—at least I think that is what he said. But there was no element of personal vainglory in his tone. The voice that spoke to me with such burning intensity was curiously impersonal. If it came from Davers's self, it expressed a higher, more spacious self than most of us know that we own. Good Lord. He has got me doing it now. I'll spare you a dissertation and come to the point, or what, as a practical man, not to mention an officer of His Majesty's Indian Department, I determined to be the point at that time.

"We are in this world," said Davers, "in order to dream. We must bring the knowledge of higher worlds and of higher beings into this existence. We must heal the wound between earth and sky. Otherwise we risk the destruction of our present world and something unimaginably worse.

We risk losing our souls. This is the message of the
Prophet, and it is not a message for one nation, or one race
only. It is not a call to war, but a call to spiritual life."

I pricked up my ears at the mention of the Prophet. The
intelligence that Davers had actually met this mysterious
personage, of course, is what had brought me hurrying
back to Detroit. I risked a few direct questions. What was
the Prophet's tribe? Where was he living? What was the
size of his following?

"You must bear with me, Shane."

I sneaked a mouthful of brandy from my traveling flask
and did what I was told.

"The Prophet comes from the east," thus Davers, "from
the direction of the sun's first rays. He is not who Pontiac
and the warmongers say he is. He does not call for slaughter and bloodshed. He teaches that all the races of men—
the Africans are the oldest, the Indians the youngest—were
given the same drums and the same songs by our Creator
to commune with the spirit world, but that little by little,
we have forgotten. The natives of North America, being
the newest of the races, are no strangers to soul-flight, as
white men have become. But they risk losing their paths to
the Upper World and the Land of the Dead by acquiring
our vices and/or indifference to things of the spirit. This is
the wound the Prophet is come to heal."

I could not help myself. "You said that you met him,"
I reminded Davers.

"It was after my battle with Hole in the Day, the *wabeno*," he said, remembering. A *wabeno*, I gather, is a fire
conjurer who goes about with a kettle-drum with a horned
figure with wings on the top. "I can still hear the *wabeno*'s
voice.

> '*Nah me ba o sa yaun.*
> I walk about in the night.
> I come out of the ground
> I that am a lynx.
> See what I am become!
> How do you like my looks?'

Davers did not translate more than few of the lines, but I don't mind telling you that this insinuating dirge gave me the shivers. I gather that it was Hole in the Day's boast that he could draw the souls of his victims out of their bodies, to enchant them or to kill them. He became jealous of Davers, the parvenu, and decided to bewitch him. Davers found some way to turn the sorcery back on the sender, and don't ask me to explain it to you. I can tell you that it involved more than a stiff uppercut.

"When my vigil was over," Davers went on, "I lay close to death. I think, for a long time, I was dead to my body. My mother, my adopted mother, told me afterwards there was no sign of life except for a warm spot over my heart. It was in this time that the Prophet called me to him, and I journeyed with him to the Upper World. He brought me to the seat of the Master of Life and showed me his will."

I experienced a stab of disappointment. It seemed that all Davers had to give me was more of his hallucinations. I began to think differently as I heard him out.

"The Prophet's eyes shone like mirrors. He told me, 'The Master of Life heard me when I was weeping and singing under the stars because my people had forgotten their way. He said: I have heard your prayers. I have seen the grass wet with your tears. I have put this earth into your hand. It is a sign to the races of men. Look, it is round like the world when I danced it into being. It is clean and whole. You must remake the world you have fouled in this likeness, as it was when I breathed life into clay. Go among your people. Give them this sign. Tell them that all the filth and corruption of your lives must be swept away. Everything must be cleansed and made new.'

"The Prophet spoke with his hands cupped in front of his chest. When he moved his hands apart, a ball of red clay formed between them, a world the size of a man's head.

"The Prophet told me that he had once been given over to white men's vices, to liquor and greed, and that his spirit guides were so disgusted with what he had become that they abandoned him, and called on his soul to follow, departing from his body. He died and was reborn. It is the same for all men. We must die to the old life in order to be born again in the life of the spirit. If we forget this in our present lives, we will be obliged to learn it again after death—after many deaths. If you imagine that this has nothing to do with you, Shane, I must tell you that you are gravely mistaken."

I stole another gulp of brandy. This was proving to be damnably thirsty work. Davers gave me to understand that the Prophet invited him to accompany him on his journey to the Upper World. Now if you or I could puzzle this out, we would say, "another journey." That is not the way Sir Robert talked. He talked as if he had walked with the Prophet on his *original* journey—the famous one that was depicted on the dream-maps on buckskin that circulated everywhere in the Indian country, and that native warmongers quoted as a mandate for their deviltries. I have quoted Johnson's observations about how traditional natives do not share our notion of past, present and future moving forward in a neat progression. Davers had said something about dissolving time. If you want to know more about the mechanics, you will have to dream as he did.

What's that?

You want me to shut up and let Davers finish his own tale? I know I said I would, but I find I cannot hold to this promise. You see, I think I would make a poor job of it. I was not taking dictation, and even if I had been, I doubt that I could convey to you how Davers was able to relate a fairy-tale peopled with underwater monsters, and bone-crunching demons, and mountains of crystal, and make it sound *real*. He reminded me, at times, of the tale of Con-Edda, on his hero's quest to a magic kingdom at the bottom of the lake, except that Sir Robert was telling it in the first person. His own experiences and those of his phantom Prophet became hopelessly entangled. When he came to their interview with the Master of Life in a shining city on a hill, I could not tell where Davers's identity left off and that of the Prophet began. It occurred to me, of course, that perhaps there never *was* a Prophet, not in the sense of a man of flesh and bone, that he existed only in a collective hallucination of the native tribes which Davers had entered because he was so totally vulnerable to their dreams and sorceries.

To get to the grist of this episode, Davers's version of the Dream of the Prophet was similar to the reports Sir William and I had heard, yet entirely different. The Prophet wanted the natives to give up liquor and white men's goods—even guns and powder—and stop selling land and return to their old ways. He said that the Great Spirit had made this Turtle Island for the use of the natives, and that they went against his will by allowing blue-eyes to trespass. Subversive stuff, from the point of view of our traders and settlers and, I dare say, the Indian Department. But, the way Davers told it, the Prophet was not preaching literal revolt; it was hard to see how an uprising could succeed if the rebels agreed to forgo guns and steel knives and hatchets. The Prophet's call was to *spiritual* reformation. There was nothing in it about killing all the "dogs in red coats" and the other bloodthirsty stuff that Pontiac and his gang, no doubt with a little editorial advice from Saint Ange, had inserted. In short, it sounded to me as if the warmongers had borrowed the name of the Prophet without asking his permission.

Davers seemed to be saying that the Prophet was grieving because his message had been distorted.

He said, "It has been the same with our Bible. Christ said I have come not to bring peace but a sword. The armies of intolerance have used this as a commission to make wars and inquisitions, but the sword of the Savior is the sword of spirit fire."

"Now look here, Robert." I had to come up for air. "I'm a plain fellow, and I want it put to me plainly. Is there truly a Prophet?"

"Oh, yes."

"I mean, is he here in this reality, as opposed to your dream-world and that of the Indians?"

"What is the difference?"

I really was at the end of my tether. "Sir Robert Davers," I thought it helpful to remind him of who he was, because, of course, he had taken one of those Indian names which meant something like Fire Along The Sky, "you got me out here because you were worried about an Indian war, and in the short time I have been here, I have heard nothing to disabuse me of the fears Sir William and I both harbor on that account. Except that Bulldog Gladwin and the general don't think the natives are up to much. If there is a Prophet who can be viewed and heard by simple men, and who truly stands for peace, then we must get to him as quick as we can and persuade him to speak out against all rascals that are preaching sedition in his sainted name. We have to get on with it. Well? What do you say?"

Davers, the holy idiot, was somewhere else.

The best I could get from him was this: "We must not take from the tree until the fruit is ready to fall. When the Prophet is ready, he will call me, and we will answer his summons."

Not very promising material for an Indian Department report, though I put some of it in a private letter to Johnson. I returned to the fort at sun-up, to see what I could worm out of earthier informants—Sergeant Toole and the ladies of Detroit.

Dearest Shane,

While he was still living at Passy, dear Ben Franklin
told me the natives of North America believe there is a
vital energy in the universe that is more powerful
than electricity and less tangible. This mysterious life
force flows through everything and connects everything.
The American Indians call it Orenda. Mr Franklin said
the natives believe that certain people have a special
ability to tap into this force and direct it into the
bodies of the sick, and that true healing is accomplished
in this way.

Can this be true? I took these remarks very seriously, coming from the lightning wizard who discovered electricity.

I have searched your manuscript for information on
this theme, since you are so well acquainted with Indians. I find you continue to apply yourself to petticoats and battles. I wish you would put off all vanity
and place your literary endeavors under my supervision
before sharing your pages with the booksellers. The
aeon demands a spirit of scientific inquiry. Infused
with this spirit, your observations of native habits must
surely hold lessons for us, and our barbarous medical
practitioners. Last winter Sir Henry made the near-
fatal mistake of summoning a leech from Exeter to
treat his sore throat. In the name of medical science,
this wretch drained off three pints of Sir Henry's blood
before I was able to put a stop to the butchery.

I wish you would tell us if American Indians truly
know how to cure physical ailments by manipulations in
the etheric. How do their medicine people channel the

life force they call Orenda? Do they draw down planetary rays, or call up the energy of Mother Earth?

Mr Franklin was teasingly oblique on these matters. Being a true man of science, he believed fervently in the authority of experience, and was no doubt embarrassed by his lack of first-hand knowledge of native practices. In that season he was also tormented by the stone. He confessed there were days when he could only relieve himself by standing on his head. He volunteered to demonstrate before a gaggle of his female admirers, reducing one of our number to a swoon when he actually produced the chamber-pot. You know how he loved to shock. Ben confided to me in a calmer moment that he was much ashamed that, in his condition, he would no longer delight the ladies and preferred to drive them from his society rather than risk their derision. I hastened to reassure him that fame is a love potion that only the strongest head will resist.

I think what was buzzing in Mr Franklin's mind, when he spoke of Orenda, was a possible resemblance between the practices of the American witchdoctors and the séances of Herr Friedrich Mesmer, who was the talk of every salon in Paris in those days.

The Mesmer affair was blowing up into a ripe scandal, the most noisome in that noisy town. The King himself asked Mr Franklin to look into it, as the grand old man on a committee of panjandrums drawn from all the sciences. With the treaty newly signed, and America and England gone their separate ways, Ben found medical controversy a welcome diversion. It is strange to think of his royal commission now. Two of its members were beheaded under Mob Rule, by the invention of a third, the notorious Doctor Guillotine.

Did you ever meet Friedrich Mesmer, the Viennese conjurer who charmed half the title women of Versailles? I can picture you two in partnership, dividing up the phalanxes of fashionable ladies who swarmed to Mesmer's candlelit soirées. But the partnership would not have prospered for long. Place two cocks in a henhouse, and they will peck out each other's eyes.

All Paris, and half the Continent, was divided over Mesmer's claims to work wonder cures by animal magnetism. The King's brother swore by him. Lafayette hailed him as a benefactor of mankind. The physicians, naturally, were Mesmer's principal denouncers. They wanted him drawn and quartered, because he was a threat to their fees. That has always been the response of the established medical profession to all other practitioners. My mother told me her grandmother was denounced by a doctor, and threatened with burning, because she presumed to deliver babies in return for buttermilk and fresh eggs.

The fact that the physicians called Herr Mesmer a charlatan and a quack inclined me to his side of the debate, as did the fact that some of the most odious hypocrites of the merchant class denounced him as a threat to public morals. I was charmed when Mr Franklin invited me to assist him in establishing whether Mesmer was a fraud, by presenting himself at one of his séances as a patient.

Herr Mesmer's receiving room was all velvet and damask. The atmosphere reminded me at once of an undertaker's and a bordello. There were twenty women, if not more, all turned out in their glossiest plumage, quivering to the dirge-like music of a machine called an armonica.

The Viennese magician made a grand entrance in a suit of violet silk, brandishing a great iron wand. He arranged us to his satisfaction around his famous *baquet*, a sort of trough filled with glass bottles and iron filings and Lord knows what else that is supposed to conduct the great doctor's magnetic effluvium to as many as can take hold of one of the metal straps that protrude from it.

In a vile accent, his speech barely intelligible, Herr Mesmer explained his principles. Our life energy flows from the planetary bodies in the form of a salvific fluid, perceptible only to clairvoyants. When the flow is blocked, we sicken. Health may be restored by the animal magnetism of a powerful personality, none equal to Herr Mesmer.

I cannot remember more because the low solemnity of the Austrian's speech had me nodding off. I saw that most of the ladies were glassy-eyed, like mice before a cobra. There is no doubt that Mesmer is a fascinating man. A good-looking brute, with bad, washed-out eyes.

He favored some of us with more intimate attentions, butting knees, rubbing thighs. When his hands went straying into the deeps of my décolletage, I demanded to know what he was doing. "I must put myself *en rapport* with the source of your affliction, *cher madame*," was all his explanation. He whispered later that he must consult with me privately.

For the sake of science, I attended an assignation in his private chambers. He must have put me to sleep with his drowsy monotone and unblinking eyes, because I roused to find his wand replaced by a fleshier organ, and my clothes in spectacular disarray. He had the gall to clap his hands, turn a little jig, and pronounce me cured of my convulsions (the pretext for my visit, though I have never been convulsed by anything except laughter).

This incident, by itself, would be cause enough to dismiss the man as a charlatan with a priapic disorder that rivals your own. Yet I saw other patients with true afflictions who left Mesmer believing themselves to be fully healed, and acting the part.

Mr Franklin concluded, in the public report, that Mesmer is a fraud but may, through the curious force of his personality, encourage helpful delusions. In short, people are healed by him because they believe he can heal them. In this sense, his "animal magnetism"— now thoroughly discredited in intelligent circles—may be a real phenomenon.

Mr Franklin showed me the secret part of the report, which caused grave offense to poor Marie Antoinette and titillated her royal husband. It is there concluded that women are more susceptible than men to being Mesmer-ized because we are held to be less stable, more prone to flights of imagination, and more combustible in every regard. "Touch a woman in one spot, and you touch her everywhere." I gave Ben a good hard pinch for that line!

The Mesmer affair is now used by our medical monopolies as a pretext to deride and oppress all approaches to healing that are not owned by them. This is why it would be particularly helpful to have some reliable account of American Indian practice. I suppose there are charlatans in all countries, but if the mind can be changed by their pretenses, and so change the body, might not that be healing all the same?

I wish Ben Franklin could goad you to apply some of your experience to these questions. How I miss him! Except when he was racked by the stone, I saw his good humor fail him only once, when they sent him a copy of the Great Seal approved for the new Republic. He was enraged that they overrode all his protests and anointed the bald eagle as the national bird. He always maintained the bald eagle is a cowardly, useless animal. The turkey (said Ben) is the true embodiment of American character.

Merry Christmas.

Your
Valerie

12

The Quest for the Prophet

BEFORE THE RIVERS FROZE, I went fishing at night with the Huron women. They throw their nets out into the deep of the water, weighting the lower corners with rocks, hitching the upper corners to floating paddles so they can take their catch with ease come daylight. It snowed in the night; in the morning, we found the trout and perch frozen stiff. This was the very image of my catch at Detroit that winter.

Angélique, the tickler, had gone and got herself betrothed, not to another frenchie, but to needle-nosed James Sterling, one of the most prosperous of our British traders about the post. I suppose there wasn't much the matter with Jemmie Sterling, except that he had the wrong business partners and had claimed sole possession of what I and certain other gentlemen had viewed as common pasture. Sterling was the western agent for the Schenectady firm of Livingston, Rutherford, Duncan, and any enterprise that had a Livingston, however lowly, on its shingle was viewed with the blackest suspicion by Sir William. Livingstons were at the back of Uri Klock's claim to the lands of

the Upper Castle of the Mohawks. Livingstons—top dogs
in the interior of the Province of New York until Johnson
had come upriver a quarter-century before—were for ever
conniving against Sir William and scheming to give him a
lift out of his stirrups. Johnson had warned me to keep an
eye on Sterling. The Livingston agent had already in-
flamed the Senecas, not that they needed much priming,
by building on a choice piece of land around the upper
landing at Niagara that he had got deeded to him and his
partners by the usual method of getting a few loafers
drunk, all this with the blessing of Sir Jeffrey Amherst,
that great student of the workings of the native mind.
Johnson suspected that Jemmie Sterling was secretly engaged in buying deeds to Indian land in the vicinity of Detroit against the day when his patrons hoped to succeed in
ousting Sir William and opening the western frontier to
white settlers and speculators. It was this kind of underhand business, of course, that persuaded the tribes that we
were come to exterminate them.

I decided I could best execute Johnson's instructions by
acting in his spirit and pleasuring Jemmie Sterling's
fiancée on the sly. An exchange of notes—discreet addresses at a winter ball, a sleigh-ride on the frozen river,
where I seized the opportunity to remind her of what she
was missing under our lap-rug—it required only a week or
two to arrange what the frenchies call *l'heure du berger*,
the hour when the shepherd comes for the fleece. I think
the decisive moment in my renewed courtship came when
I was fumbling with her skirts behind our steaming nag on
the river.

"What, sir," demands Angélique, "do you wish me to be
inconstant to my lover?"

"Ah, if only it were possible to be constant, my dear."
I gave her my bedroom eyes. "But we cannot love for two
successive instants in the same fashion, because we are not
the same people. We must not hesitate for an instant to be
fickle when we are tempted or else we would be unfaithful
to our own natures which are always in flux."

I do not recommend that you try this approach on a girl
of romantic disposition, or of healthy, uncomplicated ani-

mality. I doubt that it will assist you with any English girl. I suspect, indeed, that it works only in the French tongue, and only with that peculiarly French type of Cartesian tickler whose secret credo runs, *cogito, ergo fornicato*. If you have caught an echo of Marivaux in my speech, you are not only correct, you are on your way to winning your Angélique. I do not doubt that the lady had several reasons for going to bed with me—she was eager to sniff out intelligence of Johnson and our Department for the benefit of both father and lover—and as I have reported without false modesty, I generally know a girl's spot.

But I think Angélique decided to cuckold her fiancé on principle. Like the Marquise de Merteuil, whom she much resembled, she never made the mistake of thinking that the man with whom she sought pleasure was the sole depository of it. As Peg says, there are women who regard it as their vocation to avenge themselves on my sex.

As spies, I believe that Angélique and I held each other in check. She fed me gossip and rumor that evaporated under close inspection faster than river fog in the morning sun. She tried to prejudice me against François Bâby, a prominent merchant across the river in the section the French called the Faubourg St Rosalie, as if they were living beside the Seine; in fact, when we needed friends during the revolt, this Bâby proved to be one of the staunchest. If Angélique knew anything of Saint Ange, she did not confide it to me, neither on the pillow nor the nether end of the bed. I was no less duplicitous with her, exaggerating the size of our garrisons and of the shipments of Indian gifts that Sir William would send to gratify the natives when they returned from their winter hunt. If either of us came out on top in this shadow-play, I believe it was Angélique because, by favoring me with her infidelities, she made me relax my suspicions of her father. Dandy Cuillérier was as obliging as ever, thoughtfully absenting himself so Angélique could entertain me at home, serving me a glass of wine as he showed off his new set of buttons, sheathed in flowered silk in the elaborate style that the frenchies call *passementerie*. Never put your trust in a

man who pays excessive regard to his buttons. Had I
known the full extent of Dandy Cuillerier's complicity
with the engineers of the Indian revolt, I would have
pressed Major Gladwin to place him in irons.

Joseph and the Mohawks were invaluable to me in my
efforts to gain hard intelligence on the threatened uprising.
They could pass for Hurons, and they traveled further and
faster on their snowshoes than any white man could have
managed. Conrad The Song went as far as La Baye on the
western shore of Lake Michigan, and brought me a letter
from Lieutenant Gorrell of the 60th that was pretty typical
of the reports that we had from our outposts. He had had
a visit from "a King of the Sac Nation," flying the French
colors from the prow of his canoe. When quizzed about
his choice of ensigns, the chief excused himself on the
grounds that he "did not know any better." Gorrell complained about the deceits of one of our traders selling watered rum, about a lying French interpreter called Gouchea
who deliberately misrepresented his statements to the Indians, and about a furtive bunch of Ottawa agitators slipping
through his territory. He wanted to know why he was not
being sent wampum beads and powder to keep the natives
sweet.

General Amherst's parsimony, French sedition, native
resentment over cheating traders and licentious soldiery—
these were constant elements, and you have heard enough
of them already. Over that winter, into the early spring,
they produced a nasty series of incidents. Traders toma-
hawked and scalped, military expresses ambushed and
robbed, truck houses looted, secret war belts carried between the tribes.

I found more and more evidence that French agents
were conspiring to weld the tribes together in a general-
ized revolt. Toole's Chippewa squaw said that a war belt
from Belêtre, the former French commandant at Detroit,
was circulating among the chiefs of her people, from
Saginaw Bay to Crooked Tree. A trader returning from the
Twightee country told me that a frog named Clermont was
spreading the old tale that King Louis had woken from his
nap and was coming with all his horse and foot to knock

the English on the heads. Joseph brought in a thirsty Ottawa called Wausso, which means Lightning, who told me that "Santang" had been traveling with a band of his people led by the war chief called Pontiac.

It may surprise you that Pontiac has not figured more prominently in these pages up to this point. Frankly, Pontiac was quite unknown to the Indian Department until the eve of the revolt that bears his name. We first heard that name from Angélique in 1761, not because Johnson's people were dozy or incompetent, but for the perfectly simple reason that the war chief had changed his identity. Indians are apt to adopt a new name when something memorable happens to them. Pontiac is a friendlier version of the Ottawa word Obwandiyag, which means He Stops It Up, a reference to one of those astonishing episodes in which the chief bunged up a keg of liquor during an Indian council. A man who can compel his fellow-natives to forgo spirits must be taken seriously, and I set about gleaning such information on Pontiac as I could from the sources available. Saint Martin and La-Butte, the French interpreters at the fort, were among the most useful, though it was hard for me to know how far they were to be trusted, since they had so recently served King Louis.

Ironically, while Saint Ange and his gang were stirring the pot, I received heartening news from Sir William with the first boat from Niagara after the thaw, that Britain and France had declared a cessation of arms. Bulldog Gladwin organized a feast for the *habitants* at the fort to give them the good news, and I passed it on to the bands of Indians who came drifting back to their summer villages with peltries to sell and powerful thirsts to be serviced. Our commandant thought that the news that peace was about to break out would put an end to French cabals and native conspiracies. By my observation, the news had precisely the reverse effect. The lost soldiers of France and the chiefs who hated us, maddened by the prospect of final abandonment by King Louis, resolved to hazard all on a wild and desperate stroke.

I did not know what form this would take, but the warning signs continued to multiply. The Indians returning from the winter hunt were lean and surly. They complained they had fewer buckskins and beavers to sell than was usual, because they had exhausted their powder and ammunition thanks to the general's "retrenchments" and the high prices of our traders. Sergeant Toole's lady friend told us that four or five hundred warriors had held another secret powwow at the Rivière des Ecorces and sent runners north to the Chippewas at Saginaw Bay, the western Ottawas at Crooked Tree and the Mississaugas at the Rivière à la Tranche.

Three days after this, on the last day of April, Pontiac and fifty of his tribe came to pay a social call on Bulldog Gladwin and I got my first good look at the general of the revolt. I have seen Pontiac described in other men's memoirs as the King of the Ottawas. He did not look very much like a king. He was only of middling height, but his chest was as round as a hogshead. His hair fell to his shoulders from under a headdress that reminded me of a birdcage. The beaks of four unfortunate woodpeckers lolled over his brow. Father Pothier informed me that the woodpecker has a supernatural significance for some of the Woodland Indians, because it hunts the unseen, poking through the bark after the grubs and insects inside. Pontiac wore a short cape composed of the skins of many different animals with the design of thunderbirds and other such mystical beasts on the inside. He carried a pouch of raccoon skin. Saint Martin, who was with us, told me that the raccoon is a personal fetish of Pontiac's and indeed, as the war chief came closer, I saw that he had daubed great circles of potblacking about his eyes in imitation of the animal's bandit markings. The eyes themselves glinted like onyx.

The man had a presence, I will not deny that. I am positive he was not among the Ottawa chiefs who had attended Sir William's native councils at Detroit in 1761. Nor did I see any of the principals from those sessions in Pontiac's present company. A change had evidently come about in the leadership of the Ottawa nation. In place of careful old grayhairs, we now had to deal with the Wild Men. I knew that some of this tribe, and probably Pontiac himself under a previous name, had crouched in the woods beside the Monongahela, shot General Braddock from his horse and routed a whole British army.

Bulldog Gladwin may not have been scared of them, but I do not mind admitting that I was more than a little uneasy. The Ottawas had sent a message that they wanted to smoke the calumet with us, and the major put on a bit of a show with drum and fife and bagpipes too, because I had insisted on them. Sir William and I were of the same mind on this matter—the war pipes are the one thing you can count on to defeat the hideous din of native music.

The calumet, an enormous pipe hung with dead birds and feathers, was passed around; the Ottawas exchanged a couple of mangy beavers for trinkets and salt pork from the commissary; we jogged around in a shuffle-dance, with Gladwin evincing signs of distress that became quite comical when Sergeant Toole trawled past humming Old Derby.

I thought the Ottawas were behaving in a distinctly shifty fashion. Some of them slipped away from the main party. Toole came back after a bit and whispered to me to come and look. I saw our visitors wandering around the barracks and peering inside the magazine, taking careful note of the deployment of our sentries and the state of our powder.

When we had seen the back of them, I asked Gladwin if I could talk to him in private.

I told him, "I believe they are planning to attack the fort."

"Hogwash," said the major. "It is unheard of for Indians to attack fortified positions."

I reminded him that Pontiac's mob had French advisers and were in any case capable of ruses. Indians were always wandering in and out of the fort. Our visitors today could have brought concealed weapons.

"They would have had a warm welcome, by God," said Gladwin, supremely confident of the superiority of regulars.

I suggested to him that he should double the watch while the Indians were gathered in force at their villages nearby and restrict traffic at the gates. He said he would consider my recommendations.

After this, I received a spate of alarming reports. One of my Mohawks came back from the Huron village and said that a band of Wild Men led by a pagan chief named Takea had sworn to fight with Pontiac against the British. Teata, who was one of Father Pothier's converts and a moderate, was wavering. Chippewas were coming down from the upper lakes and could tilt either way. The Potawatomis—Toole's Potti-Wottis—were dominated by a chief called Ninivois, who was a confirmed enemy of Britain, having lost several of his sons and nephews to our forces during the war.

I tried to play things as I conceived Johnson would have done, inviting chiefs to dine with me in ones and twos, passing out bribes and assurances, playing them off against each other. I even invited Pontiac to have a drink with me. He sent a runner to tell me that he had to mourn his uncle and would come in the new moon. I learned that he was living on an island at the mouth of Lake St Clair, upstream from the Ottawa village, with a personal bodyguard of warriors. I had a mind to beard him in his own den, but Joseph came to me first with the specific tip I had been hoping for. He told me he had been fishing near the Potawatomi village, and that there was a big discussion going on there. He had seen a couple of strange Frenchmen; they were staying at Mini Chêne's house, which was only a few musket-shots away.

I knew Mini Chêne slightly. His nickname was a joke. He stood half a head taller than me, and must have weighed three hundred pounds. His skin was tanned like cordovan leather. He was one of those rough bushlopers the French call *coureurs des bois*, as wild as any Indian. He hated all authority, but above all he hated the British. I thought he was just the fellow to provide bed and board for the ringmasters of a revolt and wondered if I would find the Chevalier de Saint Ange among them.

I resolved to go and see for myself. You must understand something of my frustration and my fears. We had two companies of the blue-trousered Royal Americans in

the garrison at Detroit. According to the book, there were
seventy-eight men in each; in fact, their combined strength
was less than that. We had one company of the Queen's
Rangers, mustering only twenty-two men and commanded
by a crooked Marylander, Captain Joseph Hopkins, who
spent the greater part of his time, by my observation, fiddling his unit's accounts and stealing rum rations from his
men to peddle to the Indians. Add the crews of the sloop
and the schooner anchored in the river on either side of the
fort and we had a grand army of a hundred and twenty
men to defend Detroit. The English traders could be expected to help out at a pinch. The *habitants* could not; my
guess was that more than half of them would go over to
the rebels if they seemed likely to succeed. Against us, if
it came to a fight, were perhaps two thousand Indian warriors in the immediate neighborhood with more bands reported to be converging on Detroit from the Grand River,
Saginaw Bay and places farther north and west. Our powder and stores were low and the convoy from Niagara was
late. Clearly, whatever was being plotted in the native encampments, we were in no condition to contemplate any
sort of serious offensive. The nearest British posts to us
had puny garrisons of ten or twenty men.

All the same, if the enigmatic Saint Ange was in the vicinity, I meant to see him again. I am not sure that my
plan was clearly formed. I had some vague notion of trying to make him see reason by explaining to him that the
war was over, that it could only be a matter of months before a formal treaty was concluded, that there was no
profit in sparking a war in the name of a lost cause. I had
some idea of arresting him and holding him prisoner if he
refused my overtures, because I took Toole and two soldiers with me, as well as the Mohawks, when I paddled
downriver. I dare say this sounds muddled to you. I will
plead only that, in my experience, the boldest enterprises
are conceived and executed in a warm fog; an excess of
calculation distances a man from his purpose and pays
scant regard to luck, the best friend a fellow can have.

We dressed in native garb and blackened our faces. We
coated the barrels of our guns with tallow to avoid reflect-

ing the moonlight or the glow of Indian campfires. Gladwin had authorized me only to make a reconnaissance, but that is a wonderfully capacious word. In French, it is a euphemism for a man's mistress, and also for the last rites.

It was after midnight when we crept on shore and drew the canoes into the shelter of the brush, a few rods below Mini Chêne's cabin. The house was in darkness, and all seemed still. Shouts and singing carried from the Potawatomi village, where the natives seemed to be playing at being war-eagles and grizzly bears.

My purpose began to falter. If I simply barged into the Frenchman's house, without overt provocation, terrorizing his womenfolk, I might cause an incident that would have all the *habitants* up in arms.

"We will wait for a time," I told Toole and the others. "Perhaps the game will come to us."

We concealed ourselves behind a great heap of firewood and among the birches behind the house.

Within an hour, I was rewarded by the view of Mini Chêne shambling back from the native village in the company of several others, one of them a white man with a two-barred French cross about his neck.

Saint Ange. I felt sure it was him, though I could not see the face distinctly. The lean hips. The loping gait of a timber wolf.

They were less than a bowshot away.

I resolved to step out and confront them boldly when one of the Mohawks started cawing like a crow. I saw shadows flitting through the woods. Mini Chêne and his friends had come with an escort. I could not risk an exchange of arms.

Reluctantly, I waved my men back to the canoes.

Mini Chêne saw me as I slipped through the brush.

He yelled after me, telling me to stop or he would put a hole through my back. I paused and decided to risk a simple conversation with Saint Ange, whatever the number or temper of his companions.

The man with the two-barred cross had vanished.

Mini Chêne bulked huge among the shadows, flanked by a score of warriors covered in warpaint.

I told him as coolly as I could manage that I had received a report of illegal liquor-peddling.

I added, "It is plain that I was misled."

Mini Chêne swore and called me a thief and a liar.

"And you, sir," I informed him, "are a pimp and a mackerel."

"*Tais-toi, pendard!*" the brute bawled. "Shut up, you gallow's meat! Say one more word to me, and I'll break your bones!"

He growled something in the native tongue to his escorts, and they advanced on me in a distinctly unfriendly manner.

There was an unmistakable click as one of my men cocked his firelock. Joseph, God love him, was up in a tree, aiming at the unmissable target of Mini Chêne's swag belly.

"I think it's a stand-off, won't you agree?" I proposed to Mini Chêne.

He called off his braves with bad grace, and I told him that I looked forward to our next interview.

He bade me good-night by remarking, "*Vous, monsieur, êtes une sauterelle d'enfer.*"

I confess that this puzzled me. I have been called names saltier than ammonia, on land and on sea, but I had never been called a grasshopper out of hell.

After this, it was plain even to the blockheads at the fort that we were in for serious trouble. I wrote urgent reports to Johnson and to Major Wilkins, our new commandant at Niagara, praying that they would get through, but without much optimism about what they would bring. Wilkins had struck me as an idle, listless windbag, and though Sir William would move heaven and earth to assist us, he was far away and the regulars who had won the war were on troopships out at sea or in sick beds, fighting the malarial fevers that had claimed more casualties at Havana than the Spaniard. For a good while yet, we would be obliged to live on our wits, while the Indians did the war-dance all around us and Saint Ange, no doubt, lectured them on how poky King Louis was feeling after his noonday snooze.

It was at this juncture that Robert Davers surfaced again, to tell me he had got his marching orders from the Prophet.

I had gone across the river to the Huron village to try to get some intelligence from Teata, the Christian chief, and to raise our stake in his hedge with a judicious distribution of rum and silver dollars. I decided to stay the night at Madame Chauvin's establishment, which was not far off, because of a pressing itch in my breeches. Angélique had taken to refusing my assignations, pleading Jemmie Sterling's rising suspicions. I know now that her family did not want a fellow from the Indian Department hovering about their house where Dandy Cuillerier was sitting in secret conclave with Saint Ange and the Indians. Angélique's coolness was less of a disappointment, now I had come to an understanding with Madame Chauvin's elder daughter, Babette, a brisk little filly who saw no harm in rehearsing for the married estate.

Babette was a spoiled, sulky, fine-boned girl with a quantity of frizzed hair, somewhat narrow above the waist, but plump as a pear below, where two dimples paid court to her tailbone. She was as sallow as a native, but her own color was well hidden by paint and priming until she took her clothes off, which is when she shone. She was less of a beauty than Angélique, but she improved what God had given her with artifice and acrobatics I had never thought to find on the edge of virgin forest. We punished the paltry rush-bottomed chair in her bedroom until the legs folded under us. Madame Chauvin charged me for that as she charged for everything. *Il faut marchander* was her watchword.

The house was crowded with company that night and there was no recourse but to sleep three-in-a-bed with Babette and her younger sister Martine, a rosy, fair-haired thing, soft and round as a butterball. This situation reminded me most agreeably of my afternoons at Fish House with Sir William and the Wormwood girls, and you may believe that I did not waste my opportunity. The girls were most accommodating after I showed them a fine piece of Irish linen I had decided not to waste on the Hurons.

Martine was fresher to the game than her sister, but her appetites were no less exacting. I rekindled my fire with a bumper of good Nantes brandy, and we banged the high bedposts against the wall until the tester came down and gruff curses exploded from the chamber next door. I may have said it already, but I shall say it again: I have rarely encountered such eager trotters as it has been my privilege to know in North America. There was no holding the Chauvin girls once they were off and running. It may be that the natural environment of the colonies pushes temperament to the extremes. In the north of America, winter saws the skin off your face; summer flays it off. The rivers run faster and colder than at home; the mountains stand taller. Even the sky is bigger, when you can see it above two-hundred-foot trees. The horizon is not circumscribed by hedgerows and stone walls and cozy hills. Ambitions and appetites run free, beyond convention, beyond proportions. A praying man becomes a saint or a babbling fanatic. A whore becomes the mother of all whores.

When the sisters allowed me to rest, Babette tied a black ribbon round Captain Standish and hummed a funeral dirge.

I informed the ladies I intended to sleep until noon.

I dreamed of Davers. He was leading me along a dim passageway, lit by flickering sconces. We came to many doorways. At each one, he paused and ushered me into a chamber where I saw people of different races, attired in the clothing of different times, enacting dramas whose nature I cannot recall, except that the protagonist in all of these plays, or events, I cannot say which, was always Robert Davers, though he never looked the same and was always hovering, at the same moment, at my shoulder. As I re-read this statement, I realize how preposterous it seems, even by the standard of dreams. I will say no more about it except that, in one of the sequences, Davers, in the semblance of an ancient Indian, with a storm of white hair about his shoulders, was explaining something to me at tremendous length, using drawings on birchbark and strings and circlets of wampum beads to illustrate his message. We sat on opposite sides of a fire, and the strangeness of this fire was that its flames glowed deep purple, like the heart of an amethyst. I woke with a start, to hear Robert Davers singing in a language I cannot translate. The words echoed in the darkened bed-chamber. I would swear that they set the cheval-glass on top of the cupboard shaking in its stand, except that of course you would not be able to credit it. I looked for Davers, inside the house and outside, in the courtyard and along the river road. I found only the inert bodies of well-oiled Canadians and a couple of Hurons, dozing at the kitchen door. I did not know the language Davers used, yet I recognized his meaning. He had heard the call of the Prophet. He was going somewhere I could not follow. This was his farewell.

I was seized with the sudden terror that, naked beneath the mantle of his dreams, Robert Davers was going to his death. I had long since stopped agonizing over my wager with Gaius Walsingham. Whatever became of Davers, Gaius owed me one hundred guineas, which I proposed to collect as soon as I got back to London, whenever that would be. London! Silky mornings at Peg's, three-hour lunches at the coffee house, a smart box at Drury Lane with a view of the finest décolletages in England, the friendly cries of boys selling pippins and warden pears—to think what I had given up!

I cursed myself for these homesick maunderings. I cursed myself even harder for still feeling responsible for Davers. But I did; there was no getting round it.

I hurried back to the Huron village before dawn, to collect Joseph. He rose light and quick as a cat from his sleeping-mat in the lodge of a Wolf Clan matron. You know that among the natives the clan commands a loyalty independent of the tribe; members of the same clan from different nations look after each other, as distant relatives.

We skimmed downriver. I hardly hoped to find Davers on his white wood island. I had looked for him there several times since he had talked to me of the Prophet, without finding him. But he was there now, at the same landing, his face reddened by the rising sun.

"I was expecting you," he told me. "I waited for you to come."

His canoe was already laden with neatly rolled bundles. No liquor. Only a solitary fowling-piece.

He told me he had received his summons and must go upriver and across the lakes to a place called the Island of Souls. He had only one companion, a Pani slave he had bought from a Frenchman. He looked like a shiftless, hangdog specimen to me, even worse than Daniel the Wild Man. Don't ask me what had happened to Daniel. I neither knew nor cared after the scare he had caused in the Valley.

"Wait," I said to Davers. "You said you would take me. If the Prophet truly means peace, then his voice must be heard about Detroit before all the nations take up the hatchet. Give me a day or two to get things organized. It's not safe for an Englishman to go roaming about on his own. I nearly got knocked on the head over at Mini Chêne's."

"It is safer for one than for many," said Davers. "The Indians will not harm me. I travel under a special protection."

I wrangled with him. I even threatened to come after him and bring him back by force if he persisted in leaving without me. I begged him to allow me twenty-four hours to work things out.

"As you wish," was the closest he came to compliance. "But it will end badly."

If I had swallowed even one tenth of what he had told me about dreams and clairvoyance, I would have listened. I didn't, and I suppose, in that sense, I have blood on my conscience. Robert Davers does not blame me. He knew what was coming to pass. He accepted it.

I talked Bulldog Gladwin into letting me make a party of it, with some assistance from Captain Robertson, the admiral of our two-ship navy at Detroit. Charles Robertson was a jovial sort, a sound bottle-man with an inexhaustible store of dirty ditties. He shared the general contempt of our regulars for the natives, but he had an eye for strategy. I had heard him talk wistfully during the shut-up winter months about wanting to sound the channels to see whether it was possible to take ships of war to Michilimackinac and beyond. I reminded him of this now, adding the thought that if the natives did stage an uprising, it would vastly improve our position, and those of the smaller posts to the west, if we were able to ferry men and supplies back and forth on the sloop or the schooner. We were confident that our ships of war could repulse any Indian attack unless the watch were all drunk.

"Capital!" exclaimed Robertson when I proposed sending a gunboat upriver, on the pretext of dropping lines to fill in the holes on our navigational charts. "Strap my vitals! I'm rotting for a bit of action!"

For Gladwin's benefit, I slipped in the hint that the Indian Department had an intelligence requirement.

"We will be able to discover whether the northern Chippewas are really coming in force, or whether this is only a scare story circulated by our enemies to induce us to abandon the fort."

It really had been put to us, by Dandy Cuillerier and some other frenchies who purported to have our well-being at heart, that we ought to close up shop and get out of Detroit before the Indians lost their tempers.

Bulldog Gladwin looked unhappy. He may have been experiencing one of his malarial spasms with the change in the weather. Then again, he always had trouble getting acquainted with a new idea.

"Furthermore," I tried to encourage him, "there's a chance we may bag this native witchdoctor they call the Prophet."

Davers would have howled had he heard me. But how would you have explained about Davers and the Prophet to a sturdy woodenhead like the Bulldog?

The bit about the Prophet seemed to cheer Gladwin up. We had been hearing the name of this personage more and more frequently, as Pontiac and his rabble-rousers went about doing their stuff. I had actually laid hands on one of the famous dream-maps as a souvenir. It looked a bit like a plan of our fort, drawn on buckskin with gaps in the wrong places, and a thin deer inside and a fat deer on top, in what I presumed to be the happy hunting-ground.

There was no question of taking the sloop or the schooner; there was too big a risk that the ship would get snagged on the sandbars about the mouth of Lake St Clair, and lie as easy prey for a war-party as a beetle lying on its back. But Gladwin agreed to give us a flatboat, and a few Royal Americans together with Robertson's tars, and the captain asked permission to include a keen young subaltern called John Rutherfurd in the party.

I slipped back down the river to give Davers the glad news.

He shrugged and asked how soon our party would be ready to leave.

When we formed up below the river gate, Davers and his Pani, whose name, I believe, was Redwing, came paddling along near the bank.

"Come on board, Sir Robert!" cried Captain Robertson. "We have some capital punch for the voyage!"

"Thank you, Captain. I must go with Redwing."

He must have sensed how curt this sounded, because he quickly added something about how it would be easier in the native craft to slip up the smaller creeks and inlets and scout the lie of the land.

I announced that I had a mind to mimic him and go with Joseph in our own canoe, though I would of course be delighted to share in the captain's liquid hospitality.

It is as well for Bulldog Gladwin that I did this, because some hunch I could not have communicated in words prompted me to tell Joseph to make a turn at the mouth of the creek near the Ottawa village on the south-east side of the river. I had spotted some women gathered in a circle. They were probably doing their laundry, but the speed with which they started to pick themselves up and scuttle towards their bark huts made me suspect that something more interesting was afoot.

A granny fatter and heavier than the rest lagged behind, and we soon overtook her once we had pulled our canoe up into the sedge.

ages try my patience, I shall give them a taste of Shef-
d steel!"

Robertson's confidence in the superiority of his own
ck was magnificent in its way. It was a similar arro-
ce that carried the British flag, usually in the hands of
try bands of cracks and projectors, from Madras to the
ve coasts of Africa. The same bomb-proof vanity led
or General Braddock to march his army, without native
uts, to the slaughter-ground near Fort Pitt, and dull-
tted Abercrombie to despatch our finest grenadiers to be
tted like fatted hogs on Montcalm's breastworks beside
ke Champlain.

Davers said to the captain, "So you will not change.
u have chosen your own path. It is on your head."

"What the devil do you mean, Sir Robert?" Robertson's
bwig danced on his pink scalp. "What is on my head?"

"What I have foreseen."

e Chippewas were waiting for us at the narrows where
e river boils through the opening from Lake Huron. I
essed that there were four hundred of them, pressing
wn along the sandy beach, which was gunmetal gray
th garnet lights.

Davers called over to the flatboat. "Captain Robertson!
is is your last chance! I am going on shore to talk with
m. I implore you to turn back!"

You may conceive that when I heard Davers's an-
uncement that we were going on shore, I regretted my
ice of transportation. Not that it would have made any
erence. Captain Robertson staunchly refused to enter-
 any change in his dispositions. Once he had a plan in
 head, it stuck there like a nail. Besides, there was a
ctical objection—it would be ticklish work, bringing
 clumsy flatboat around in those treacherous currents,
 a strong likelihood of getting stuck on a bar adding
 lt to possible injury from the savages. Furthermore, as
 ertson yelled back, "The natives look friendly!"

Hand to God, but they do, your honor!" This came
 Sergeant Toole, who was riding on the bateau.
 soon observed the source of his good humor. Women

"Bonjou' neejee," I hailed her in the pidgin of New
France. "Can we be of some assistance?"

She had tried to get rid of her burden among the bushes,
but the glint of the barrel betrayed it. I reached through a
clump of milkweed and retrieved a firelock. The barrel
was partly filed through, eighteen inches from the firing
pan. I assumed the old crone had dropped her file somewhere else, or concealed it about her shapeless person. It
took only an instant for me to grasp the significance of
what she, and no doubt her companions, were doing. A
sawn-off musket is a devilishly inaccurate weapon, but a
damn sight easier to conceal under an Indian blanket than
a full-length barrel. I thought of Pontiac's braves, skulking
and spying around the *chemin de ronde* and the magazine
inside the fort.

"God's breeches! They mean to take Gladwin by surprise the next time they go to the fort for a powwow. We
must warn the commandant!"

In fact, it was Joseph who warned Bulldog Gladwin. I
have seen a lot of fanciful rot, in other men's writings,
about who gave Gladwin the warning that Pontiac was
planning to smuggle guns inside the fort in order to make
soup of the commandant and the garrison. It has even been
stated that the major got his intelligence from a steamy encounter with a Chippewa squaw, which is a pretty good
joke if you ever knew the Bulldog. Here is an end to the
mystery: we saw native women filing down guns with our
own eyes, and you do not need the second sight to know
that hunting men don't want sawn-off muskets to shoot
squirrels.

I suggested to Captain Robertson that we should turn
back. The fort was clearly in imminent danger. At best, we
would be cut off. At worst, we would be cut down.

Robertson wouldn't hear of a change of plans. Davers,
as always, responded only to his own inner compass.

We went on. For the most part, I traveled with Davers
and his Pani in their long birchbark canoe, talking and poling for fish and exploring the inlets. The mild spring
weather mocked my fears of approaching catastrophe. The
south wind blew soft and warm at our backs as we

rounded Pontiac's island, which seemed untenanted. Up-river, the green-black shadows of the woods were splashed with color: yellows and pinks and blues, the pearly streamers of laurel. Clouds of pigeons rolled under the boughs of the red maples, taking the new-fallen seeds.

We saw a woodcock paying court to his lady.

Peeeeent!

The bawdy fellow threw back his head and let out a string of raucous screeches.

Peeeeent!

Then he shot straight up into the air. High overhead, he made a new sound, like tinkling glass, as he turned a wide circle. The sound came from under his pinions, as if he had fitted himself with a set of windchimes. I had my gun charged and cocked, but I could not bring myself to pot such a rakish fellow.

For two days and nights, we saw no sign of human life. Davers and I paddled upstream to a village of bark huts shaped like sugar loaves that had been used by Chippewas the summer before. It was deserted. Dead husks of corn blew about the clearing. Bark sheets flapped against the roof poles. A bald-headed vulture squatted on the ruins of the stockade, wrinkling its ugly red neck as it gave us a leisurely inspection.

I felt the immensity of the wilderness all about us. I felt shipwrecked: fragile and infinitely vulnerable in that vast green ocean. As my spirits drooped, Davers's seemed to soar.

He sat among the roots of a white birch and appeared to lose himself somewhere inside it for fully half an hour.

"You don't know life until you have entered the dream of the heartwood," he said. "Higher beings enter the dreaming of a tree and rest there for centuries. The Prophet has told me these things."

He saw my face.

"Ah, Shane, Shane! There is more in heaven and earth than you can ever guess in this lifetime. You don't even know that trees are as individual as people, do you?"

With some difficulty, I got him back to the river. That

was better. I could begin to breathe again
smiling dementia and the encirclement of th
started to feel I was suffocating. I had to list
bling on for what seemed like hours, on the
groves are God's first churches.

"The Romans cut down the sacred oaks i
the papists chopped down the holy groves of
were terrified of the spirits they contained,
eyed druids, priests of oak."

You can imagine the rest.

If you think I am not being sufficiently sy
Davers, you are right. The truth of it is, I cou
to indulge his point of view, out in those wild
imagination becomes so easily disordered.

We met Indians on the third day—a family
was in a canoe. We traded bread from the fo
twists of tobacco for some of the bright-eye
they had thrashing about among their thwarts.
civil, but impassive. Davers talked to them in
lingo. They affected not to know anything about
ments of Chippewas from Saginaw Bay and

Across the broad basin of Lake St Clair, w
rolling away to the west, Robertson's sailors
the fierce currents of the Huron River surgin
to hurl its water into the lake.

We came to a neck of land with a sawmi
of French carpenters milling pine logs. Ro
them some flour from our bakery for deerm
made wine. Their leader seemed to be a de
took some of us aside and counseled us to
had heard that a Chippewa war-party was
and was sworn to eat the livers of the Engli

Davers said, "Jacques is right. You mus
not have your blood on my hands."

"Confound it," thus Captain Roberts
your personal bodyguard, Sir Robert! I h
perform on His Majesty's service, and th
if I will be deceived by shadows, or a wh
cowardly, skulking banditti. We Brit
sterner stuff, are we not, Mr Hardacre?

and children formed the first rank of the Indians along the beach. The children were beckoning to us, holding up offerings of gleaming trout and whitefish and little *mukaks* of maple candy. The sugarwood boxes were nankeen yellow. That color haunts my memory.

The older girls, and some of the women, were offering sweeter enticements. Though their words meant little to me at the time, their gestures were plain enough for a dotard to comprehend. One native princess thrust her hand under her deerskin kilt and ground her wide hams. Another fretted her right thumb in her left fist, ogling and puffing kisses. The best-looking of the bunch waded out into the river, opened her shirt, and jiggled her tits.

One of the privates on the flatboat could not contain himself.

"I'm coming, sugarbox. Oh Gawd, I'm coming!"

This brought thunder from his commanding officer.

Davers's mouth was a straight line. As we nosed into shore, he muttered something that might have been, "They are dead men."

I do not profess to be a world authority on Indians, but I did not need Davers to tell me something was amiss. A trade squaw in liquor may do things that would make a Covent Garden trollop blush, but you do not see a whole village of native women behaving like sluts unless there is a deeper purpose behind it than acquiring a case of jew's harps or a keg of rum.

"I trust you know what you're doing, Robert," I said to Davers.

I did not like the way he smiled.

"Do you know any of these people?" I pursued.

I did not catch his answer, if he gave one, because we were surrounded by a crowd of jabbering Chippewas. There were warriors among them. I was relieved to see that, though most of them were half-naked, they were not painted for war.

I followed Davers onto a rise, where he squatted down to parley with the chiefs. Captain Robertson, I saw, was pursuing his course upstream towards the lake. His boatmen were making hard going of it; perhaps their hearts, or some other portion of their anatomy, had joined the squaws.

I cannot convey the content of Sir Robert's dialogue with the Chippewas. I know that they received him with the outward signs of friendship and respect. They offered him the calumet, and he held it out to the four quarters, and to the above and below, before sending a few wisps of smoke skyward.

I would have taken this as a reassuring sign except that I noticed a great deal of activity among the bushes farther upstream, and realized, for the first time, that there were warriors half-hidden in the trees on the opposite shore, and that they were painted for killing.

"Robert—"

He waved me away with his hand.

"Robert, for God's sake. What are they telling you?"

"Be still, Shane. Be still, if you wish to live. I have told them you are not *wabishkizze*."

"Have you taken leave of your senses?"

I did not know much of the Chippewa tongue, but I new that *wabishkizze* are white men, or more specifically, in that place and time, Englishmen.

"Bear with me, Shane. I told them you are a slave of the English, no less than my Pani. I told them you belong to the tribe of the Gallicae, who live in a place like Manitou Island, and hate the English. They may accept you, if you behave yourself."

The blood rushed to my face. I had spent a good part of my life, as I have told you, pretending to be something more than Irish. Now, it seemed, my life hung on whether these savages would accept that an Irishman was something similar to them.

My attention was diverted by the movement of the younger braves. They were slipping away through the brush. I saw some of them blacking their faces with charcoal and taking up firelocks. I knew their purpose. They were going to slaughter Captain Robertson and his men, helpless as fish in a barrel as they struggled with the rapids.

Before I moved, Davers said softly, "Don't do it, Shane. They are dead men. I warned them of this."

Loyalties are terrible things.

I do not know where Sir Robert Davers's loyalties were at that instant. No doubt they were with the Prophet, if such a being existed.

As a youth, I had preened myself on my unerring fidelity to my own interest. But a change had come over me since I had found Johnson and his world. I knew that, whatever it cost me, I would not allow Robertson and Toole and the rest of them to be gunned down without a warning. I did not take time to deliberate all of this. I was on my feet before I knew it, pelting towards the river, bawling to the men on the flatboat.

I saw Robertson's open mouth. I imagined him yelling "Sheer off!" to the pole-men, and "Backsides!" to the fusiliers. I could hardly have heard this in the hellish din that erupted on all sides of me.

I suppose I got Davers killed.

I sensed, more than saw, the savage bringing his firelock up to his shoulder. I spun round to confront him, and had a clear view of Sir Robert as he threw himself between me and the ball.

I think that Davers foresaw what was coming. I do not doubt that he welcomed it.

He had breath left in him when he toppled back, enough for me to catch his last words before the Indians throttled me with a moosehide choker and dragged me away like a restive dog.

"I have turned from none of the six directions—I have faced the Abyss and returned—I have stayed my course on the good body of the mother—My father has winged my soul."

Dearest Shane,

Voltaire said that an Englishman, like a free man, goes
to heaven by whatever route he chooses.

I wonder if Davers is happy at the end of the road
he took.

I could not eat after reading your next pages.

Your

Valerie

13

Eating Fire

WHEN I SCREAMED, ONE of the brutes set his heel on my throat. The dark waterfall of my blood crashed inside my head. My tongue leaped between my teeth like a captive animal trying to break its leash. I could neither speak, nor breathe, nor swallow. I saw my own carcass laid open, as on a slab at the Smithfield market—the lizard coils of the intestines, the black bag of the spleen, the nerves waving at each other like sea anemones. The world was being sucked into a wet blackness, dark within dark. I was going with it, into the belly of the beast.

The pressure on my throat was removed. I came back coughing blood and bile. Naked feet flew up and down, driving wind-gusts that plucked at my ears. They were red and horny as a buzzard's talons, arched high, so heels and toes hardly met the earth. The savages flew over me with the yelping bark of the war-eagle and the downward-slurring, deathbed squeal of the redtail hawk.

"Kya! Kya! Kya!"

"Keeeer-r-r! Keeer-r-r!"

The whir of feathers and claws. Hard, compact muscles

rippling under the shiny casing of grease and blacking, as the serpent's coils. Not birds, but winged serpents. The unspeakable cruelty of the eyes.

"Bonjou', neejee. Regardez-moi. Lookee here."

A squat little figure waded into the circle of my captors. I saw a blur of yellow, set off by quills or dyed moosehair, like a woman's dress, the dull sheen of traders' brooches among the rank hair.

"Lookee here, Whiteface. *Regardez ici*, damn-you-by-God."

I looked up into the dark their bodies made between me and the sun. They had robbed me of the strip of cerulean blue above the river, my lifeline back to the world, laced with those fleecy, scudding, fair-weather clouds that mocked our destiny.

I saw a grinning face, round and flat as a pancake, broken out in green and yellow spots. The earlobes, weighted with silver and tufted with turkey-down, hung down to the collar-bones. Around the neck, a silver cross vied for room with a heap of fetishes and bits of furry animals.

"Regardez, regardez," this apparition sniggered, and rammed an object into my face. I tried to push it away, but my arms were tightly prisoned.

"Oh sweet Jesus."

His skin was still warm. The color had faded from his features, as the blood drained to the back of the head. But he looked very nearly alive, save for the thick clusters of flies at the top of his skull, about the fontanel, where the savages had stripped away a layer of bone, together with hair and skin. The pink-gray membranes were exposed; they pulsed sluggishly with the ghost of an idea. The lips were drawn back over the gums. No, that was not right; the bastards had peeled them away, like the skin of an orange. The eyes. They say you can read prophecy in a dead man's eyes. Robert Davers's eyes were fully open. I could see the whites along the bottom. The irises were the color of wetted ashes; the pupils were cold cinders. They gave back nothing—no image, no epiphany, not even horror. I do not know what Robert Davers felt at the moment of his death. All his features betrayed, what was left of them, was a mild surprise, the expression of a man who has recognized an old acquaintance in an unexpected place. Nothing more. The thing that Yellow Shirt swung by the forelock in front of my nose was loathsome, but untenanted. Whatever Davers had become, he was no longer this.

"Fire in the Sky! Fire in the Sky!" Yellow Shirt screeched and giggled. "*Il a de la chance!* He is the lucky one! You eat fire tomorrow, Whiteface!"

The others pushed him away. One of them seized Davers's head, no doubt for a private trophy. A huge man-mountain who had blacked his face in the design of a bear's paw, the claws raking up across his forehead, grabbed my hair and dragged me to my feet.

They tied my hands behind my back. They used wet rawhide thongs, lashed above the elbows so tight they gouged into the flesh. Bear Face threw a noose around my neck and hauled me along like a dog that must be broken to heel. My master increased his pace to a jog, then a brisk trot. Dazed and weakened, I could not keep up. The noose bit into my neck. I swayed and buckled, gasping for air. I half-ran, half-fell, after the thundering haunches of my captor, wide as calves' bellies.

Yellow Shirt skipped along beside me with a crowd of squaws and children. The boys took it in turns to run up and give me a friendly poke under the ribs with the points of their wooden spears. They rumbled and snapped like wild dogs contesting a bone.

"*Allo, neejee!*" cried Yellow Shirt in his frontier demotic. "You know what name they call you? They call you Annemoosh. They call you Camp Dog."

"My name—" The rawhide sawed at my neck.

"Annemoosh! Annemoosh!" howled that chorus of demons.

"My name—Lieuten—acre—king's service—damn-you-to-hell!"

I clung to my name. What was I without it? A miserable, slavering animal at the end of a leash, the toy for a flat-nosed she-man and a pack of vicious children, the kind you see at home, detaching the wings from flies with loving care, but here turned loose upon men. I had no

sense of direction, except that the river, and all of my life
before this moment, were far behind me. The shadows of
the forest fell thick about me. The trail narrowed to a
mudbrown furrow, snaking around rocks and fallen timber.
My tormentors fell silent. The Indians ran almost noiselessly, their toes turning inward, avoiding the treacherous
roots and brambles on which I stubbed and tore my
clumsy white man's feet. We branched from the trail,
through pathless woods. I stumbled and fell and was
dragged on, half-throttled. Thorns and dry spruce twigs,
sharp as skewers, stabbed through the rents in my clothes.
My heart banged against my breastbone. The hard knot in
my side swelled and swelled, bruising my ribs. I tripped
on a dead stump, hurting my ankle. Good. Let me die now,
in this forest that has eaten the sky.

"Annemoosh!"

My master tugged on my leash. I staggered on.

I am Lieutenant Hardacre, of the Indian Department.

I repeated the words over and over inside my head, like
a yellow lama chanting his mantra. What else did I have
to hold on to?

I am Shane. I am of Ireland, the holy land of Ireland.
Fergus and Cuchulain. The oak-priest, casting dreams. I
fear no man.

"Annemoosh!" Yellow Shirt bounced along beside me.
"Is your heart brave, *wabishkizze*? Ojibwa like brave warriors. Brave ones eat fire many times little bit before spirit
passes over. Brave ones die little bit many days, Annemoosh."

He showed me his teeth. They were very near white.

We came to a place of the dead. The forest ended at a
clearing choked by pokeweed and red sumac. Beyond it,
on a scrubby rise above a swamp, I saw the rough cedar
palisades of an Indian village. There were gaps in the
walls big enough for a stagecoach; through them, I saw the
skeletons of bark lodges gutted by wind or fire.

Bald vultures escorted our progress, tilting and skidding
overhead, flapping their black wings like broken umbrellas. A whole tribe of them was gathered on a ghost ash on

a hillock. When we came nearer, I saw they were standing watch over an open grave. The earth was newly turned, but the bodies were old. Some were merely dry heaps of bones bundled together like kindling. Where meat remained it had turned bottlefly-black or pus-green, and pullulated with alien life. The stink was bad enough to call vermin from Detroit.

"For us?" I croaked at Yellow Shirt, inclining my head towards the burial pit.

He gave no sign of acknowledgment, so I repeated myself in French.

"C'est pour nous?"

"Va t'en!" His tone was harsh. He had turned solemn now. "They hear you. They watch you eat fire, *wabish-kizze.*"

We halted a bowshot away from the palisades, while the natives formed their reception committee. I saw two of Robertson's soldiers—one of them was Conroy, the cauliflower-headed sergeant from Donegal—yoked as I was.

Women came to inspect me. I thought this was a promising sign, especially when Bear Face removed the leash from my neck and propelled me into their midst with a push between my shoulderblades. Lord knows, they were no beauties. There was a withered old granny on a stick whose skin made folds and ridges like a wrinkled apple. The youngest one might have been my mother's age; she was as round as she was broad and smelled like a rabbit left hanging too long. The ringleader was the worst of the bunch. She was a walking buffalo. Those biceps and triceps might have made even Bear Face blanch. Indeed, I would have mistaken her sex save for dried flaps that hung down beneath the filthy calico shirt. Not promising material, but I fancied I knew a thing about older women, and what did a man in my extremity have to lose?

"Your servant, ladies," said I, graciously. "I regret that you see me at something of a disadvantage. I had not hoped to encounter such refinement in the wilderness."

Rabbit Breath greeted this declaration by blowing a prodigious gob of spittle over my cheek. Buffalo Woman stamped on my raw, bleeding feet. Granny laid about my

"Bonjou' neejee," I hailed her in the pidgin of New France. "Can we be of some assistance?"

She had tried to get rid of her burden among the bushes, but the glint of the barrel betrayed it. I reached through a clump of milkweed and retrieved a firelock. The barrel was partly filed through, eighteen inches from the firing pan. I assumed the old crone had dropped her file somewhere else, or concealed it about her shapeless person. It took only an instant for me to grasp the significance of what she, and no doubt her companions, were doing. A sawn-off musket is a devilishly inaccurate weapon, but a damn sight easier to conceal under an Indian blanket than a full-length barrel. I thought of Pontiac's braves, skulking and spying around the *chemin de ronde* and the magazine inside the fort.

"God's breeches! They mean to take Gladwin by surprise the next time they go to the fort for a powwow. We must warn the commandant!"

In fact, it was Joseph who warned Bulldog Gladwin. I have seen a lot of fanciful rot, in other men's writings, about who gave Gladwin the warning that Pontiac was planning to smuggle guns inside the fort in order to make soup of the commandant and the garrison. It has even been stated that the major got his intelligence from a steamy encounter with a Chippewa squaw, which is a pretty good joke if you ever knew the Bulldog. Here is an end to the mystery: we saw native women filing down guns with our own eyes, and you do not need the second sight to know that hunting men don't want sawn-off muskets to shoot squirrels.

I suggested to Captain Robertson that we should turn back. The fort was clearly in imminent danger. At best, we would be cut off. At worst, we would be cut down.

Robertson wouldn't hear of a change of plans. Davers, as always, responded only to his own inner compass.

We went on. For the most part, I traveled with Davers and his Pani in their long birchbark canoe, talking and poling for fish and exploring the inlets. The mild spring weather mocked my fears of approaching catastrophe. The south wind blew soft and warm at our backs as we rounded Pontiac's island, which seemed untenanted. Up-river, the green-black shadows of the woods were splashed with color: yellows and pinks and blues, the pearly stream-ers of laurel. Clouds of pigeons rolled under the boughs of the red maples, taking the new-fallen seeds.

We saw a woodcock paying court to his lady.

Peeeeent!

The bawdy fellow threw back his head and let out a string of raucous screeches.

Peeeeent!

Then he shot straight up into the air. High overhead, he made a new sound, like tinkling glass, as he turned a wide circle. The sound came from under his pinions, as if he had fitted himself with a set of windchimes. I had my gun charged and cocked, but I could not bring myself to pot such a rakish fellow.

For two days and nights, we saw no sign of human life. Davers and I paddled upstream to a village of bark huts shaped like sugar loaves that had been used by Chippewas the summer before. It was deserted. Dead husks of corn blew about the clearing. Bark sheets flapped against the roof poles. A bald-headed vulture squatted on the ruins of the stockade, wrinkling its ugly red neck as it gave us a leisurely inspection.

I felt the immensity of the wilderness all about us. I felt shipwrecked: fragile and infinitely vulnerable in that vast green ocean. As my spirits drooped, Davers's seemed to soar.

He sat among the roots of a white birch and appeared to lose himself somewhere inside it for fully half an hour.

"You don't know life until you have entered the dream of the heartwood," he said. "Higher beings enter the dreaming of a tree and rest there for centuries. The Prophet has told me these things."

He saw my face.

"Ah, Shane, Shane! There is more in heaven and earth than you can ever guess in this lifetime. You don't even know that trees are as individual as people, do you?"

With some difficulty, I got him back to the river. That

was better. I could begin to breathe again. Between his smiling dementia and the encirclement of the forest, I had started to feel I was suffocating. I had to listen to him babbling on for what seemed like hours, on the theme that the groves are God's first churches.

"The Romans cut down the sacred oaks in England, as the papists chopped down the holy groves of Ireland. They were terrified of the spirits they contained, of the gray-eyed druids, priests of oak."

You can imagine the rest.

If you think I am not being sufficiently sympathetic to Davers, you are right. The truth of it is, I could not afford to indulge his point of view, out in those wilds, where the imagination becomes so easily disordered.

We met Indians on the third day—a family of Chippewas in a canoe. We traded bread from the fort and a few twists of tobacco for some of the bright-eyed whitefish they had thrashing about among their thwarts. They were civil, but impassive. Davers talked to them in their own lingo. They affected not to know anything about the movements of Chippewas from Saginaw Bay and Grand River.

Across the broad basin of Lake St Clair, with blue hills rolling away to the west, Robertson's sailors had to fight the fierce currents of the Huron River surging over rapids to hurl its water into the lake.

We came to a neck of land with a sawmill, and a gang of French carpenters milling pine logs. Robertson traded them some flour from our bakery for deermeat and home-made wine. Their leader seemed to be a decent fellow. He took some of us aside and counseled us to turn back. He had heard that a Chippewa war-party was headed our way and was sworn to eat the livers of the English without salt.

Davers said, "Jacques is right. You must go back. I will not have your blood on my hands."

"Confound it," thus Captain Robertson, "we are not your personal bodyguard, Sir Robert! I have a mission to perform on His Majesty's service, and the devil sweep me if I will be deceived by shadows, or a whole army of these cowardly, skulking banditti. We Britons are made of sterner stuff, are we not, Mr Hardacre? By God, if these savages try my patience, I shall give them a taste of Sheffield steel!"

Robertson's confidence in the superiority of his own stock was magnificent in its way. It was a similar arrogance that carried the British flag, usually in the hands of paltry bands of cracks and projectors, from Madras to the slave coasts of Africa. The same bomb-proof vanity led poor General Braddock to march his army, without native scouts, to the slaughter-ground near Fort Pitt, and dull-witted Abercrombie to despatch our finest grenadiers to be spitted like fatted hogs on Montcalm's breastworks beside Lake Champlain.

Davers said to the captain, "So you will not change. You have chosen your own path. It is on your head."

"What the devil do you mean, Sir Robert?" Robertson's bobwig danced on his pink scalp. "What is on my head?"

"What I have foreseen."

The Chippewas were waiting for us at the narrows where the river boils through the opening from Lake Huron. I guessed that there were four hundred of them, pressing down along the sandy beach, which was gunmetal gray with garnet lights.

Davers called over to the flatboat. "Captain Robertson! This is your last chance! I am going on shore to talk with them. I implore you to turn back!"

You may conceive that when I heard Davers's announcement that we were going on shore, I regretted my choice of transportation. Not that it would have made any difference. Captain Robertson staunchly refused to entertain any change in his dispositions. Once he had a plan in his head, it stuck there like a nail. Besides, there was a practical objection—it would be ticklish work, bringing the clumsy flatboat around in those treacherous currents, with a strong likelihood of getting stuck on a bar adding insult to possible injury from the savages. Furthermore, as Robertson yelled back, "The natives look friendly!"

"Hand to God, but they do, your honor!" This came from Sergeant Toole, who was riding on the bateau.

I soon observed the source of his good humor. Women

and children formed the first rank of the Indians along the
beach. The children were beckoning to us, holding up offerings of gleaming trout and whitefish and little *mukaks*
of maple candy. The sugarwood boxes were nankeen yellow. That color haunts my memory.

The older girls, and some of the women, were offering
sweeter enticements. Though their words meant little to
me at the time, their gestures were plain enough for a dotard to comprehend. One native princess thrust her hand
under her deerskin kilt and ground her wide hams. Another fretted her right thumb in her left fist, ogling and
puffing kisses. The best-looking of the bunch waded out
into the river, opened her shirt, and jiggled her tits.

One of the privates on the flatboat could not contain
himself.

"I'm coming, sugarbox. Oh Gawd, I'm coming!"

This brought thunder from his commanding officer.

Davers's mouth was a straight line. As we nosed into
shore, he muttered something that might have been, "They
are dead men."

I do not profess to be a world authority on Indians, but
I did not need Davers to tell me something was amiss. A
trade squaw in liquor may do things that would make a
Covent Garden trollop blush, but you do not see a whole
village of native women behaving like sluts unless there is
a deeper purpose behind it than acquiring a case of jew's
harps or a keg of rum.

"I trust you know what you're doing, Robert," I said to
Davers.

I did not like the way he smiled.

"Do you know any of these people?" I pursued.

I did not catch his answer, if he gave one, because we
were surrounded by a crowd of jabbering Chippewas.
There were warriors among them. I was relieved to see
that, though most of them were half-naked, they were not
painted for war.

I followed Davers onto a rise, where he squatted down
to parley with the chiefs. Captain Robertson, I saw, was
pursuing his course upstream towards the lake. His boatmen were making hard going of it; perhaps their hearts, or

some other portion of their anatomy, had joined the
squaws.

I cannot convey the content of Sir Robert's dialogue
with the Chippewas. I know that they received him with
the outward signs of friendship and respect. They offered
him the calumet, and he held it out to the four quarters,
and to the above and below, before sending a few wisps of
smoke skyward.

I would have taken this as a reassuring sign except that
I noticed a great deal of activity among the bushes farther
upstream, and realized, for the first time, that there were
warriors half-hidden in the trees on the opposite shore, and
that they were painted for killing.

"Robert—"

He waved me away with his hand.

"Robert, for God's sake. What are they telling you?"

"Be still, Shane. Be still, if you wish to live. I have told
them you are not *wabishkizze*."

"Have you taken leave of your senses?"

I did not know much of the Chippewa tongue, but I new
that *wabishkizze* are white men, or more specifically, in
that place and time, Englishmen.

"Bear with me, Shane. I told them you are a slave of the
English, no less than my Pani. I told them you belong to
the tribe of the Gallicae, who live in a place like Manitou
Island, and hate the English. They may accept you, if you
behave yourself."

The blood rushed to my face. I had spent a good part of
my life, as I have told you, pretending to be something
more than Irish. Now, it seemed, my life hung on whether
these savages would accept that an Irishman was something similar to them.

My attention was diverted by the movement of the
younger braves. They were slipping away through the
brush. I saw some of them blacking their faces with charcoal and taking up firelocks. I knew their purpose. They
were going to slaughter Captain Robertson and his men,
helpless as fish in a barrel as they struggled with the rapids.

Before I moved, Davers said softly, "Don't do it, Shane. They are dead men. I warned them of this."

Loyalties are terrible things.

I do not know where Sir Robert Davers's loyalties were at that instant. No doubt they were with the Prophet, if such a being existed.

As a youth, I had preened myself on my unerring fidelity to my own interest. But a change had come over me since I had found Johnson and his world. I knew that, whatever it cost me, I would not allow Robertson and Toole and the rest of them to be gunned down without a warning. I did not take time to deliberate all of this. I was on my feet before I knew it, pelting towards the river, bawling to the men on the flatboat.

I saw Robertson's open mouth. I imagined him yelling "Sheer off!" to the pole-men, and "Backsides!" to the fusiliers. I could hardly have heard this in the hellish din that erupted on all sides of me.

I suppose I got Davers killed.

I sensed, more than saw, the savage bringing his firelock up to his shoulder. I spun round to confront him, and had a clear view of Sir Robert as he threw himself between me and the ball.

I think that Davers foresaw what was coming. I do not doubt that he welcomed it.

He had breath left in him when he toppled back, enough for me to catch his last words before the Indians throttled me with a moosehide choker and dragged me away like a restive dog.

"I have turned from none of the six directions—I have faced the Abyss and returned—I have stayed my course on the good body of the mother—My father has winged my soul."

Dearest Shane,

Voltaire said that an Englishman, like a free man, goes
to heaven by whatever route he chooses.

I wonder if Davers is happy at the end of the road
he took.

I could not eat after reading your next pages.

Your

Valerie

13

Eating Fire

WHEN I SCREAMED, ONE of the brutes set his heel on my throat. The dark waterfall of my blood crashed inside my head. My tongue leaped between my teeth like a captive animal trying to break its leash. I could neither speak, nor breathe, nor swallow. I saw my own carcass laid open, as on a slab at the Smithfield market—the lizard coils of the intestines, the black bag of the spleen, the nerves waving at each other like sea anemones. The world was being sucked into a wet blackness, dark within dark. I was going with it, into the belly of the beast.

The pressure on my throat was removed. I came back coughing blood and bile. Naked feet flew up and down, driving wind-gusts that plucked at my ears. They were red and horny as a buzzard's talons, arched high, so heels and toes hardly met the earth. The savages flew over me with the yelping bark of the war-eagle and the downward-slurring, deathbed squeal of the redtail hawk.

"Kya! Kya! Kya!"

"Keeeer-r-r! Keeer-r-r!"

The whir of feathers and claws. Hard, compact muscles

rippling under the shiny casing of grease and blacking, as the serpent's coils. Not birds, but winged serpents. The unspeakable cruelty of the eyes.

"Bonjou', neejee. Regardez-moi. Lookee here."

A squat little figure waded into the circle of my captors. I saw a blur of yellow, set off by quills or dyed moosehair, like a woman's dress, the dull sheen of traders' brooches among the rank hair.

"Lookee here, Whiteface. *Regardez ici,* damn-you-by-God."

I looked up into the dark their bodies made between me and the sun. They had robbed me of the strip of cerulean blue above the river, my lifeline back to the world, laced with those fleecy, scudding, fair-weather clouds that mocked our destiny.

I saw a grinning face, round and flat as a pancake, broken out in green and yellow spots. The earlobes, weighted with silver and tufted with turkey-down, hung down to the collar-bones. Around the neck, a silver cross vied for room with a heap of fetishes and bits of furry animals.

"Regardez, regardez," this apparition sniggered, and rammed an object into my face. I tried to push it away, but my arms were tightly prisoned.

"Oh sweet Jesus."

His skin was still warm. The color had faded from his features, as the blood drained to the back of the head. But he looked very nearly alive, save for the thick clusters of flies at the top of his skull, about the fontanel, where the savages had stripped away a layer of bone, together with hair and skin. The pink-gray membranes were exposed; they pulsed sluggishly with the ghost of an idea. The lips were drawn back over the gums. No, that was not right; the bastards had peeled them away, like the skin of an orange. The eyes. They say you can read prophecy in a dead man's eyes. Robert Davers's eyes were fully open. I could see the whites along the bottom. The irises were the color of wetted ashes; the pupils were cold cinders. They gave back nothing—no image, no epiphany, not even horror. I do not know what Robert Davers felt at the moment of his death. All his features betrayed, what was left of them, was a mild surprise, the expression of a man who has recognized an old acquaintance in an unexpected place. Nothing more. The thing that Yellow Shirt swung by the forelock in front of my nose was loathsome, but untenanted. Whatever Davers had become, he was no longer this.

"Fire in the Sky! Fire in the Sky!" Yellow Shirt screeched and giggled. "*Il a de la chance!* He is the lucky one! You eat fire tomorrow, Whiteface!"

The others pushed him away. One of them seized Davers's head, no doubt for a private trophy. A huge man-mountain who had blacked his face in the design of a bear's paw, the claws raking up across his forehead, grabbed my hair and dragged me to my feet.

They tied my hands behind my back. They used wet rawhide thongs, lashed above the elbows so tight they gouged into the flesh. Bear Face threw a noose around my neck and hauled me along like a dog that must be broken to heel. My master increased his pace to a jog, then a brisk trot. Dazed and weakened, I could not keep up. The noose bit into my neck. I swayed and buckled, gasping for air. I half-ran, half-fell, after the thundering haunches of my captor, wide as calves' bellies.

Yellow Shirt skipped along beside me with a crowd of squaws and children. The boys took it in turns to run up and give me a friendly poke under the ribs with the points of their wooden spears. They rumbled and snapped like wild dogs contesting a bone.

"*Allo, neejee!*" cried Yellow Shirt in his frontier demotic. "You know what name they call you? They call you Annemoosh. They call you Camp Dog."

"My name—" The rawhide sawed at my neck.

"Annemoosh! Annemoosh!" howled that chorus of demons.

"My name—Lieuten—acre—king's service—damn-you-to-hell!"

I clung to my name. What was I without it? A miserable, slavering animal at the end of a leash, the toy for a flat-nosed she-man and a pack of vicious children, the kind you see at home, detaching the wings from flies with loving care, but here turned loose upon men. I had no sense of direction, except that the river, and all of my life before this moment, were far behind me. The shadows of the forest fell thick about me. The trail narrowed to a mudbrown furrow, snaking around rocks and fallen timber. My tormentors fell silent. The Indians ran almost noiselessly, their toes turning inward, avoiding the treacherous roots and brambles on which I stubbed and tore my clumsy white man's feet. We branched from the trail, through pathless woods. I stumbled and fell and was dragged on, half-throttled. Thorns and dry spruce twigs, sharp as skewers, stabbed through the rents in my clothes. My heart banged against my breastbone. The hard knot in my side swelled and swelled, bruising my ribs. I tripped on a dead stump, hurting my ankle. Good. Let me die now, in this forest that has eaten the sky.

"Annemoosh!"

My master tugged on my leash. I staggered on.

I am Lieutenant Hardacre, of the Indian Department.

I repeated the words over and over inside my head, like a yellow lama chanting his mantra. What else did I have to hold on to?

I am Shane. I am of Ireland, the holy land of Ireland. Fergus and Cuchulain. The oak-priest, casting dreams. I fear no man.

"Annemoosh!" Yellow Shirt bounced along beside me. "Is your heart brave, *wabishkizze*? Ojibwa like brave warriors. Brave ones eat fire many times little bit before spirit passes over. Brave ones die little bit many days, Annemoosh."

He showed me his teeth. They were very near white.

We came to a place of the dead. The forest ended at a clearing choked by pokeweed and red sumac. Beyond it, on a scrubby rise above a swamp, I saw the rough cedar palisades of an Indian village. There were gaps in the walls big enough for a stagecoach; through them, I saw the skeletons of bark lodges gutted by wind or fire.

Bald vultures escorted our progress, tilting and skidding overhead, flapping their black wings like broken umbrellas. A whole tribe of them was gathered on a ghost ash on

a hillock. When we came nearer, I saw they were standing
watch over an open grave. The earth was newly turned,
but the bodies were old. Some were merely dry heaps of
bones bundled together like kindling. Where meat remained it had turned bottlefly-black or pus-green, and pullulated with alien life. The stink was bad enough to call
vermin from Detroit.

"For us?" I croaked at Yellow Shirt, inclining my head
towards the burial pit.

He gave no sign of acknowledgment, so I repeated myself in French.

"C'est pour nous?"

"Va t'en!" His tone was harsh. He had turned solemn
now. "They hear you. They watch you eat fire, *wabishkizze.*"

We halted a bowshot away from the palisades, while the
natives formed their reception committee. I saw two of
Robertson's soldiers—one of them was Conroy, the cauliflower-headed sergeant from Donegal—yoked as I was.

Women came to inspect me. I thought this was a promising sign, especially when Bear Face removed the leash
from my neck and propelled me into their midst with a
push between my shoulderblades. Lord knows, they were
no beauties. There was a withered old granny on a stick
whose skin made folds and ridges like a wrinkled apple.
The youngest one might have been my mother's age; she
was as round as she was broad and smelled like a rabbit
left hanging too long. The ringleader was the worst of the
bunch. She was a walking buffalo. Those biceps and triceps might have made even Bear Face blanch. Indeed, I
would have mistaken her sex save for dried flaps that hung
down beneath the filthy calico shirt. Not promising material, but I fancied I knew a thing about older women, and
what did a man in my extremity have to lose?

"Your servant, ladies," said I, graciously. "I regret that
you see me at something of a disadvantage. I had not
hoped to encounter such refinement in the wilderness."

Rabbit Breath greeted this declaration by blowing a prodigious gob of spittle over my cheek. Buffalo Woman
stamped on my raw, bleeding feet. Granny laid about my

hind end with her stick. This certainly diminished my ardor. I made a sorry show as the ladies clawed off what remained of my clothing. Even so, the theft of my breeches produced a palpable change of mood. Granny, in particular, fell to clucking and twittering. The old slut even presumed to give my ballocks an experimental squeeze.

Yellow Shirt came wobbling up, eager to join in the sport. He exchanged witticisms with my gentle hostesses, of which I can only convey what he deigned to translate for my benefit.

"This one," he pointed at Granny, "she say you got good strong fish, maybe jump high little bit. Maybe you go make baby with her."

The freak twittered like a loon.

There were more exchanges in the native gibberish, illustrated with hand signals any monkey could understand.

Yellow Shirt snorted. "This one say," he indicated Rabbit Breath, "maybe you go to be *my* husband."

He stuck out his belly and ground his hips in front of me, causing general merriment.

"Bugger off!" I was in a dangerous mood. "God's pistols—"

Crrrk-crrrk-crrrk-crrrk!

It might have been a dozen rattlesnakes, rising up in the long grass in the same instant to lash out their warning. That peremptory signal, cracking and hissing, cut short our entertainments. With speed and precision astonishing in a creature of her girth, Buffalo Woman felled Yellow Shirt and set about smearing me with a lump of soft charcoal. From the rapture that these motions commanded from the rest of the savages, I understood that I had nothing to look forward to.

Crrrk!

The rattle snapped again, close to my ear, and I felt a sudden chill at the back of my neck. I turned as far as I was able and saw the most frightful man I expect to see this side of Hades.

A nose that could split firewood jutted out from a face that ceased to be human when its owner turned his profile. His paintwork was elaborate beyond the dreaming of the

Palais Royal. From one side, he was the image of a cruel,
raptorial bird, from the other, a carp about to devour a
lesser fish. His eyes, head on, burned as live coals. A
storm of white hair blew about his shoulders. The beaks of
decapitated birds bobbed along the hard ridge of his forehead. The wing feathers of larger birds—hawk and raven,
eagle and owl—waved from the gables of his headgear. A
curious cape, a patchwork of skins of various animals,
hung off his shoulder. His belt was a writhing thicket of
rattlesnake skins. A little drum was suspended over one
hip; it bore the design of a horned figure with wings.
Among his many pouches and amulets was a sack made
from the skin of a human hand; the thumb remained intact.

In one hand, he brandished his rattle. With the other, he
clutched a staff as twisted and misshapen as his own form.
He moaned a dreary dirge that sounded even worse than
the Mohawk songs. The other Indians seemed in awe of
him. They gave him space. They kept their eyes on the
ground when he shuffled near them.

He touched my sternum—or perhaps I only imagined it.
I must have imagined the shock that passed through my
body, as if I had been brushed by lightning.

"Who in hell was that?" I demanded of my interpreter,
when our visitor had passed on his way.

"Wabeno," said Yellow Shirt, nodding his head. "Very
powerful one. Many *jebi* go with him. He says you make
jebi happy. *Jebi* very hungry since many moons."

Had I listened to Davers more carefully, I would have
remembered that the *wabeno* is the Master of Fire, a sorcerer of a particularly dangerous and often malevolent
kind. I did not know that *jebi* are ghosts, and the only
ghosts I had seen were on stage.

I suppose the *wabeno* had come to shrive us, in a manner of speaking. The reception committee was ready along
the track up to the village that must have been abandoned
many seasons past and resurrected in our honor. Men,
women and children, in no apparent order, had formed
themselves up in a double file, leaving a narrow path between. They had armed themselves with whatever weapons took their fancy—split poles, clubs, digging sticks,

knives, and the heavy brass-stemmed pipe-tomahawks the traders sold to the natives in such abundance.

I saw three or four survivors from the flatboat, including Sergeant Toole, who had a Chippewa woman for his common-law wife. Whatever she had taught him of her nation's customs did not avail him here.

They took Toole first. He had lost his bobwig. Perhaps they liked the flame-red color of the stubble that was left on that sooty, bulging head.

The Indians stamped on the ground as if they meant to shake the world to its core.

"Good luck to you, Mick!" I bawled to him.

I doubt whether Toole heard me through the howls and the drums and the pounding feet. I saw him brace himself and drop his chin to his breastbone. Good man. He charged among the Indians like a bull. Who would have thought he could run like that? He was halfway to the gate, his meaty buttocks rolling like a pacer's. He was going to make it. No.

Buffalo Woman brought him down with a chopping blow at the base of the neck. What was that in her paw? An axe? A hammer?

But the sergeant was a game one. He was on his knees, he was willing himself up.

"Come on, Mick!" I yelled, as if we were in Phoenix Park. "Ten to one you'll do it!"

I saw Toole's mouth open and shut. The natives were jabbing and poking, goading him like picadors around a little Spanish bull. A boy no higher than my belly-button jumped out with a gun—no, a fowling-piece, perhaps the one Davers had with him in the canoe. He rammed the muzzle up against Toole's side. Did they mean to let him die so quickly? I saw the belch of smoke.

I heard Toole's wail, keening above the Indian death shouts—

"Holy Mary Mother of God—"

I saw him slump forward, black treacle spilling out from below his armpit.

The natives carried him face down like a drowned man

through the gap in the palisades. I did not know whether
he was dead or alive. I tried to find the words of a prayer.

In nomine Patris et filii et Spiritus sancti.

In extremis, every Irishman remembers the words of the
Roman prayers, or older words, from the time when there
was no time.

I am a tear the sun lets fall.

Now they were taking me off. I won't disgrace you,
Mick Toole. Lend me your guts.

But I lacked both Toole's doggedness and Davers's res-
ignation. If all the life that remained to me was that noisome corridor into hell, then I meant to squeeze some last
dregs of satisfaction out of it. I would not go like a damp-
eyed ox, tamely treading the gangway to the butcher's
mallet.

So, when Yellow Shirt and the sour-faced ruffian who
stood guard over me shoved and kicked me along Toole's
path, I broke from them and ran outside the lines. I hurled
myself on the first man who came after me. He was a sinewy young brave, greased and slippery, but I got him by
the throat and wrestled his war club away from him. I
heard bones crunch as I twisted his arm up behind his
back; I hope I broke it. He sank his fangs into my left
hand. He made a fair bid to worry my middle fingers off
before stronger hands wrenched us apart. I struck out with
the club, and brought down a shaven-headed specimen
with a necklace of bones. They got the club away from
me. I used my fingers for knives, gouging into eye-
sockets, stabbing behind windpipes.

I was no longer the man who had boarded a ship with
Davers. I had never heard of Drury Lane. I was something
feral, a thing of teeth and claws, driven by the stench of
blood. I drew gasps and hisses—the natives count it a
grave dishonor for a man to cry out in pain—and the hot
spurt of blood across my cheekbone. I was on fire. I was
howling the old words, the ones my anglicized family had
long forgotten. I did not know it until the silence fell and
I found myself alone on my haunches on the beaten earth
inside the circle of my enemies, foaming with sweat and
blood, screaming the name of an ancient hero. Of Cuchu-

lain whose wrath in battle blazed so fierce that when his kinsmen set him in a tub of cold water afterwards to quell the fever, the liquid boiled into bubbles as big as your fist.

Confused by the stillness and the red fog in front of my eyes, I waited for the next assault.

The circle opened, and Bear Face walked through.

"Very well, you whoreson. I am ready for you. Come and take me if you can!"

His ugly mug was void of expression. He flicked his wrist, and the thong in his hand leaped out and took me by the throat. The next instant, I was laid out in the dirt.

Bear Face padded over and put his hind leg on my belly. He made a little coughing sound that seemed to rise out of his gut and brought grunts of approval from our audience. He pulled on my noose. He might have put a hole through my lungs.

My master.

Do you know that since I returned from America I have never *once* put a dog on a leash?

They took me to the House of Severed Heads, though of course it was not until I was better versed in their tongue that I was able to interpret its name. It was the grandest building in the village but had fallen into disrepair, like the rest. Over one half, the roof gaped open to the sky. At this end, they set up the poles. Three of them. Toole was tied to the one in the middle. A Yorkshire fusilier—I learned his name was Plumb—and I were on either side.

"Just like Calvary," I remarked in a poor attempt to recruit our spirits. "Plumb and I, I'm afraid, are the thieves."

"Faith, and it's no time to be blaspheming, saving your honor, Mr Hardacre," says Toole.

"Quite right, Sergeant." I was chastened. "No offense meant, to be sure."

The wound under Toole's armpit looked frightful. Gangrene could not be far off, but this was hypothetical, since the natives plainly did not intend any man among us to die from infection. It seemed that the boy who had drilled Toole with the fowling-piece had loaded only with powder.

This, I am sure, was no oversight; it is not their way to allow a captured enemy a simple death.

There were piles of firewood thoughtfully stacked like stepped pyramids near the base of each post.

Fires were already blazing in pits scooped out of the dirt floor of the lodge. Acrid billows of smoke pained my eyes, although the roof overhead was open. It is not surprising that native herbalists know twenty simples for treating sore eyes; they need them. The warmth, or the prospect of fresh meat, had brought a profusion of animal life. Mangy yellow dogs licked at the wounds in my feet and my left hand; gnats and mosquitoes dined on my naked skin. Something was trying to bore into my inner ear.

At the far end of the lodge, shadow-giants leaped and cavorted on the bark walls, above the heads of the native potentates who squatted on rude benches, where they had a clear view of the press of young braves and hooting squaws who formed an elongated noose that enclosed us.

They brought punkwood and a flaming splint and ignited the fire beside Toole. The color red has a special significance for the natives of the New World. It is not only the color of blood and war; it is the color of rebirth. I suspect that, once again, Sergeant Toole's carroty curls had won him the dubious distinction of going ahead of us on the long trail.

He prayed, and I tried to pray with him, envious of his certainties.

He looked up and, following his gaze, I seized on a fugitive hope. Suppose it were to rain. Suppose the skies opened, like a scene from the Old Testament, and the Lord of Hosts quenched the fires of the heathen while he punished them with the fury of his lightnings.

Sorry, Mick.

The sky was clear and full of stars. The Dog Star winked red. It seemed very near.

They loosed Toole's bonds. They paid out two yards of rawhide and hitched him to the stake by the neck once again. They made him dance around it like a bear in the pit at Hockley-in-the-Hole.

The warriors made room for a very old woman, tiny and

shrunken. With her hair tied back in a bun and her modest
shirt-dress of mazarin blue with embroidered flowers, she
looked tidy enough for a tea-party in Sir William's parlor.
She was chattering away to herself, or the other natives,
wagging her head. It was wonderful how her smiles lit up
her face; she might once have been pretty.

She petted Toole's arm. She inspected the black wound
under his armpit. She seemed angry about it; she spoke
sharply to the Indian men, pointing and scowling. They
jumped as if they had received a blow.

Toole exchanged a few words with her. He was smiling.
The woman was holding a dried herb under his nose; perhaps it was only sweetgrass. The braves fetched her a kettle of broth. She spooned the soup into the captive's mouth
with a ladle, as if she were succoring a baby.

Good for you, Mick Toole. She's taken a shine to you.
Maybe she'll adopt you. She looks like a medicine
woman; she can fix your wounds. Look, they're bringing
her something for you now.

Reverently, Bear Face approached the old lady. He offered her a tool as daintily as a waiter presenting a chilled
fork on a napkin. It was a hatchet. They must have it
warming for hours in one of the firepits. The blade glowed
blood orange.

Cooing and smiling, Wind Weaver—I may as well give
these natives the names by which I came to know them—
took the axe by the handle and went to Toole. He backed
away from her, of course, but some braves ran up and pin-
ioned him. I watched the woman press the flat of the blade
against Toole's side, and hold it there. I heard the hiss of
seared flesh, under his screams.

"Sing, Mick!"

I bawled the first ditty that sprang to my lips. It was a
favorite at Fort Johnson. I can still hear Sir William, Guy
and the Butlers killing the verses together with a bowl of
shrub.

Sing didro sing bobro
sing Gra-ania Wai-ll—

I sang unaccompanied. Maybe Plumb, being a Yorkshire-man, did not know the words of the old Irish ballad, though I had heard our lobsterbacks murdering it drunk under the ramparts of Detroit. Maybe Toole was beyond hearing. The women were dabbing at his wounds and bruises with firebrands and hot metal, with the facial expressions of solicitous nursemaids.

"Sing, damn you!"

I bellowed the chorus again.

> Sing didro sing bobro
> sing Gra-ania Wai-ll
> The fox in the trap
> we took by the tail—

Now Plumb took up the refrain, unsteady, but doing his bit. Good lad. Women and braves together began a shuffle-dance around Toole. They flapped their arms. Each fist held a skinning knife or a burning splint.

I did not want to look any more. I tilted my head back as far as my collar would let me. I saw a dark ribbon of smoke curling up through the hole in the roof. It was gray against the inky dark between the stars. Wait. There was someone—some *thing*—squatting on the rooftrees, drinking in the odor of burned meat.

Davers said that earthbound spirits hover close to the cooking fires of the living.

What piffle. My mind must be going. It was one of those native brats. Or a night bird. That's it. An owl. Keen, unwinking eyes, useless in daylight. Strange how the thing reminded me of the sorcerer—the *wabeno*.

"Oh Christ, sir." Plumb's sobbing called me back. "That poor Mick. That miserable bleeding sod."

I looked. Buffalo Woman had a grip on Toole's wrist. She leaned over it, the way I might lean to tickle the inside of a woman's palm with my tongue—it's a trick that rarely fails, believe me—except she had got his thumb between her jaws. She ground her teeth, back and forth, back and forth, in no great hurry. The blood spilled over her chin. She must have gnawed through the bone, because

she put her hand to her mouth and extracted Toole's
thumb. No. It was still attached by the sinew. She drew it
away gently, lovingly, like an angler on the bank of a
troutstream. The sinew stretched to a length I would not
have believed without seeing it. The monster wound it
around Toole's forearm, like thread on a spool.

> So fill up your bumpers
> and drink without fail
> Success to the sons of
> great Grania Waill

I do not know if the words came out of my mouth, or were
merely banging around inside my skull.

It is not death that is terrible, said Davers. It is the process of dying.

Grania Waill was a pirate woman, tougher than her men.

I cannot say how many hours they took to kill Sergeant
Toole. I know he clamored for death many times before it
was granted to him. When the Indians warmed to their
work, they operated with the slow precision of a surgeon
performing a vivisection for the edification of his students.
They wanted a conscious patient. Each time Toole fainted,
they paused to bring him round. They jollied him along
with their rare sense of humor.

"Uncle is cold. He needs warming."

"Our friend is a leaky canoe. He is full of holes. Quick.
We must caulk him up!"

They fed and watered him. They gave him cornmush
and rum-shrub pilfered from our boats, which of course
his stomach could not hold. Later, with the airs of a courtesan feeding her lover grapes, they filled his mouth with
strips of his own flesh.

Toole was still alive when Katchetosh, his master, drew
a circle on his head with the point of a knife and lifted the
scalp with his teeth. I hope, for Toole's sake, that his spirit
had passed over before the savages set to measuring the
length of his entrails.

Do you really wish to know more?

If so, you may seek out the vile reveries of the infamous

Marquis, or of others perverse enough to revel in horrors they have only imagined. You will get nothing more from me on the subject of Sergeant Toole's death. I had to halt my pen just now, and take a long stroll on the terrace. When the memory of that night returns to me, I still fall to violent shakes and morbid fevers, as if in the grip of a quatern ague.

I suppose that in our age, no man, however pacific, however shrinking, is entirely a stranger to the rituals of public death. I have witnessed burnings and hangings and beheadings; I have seen a poor wretch broken on the wheel at the Châtelet and an alleged traitor drawn and quartered at Tyburn. But I have never seen, nor hope to see, cruelties equal in refinement to those inflicted on captives consigned to execution by the natives of North America.

I have heard well-meaning persons, who have never set foot outside a city and know books better than men, dismiss native cruelty as the invention of land-sharks and cowherds. I encountered kindness and wisdom, even poetry and beauty, in the life of the Indians. At one stage in my life, tutored by Sir William, I constructed apologias for native savages. I quoted the stern rebuke of Moses to Phinehas, when he returned from battle to report that he had neglected to slaughter all the women and children of Midian together with the men. I reasoned that in proportion to the might of arms and population of our European empires, the Indian nations were little peoples on the edge of extinction. What were their cruelties compared with the deliberate genocide plotted against them by some of our most distinguished citizens? When Sir Jeffrey Amherst and Colonel Bouquet canvassed a scheme to exterminate unruly savages by circulating hospital blankets infected with smallpox, who are we to call the natives inhuman? Then, too, I came to realize that the Indians are better judges of human behavior than many of our strategists. By calculated atrocities, they seek to terrify their opponents into instant flight or submission. In this way, they try to win their wars without having to fight anything we would recognize as a pitched battle. It is the *intimacy* of torture that is so terrible to us. It may be debated whether, in the larger scheme of things, it is more cruel to skin a few prisoners than to march a great body of unwilling young men into an open field to the harmony of fife and drums, to stand up and be knocked down like ninepins.

I have even argued—and once had a pot of scalding toddy flung at my head for so doing—that native cruelty is the less reprehensible because Indians inflict no punishment on others that they do not school their own braves to endure.

But if any man had presumed to talk to me like this on the night I watched Sergeant Toole eat fire, I would have knocked him down, had my wrists been free. I might even have been willing to cut out his liver, as I saw the Chippewas do to Toole. I would have given everything I possessed to smoke the liver of every man and woman in that House of Severed Heads.

In the pink dawn, I watched one of the chiefs carve a hole through Toole's ribcage. He ripped out the heart and held it up, steaming, to greet the sun, before he dropped it down his gullet.

15th January

My dear Shane,

What does it mean, to wake from your dream and discover you are still dreaming? This happened to me last
night, not once, but six or seven times. I was with
you, my skin a web of nerve endings, as we lay together. You were gentle and knowing, serving my time
and rhythms. You were tireless. You served me again
and again, never tiring or wilting, until I cried out for
joy and mercy, "Where is the bone?"

Then I realized our position was impossible. You
were a young buck, not twenty years old, the hair on
your face still a fine, silky down. You were as Peg
Walsingham must have known you, damn her good
fortune.

At that moment, I woke, knowing myself deceived by
a dream. I never knew the pleasure of entertaining
you between bedsheets until you had kissed good-bye
to sixty summers, and your vanity required a corset as
well as a peruke.

Then I saw you across the room, writing at my
secretary by candlelight. Scratch, scratch. I can still
hear the strokes of your goose-feather quill. I was so
glad to have you with me, even in this sagging flesh,
gone pouchy under the eyes, swathed in a velvet
wrapper, that I flung myself on your neck, kissing
and stroking.

You put down your foul black Brazilian cheroot, and
peeled off your spectacles. I remembered, in that moment, that I had a bone to pick. How could you put
down the horrors of your last chapter where any innocent might read them? I do not doubt that the savages
who captured you were as bloody or sadistic as you

make them out to be, but must we know all the grisly details? Can you not leave something to the imagination? And what are their cruelties, in any event, compared to what people of our stock have done to our own fellows? My father spoke to me often of the butcheries in Ireland, under the yoke of Elizabeth and Cromwell. Of children spiked on bayonets, of good men quartered by the violence of horses, of true priests harried and spitted by roistering drunken louts. Such memories live in both our bloodlines. And it is a tale known to others. All Scotland remembers the carnage after Culloden, when a fat prince triumphed over clansmen who had only clubs and claymores to match his cannon, and women and girls were ravished and disembowled, among the smoking ruins of their cottages, for a hundred miles on either side.

Whom do you serve by drenching us in the blood of a few Britons captured by Indians, on land that was never theirs?

I said these things to you, while you clouded the lenses of your spectacles with your breath and wiped them off with a kerchief.

Then I realized I was only dreaming again, with Sir Henry snoring at my elbow in the bed.

And woke in the thickest woods I ever saw. I thought I was in the oak forests of the Dordogne, on a summer jaunt, and marveled that I had dreamed myself back in bed with Henry. Then I entered a clearing, and saw my mistake. A cruel warbird shot down at my head from the sky, in a blur of tawny feathers. He sank his talons into my hair, which I wear piled up as high as a grenadier's bearskin, according to the fashion. (Neither you nor Sir Henry would expect anything less!) I saw his yellow eye, very close to my own. We struggled together. We rolled in sun-dried grass. I thought I was fighting for my life. Yet I did not wish to harm this bird—hawk or eagle, I cannot say—because he was somehow connected with you.

With that thought, I woke from this fierce struggle. I found myself, to my great relief, back with you. I saw you replace your reading glasses on the bridge of your nose. You smiled at me indulgently.

I told you my dream of the warbird, and my feeling that there was·a message here of the most urgent nature. Something tearing at my head, that I cannot yet understand. What can it be? I asked for your counsel.

Then I remembered: This cannot be. You are in Sintra, dipping your sweet face in the inhalations—or exhalations—offered by some Portuguese maid with hairy armpits.

I woke with relief. I resolved to waste no more time with chimeras. I went about the business of the day. I discussed the luncheon menu with the cook. I interviewed three candidates for the assistant butler's office, which has fallen vacant due to extracurricular involvement with the upstairs maid. I even went to Covent Garden to supervise the purchase of our kitchen greens. While I was looking at cabbages, a tattooed brute leered at me and said he had the pick of the crop. He beckoned me behind the display with a crooked finger. Despite my better judgement, I followed.

He unveiled his prize. It was the head of a man, with the most prominent features peeled away. I screamed when I saw the bloodied eye-sockets.

And woke to Sir Henry's hacking and fussing, as he busied himself with the chamber-pot. He demanded to know if I was having a seizure. I pulled his whiskers, to assure myself, by his yelps, that I was finally out of my dreams.

Dreams within dreams, nested like those dreadful Russian matriosha dolls. I blame you for this giddying night, Shane. You and your horror stories. Am I quite mad? Will you explain to me what is happening?

Can you assure me I am not dreaming, as I write these lines?

In dreams,

Valerie

Sintra

4th February

Dearest Valerie,

Sorry about your rocky night. I experienced something
like after consuming bad shellfish at Cascais. Or perhaps
it was a bad bottle of champagne.

I cannot help you with your question about dreaming and waking.

I have heard that the swamis of India say this life is
a dream from which we wake up when we die. That
would make birth the first of our false awakenings,
if that makes any sense at all.

I expect Davers would know. I'm not sure whether
I'll wake from this life into a sleep without dreams,
or a bloody nightmare, or a paradise where I can
pleasure you as a perennial twenty-year-old. (I stiffen at
the prospect, I really do.) But if I wake up after dying,
I'd like Robert to be waiting for me. One always
wants to be properly introduced.

Your own

Shane

14

Pontiac's Daughter

THEY CUT ME DOWN from the hickory pole and kicked me into a corner to rest. I expect they wanted me fresh for my own fire-dance. They had my arms bound so tight that the cord was hidden in the flesh. Stealthily, I rolled on my left side and tried to strip the thong from my right arm, willing it to slip over the bulge of my elbow. The pain was terrible. I carried away my own skin and flesh with my fingers. But I had the cord over my elbow. It slipped easily down my forearm to the wrist. I gritted my teeth for one last effort.

Yellow Shirt, the *agokwa*, the she-man, bounced up and down on his heels beside me, giggling.

"You want your hands, Whiteface? *Voyez, voyez.* I give you your hands."

He whipped out a long blade and severed the cord.

He held the tip against the septum of my nose while I chafed my wrists, trying to restore circulation. Where the thong had bitten deep, my arms were a nasty shade of purplish-black, like trodden grapes.

Yellow Shirt rocked and snickered.

He put the knife away and offered me a bowl of soup.
"Eat! Eat! You must be strong for tonight, *wabishkizze.*"

I was consumed by a ravening hunger. You may wonder
how I could find appetite after what I had witnessed. The
body has its own wisdom and will not be denied.

I grabbed for the ladle. My hands were not steady
enough to hold it. I lowered my face over the bowl, and
lapped at the broth like a dog.

"Annemoosh!" Yellow Shirt crooned with delight.
"Camp dog!"

The soup was greasy and thick with chunks of meat.
From the sweetness, I guessed I was feeding on bearmeat,
or on salt pork taken from the flatboat. A larger chunk
bobbed up to the surface of a gray-brown stew. It was a
man's ear, flapping open where a knife or a hatchet blade
had narrowly failed to cut it in two..

I vomited like a child. Wave after wave of warm puke
washed up from my belly to my eyebrows and spewed for
a prodigious distance over the dirt floor of the House of
Severed Heads.

Yellow Shirt hooted. "You no like English meat? Take!
It will make you strong!"

He tried to cram the severed ear between my teeth.

I shoved him away and spat in his face.

"The devil sweep you! I'll see you in hell!"

I do not know which of my companions provided my
breakfast. It may have been Captain Robertson or Sergeant
Toole. It was not Robert Davers. For that, at least, I give
thanks. The she-man told me that they gathered up
Davers's parts and buried him as a native, flexed like an
infant in the womb, facing the Path of Souls, because he
was a dream-hunter, and the natives treat dreamers—even
those of hostile nations—with a solicitude denied to common men.

The Chippewas got drunk on the rum-shrub Captain
Robertson had brought on the boat. I was obliged to watch
them dancing and capering in the clothes of my friends.
Their cannibal feast lasted all day. They ate the men slain
on the river boiled or roasted.

My master, whose native name was Kakaik, or Little Hawk, brought me a rumpsteak on a spit.

The she-man translated. "Very good to eat. He say you must eat. You must learn the customs of real men. You must learn the *goût sauvage*. You are never going back to the English."

This was the first hint that I was not, after all, to share the fate of sergeant Toole. I did not feel any sense of liberation, with that black-faced savage leering over me with a half-raw hunk of a British soldier on a stick.

"Tell this fellow I decline to dine on my friends."

They jabbered and cackled, and finally allowed me to fast. Buffalo Woman, the harpy who had gnawed off Toole's thumb, came with some of the women. They yoked me and dragged me down to the river, where they dunked me repeatedly and washed me clean of blood and ash. They indicated, by signs and shoves, that I was to be Wind Weaver's slave. They took me into the woods and heaped my back with firewood until I was reduced to creeping on all fours, which brought more ribaldry.

"Annemoosh! Annemoosh!"

I am not sure whom I should thank for my reprieve. The adoption of captives to replace dead sons or husbands is, of course, commonplace among the Indians. But my adoption came later, when I became the property of another nation. I believe that Pontiac, counseled by Saint Angé, had sent word among the tribes that British prisoners were to be held as hostages. This no doubt explains why a few of the survivors, including young John Rutherfurd, who was taken by a band led by Perwash, a war chief of the Chippewas, were spared from eating fire.

As soon as I had recovered a little strength, my mind turned to thoughts of escape. We were closely watched, and there was no chance of communicating with the other English captives. I did not even know whether Detroit had fallen, and the fort was eighty miles off by my calculations, through woods full of hostile Indians. Even if I could break away from my captors, I would need a boat and provisions.

I saw my chance in the apparent liberty of Redwing,

Davers's Pani slave. Perhaps because he was a fellow Indian, the Chippewas allowed him to come and go at will.

At night, when I was lying tethered to my spot just inside the door of Wind Weaver's hut, where anyone entering or leaving could give me a friendly kick in the kidneys, I risked whistling to Redwing as he sauntered past. He idled over towards me and squatted down, with his back to the bark screen between us, and busied himself filling a pipe.

Wind Weaver and her children appeared to be sleeping sound. The old woman's breath, through her open mouth, sounded like distant surf.

"Redwing. Help me get to the fort, and I'll see you have ten dollars and all the rum you can use."

The Pani made a noncommittal grunt.

I improved my offer a little, invoked the names of Davers and Sir William Johnson, and coaxed noises from him that I took for assent to my plan. He was to smuggle me a knife and lay hands on a canoe and as much fish and cornmeal as he could muster up—I did not trust the meat around that slaughter-house—and lie in wait for me at midnight the following day.

Wind Weaver worked me all day like a dog, hauling firewood, trawling for perch and whitefish in the river.

After dark, Redwing slipped me the knife. I could only guess at the time. I lay flat on my back for a long while after I cut through my bonds. The lodge was still. I waited for my heartbeat to settle before I crawled under the deerskin flap and crept between the Indian huts, hugging the shadows. Several warriors were gathered in a noisy circle around a drunken brawl or a game with deer buttons for dice that the Chippewas call bugger-sag, or something like. They had no eyes for me.

I was out among the hemlocks.

WhooooOOM!

A boom like a coehorn mortar exploded close at hand. I dropped down, shivering with fear more than the chill in the night air. I sensed a small bird flapping away through the dark. The natives have a superstitious awe of a kind of wren that has a habit of exploding out of hollow stumps.

They say it is an evil portent. If that is what I came across in the hollow of the night, I must say they are right.

It took me half an hour or more to find our place of rendezvous, downriver from the camp, below the place of the ambush.

There was no sign of the canoe, or the Pani.

An arm of the forest reached out and took me by the throat.

The mountainous form of Kakaik, my master, loomed above me like the death of all hope.

They changed my sleeping arrangements. Kakaik cut a thin wooden post. He planted one end in the floor of the hut and tied the other to the rooftrees. He made a notch in the pole with his hatchet, two feet off the ground. He signed for me to lie on my back. He seized my right leg, a little above the ankle, and thrust it into the notch. He lashed it between the pole and another piece of wood like a splint. I could not turn on my side. I was obliged to lie there like a cripple with my leg in the air and my hands tied behind my back, with the end of the cord secured under my master's body.

Yellow Shirt amused himself by tickling the sole of my foot and the underside of my knee with a turkey feather. He told me that Redwing had been allowed to go home to his own people, somewhere far to the west, in return for his treachery.

In case my new condition was not sufficient to break my spirit, Kakaik gave me a lecture in strategy. With the aid of some pebbles, he showed me that Detroit was closely besieged by four Indian nations. He deployed more pebbles, to show the war-parties that had been sent to the mouth of Lake Erie and beyond to cut off any relief expeditions from Niagara, and to wipe out the smaller outposts at Sandusky and Presqu'Isle.

"Before the new moon," he told me via the she-man, "there will not be one Englishman left alive at Detroit."

His lecture afforded me some hope—at least Gladwin had not been taken by surprise. Joseph must have reached him in time. But I knew that the situation of Detroit was desperate. At the time I left, the garrison had provisions for only three weeks. Without help from Niagara or from the French about the fort, a doubtful quantity, Gladwin's men would soon be reduced to hunting rats.

Kakaik showed me the remains of Robertson's men. The Chippewas threw some of their mutilated bodies into the river, to float downstream and give heart to our men. Mangy yellow dogs fought over the bones of others.

The women shaved my head, leaving me a tuft on the crown and two wretched locks hanging over my face, which they daubed with red and yellow paint until I looked as if I was broken out with a peculiarly virulent form of the pox. They dressed me in a breechclout and gave me a blanket which appeared to have been fouled by every dog in the encampment.

I came down with the bloody flux which weakened me so much that for several days I could neither stand nor walk.

"You lucky, Whiteface!" shrieked the she-man. "Chippewa don't eat man who dies with bad *merde au cul.*"

The conjurer, that hell-hound I encountered before on my way to the encampment, came and danced a jig over me.

He inspected my palm and jabbed at the lifeline.

"He say," thus Yellow Shirt, my indispensable interpreter, "you come soon to this place where wolves and vultures are gathered to pick at your bones."

You may conceive what this did for my humor. At least I was spared a personal demonstration of the witchdoctor's skill with his eagle bones. I did observe him ministering to some of the natives who were ill. Moaning and shaking, he would crouch over them, clamp a bone to chest or belly and suck away like a thirsty Irishman in a tavern. He would stumble away, pretending to have extracted the hidden cause of the disease. He would spit out a foul, bloodied mess of white stuff like a wriggling worm. My guess is that he performed this trick by concealing a bit of fluff next to his gum and biting on his tongue to produce the blood.

Davers, no doubt, would say that I did not observe what was really going on, because I saw only with my eyes. I

did observe that all the natives lived in holy terror of the
sorcerer. Their intention, it soon became plain, was to join
up with Pontiac's horde around the fort. But they did not
decamp until the conjurer held a consultation with his spirits. He had himself bound hand and foot and carried inside
a tent of skins with a small hole left open to the sky at the
top. In due course, we heard snarling and barking and
snuffling from inside, as if a whole menagerie of wild
beasts were worrying over a bone. These were followed by
a soft yapping, like a puppy-dog that has lost his way,
which was received with great jubilation by the natives,
because they believed this was the spirit of the Great Turtle come to counsel them. I will not tax your patience with
the rest of it. I gather that their bloody mission was
approved by this higher authority. When the tent was
opened, the sorcerer was revealed, free of his bonds,
which were discovered, with expressions of wonderment,
on the far side of the clearing; I could have made use of
this trick in Wind Weaver's lodge. The conjurer was rewarded with presents, and the war chiefs were licensed to
go downriver, on condition they strangle two misfortunate
white dogs and offer them to the spirits of running water.

A four-day voyage brought us to Parent's Creek, which
will always be remembered as Bloody Run, for reasons I
shall presently describe, some distance above the fort.
Here we disembarked. I had a distant view of smoking
ruins and the charred frames of houses and barns outside
the stockade. I learned later that most of this destruction
had been wrought by Bulldog Gladwin in his efforts to
deny cover to Indian attackers as they made runs towards
the fort with their fire-arrows. Fire, next to starvation, was
the principal danger for the defenders, since most of the
houses inside the walls are roofed with thatch.

I could see Dandy Cuillerier's house, as busy as an inn,
with Frenchmen and Indians coming and going. I paused
to see if I could catch a glimpse of Angélique, wondering
if she could do anything for me. Wind Weaver fell on me
with a paddle and gave me a hard drubbing that left my
shoulders raw.

The Ottawas seemed to have moved their whole village

across the river. While the Chippewa war chiefs went to
confer with Pontiac, the women set me to work construct-
ing new bark houses or pounding corn in a pestle until my
hands were a mass of blisters.

The Indians took time from their military maneuvers to
play loud, violent games of lacrosse, hurling a hard ball at
each other's heads and sometimes, for diversion, at mine.

My master loved to show me off during these entertainments.

"Look at my little white man! Look at Annemoosh, my
camp dog!"

Kakaik took me with him on a visit to Pontiac's grand
encampment which stood a little way back from the river,
screened by a swamp from the guns of our men-of-war.
Fresh scalps, dressed with eagle feathers, hung from poles
before the council-house. I saw several Frenchmen. One of
them was Saint Ange. He was wearing the white dress regimentals of an officer of the Regiment of Roussillon.

I hailed him and asked him if he would help me.

"Je le regrette beaucoup," he said, with a little bow.
"You are the guest of one of our allied nations. Your disposition depends on their pleasure. I have argued for temperance. You are not alone. And when the fort is taken,
which will not be long from now, I assure you, you will
have a good deal of company."

I called him a grasshopper out of hell—I never forget a
ripe insult—and he gave me another bow.

To my surprise and initial delight, I found Captain
Campbell and Lieutenant McDougall of the 55th among
the Ottawas. I say delight, because I assumed that they had
come from the fort as an embassy. I found that this was indeed the case, but that Pontiac had cheated by retaining
them as hostages.

Donald Campbell told me the story of what had happened at the fort after I went upriver with Davers. Pontiac
had turned up with three hundred warriors in tow, all of
them hugging sawn-off guns and tomahawks under their
blankets and matchcoats, on the pretext of staging a
friendly contest for the entertainment of our garrison. Bulldog Gladwin was ready for them, thanks to Joseph. He let

them inside the gate and presented them with the sight of
a hundred redcoats with loaded firelocks and fixed bayonets gleaming like icicles on a midwinter morning. This
unsettled Pontiac's resolve. He sat down with Gladwin in
the council-house with a few of his chiefs, grumbling
about British distrust. Why Gladwin let him out of there in
one piece I cannot fathom. Perhaps it was that unshakable
self-confidence of an Englishman abroad. Perhaps, even
now, he could not bring himself to see that the conspiracy
was serious business. In any event, Pontiac was allowed to
go free. He tried some more tricks; he must have been
convinced that our woodenheads *never* learn. When these
ruses failed too, his braves ran amok. They had been
whooping themselves into a blood-frenzy for several days.
They fell on every Britisher they could find outside the
stockade. One of them was a harmless old widow living
near the Roman church. Another was a retired army sergeant living with his native woman at a place on the river
the frenchies call the Ile des Cochons. From the way they
were despatched, I can tell you the Ottawas concede nothing to the Chippewas in savagery.

Despite all this, when Pontiac's envoys came with
Dandy Cuillerier and some other Frenchmen to talk peace
terms with Bulldog Gladwin—peace meaning the surrender of the fort—our commandant was fool enough to agree
that some of his officers should return with them to the native encampment, and Campbell was fool enough to volunteer.

"I can't believe that you did it," I reproached Campbell.

"I can hardly credit it myself. But you see, there were
Frenchmen with them—"

"Frenchmen! Renegades!"

"And we're damned low on food and powder, Shane."
He dropped his voice to a murmur. "It seemed worth a
shot."

It did not appear that we had many shots left as jubilant
war-parties trooped back with prisoners from other posts.
There was pretty, olive-dark Ensign Paulli from Sandusky,
spared the fire that consumed his men because a squaw
liked his looks. There were ragged survivors from a con-

voy Major Wilkins had sent from Niagara, ambushed and
butchered near the mouth of the Detroit River—so much
for our hopes of relief. Their captors were roaring drunk,
and Pontiac and Saint Ange either could not intervene, or
would not, as they hacked our men to pieces and floated
the parts down the river to feed the perch. A blackrobe
arrived from up north with a letter from Lieutenant Ether-
ington at Michilimackinac. The fort had been taken by
Chippewas, followers of a famous chief called Minavanana, who pulled off the same kind of ruse Pontiac had tried
on Gladwin. The natives arranged a game of lacrosse
under the stockade and hefted the ball inside the gate as if
by accident. As they chased after it, whooping and yelling,
they snatched guns and hatchets from their female audience and made short work of our garrison.

I was summoned to Pontiac to read this letter aloud,
which gave me my first close-hand look at the general of
the revolt. He was illiterate, of course. I gather that he
would trust no written intelligence unless he was advised
of its contents by at least two independent interpreters.

Pontiac wore a French officer's tunic over his native
garb; I believe that the coat was part of a costume presented to him by Montcalm after the fall of Fort William
Henry on the shores of Lake George, when the French Indians massacred our survivors.

He had a battery of secretaries—two Frenchmen, to take
letters, and native scribes who scrawled messages on
birchbark. Some of these scraps of bark were his famous
IOUs. To supply his army, he had taken to commandeering
cattle and grain from the *habitants* along the river. Each of
these unfortunate landholders was issued with a receipt in
the form of Pontiac's personal device, the raccoon, and
some drawings of beavers and buckskins, and promised
that payment in full would be forthcoming as soon as the
Indians had the keys of the storerooms at Detroit.

I observed that Pontiac had something no less novel for
a native general waging war. He had military maps of the
area, with zigzag lines that appeared to indicate entrenchments that were to be dug, so the Indians could advance
up to the walls of the fort under cover from the sentries on

the rampart. These, I assumed, were another contribution from Saint Ange.

I took the opportunity to ask Pontiac if he was not aware that Britain and France had called an end to the war and were drawing up a peace treaty.

He told me, through a French interpreter, that this was a lie spread by the English.

"I know the heart of my father. He will never abandon his children. Even now, he is coming with cannons and floating castles. Their voice will sound louder than rolling thunder."

Pontiac was not amused by my interruption. I was dragged back to the Chippewa camp, and I might have stayed there until they made soup out of me, pounding corn and hauling firewood, but for our grog-peddler Captain Hoskins and a mule-driver from Lancaster County, Pennsylvania.

Indian snipers were taking a toll of the soldiers up on the ramparts, shooting from around the corner of a Frenchman's barn that had been left standing, and from foxholes they had dug nearby. The snipers were mostly Chippewas. Kakaik, my master, was with them on the day I remember most vividly, together with a band of warriors led by Wasson, the head chief from Saginaw Bay.

That morning, Bulldog Gladwin organized a sortie to flush the snipers out of their hides. It was led by Hopkins, though I did not know that at the time. It happened too far off for me to witness much of the action, though I wriggled up into an apple tree when I heard all the commotion to see as much as I could. Our Rangers made quick work of the native positions, firing from the shoulder, then rushing in with cold steel. The rest of the Indians buzzed around like maddened hornets and our men ran for their lives, with two or three hundred warriors on their tails. One of them—this was the Lancaster County man—could not resist the chance to tease the natives in a style they would understand. He lifted the scalp off one of the dead Chippewas and brandished it in his fist before showing the others his backside.

All hell broke loose. It seemed the native the Ranger had scalped was the favorite nephew of Wasson, the chief from Saginaw. The Chippewas were howling for English blood and, after they were driven back from the fort by concentrated volleys, they went after the prisoners.

For the first and only time, Wind Weaver showed herself as a friend. I suppose she did not wish to lose family property. She helped me conceal myself in the hayloft of a Frenchman's barn, buried to the nose in old straw smelling of cowdung and crawling with lice and vermin.

The first captive Wasson's gang laid hands on was poor Donald Campbell. I believe they were holding him up in a garret as Baptiste Méloche's house next to Bloody Run at that time. They carved him up on the spot. They ate his heart raw and fed the rest of his carcass to the dogs. They preserved some of the skin of his forearms to make pouches. I understand that McDougall, his companion, managed to avoid a similar fate by hiding behind some wine barrels, though this would seem to me to be a most unpromising place to seek refuge from Indians on the rampage.

Now Captain Campbell, of course, was the prisoner of Pontiac and the Ottawas. Thus his slaughter provoked what might be described as a diplomatic incident. The Ottawas wanted a Chippewa prisoner to compensate for the loss of their property. The Chippewas agreed, on the understanding that this captive would be used for a feast to mourn the loss of the nephew of Wasson, the great *sugema*. I am stating all this as calmly and as decorously as possible. My emotions were not so orderly at the time, since I was the captive the Chippewas agreed to deliver up for this ceremonial.

I saw what was left of jolly Donald Campbell, lying on the river road. Crows and dogs were his visitors.

I was stripped and confined more closely than before, in a lodge in the Ottawa camp near the creek. I lay with my hands tethered behind me, and both ankles lashed to poles, high above my head. The blood drained from my legs and flowed down to my temples. I imagined my face was turning purple-black like the underside of a corpse.

The endless pounding of the war drums throbbed between my ears. My mind fled from terrifying images of the thousand ways the Indians can kill a man slowly, playing nerve and sinew like woodwind and strings. I found refuge in fantasy and delusion. I was sporting with Sir William at Fish House. I was lazing among the bedclothes at Leicester Fields, with the smells of tea and oranges and lavender in the room, and Peg's warm bosom swinging in my face. I was with Davers. He was happy. He was whirling like a dervish in a field of white-blue light.

One of my fantasies became palpable.

A slight, pretty Indian girl was hanging over me. She was toying with Captain Standish. He stood to attention. Is it true that hanged men die with stiff cocks? Her laughter carried the froth of white water. She was very like the girl we freed from McDonner's riffraff down by the Cuyahoga. She murmured something which I seemed to know, though her tongue was strange to me. "It is a shame to waste the seed." She slipped out of her doeskin kilt. The deerhoof rattles on her leggings made teasing music as she straddled me. Ah, let me die like this, with my jumper deep inside a true woman!

She was real.

I have known some forward girls in my day, but I think this is the one time I can say, without qualification, that a woman has taken *me*. I was obviously in no state to resist, had I a mind to do so. She was somewhat wooden as a lover, grinding me relentlessly as a fire-drill. But, because I suspected this was my last time, I doubt that I have ever enjoyed the act so profoundly.

Once she had taken my seed, she darted away.

"Wait a bit!" I called after her. "Can't you get me out of this?"

"Demain," was all I got out of her. Tomorrow. I had no great hopes about *demain*.

But luck had not altogether deserted me. *Demain* brought the discovery that my succubus was not only the same Ottawa maiden we had rescued from McDonner's banditti, she was Pontiac's daughter. Her long native name meant something like Three Loons Against A Red Sky, which I suppose is what her mother saw when she squatted under a tree, trying to get her daughter's head out from between her thighs. I shall call the girl Magid, which was the native version of Marguerite, the name the blackrobes gave her at her baptism. Pontiac was so deeply involved with the French that he gave out that his family were Catholics when they were with frenchies, though I never noticed that the Good Book meant much to him on other occasions; indeed, he had something of a reputation as a conjurer, a priest of the Metai.

Magid's favor brought a radical improvement in my circumstances. In the morning I was cut out of my harness and given to understand that I was to be adopted by the Ottawas, as a preliminary to becoming Pontiac's son-in-law. I was submerged in the river again, and re-painted to suit Ottawa taste, and some lady hairdressers removed offending bristles from my cheeks and scalp with copper wires and clamshell pincers, which are no substitute for my Jermyn Street barber. At night, I was pushed back and forth around the edge of an open grave while women wailed and covered their heads with ashes, and at length a savage unknown to me announced that I was flesh of his flesh and bone of his bone and thereby a member of the Cut-Foot Clan. I was no longer Annemoosh, the Camp Dog, but Standing Dog, officially licensed to state, *Nee nin dauw,* "I am a man."

Things were improving, though I was not enamored of the prospect of living indefinitely with the daughter of a rebel who deserved the firing squad or worse, in my opinion, because of what I had seen his followers do to my friends and countrymen.

However, there was a delay in the marriage proceedings, perhaps because Pontiac had misgivings about Magid's choice. Nonetheless, I was brought to more of his councils in the guise of secretary and interpreter, a role familiar to me from my work in Johnson's Indian Department which I had never thought to exercise at the whim of a cannibal.

The most memorable of these conclaves was held in Dandy Cuillerier's house.

It was a rather different scene from the one that had

greeted me when I arrived here with Sir William for the ball in his honor, but no less colorful or populous. Some two hundred Indians crowded into Cuillerier's great room, which was stripped of all furnishings save for a small table, four chairs for the chiefs of the allied nations, and a fifth for myself, as secretary. The principal order of business was the question of whether a peace between Britain and France was now truly in force. The Hurons and some of the Chippewas were distinctly nervous about the prospects for the revolt if assistance from the French, in the shape of troops and arms, could no longer be counted on. I learned that Mini Chêne had gone to the Illinois country to confer with Neyon, the French commandant there. He had sent back some hapless English traders as captives, with the message that he had reserved a few more for the tribes of the Illinois "to make soup in order to spirit up will for the fight."

I saw that Pontiac was having trouble holding his allies to his purpose. This might be good news for Bulldog Gladwin, and our side in general, but I suspected that the captives, myself included, would be the first to pay the price of Indian frustration if Pontiac's army decided to fold its tents.

Saint Ange was not present. I gather he had gone to try to obtain some more powder for the Indians, who, though generally excellent shots, were using up incredible quantities between their noisy feasting and their daily sniping at the fort.

When the Huron Takea and Pontiac were jawing away at each other, I found an opportunity to slip out of the room in search of Angélique. I found her sitting at her tapestry frame, as cool as if she were on the Ile St Louis in the shadow of Notre Dame.

"Shane!" she stared at my wild appearance. *"Mais vous êtes vraiment sauvage."*

I had managed to retrieve my shirt for this formal occasion, but it had not been washed in nearly a month and had a nasty habit of sticking to the septic wounds on my back. My head, as I have told you, was shaven, apart from the scalp lock which Magid had garnished with beads and little silver trinkets.

"You seem to be enjoying yourself," I said to Angélique sourly.

"But what can we do? As you see, we are the servants of our guests."

"A little more than servants, it seems. I heard Pontiac has promised to make your father commandant at the fort if Gladwin surrenders." This offer was no secret about the native encampment and the French settlement, and it shows you how deeply M. Cuillerier was compromised in the conspiracy.

"My father is the prisoner of circumstance," said Angélique. "If he denies them anything, they will kill him."

"He is less at risk than some of us. Do you know what those fiends did to Davers? And to Robertson? And Campbell?"

She had the grace to turn her face from me.

I said to her, as calmly as I could manage, "I want you to get your father to buy me from the Ottawas. I will repay him whatever it costs when this thing is over. It may even save his neck from gracing a halter."

She said, "I can ask. But I heard you were to wed *une belle sauvage.*"

I disdained to comment on my relations with Magid. "Something else. I want fresh clothes."

"Bon."

"And I want you to get a letter to Sterling. He is still your fiancé, isn't he?"

She pricked her thumb on her needle, so I know she was not as entirely a stranger to emotion as she liked to pretend.

"Tell him Pontiac is preparing entrenchments."

"He knows that."

That smooth, flawless face. Was there no man she did not deceive?

"Well, then."

She brought me fresh clothes, Indian trade goods, from her father's store—a ruffled shirt, a fresh breechclout, a mantlet that looked like one of Angélique's old bedgowns made over, which is no doubt what it was.

That is all the Cuilleriers did for me.

I returned to the powwow. Some of the warriors eyed me hungrily. I learned afterwards that Pontiac had promised them that more prisoners would eat fire to gratify their restless dead. After the meeting, one of the Ottawas robbed me of my mantlet and another took my ruffled shirt. Being Pontiac's prospective son-in-law, it seemed, did not carry many privileges.

But the daughter saved my life.

She came to me in the night and cut my bonds—they still kept me tethered. She whispered in French, "My father says you are a spy. You must go now. They will come for you before morning."

I do not own that mad kind of courage that sets life at nothing compared with a cause. But I knew the location of Pontiac's powder magazine, and it occurred to me that I should strike a blow for all the slaughtered Englishmen I had known before making for the fort. No doubt I should have rogered Magid again instead, for a keepsake. The tinkle of windchimes or of sleighbells still brings warm memories of those rattles on her leggings.

I prepared myself as best I was able. I rubbed my face and chest with slime and black mold from the edge of the swamp to darken my skin. I wrapped myself to the throat in a native blanket.

I was fully prepared to abandon my purpose if I found the magazine—in a hut behind Méloche's outhouse—well-defended. But there were no guards in view. Here, in the heart of the native encampment, Pontiac's men had grown cocky. Or perhaps they were busy making a stew of the traders Mini Chêne had sent back, which is indeed what they did.

I found a dry splint and ignited it in the embers of a fire that was nearly out. I set a train of powder from one of the kegs in the hut and was about to light it when a pair of Ottawas reared up out of the shadows and accosted me.

My knowledge of their tongue was not sufficient for

repartee. When one of them brought out his pipe-
tomahawk, no doubt a council gift from Sir William who
used to hand them out by the score, I leaped to the magazine and stood with the burning splint in my hand, daring
them to send all of us to Hades.

They hesitated just long enough for me to form my own
resolve. I threw the splint at an open keg, and hared off
into the orchard behind.

A series of muffled explosions buckled the earth beneath my feet and stretched me face down in the mud.

The blaze I had left behind me lit up the whole encampment. Indians came bulling and howling from all
directions. I do not know if I had enlisted the support of
someone higher up, but the thunderstorm that had been
menacing all day was unleashed pretty soon afterwards,
and between the chaos in Pontiac's camp and the drum-
rolls from the heavens, I was able to get away into the
thick of the woods.

It took me several hours, arcing up into the foothills, to
put some distance between myself and likely pursuers,
struggling with briars and thorns, to come within sight of
the fort. Thanks to Gladwin's scorched earth approach,
there were easily two hundred yards of open ground to
clear before I could reach the nearest of the gates—and
any number of watchful eyes concealed behind trees and
barns and stacks of firewood.

I had no choice but to risk it.

I let out a war whoop, "Ayeeee-OH!" to wake up the
sentries, and made a dash for the stockade.

I was greeted with bullets.

They came not from behind, but from up ahead. The
soldiers took me for one of Pontiac's gang, as well they
might have, with my shaven head and blackened skin. One
of their balls plowed a shallow trench along the side of my
scalp lock that I carry to this day, though I trust I shall
never go bald enough for the ladies to require explana-
tions.

"God's breeches!" I screamed. "I'm British!"

I sensed muddled consultations going on along the ramparts.

"Let me in, for God's sake!" I was up against the northern gate, pounding on it. I could see Indians massing behind me, like wolves.

"Give the password," bawled some soldier.

"I don't know the bloody password! I'm Lieutenant Hardacre of the Indian Department."

More confabulations. They were coming after me now, low and deadly.

"Sorry, Mr. Hardacre," the fool called down, "this gate's been nailed up. You'll have to go round the river side."

You can imagine the names I called them. A grasshopper out of hell wasn't even in the running. It was too much, to get away from Pontiac and be scalped under the very walls of the fort because of our bumbling regulars.

My fury must have given me speed, because I got round the river side of the fort ahead of the savages who came pounding after me, and, God be praised, a few wide-awake tars on the sloop in the river welcomed them with a dose of iron spikes from the mouth of their cannon.

I fell more than ran through the river gate as it swung open on groaning hinges.

"Good Lord," Bulldog Gladwin greeted me, "we all thought you'd been eaten."

If you had told me then that any woman, let alone a society cock-teaser from Manhattan, would have induced me to try my luck with Pontiac again, I would have said you were crazier than poor Davers.

London

20th February

Dearest Shane,

It is good you have suffered. Through suffering, we become human.

Your

Valerie

15

Bloody Bridge

THEY FED ME HARDTACK and soldier's grog enlivened by a few cucumbers and a little beef jerky smuggled across the river at night from François Bâby's farm on the other side. I would not touch the salt pork. It reminded me too strongly of Chippewa cuisine. There was no man inside the fort who was a stranger to the dull ache of hunger after two months of the siege, and hardly a single fusilier of the garrison who was not the victim of scurvy or the bloody flux. I saw a sentry faint on the ramparts; he toppled down onto the *chemin de ronde* and broke his neck.

We had the fort pretty much to ourselves. Most of the frenchies had taken leave of the place, preferring to try their luck among the Indians rather than live with the certainty of slow starvation. Soldiers off-duty, went hunting rats in cellars with their bayonets; they were forbidden to shoot them because we were desperately low on powder and ammunition. Gladwin had taken to stripping lead from roofs and windows, to be melted down to make bullets.

Jemmie Sterling cut a fine figure in his green coat and laced hat, drilling the militia—a dozen grumbling traders—with a monstrous broadsword at his side that looked like some relic of Culloden.

Joseph and the Mohawks were gone, to carry Bulldog Gladwin's letters to Niagara and Sir William, pressing the urgency of a relief expedition. We prayed that Sir Jeffrey Amherst would finally hear us. Detroit had survived the Indians' fire-arrows, thanks to some good shooting from the ramparts and the barrels of water and leather buckets Gladwin had deployed all around the wall. Protected by the cannons of the sloop in the river, our men could pass in and out on that side, bringing back fresh water and the occasional haul of fish. I warned Gladwin that I had heard talk in the native encampment of a plot to destroy the ships with fire-rafts, and he put a chain across the river to avoid a nasty surprise. This saved us from disaster on the night when flames leaped across the water like the very mouth of hell, followed by canoe-loads of savages who tried to board the sloop and had to be beaten off with poles and grappling hooks.

Gladwin was holding in. But General Hunger and the need to be on guard day and night were wearing us down. We slept in our clothes with our firearms close at hand. And then there was the bitter sense of isolation and abandonment. From the reports that seeped through the lines, by messengers Pontiac allowed to reach us, in order to beat down our morale, Detroit was the only British post west of the Alleghenies where the cross of Saint George still flapped at the masthead. Michilimackinac and the western outposts, Ouitanon on the Wabash, Fort Miami on the Maumee River, were lost. So were Sandusky and Presqu'Isle along our lifeline across Lake Erie. The forts in the Ohio country—Venango, Le Boeuf—had fallen too. We heard that even Fort Pitt was taken, though this proved to be a deception. Niagara was beleaguered by Senecas who had joined the revolt.

Bulldog Galdwin had risked sending the schooner to Niagara in pursuit of supplies and some hard intelligence of the larger world. The captain survived an attack by the Potawatomis and came back with damned little powder or beef but with news that almost made up for our rations.

There it was, in Guy Johnson's flourishing copperplate—
the ambassadors of England and France had sat down in a
perfumed ballroom at Versailles and signed a treaty to end
the war that had dragged on for seven years across three
continents. Canada and the whole continent east of the
Mississippi down to New Orleans was the property of the
British Crown. With a stroke of the pen, King Louis's men
had made Dandy Cuillerier and Saint Ange and the rest of
their gang British subjects, so long as they stayed on our
side of the river. Their hopes of drawing the French Empire into a new war in our neighborhood were all exploded. Pontiac's great white father had abandoned his
own kind in North America, as well as his red children.

We feted the news of peace with bell-ringing and fusil-
lades, and Gladwin rounded up the frenchies that were left
inside the fort and told them to summon the *habitants*
from along the river to a grand council, while I used Father Pothier and some Hurons who were playing both sides
to spread the word in the native encampments. I was less
confident than Bulldog that our troubles were over, because I had seen the depth of Pontiac's hatred of the British and of Saint Ange's addiction to a lost cause, and
because the native rebels had already accomplished things
few white men in the colonies would have dreamed possible before the uprising. They had sustained a siege of a
powerful fortified position for above two months, they had
captured six or seven other posts, and above all, they had
held together a grand alliance of Indian nations, all across
the Great Lakes and deep into the Ohio country, that included tribes that had been locked in bloody vendettas until only a season or two before.

While we waited for the Frenchmen to assemble, I read
and re-read my private letter from Sir William. He had had
a devilish job holding the Six Nations to our side. He had
risen from his sick bed to hold an Indian council, which
was boycotted by the Senecas, who seemed to have definitely slipped the leash. The Onondaga speaker had requested him to give General Amherst the message that if
the English persisted in depriving the Indians of the customary powder and presents, and in stealing their lands,

the Great Spirit would punish them. The Mohawks were jumpy because Uri Klock would not stay in his box. The governor's council, no doubt oiled by the Livingstons, had declined to rule his land deeds invalid; the Mohawks were sitting on lands that still belonged, on paper, to a gang of swindlers and sharpers.

"I hope that this finds you and Sir Robert in good health," evidently Sir William had written before Joseph's coming, "and that your circumstances do not deprive the belles of Detroit of the pleasure of your company. I know not whether anything good may yet be derived from this bloody business, but I am determined to use it to make the king and his ministers accept the necessity of a Boundary Line between the Indians and white settlement in this continent. I have drafted the text of a royal proclamation on this question, and have forwarded it to London by sure hands. I doubt not that this proclamation will do more to extinguish the embers of revolt than the Treaty from Paris."

Fifty or sixty of the *habitants* arrived at the river gate and filed into the council hall to hear Gladwin read the terms of the peace treaty. Dandy Cuillerier was with them, and Jean Baptiste Méloche, his neighbor.

"Henceforth," said Bulldog, "any resident of the French settlement found giving aid to the rebels will be held guilty of treason and will stand liable to have his property expropriated and be court-martialed and shot like a rabid cur."

"Forgive me," said Angélique's father. "It would of course be our privilege to obey the commandant's wishes, but I find that he is a stranger to our circumstances. We are not at liberty to deny the savages food and shelter. We do not enjoy the luxury of blockhouses and cannon. If we refuse Pontiac's demands, he will destroy our homes and our families."

"Then explain to Pontiac that he must sue for peace! Can't you make him understand that the war is over?"

"He will not trust the word of your general, nor of Sir William. Couriers have gone to Commandant Neyon, among the Illinois. If Neyon confirms that a treaty is made, then perhaps something may be accomplished."

Gladwin swore afterwards that he would not lie content until he saw Dandy Cuillerier's head on a pike. We soon learned that he had told us only part of the story. Pontiac had summoned the Frenchmen of Detroit to a council of his own, and demanded that they take up arms on his side. The merchants pleaded that they were too old and infirm, but some of the rough voyageurs and bushlopers cast their lots with the revolt. We saw a few of them in their red caps trying to steal up on a makeshift bastion Gladwin had set up between the backside of the fort and a little creek called the Ruisseau des Hurons. One of our gunners bowled half a dozen of them out of the branches of an apple tree with a six-pound ball.

Father Pothier brought me the happy intelligence that Teata's band of Christian Hurons had sworn to part company with Pontiac, and one of my Huron spies informed me that the Potawatomis had publicly denounced the butchery of English captives, around the council fire in the native encampment, and seemed to be on the verge of defection. Yet none of this allowed me to rest easy at night. With his native army breaking up, Pontiac was a cornered man, and a man with his back against the wall is capable of anything. He needed to strike a decisive blow, to rally his faltering ally to his cause. It was only a question of when and where this blow would fall. I could picture him with his sorcerers, taking counsel from puppy-dog snufflings from inside a shaking tent.

I decided to test the sincerity of Father Pothier's Hurons by tasking them to bring me a prisoner or two. They came to the river gate before dawn with a Jewish merchant named Chapman in much the same condition that I was when I made my escape to the fort. His was an interesting tale. He told me that the natives had tied him to a stake and amused themselves by sticking burning splints into his flesh. They were preparing a bonfire about his feet when he begged for something to drink. It is the custom of the Indians, as it is ours, to offer a condemned man some refreshment before he gasps his last. They brought him the last thing they had put in their kettle—a scalding broth that burned Chapman's tongue and palate. In his unreasoning rage, he hurled the pot at the head of the nearest savage, who proved to be one of their high panjandrums. This act of gallantry saved Chapman's life. The natives concluded that he was a lunatic, and they hold the deranged in superstitious respect, as you may have gleaned from Davers and the stories of the Prophet. Chapman was allowed considerable liberties, and even asked for weather forecasts, before the Christian Hurons brought him to me.

We lived on rumors. Exhausted sentries patrolled with fixed bayonets, starting at shadows.

In this time of strained nerves and short tempers, Angélique trotted up to the fort, bright as a new penny, in her little fiacre. They let her in by the river gate, and she flounced up to Sterling's house, sporting the daintiest pair of high heels I have seen west of the Palais Royal. Balancing on them required hip-rolls certain to hold the attention of any man in possession of his parts.

· I resolved to join the interview, though I knew I would not be a welcome visitor under Jemmie Sterling's roof.

I found him high in color, with his neckcloth in suspicious disarray.

"You call at the most unconscionable time, Mr Hardacre!"

"I hoped that Miss Cuillerier might have brought us some fresh news."

"Well, well, you may ask for yourself."

He had poured Angélique a glass of canary wine. Since he did not offer the decanter to me, I served myself.

"You almost look like a white man, Shane," she teased me.

I was wearing one of M. Navarre's elderly bagwigs, to cover the raw stubble over my scalp where the hair was beginning to grow back.

She fluttered her turkey-feather fan under her eyes.

"I find that paying court to Indians does not disagree with you, mademoiselle. May I inquire if you have any news for us?"

She glanced at Sterling and said, "Mini Chêne is returned from the Illinois with a letter from the Chevalier de Neyon."

"And?"

"Neyon says the war is over. He received letters from New Orleans. He refuses to give any help to the rebels."

"Thank God! Now Pontiac must cut his losses."

"It is not so easy," Angélique beat her fan. "Some of our people told Pontiac that Neyon is a traitor, that he does not speak for the king and will be shot before this affair is over. Pontiac listens to what he wishes to hear."

"Is your father one of these people?"

"Oh, Shane! You must not think too harshly of him! He has made mistakes, but he is not his own master! If he stands against them, Mini Chêne and Saint Ange will kill him."

"We must tell the major!" cried Sterling.

"Why don't you run along and do that?" I said to him, battening on the chance of a few private moments with Angélique.

Sterling was too canny for that. He insisted we must all go.

"I don't know what to make of it," said honest Bulldog when we bearded him in his stone house.

"Well, I have a notion," I piped up. "Pontiac is the soul of this revolt, but Saint Ange is its brains. We must seize him and lock him up. We can do it under cover of a parley as they did to poor Donald Campbell."

Gladwin thought this suggestion despicable and unworthy of any gentleman. If I had had my Mohawks with me, I might have proposed a covert raid, but I would not trust this venture to the Hurons or to Hopkins's Rangers—the Tosspot's Troop I called them, in honor of their captain's hand with a bottle.

We waited and stewed in the sultry summer heat, with Jemmie Sterling stoutly upholding his property rights over the only likely satinback in sight. Word came from the Hurons that Pontiac had strung up some more white dogs and sworn never to leave Detroit until he had dyed the forests red with our blood.

By the end of July, I found it almost impossible to sleep during the hours of darkness. If I threw off my clothes, I made a feast for the mosquitoes that penetrated any quantity of gauze. If I left them on, my sweat flowed so freely that soon I was rolling in a warm, stagnant bath.

Long after midnight, on the last Thursday of the month, I lit a pipe and went to air myself along the ramparts. An eerie fog was rolling up from the river as dense as a snow-drift. Soon I could see no more than an arm's length in front of my face as I groped my way towards the south-west bastion.

"Halt! Who goes there?"

A red, sweaty face peered out at me over the point of a bayonet. I recognized Corporal Horsfall of the Royal Americans.

"Oh, it's you, Mr Hardacre."

"I am glad I am not the only man awake, Corporal."

"Damned murdering weather, sir. I wish some of them shitten elves would come on, if they be coming. By salt and vinegar, I'd made a meal of 'em."

As he spoke, we heard the crack of musketry from downriver where the schooner bobbed at anchor. Beyond it was the village of the Potawatomis, commanding the mouth of the river.

"Careful what you wish for," I murmured to Horsfall.

We hurried up onto the roof of the bastion where a drowsy private was squinting into the fog.

"Can't see a bleeding thing," he reported. "Those hell-hounds could be in the major's garden, for all I can make of it."

We heard ululating war whoops and white men's voices, hoarse in anger and pain.

"They're after the ships again," said Horsfall. He dis-charged his firelock into the air, and the sentries returned the signal from the four corners of the fort. Soon the alarm was echoed by the tolling of the church bells, and the whole area was astir. Gladwin, his wig askew, came puff-ing up to join us on the wall. Jemmie Sterling rushed about down below, brandishing his killing-iron.

The shooting was nearer.

From the woods behind the fort and the encampment upriver, we heard the pulse of Pontiac's war drums.

Bulldog Gladwin ordered the gunners to put their balls in

the air and reload with spikes—nails commandeered from our traders, shrapnel salvaged from previous engagements—in readiness for a close encounter with our enemies.

When the din of the six-pounders ebbed away, I heard the distinctive thump of coehorns answering us from downriver.

"By George," said Gladwin, "I believe our visitors are our own kind!" He yelled to Josh Hopkins, who was quietly tippling from his canteen down by the river gate, to have one of the row-galleys manned and ready.

I followed close on Gladwin's heels and joined him in the galley with a dozen fusiliers.

The fog thinned a little. On the black water of the river, skidding like dragonflies, I saw a whole armada of bateaux. I lost count at twenty. The lead boats had swivels and mortars riveted to their decks. There were ten or a dozen men in each boat in the scarlet coats of the 55th and the blue trousers of the Royal Americans. Some were green striplings, some were near-invalids, shaking with fever, a few had been bloodied by Indian snipers. They did not cut much of a dash, but I doubt that any men in uniform have been welcomed with greater applause than was this relief column of two hundred and eighty regulars by the defenders of the fort, who had been cut off from the wider world for nigh on three months.

"Where is your escort?" Gladwin hailed the pilot, who turned out to be a Montreal trader named Lascelles, with some connection with Daniel Claus, Sir William's deputy.

"We are as you see us!"

We learned that the flatboats had left Niagara without the protection of a ship-of-war. This was the first bad news. It meant we would have to feed nearly three hundred additional mouths from our dwindling stores.

There was worse to come.

"Where is your commander?"

"At your service, sir!" that personage replied for himself.

There, in the second boat, was a face I had never hoped to see west of Hudson's river. The sun was coming up beyond Pontiac's camp on the edge of the Grand Marais. It

had burned off enough of the fog for me to see Captain
James Dalyell's features distinctly. He was puffy about the
eyes from the night's ordeal, slinking past Pontiac's watch-
dogs on muffled oars. But his tailored regimentals betrayed hardly a wrinkle. He greeted us with a smile of
invincible self-satisfaction.

Bulldog Gladwin invited me to the banquet in Captain Dalyell's honor. We had stewed kid—François Bâby was doing
his best—and I accounted for more than my share of the
commandant's last pipe of madeira. I needed fortification to
endure Dalyell's bulling and name-dropping. He spoke of
crossing Lake Erie as if he had discovered the north-west
passage to China, or licked the Persians at Marathon.

Sterling hung on his every word, which did not surprise
me, since No Deal, of course, was General Amherst's major-
domo, and Sterling was still hoping to get round Sir William
and secure his claim to that fat chunk of Indian land about
Niagara. Tosspot Hopkins fawned on Dalyell openly, hoping
for a patron who would overlook the way he had been robbing his men blind. I was more disgusted by the show of
deference from the professionals, even Bulldog Gladwin.

The newcomers included a swart, thick, well-timbered
New Hampshireman in the green bucksin of the Rangers. I
knew him by reputation—who in the colonies did not? His
name was Robert Rogers, and he held the rank of major in
the provincial forces. He was said to know as much about
killing Indians as any man who took the king's side in the
late war. He had gone up to Canada over fierce back trails,
and squashed the hornets' nest at St Francis. He had scouted
for Sir William, who once said of Rogers: "If a man is
needed to bang hostile Indians, I would choose Major Rogers over any except a Mohawk. But in time of peace I
would put him in irons, because it is easier to make sheep
from wolves than to gentle so unmitigated a ruffian."

I cannot judge if Johnson's opinion was altogether fair;
I know that Sir William never tolerated a man who threatened his suzerainty over Indian affairs, as Rogers did later
on at Michilimackinac, and met his ruin for it. But I will
say that Rogers seemed woefully tame that evening under

Gladwin's roof. He applied himself to his bottle, speaking only when spoken to, and then to flatter No Deal by supporting whatever he had said last.

I supposed that Rogers, too, felt in need of a patron for the ambitious designs he nurtured in that barrel chest, and that he counted on Dalyell, who dropped Sir Jeffrey's name with every second breath, to enlist the general in his interest. I can think of no better explanation for Rogers's docility which damned near got both of us scalped.

As for Gladwin, he was worn-out and ill, and would have loved nothing better than to lay down his commission and go home. He allowed Captain Dalyell to preen and puff until No Deal came out with the following speech:

"The general was saying at Mr Van Horn's—they keep the best table at York, don't y'know—that he cannot fathom how a pack of skulking banditti have been permitted to hold the regulars of this garrison to ransom all these weeks past."

"I do not believe that Sir Jeffrey has ever met our adversaries," Bulldog shot a sideways look at me, "and I doubt that he would have thanked me for risking this post by some damnfool act of bravado. Mr Hardacre can confirm it. Pontiac is no ordinary native."

Dalyell, who had been ignoring me all evening, disdained to ask my opinions now.

"Pontiac!" he sniffed. "You talk of a naked savage as if he were the veritable Cáesar of the forest! By God, I have examined that hellion's work! We inspected the ruins of Ensign Paulli's fort on the lake. We picked the bones of British regulars out of the ashes. They will pay for it, I promise you! They took certain of our posts by stealth and treachery. They will not enjoy the same fortune again. They are good for shooting a man from behind a tree, or for shaking your hand while their accomplices knife you in the back. Sir Jeffrey's own words, gentlemen! What do you say, Major Rogers?"

The Ranger belched. In honor of the company, he covered his mouth with the back of a hairy paw, big enough for a grizzly.

"It don't gall a snake to hide in the grass nor a buzzard

to feed on a critter who's down," quoth Rogers. "No more an injun to cheat in a fight."

"Well put, well put, by Gad!" No Deal warmed to his theme. "Gentlemen, Sir Jeffrey is persuaded that we must not delay in breaking the backs of these rattlesnakes. I have had a full day to inspect our position. It is my considered opinion that we should advance on Pontiac's headquarters at once. Is there a man among us who does not want to put an end to him? I say, let's put it to him tonight! We'll smoke him like a kipper for breakfast!"

This met with a mixed reception. Gladwin and the officers of the garrison, apart from Tosspot Hopkins, were wary of a sortie. They had held off the Indians for three months. With Dalyell's reinforcements, it seemed highly unlikely that Pontiac's crew would attempt any general assault on the fort. As the end of the summer approached, Gladwin argued, Pontiac's allies would start drifting off in greater and greater numbers towards their hunting camps. Meanwhile, Colonel Bouquet, a competent Swiss professional, was on his way to Fort Pitt with another relief column. Once he had fulfilled his mission there, his troops could be assigned to Detroit to mop up what Indians remained.

"End of summer?" Dalyell echoed. "Bouquet? What the devil are you talking about, Major Gladwin? But you don't seriously mean me to sit here twiddling my thumbs! D'you fancy that is why Sir Jeffrey sent me out here? The general expects results, Major Gladwin. By Gad, I mean to supply 'em. We'll do it tonight, what?"

It seemed that the siege of Detroit had suddenly become No Deal's private campaign.

None of the officers spoke up.

Gladwin's blue eye swiveled towards me.

He said, "Perhaps Mr Hardacre will give us the benefit of the view of the Indian Department. He has more intimate acquaintance with our adversaries than any man here."

No Deal looked over my shoulder as if he were expecting someone more worthy of his attention.

This removed whatever inhibitions I might have harbored about speaking my mind to Captain Dalyell in the presence of the others.

I said to him, pretty briskly, "I gather you have some experience of banging the natives. I am told you burned the Hurons out of their village near Sandusky."

I had heard about this episode from Conrad The Song, Joseph's friend, who had arrived with Dalyell's party, bearing private despatches from Johnson country.

Captain Dalyell gave me the sort of look you would give a servant who spilled soup in your lap.

"Sandusky? Hurons? Most certainly I burned them out! The savages burned our fort and killed our men! What would you have me do?"

"Might I ask how many Hurons you took prisoner?"

No Deal stuck out his jaw. "No prisoners. No casualties. The cowardly dogs ran away. I told you these animals don't fight like men."

"In short, the Hurons knew you were coming."

"Your drift is tediously obscure, Mr Hardacre."

"My drift is exceedingly simple. Surprise and good intelligence—which is the art of avoiding surprise—are the heart and soul of Indian fighting. I learned that from Sir William Johnson, and I have found it amply confirmed by all our experiences about this post."

No Deal could not refuse the bait. "I am greatly surprised to find you an authority on native warfare, or any other sort of fighting, Mr Hardacre. I thought your knowledge of battle was limited to costume parties to please the ladies."

"Then you might recall, Captain Dalyell, that it is possible to be caught off-guard, in fancy dress or out of it."

No Deal gave me a lowering look as if he were pawing the boards under the table.

I could not resist. I said, "How is Miss Van Horn?"

Dalyell's color rose dangerously. He said, "I think it damnably impertinent of you, sir, to mention the name of my affianced in a council of war."

I might have risked another cast of the line, but Rogers interjected a practical question. He wanted to know the lie of the land between the fort and Pontiac's encampment.

"We have no chance of taking Pontiac by surprise," I told him flatly. "See here." I arranged salt cellars and celery sticks to make a model of the river road and some of the buildings along it.

"The road to the Grand Marais," I observed, "runs for a little under three miles. As you can see, it is open to the river on the right hand. On the left, it is screened by the frenchies' houses and barns and orchards and picket fences. We cannot move a column of regulars along that road without causing a buzz throughout the whole settlement. There's a narrow bridge that must be crossed." I laid a fork crossways to show the rough gorge of Parent's Creek. "And beyond it, the front of Pontiac's camp is defended by a sucking swamp. There are several places that are made for an Indian ambush, and you can wager your *affianced*," this, of course, was for No Deal, "that Pontiac's spies will be watching us every inch of the way. They will know we are coming even before we step outside the stockade."

"What in blazes do you mean?" cried No Deal.

"I mean only that there are many eyes and ears inside the fort. Not all of them are friendly to our cause."

I avoided looking at the French interpreters, Saint Martin and La Butte, who were seated at the table. I thought them both decent fellows who had been the source of some useful Indian intelligence for me, but I could not trust them not to share what they heard with their countrymen.

I added that I thought that a well-planned raid, coordinated on water and land, using hand-picked men disguised in native garb, might have better hopes of success than a more conventional assault. I said I would like to discuss this in private with Major Rogers before making a formal proposal.

Rogers looked fairly keen, but returned to his bottle when Dalyell resumed his attack.

My biggest mistake, I realize now, was to invoke the name of that little wriggler Suky Van Horn. I had pricked No Deal on his most vulnerable spot. Our military discussion shriveled into a wrangle over which of us had the balls for the job in question.

"The general and I," thus Dalyell, "have noted an unfor-

tunate tendency within the Indian Department to jaw on
the sidelines when there is any real fighting to be done. I
mean to hit Pontiac tonight. Major Gladwin, I would count
it as a personal favor if you would give me charge of this
mission. I shall hold myself accountable to Sir Jeffrey for
the results."

"In that case," said Gladwin, "you may do as you
please. But I will not strip my garrison."

"I have men aplenty," said Dalyell. He was not finished
with me. "Mr Hardacre. Are you man enough to go with
us?"

"I am man enough to recognize a fool's errand when I
see one."

"Gentlemen," No Deal appealed to the company, "Mr
Hardacre and I know something of each other. I will not
detain you with our private differences. I observe only that
Mr Hardacre thinks himself much of a swordsman with the
ladies but shrinks from an honest fight. We were rivals
once in the court of Venus. I find we will never be rivals
in the court of Mars. Whatever regard Miss Van Horn ever
had for you, Mr Hardacre, she will be entirely disabused
by your craven performance tonight."

No doubt Dalyell was in liquor. I must have been too,
because I said something quite unrepeatable in front of the
assembled officers, to the effect that I would not join him
in the dam since I had already enjoyed the beaver. The allusion was blurred, but salty enough for Dalyell to hurl the
contents of his wine-glass in the direction of my head. He
doused Hopkins instead.

"Boys, boys!" Rogers stretched and groaned. He
reached for my arm. "I would take it as a personal favor,"
he said to me, "if you would go with us. You know the
layout, and you know the ringleaders by sight. I guess
your Miss Suky will take it as a favor too, whichever of
you she settles for."

Don't ask me why I agreed to go. It was not for any noble, or even calculated, motive. I did not allow Dalyell's expedition much chance of success, but then I could not have
believed that it would end as badly as it did. I suppose I
was a little jealous of the fool who had bagged Suky Van

Horn. I wanted to see his face when he recognized that I was right and he was wrong. I know, I know. It was not one of my better moments. They gave me a medal for what I did afterwards, but Sir William understood better. He cautioned me that one of the greatest mistakes men make is to confuse courage with selling your life too cheaply.

As soon as I had made my commitment, I realized I did not want to go trooping along that shooting-gallery of a road by night without good scouts and flankers. I went in search of Conrad The Song, and found him in much the same condition as me, which is to say, several sheets in the wind.

I explained the nature and the size of the expedition Dalyell was drumming up.

The Mohawk's speech was slurred, but his import was clear enough. "Too many soldiers to die. Too few to knock Pontiac on the head."

He announced that he intended to sleep until daybreak.

Mohawks generally have a fine sense of the odds.

It was two in the morning by the time our column was assembled. I was glad to see that No Deal was not entirely devoid of common sense. The soldiers had been stripped of their packs and their heavy equipment, unlike Gage's lobsterbacks when they were sent to knock the American mutineers off the hills about Boston. But Dalyell's men had retained their thick scarlet coats and their scratchy horsehair wigs, which must have made them infernally uncomfortable on that steamy summer's night.

It was as dark as a coal-hole when we stepped out down the river road. Dalyell took this for a promising sign, but the lack of light did not improve my confidence. I knew that if Pontiac's followers were waiting to fall on us from ambush, blackened for war, they would be pretty near invisible and had no need of moonshine or starshine to find us. There was only one road, and only a deaf man could fail to hear the creak of boot-leather and the jangle of metal up to a mile away across the sleeping farms and cottages of the *habitants*.

Rogers threw a friendly arm around my shoulders and whispered, "I'm glad you're with us."

I was surprised that he was marching in the main party like a common footslogger. I had expected him to be out in front with Lieutenant Brown's party, or leading flankers through the cornfields and kitchen gardens on our left where we were badly exposed. I told him so.

"This is a party for the woodenheads," he responded cheerily. "I am here merely to take the air."

Dogs started yapping and baying. Their howls rose ahead and behind our little column. So much for the element of surprise. We marched two abreast. A pair of row-galleys, armed with swivels, splashed upriver on our right; there was only a narrow strip of sand between us and the tar-black waters. But the danger was on the other side.

I pointed out the dim profile of a Frenchman's house to Rogers. A boy had shinned up the steep roof and was perched on the top like a sparrow, gaping at us.

Rogers nodded and said blandly, "I expect Captain Dalyell knows what he's about."

I expect that some of you will think that I had it in for Rogers, because of his notorious feud with Sir William, which many held to be the root cause of Robert Rogers's ruin. I think that their judgement is wrong. Before blaming our failures on others, each of us must look within himself for the flaw in the potter's clay. But Rogers's fall is a different story. He was at the height of his influence and renown when I met him at Detroit, and I knew nothing of any bad blood between him and Johnson. What surprised me was his innocence. In his *Concise Account of America*, published at London two years afterwards, he claimed to have held a dramatic interview with Pontiac near the mouth of the Cuyahoga in 1760, when he was on his way to Detroit to claim possession of the fort from the French. When I encountered Rogers, he owned to no personal knowledge of the rebel chief. I will not tax a man overmuch for improving his story for the purposes of publication. But I do hold it against Rogers that he would not risk speaking his mind to a tin soldier like James Dalyell. I have no doubt about Rogers's physical courage. He was

ever at his best in a tight corner, and he proved that again
before the sun came up over the Detroit River. But moral
courage is of a different order, and that is where I found
Rogers wanting. Had it been otherwise, had Rogers insisted on taking command of the expedition himself as the
man who was clearly best qualified, had he merely insisted
on using his Rangers as scouts and flankers, which was
surely their job, we might have had some prospect of success. But his mind was on other things—on currying favor
with Sir Jeffrey and the general's friends in London, to
promise a windy scheme of fortune.

What's that? You say I protest too much? I admit it. I
was not at my best that night either.

The air smelled of woodsmoke and ripening plums. A
whippoorwill sounded from the back of an orchard. It was
followed by three hoots from a screech-owl, away towards
Parent's Creek. I saw Rogers bristle and cock an ear. He
quickened his stride to overtake Dalyell who was walking
with Captain Gray. Our commanding officers sent orders
through the ranks—if we came under attack, we were to
form up into platoons and answer the Indians by street firing.

I took a long look at Baptiste Méloche's house as we
passed. The inhabitants showed no lights, but I thought I
saw shadows moving behind the windows.

Our advance party was already nearing the narrow
wooden bridge over the creek. I had tried to warn Dalyell
about this spot. A mile and a half north-east of the fort,
Parent's Creek flows down through a wild, rough hollow
to join the Detroit River. There is mucky swampland
around its mouth, the preserve of frogs and snakes and
wildfowl and, in normal times, of small boys with fishing
lines or pans to catch tadpoles. The road passes over the
bridge only a few rods from the mouth of the creek. Beyond this point, the land rises abruptly, buckling into tight
ridges that run parallel to the creek. Along these crests
were the remains of the entrenchments Pontiac had placed
around his original camp before he moved to the back side
of the Grand Marais to place himself beyond the range of
gunboats on the river. There was plenty of other cover for
enemies lying in concealment—fruit-trees, wood-piles, and

those high picket fences the *habitants* placed all around their long, narrow plots.

Archie Brown of the 55th, leading our van, halted his men just before the bridge. I saw him squinting into the blackness, trying to survey all those possible sniper-holes. Our party kept on marching until our front rank bumped up against Brown's rear.

I heard Dalyell say to a runner, "Tell Mr Brown to get on with it."

The logs of the bridge complained under the steady tramp of army boots. Brown's men were halfway across when somebody raised a hoarse cry of alarm, cut off abruptly by the snap of firelocks and the banshee wail of the Indian war cry. Ottawas swarmed out from under the bridge, and from hiding places in the rank swampgrass at the edge of the road. Some of them were so close to our men that their muzzles touched them when they pulled the triggers. I believe that half the advance guard, including Lieutenant Brown, were felled by the first volley.

"Fix bayonets!" Gray was yelling. "Give 'em a taste of Sheffield steel!"

I doubt that his orders were heard in the pandemonium that swallowed us up. Our main party had come up on the heels of Brown's detachment. The fire he had drawn peppered us too. One of our Highlanders took a ball in the throat; it had passed through a fusilier of the 55th in the party ahead of us. Men reeled backwards, spreading confusion and terror. The Indians were firing on our left flank, from the trees and pickets around a nearby barn, and from the breastworks on the slope above the creek. The guns on the row-galleys on the river were no good to us here; the shots were as likely to fall among our men as among Pontiac's.

Rogers growled, and hurled himself into the smoke. I saw him stretched full-length behind a stump, sighting along his barrel. This looked more reasonable than standing about, to be potted like a woodcock; I began wriggling towards him on my belly.

Dalyell chased a would-be deserter, grabbed him by the scruff of the neck and laid about him with the flat of his sword.

"White-livered villain!" he was bawling.

He hopped about, trying to restore some kind of order. He could only conceive of one thing to do, which was to press his attack. He took command of the van, and the Indians about the creek melted away as our men jogged across the bridge. Dalyell and his troops charged on up the ridge, ready to skewer the Indians lurking behind the breastworks on the points of their bayonets. Soon curses and gruff cries of disappointment carried back. Dalyell's quarry had slipped away, leaving him fumbling in the dark.

Our enemy allowed our leaders no breathing space to weigh our situation. New volleys sounded from behind us. It seemed that Grant and Hopkins, with our rearguard, were under fire.

"Face left!" Grant roared at his men. "Face left!"

They cleared the snipers from Méloche's house with a bayonet charge, an brought up Baptiste Méloche in his nightshirt, with a comical turban on his head, to be questioned. Méloche was sniveling, trying to play the terrified innocent. His performance was the only thing that gave me pleasure that night.

"Hardacre!" Dalyell summoned me. "You know these people! This one pretends to know no English! Come and translate for us!"

Reluctantly, I crawled out of my burrow. I had scraped a shallow hole for myself, like a woodchuck, at the base of my stump.

Méloche pretended he had been taken as much by surprise as our officers. The Indians had taken possession of his house by force; he was grateful to us for his rescue. I had an idea that Baptiste Méloche's involvement in this business went rather deeper than that.

"Don't delude yourself that Captain Dalyell will be tartuffed as easily as that," I warned him. "He is a hasty man. He would as soon shoot a Frenchman as a savage."

"Que diable vas-tu faire?"

"You had best tell it all, and quickly. I cannot vouch for the captain's good humor if you delay."

Méloche told us then that Pontiac had sent war-parties to encircle our rear. His plan was to deny us both retreat and reinforcements. In his good time, when his warriors had wasted our strength with sniper-fire, he would order a general attack on us from three sides.

"It's unthinkable!" said Dalyell, when this was translated. "Indians encircling regulars! It's unheard of!"

The men who lead soldiers into battle are for ever fighting the last war. All the same, No Deal had a point. I suspected that Pontiac's plan had been refined with the aid of a certain professional.

"Where is Saint Ange?" I demanded of Méloche.

He scratched his stubble.

I saw Corporal Horsfall, and called to him, "Corporal, I think our friend is in need of a shave."

When Méloche felt the edge of Horsfall's bayonet under his jawbone, he became more amenable. He allowed that Saint Ange might have been seen at Chauvin's cottage, which was half a mile back along the road.

Our chat was interrupted by a new burst of sniper-fire. Méloche and I did the sensible thing and made ourselves worms among the crabgrass beside the road. Dalyell held his ground and took a ball in his thigh. He affected to feel no pain, though a red cockade flowered on his breeches.

Our commander seemed strangely disoriented. Perhaps it was the effect of the balls falling thick about us, the frenzied whoops of our attackers, the moans of our wounded as they were carried down to the flatboats.

Captain Grant had the sense to say, "They are drawing a noose about us sir. We must retire before we are cut off."

"Retire, sir? Over my body. I will not be made a laughingstock."

Yet Dalyell havered, moving neither forward nor back.

James Grant tried to animate him. "We must not give the enemy time to recollect. If you mean to go on, sir, by God, let's push 'em. If not, let us go before they have us by the hindquarters."

Dalyell did not reply to this. He tramped back and forth, stamping down hard on his wounded leg as if he expected the pain to inspire him.

"I think, sir—"

"You have no business, sir, to think!"

The sober, mannerly Grant was at the edge of mutiny.
He called up Lieutenant McDougall and ordered him to go
to Captain Gray, who had assumed command of the van,
and inform him of what had been said.

I began to feel Pontiac's noose tightening around my
own throttle. The moon had ridden out from behind the
clouds and made us even choicer targets for Pontiac's
marksmen. I had no intention of lounging about in that
shooting-gallery while Dalyell tried to clear his head. You
know his sort; once they get an idea in their thick skulls,
it sticks there like a three-inch nail.

Crouched down, I ran to where Rogers had gathered
some of his Rangers behind a pile of cordwood.

"Three down, if I can count," Rogers grinned. He
seemed to have come to life; he was actually enjoying
himself. "Whose place is that?" He jabbed his finger at a
neat, whitewashed house a musket-shot away.

"I believe it is Jacques Campau's."

"Then Jack Campau will have the honor of playing host
to the Rangers. That's the house we need, if we aim to get
the woodenheads out of this. I hope Jack keeps a fair cellar."

"Well, then. Let's do it!"

"Captain Dalyell!" Rogers called to our commander.
"Permission to mount a flank attack!"

No Deal puffed and hawed, which Rogers took for assent.

Old Campau was less than pleased to see us, though the
Rangers weeded a few Indians out of his front garden. Indeed, he declined to open his door to us until Rogers
threatened to break it down.

The house stood on a little rise commanding the road
and the fields around. It was furnished modestly enough—
rush-bottomed chairs, an antiquated, high-backed one with
an embroidered seat, a square table of fir boards on fold-
ing legs that stood against the wall on its end when not in
use. I knew that Campau had a good amount of silver and
a fine set of four-pronged forks, which he had no doubt
squirreled away as soon as he got wind of our approach.
He had also concealed his liquor and his womenfolk.

"Where is Madame Campau?" I asked him. "And Manon?"

"Not here." He sucked in his lip, and I was not without sympathy. No doubt he expected the worst from our rude and licentious soldiery, and no doubt he had reason. Manon was a pert *gamine*. I had not enjoyed her favors, as yet, but would not have spurned them, at least as *hors d'oeuvre*.

Rogers inspected the house, knocked out the oilpaper in the windows, and stationed a Ranger at each one. He found Campau's storeroom, and dragged out a heap of beaver plews, which he instructed his men to use as breastworks, despite our host's loud protestations.

When he was satisfied with his dispositions, Rogers licked his chops.

"Thirsty work, this," he remarked.

Campau claimed that the savages had stolen all his liquor.

"I think I'd best take a peek in the cellar," said Rogers.

Campau threw up his hands. Squeaking, he took up a stand in front of the cellar door, and from the scuffles below, it was no longer a secret to us what he had done with his women.

Rogers purred. "I begin to feel powerful lusty. What about you, Shane Hardacre?"

The language barrier dissolved at once. So did Campau's story about the Indians filching his liquor. He announced that he had just remembered that he owned a private stock, and volunteered to go down to the cellar to fetch it.

I followed him, and heard the inviting swish of stiff petticoats as the Frenchman heaved open the trap-door. Campau attempted to block my view with his broad backside.

"Eau de vie!" he called down to his women. *"Pas la meilleure!"*

"Come now, Maître Campau. You would not deny a drop of cognac to men that are defending your women."

Not without grumbling, Campau parted with two bottles of Nantes brandy. Rogers took charge of one and extracted the cork with his teeth. He took a fierce gulp, and passed the bottle around.

"That's better. A man must have spirit for a fight."

We did not have long to enjoy our refreshments. A Ranger stationed at the back of the house fired on an Indian who stole out of the shadow of Campau's barn. Fifty fusils returned the fire. One of them drilled a neat hole between the eyes of a trooper who was nailing boards across a window on the west side. We took turns at the windows. As soon as one of us fired, he ran back to reload, while another man took his place. I aimed at a darting shadow, and saw it flicker and fall.

"Save your powder!" Rogers shouted. "Don't shoot until you can see 'em plain!"

It was hard to make out, anything clearly. The Indians seemed to be all around us. If our purpose was to relieve the pressure on our regulars beside the river-beach, we seemed to have succeeded only too well. From the velocity of their musket-fire, our attackers must have numbered two hundred or more. I began to regret my decision to go with Rogers as much as my decision to go with Dalyell.

The shooting died away. The relative silence that descended, punctuated by the distant yowling of dogs and the noise of skirmishing along the river, was ominous.

From somewhere among Campau's plum trees, a voice carried the words of a war chant:

> *Todotobi penaise*
> *Ka dow wiawwiaum!*

I reached for the brandy. That harsh, screeching voice, rising from the pit of the stomach, was too familiar.

"What's 'e jabbering about?" demanded a Londoner, one of Rogers's men.

> I wish to have the body of the fiercest bird,
> As swift, as cruel, as strong.

I made the translation in a sort of daze.

"Blimey, they don't 'alf go on, do they? Where's the profit in it? More sail than ballast, if you ask me."

"I know that song," I said dully. "That is Pontiac's song."

"So he reckons he's a bird, does he?" said Rogers. "We've flushed him out then. We'll hang him till he's good and high and give him to General Amherst for breakfast!"

This cheered up most of the men, even the Ranger who was shaking under a blanket with a wound in his belly no sawbones could remedy.

But in my mind, I could hear the rest of Pontiac's battle-song:

> The eagles scream on high
> They thirst for my enemy's heart
> They look from their circles on high
> And scorn all flesh but the brave.

The words carried a remembered smell, keener than the tannery tang of Campau's beaver plews: the semen smell of charred bones.

My hands shook a little when I returned to my post at the broad, square window by the door. Campau's tobacco-box rested on a little rack over the lintel. I stretched to take a plug, but others had been in it before me.

At that instant, I felt a violent jerk in my right arm, and my firelock was torn away. My urgent need for tobacco no doubt saved me from worse than the loss of my firearm. Stretched out as I was, the sudden jolt relieved me of my center of gravity, and I tumbled backwards and sideways. The hatchet of the Indian who hurled himself through the window screaming his *sassakwi* drove splinters from the floorboards instead of the roof of my skull.

Rogers shot him through the back of the neck.

Another came after him. I saw the sharp, cruel eyes in the striped face under the bright flurry of feathers, the glint of the wicked steel point on the back of the war club, ideal for gouging out eyes.

I found my knife and slid it between the Ottawa's ribs. The blade tilted and skidded off the bone. The savage kept coming. I felt his heart pumping against my own. He

seized my knife hand in a vise, pulling it back as he
worked the point of his club round to my throat. His
strength was beyond that of ordinary men. His blood
drenched me to the skin, but I was weak as putty in that
terrible embrace.

No man came to my aid; we were under attack from all
points of the compass.

As in a dream, a singsong floated in my ears, in the Indian tongue.

> *Nahmeba osayaun*
> *Benah neenbishwe*
> *Ahnah kemenuah bumenak*
>
> I walk about in the night
> See! I am a lynx
> Do you like my looks?

I recognized the words. They were the words of a medicine song, a song of the conjurer Hole In The Day,
Davers's magical antagonist, who claimed to be able to
transform himself into a bird or an animal to overcome his
enemies. I did not realize that these words were issuing
from my own lips, until I saw the eyes of my adversary
widen in fear, or recognition. For a moment, his intent wa-
vered. In that moment, his grip loosened sufficiently for
me to drive my knife deeper, until I found the heart.

I say that I found his heart, but I suspect that he gave
it to me. When Davers first told me about the Indian attitude to death, I thought his mind was gone. I had seen
enough to understand that a man who believes he has already traveled to the beyond and overcome its terrors has
a more relaxed attitude towards dying than those of us
who don't know where in the hell we are going. This native, certainly, was not afraid of dying. I laid him down
gently, because when the blood-frenzy left him, I recognized in those bold features disfigured by warpaint and
those sad, dreaming eyes the face of a man who had once
been family. His Ottawa name was Wahgekaut—Crooked
Legs. He was my adopted father.

He was mouthing his death-song.

I caught only one phrase: "*Nee nin dauw.* I am a man." Only two months before, those words had meant more to me than a peerage.

One of the Rangers wanted to take Crooked Legs's scalp. I offered to fight him if he tried, and Rogers backed me up, though perhaps the Ottawa would have considered it an honor.

The Indians gave up trying to force their way inside the house, but they came on in waves like blackbirds to shoot at close range. The first wave would run up, discharge their weapons, and run back to reload, while another party of Indians took their place.

I don't know how long we were fighting. The Rangers had bullets between their teeth for speed in reloading and laid down a hailstorm of lead on our attackers. But they kept coming on.

I remember that, in the hollow of the night, Captain Grant came as close as he dared and yelled to us that Dalyell was killed and that he had assumed command and was leading the remnants of our force back to the fort. If it appeared that common sense had at last taken charge of our fortunes, this brought no comfort to those of us holed up in Campau's house.

"We'll cover the rear!" Rogers called back to Grant. "But we'll never get off without the boats! You'll have to send them back for us!"

In the pink dawn, we watched the redcoats marching home along that street of death. The Indians had left off their assault on the house to nip at the heels of the fusiliers; thank God they never thought of fire-arrows, or we would have been lost for sure. So Rogers gave orders to take boards from the roof, to form breastworks outside, where we could better cover the retreat and prepare for our own embarkation. Campau was close to tears as he witnessed the Rangers dismantling his house.

It was full light when the gunboats returned from ferrying dead and wounded to the landing below the fort. The swivels belched black puffs of smoke, firing over our heads to hold off Pontiac's braves as we ducked and crawled our way through the pickets and over the muskrat holes among the sedge to the safety of the stout oak siding of the flatboats. Have you ever smelled the sweetness of fresh white oak? The wood was pinkish inside the sooty surrounds of the bullet-holes on the outer side. Oak never smelled sweeter to me than when I squatted on my haunches between two Highlanders that morning.

When the stragglers came in and the tallies were made, Major Gladwin found we had lost sixty-one officers and men, killed or wounded. James Dalyell was among the missing. There are varying accounts of how he died. The general informed his kinsmen that he received the fatal bullet when he risked his life going to the aid of a wounded soldier. Alex Duncan of the 55th told me he was standing in an orchard when he was shot, still unable to decide whether to advance or withdraw.

I do not question No Deal's valor. But personally, I would prefer to go into battle with a Mohawk, who will risk his hide to avenge his father or his grandfather, but for no more abstract reason, and never without figuring the odds, than with the Dalyells of this world in whom bravery often amounts to pig-headedness carried to an absurd extreme.

Few medals were won that night, and fewer favors.

Pontiac had flogged us raw. He had bested a column of two hundred and fifty regulars and in the doing he had again revealed a sense of tactics that our soldiers thought impossible in an Indian, although I dare say Saint Ange can take some of the credit for that. We knew that word of Pontiac's victory would spread like a brushfire through the upper country and puff new life into the Indian revolt. The day before we had been toasting the relief of Detroit; now it appeared we were in greater danger than we had ever been.

Dearest Shane,

Men fight for honor, for a garter or a promise of paradise. Women fight to survive, to avoid being throttled.

Your

Valerie

16

Amherst's War

BULLDOG GLADWIN THOUGHT WE needed to do something to show the natives that we had not got the wind up, so the sloop was despatched upriver. As the ship tacked against wind and current, the long black muzzles of the guns dipped as low as the river. When the sloop rolled back, the gunners lofted their balls in the direction of Pontiac's encampment. They fell in the swamp, driving up clouds of gnats and mosquitoes. I doubt that they disturbed the Indians' digestion.

The siege of Detroit was not raised by British arms. It required another full year before a major relief party got through to Gladwin. If we were able to hold on to the fort, it was because of timely intelligence of Indian wiles, and the fact that the natives did not possess cannons, and because, far to our rear, Sir William was able to hold open the Iroquois Trail to Lake Ontario. When the hardwoods flamed red and yellow and fish-hawks wheeled in the clear, sharp air, most of Pontiac's men developed itchy feet and started to drift away to their winter hunting-grounds. Some of his allies sued for peace. But Pontiac did not leave off the siege until early November when he received another letter from Neyon, the French commander at Fort Chartres, telling him bluntly that the natives should abandon hostilities because there was nothing that King Louis would do for them. Pontiac sent Gladwin a letter. To judge by the quality of the French, his amanuensis was that rough brute Mini Chêne.

"Tous nos jeunes gens ont enterré leurs casse-têtes," he wrote. All our young men have buried the hatchet. *"Si tu es bien comme moi, tu me feras réponse. Je te souhaite le bonjour."* You may make of the rest what you please. It was something less than an olive branch. Pontiac went off towards Sandusky, and then to the Maumee River with three hundred warriors, and we soon learned from our spies and scouts that it was his fixed intention to renew the war and the siege of Detroit the next spring.

I had long since taken my leave of the fort, and Angélique. Gladwin sent the schooner back to Niagara to fetch supplies and I went with her, bound for Johnson country. You may think my last interview with Angélique somewhat wanting in gallantry; I wish I could give you a bolder and braver account. The truth of it is, I believe my experiences among the natives after Robert Davers's death had knocked me a little off my stride. But this is not the whole of it. Her looks and her extraordinary *elasticity* nurtured a cold infatuation, but it never developed into the warmth of real affection. In short, I left her to James Sterling. I am told they married after the revolt.

We got through to Niagara without incident, but at the fort below the falls there was alarming news of another massacre. On the narrow, slippery portage road, three miles below the cascades, a sheer precipice drops away to a watery abyss toothed with jagged rocks. Here, on September 14th, the Senecas fell on a train of wagons and packhorses returning to the lower landing under military escort. Lieutenant Stedman, who was in charge of the convoy, kept a cool head and got away by wheeling his horse and spurring it through a pack of screaming savages. Most of his men were killed, as were a good number of the relief party Major Wilkins sent up. They showed me the spot

where Stedman's negro drummer-boy was saved by his
drum-strap; it snagged in the branches of a tree as he fell
down the precipice into the Devil's Hole, saving his neck.

The Seneca ambush at Devil's Hole on the portage road
was characteristic of the revolt, as of native methods of
fighting in general, in a way that the sit-down siege of Detroit was not. We could hold on to a fortified position,
given proper warning. But we could not hope to beat the
natives at their own game in a war of ambush and skirmish along shadowed forest trails. We could not even
expect to keep our communications open west of Schenectady without the active complicity of the Six Nations. The
army dreamed of a stunning blow to punish the rebels and
destroy their forces. Sir William and the Indian Department labored to make them comprehend that a purely military victory was beyond our grasp. Sir Jeffrey Amherst
and our would-be war heroes drew up plans for sending
columns of regulars at vast expense across great stretches
of wilderness—to do what? To drive formless bands of
woodland fighters into deeper cover, leaving our soldiers
to burn a few wretched bark huts and a few miserable
acres of corn; the western Indians had little property of
value that they could not carry on their own backs. The
natives will not give European regulars the entertainment
of a setpiece battle unless they have chosen their own
ground and are breaking from ambush. I am no military
historian, but I doubt that even the most blinkered of that
calling would deny that, in military terms, the Pontiac revolt was an almost unbroken chronicle of Indian victories.
Some of our annalists have celebrated the Battle of Bushy
Run, when our Swiss soldier of fortune, Colonel Bouquet,
held off a pack of Shawnees near Fort Pitt, as a triumph
of British arms. I count it a slim victory for four hundred
and sixty regulars to survive an encounter with ninety-five
Indians with the loss of only sixty men—and this is the
closest thing to a British victory you will find in the record
of the Conspiracy of Pontiac. We did not contain the revolt
by force of arms, but by diplomacy and intrigue. General
Amherst gave us the war; Sir William Johnson ended it,

and proved himself, more than at any other time in his remarkable career, to be our indispensable man.

Johnson had decamped from his stone house by the river
and installed himself in his new manor, set twelve miles
back into the woods. He worked among the din of ham-
mers and saws. The plaster was still damp; the flock paper
would not stick to the walls. Sir William had planned and
constructed Johnson Hall in the year I had been away from
the Valley, hiring Samuel Fuller, the master builder from
Schenectady, to work from sketches roughed out in his
own hand for eight shillings a day. Johnson's boyhood
memories of Smithstown and Warrenstown were revived
in the design. He had put up a sturdy, hip-roofed, two
story house, sheathed in clapboards sawed and sanded to
resemble fieldstone. The Palladian window was new to the
Valley, and was Sir William's only concession to elegance.
Johnson Hall was designed for use—above all, for the in-
gathering of the clans. The stairhall was eighteen feet
wide, wide enough for a horse and cutter, or for scores of
native sachems assembled for a council, or for a hundred
Scots and Irish tenants come to toast the master on Saint
Patrick's Day. The main building was flanked by stone
blockhouses, loopholed for musketry, because Sir William
and his household were more vulnerable to enemy raiders
here than at Fort Johnson on the King's Road. Indeed, for
Johnson to move back into the woods to this gentle rise
above the Cayadutta Creek in the midst of the native uprising was a bold challenge to fate, calculated to allay the
fears of his neighbors and dependents. Of all the king's
men in our colonies, Sir William was the foremost candi-
date for assassination. In my absence, parties of hostile
Delawares and Senecas had come nosing and nipping
along the Valley with blood in their eyes for Johnson. The
Mohawks warned him that a pair of Senecas who came to
visit him at the Hall in the guise of ambassadors were assassins hired by renegade Frenchmen to take his life. He
received them in his sick bed, with his father's sword of
Damascus steel lying openly on the covers, and their purpose faltered before those steady gray eyes.

Sir William no longer spoke of the "Pontiac revolt" or the "Indian uprising." He spoke of "Amherst's war." He blamed Sir Jeffrey for starting the war. Now he was fighting to prevent the general from losing it.

When we had finished talking about Pontiac and No Deal and Davers, Johnson squired me into his bedroom office and gave me a sheaf of papers from Sir Jeffrey.

"I doubt whether a man in the king's service has ever damned himself more copiously from out of his own mouth," said Sir William. "Here, Shane. You may study the views of our commander-in-chief for yourself. While you are about it, you may choose to amuse yourself by setting them in order and making an abstract. I believe it will serve our purpose better with the Lords of Trade and the American Department than a dozen memorials from my hand."

I am not cut out for quill-driving and solitary study, but I may tell you that the general's correspondence supplied the best entertainment I had known in several months. I was so engrossed that when Joseph and some of his Mohawk friends turned up to fete my return, I made them wait for an hour. I laughed, I howled, I wept, remembering the good men who had already died because of our general's sneering ram-headedness; at last I burned with a black rage as I fathomed where his logic would lead us.

That rage still lives in me as I recall how a British commander, nettled by the fruits of his own vanity and neglect, shaped his frustrations into a warrant for genocide. But I must allow Sir Jeffrey to speak for himself, as Johnson wished.

A month after Davers was killed and several of our forts about the Great Lakes had fallen, General Amherst refused to credit all rumors of an uprising. He sniffed that posts commanded by British officers "can certainly never be in danger from such a wretched enemy" as the natives.

When Johnson sent him the first definite intelligence that Detroit was besieged, in a letter concealed in a powderhorn and carried back to the Valley by Joseph, the general flatly declined to believe it. He conceded that "the affair of the Indians appears to be more general than I had apprehended," but added, "I believe nothing of what is mentioned regarding the garrison of Detroit being cut off."

By the time I made my escape from Pontiac's camp, Sir Jeffrey could no longer shrug off the reports from Gladwin and Black George Croghan in the Ohio country. He scraped together the remnants of our regular forces in the colonies—two hundred kilted Highlanders of the 42nd, half as many fever-ridden men from the 77th—and sent them up the river to Albany, en route to Niagara and the west. He confessed his near-impotence. "Should the whole race of Indians take arms against us, I can do no more." Like many men of my acquaintance who have trouble getting it up, he tried to compensate for the feebleness of his parts by loud and raucous talk.

"No prisoners!"

"Extirpate the villains!"

"No punishment we can inflict is adequate to the crimes of these inhuman beasts!"

This was followed by a letter to Sir William received about the time I left Detroit.

"It behooves the whole race of Indians," thus Amherst, "to beware of carrying matters against the English, or daring to form conspiracies, as the consequence will most certainly occasion measures that in the end will put a most effectual stop to their very being."

Now I suppose that this, even from the pen of our commander-in-chief, might be dismissed as verbal extravagance of no greater import than a case of flatulence. It was a good deal worse than that, as Sir William had discovered from an exchange of letters between Amherst and Bouquet, the Swiss mercenary who had been sent to relieve Fort Pitt, filched by Croghan and brought to Johnson Hall.

The general hatched a practical design for "putting a stop to the very being" of inconvenient natives.

He wrote to Bouquet: "Could it not be contrived to send the smallpox among these disaffected tribes?"

And the soldier of fortune, bent on pleasing his paymaster, wrote back: "I will try to inoculate the —— with some blankets that may fall into their hands."

You will note that Colonel Bouquet was too polite to spell out the missing word. But I believe that he served the general's wishes to the very letter, because there was an epidemic of the smallpox that winter, in the Ohio country, and it killed not only rebel Delawares and Shawnees but friendly Mingoes and some Mohawk hunters as well.

I will not detain you with a polemic, but I want these things remembered, as Johnson did. It may puzzle you that I did not share Sir Jeffrey's gusto to "extirpate the villains" after what I had seen and narrowly survived. I am no stranger to the instinct of revenge; to this day, I would not trust myself alone with one or two Chippewas of my acquaintance, nor one or two frenchies either. But Sir Jeffrey Amherst sat in safety inside Fort George at the tip of Manhattan Island many hundreds of miles from the places where other men bled, pressing for the destruction of a whole race because he had made a fool of himself in the eyes of his masters in London. I hold him morally accountable, not only for the revolt, but for the atrocities committed on friendly natives by cowardly, swaggering louts all along our borders.

You must have heard something of Conestoga and the Paxton Boys. I passed near the manor of Conestoga in 1765 on my way to Black George Croghan and the Illinois country. It is on the Susquehanna, not far from Lancaster. Since the first days of the white settlement, it was peopled by a mixed band of Iroquois, mostly Oneidas, who lived on friendly terms with their neighbors. By the end of the first year of the native revolt, their number had dwindled to twenty-odd basket-weavers and broom-sellers, living in squalor in a huddle of rude cabins. Around Christmas time, some belching zealot of a Scotch-Irish Covenanter got up in Paxton town spouting Joshua, and collected fifty bully-boys to raid the Conestoga village. They killed the six or seven women they found there, lifted their scalps and fired their cabins. When the surviving Conestogans were removed to Lancaster jail for their safety, the Paxton gang pursued them there and stormed the calaboose. Some of the natives escaped to temporary sanctuary under the eye of the Quakers at Philadelphia, where they were joined by Moravian Indian converts who had been similarly driven from their homes in the Lehigh valley. Hundreds of backlands brawlers converged on the city, threatening revolution unless they were given the Indians to butcher. In terror, the city fathers tried to export their charges to New York. Sir William and the Mohawks wanted to offer them homes in the Valley, but Colden, our acting governor, declined to let them into the province; he thought, with some reason, that the story of how they had been treated would have a dispiriting effect on our allies of the Six Nations. They were dragged back to Philadelphia where I gather the greater part succumbed to smallpox—perhaps a further legacy of General Amherst, Colonel Bouquet and their contaminated blankets.

I will not pursue this chronicle of horrors. There were blacker episodes than Conestoga. The worst, to my mind, involved a Welsh deserter from our forces named David Owens, who had taken up residence among the natives and lived with a Shawnee woman. When he got wind of the scalp bounty being offered by the Pennsylvania government, he killed and scalped his own wife and children and presented their hair to the authorities. I believe he got his money.

You may think it natural that white men should seek vengeance for the killings and tortures committed all along our frontiers. I dare say it was. I am saying something different—that our commander-in-chief was openly expressing views that sanctioned the most bestial instincts of our lowest frontier scum who regarded all Indians with the same black hatred and held that none of them should be treated better than rattlesnakes. They damn near won Pontiac's war for him by a string of outrages on the heels of the general's insults and neglect that had the Six Nations up in arms. If William Johnson had not managed to hold the Mohawks and most of their Iroquois neighbors to our cause, I believe that Niagara, Detroit and Fort Pitt would have fallen and white settlers would have been driven from the interior of New York as they were chased out of the Ohio country.

This was Johnson's greatest accomplishment during the

revolt and all our hopes of winning back the continent west of the Alleghenies depended on it. You see, the Mohawks and the Confederacy of the Longhouse command the river roads to the Great Lakes and the heartlands of North America, and they are the greatest warriors and politicians you will find among all the tribes of Indians. I did not personally witness Sir William's counciling with the Six Nations during the first part of the revolt, but I can imagine it, and so can you, from what I have already written about his methods. I know there was a time, after the Chenussio Senecas bolted the stable, when it looked as if five of the Six Nations were preparing to defect from the British alliance. At that time, the Mohawks from the two castles, led by Nickus Brant and Canadagaia, gathered at Johnson Hall. They made him the solemn pledge, sealed by a twenty-row belt, that even if all other Indians in America took the warpath against him, the Mohawks would stand and die with Johnson. I believe that this single event, in the summer of 1763, when Dalyell was trying to get himself killed at Detroit, was the moment when the tide began to turn in our favor.

Now, with winter coming on, Sir William was working by guile and promises and bribes out of his own pocket to divide Pontiac's native allies and to spirit up friendly tribes to go to war on the rebels. There was a crowd of fierce Caughnawagas from Canada about the house, painted for war and scraped to a tiny scalp lock. They were kinsmen of the Mohawks, bitter enemies of Britain in the late war, but now thirsty for the blood of Ottawas and Chippewas, who were ancient enemies of their nation. They volunteered to go and knock Pontiac's boys on the head if Johnson gave them the hatchet. Sir William passed on the good news to Amherst. The general, utterly consistent in his folly, banned him from using Indians to fight Indians.

Johnson did not need Amherst's permission the next time he tried gathering up a native war-party to fight on our side. The general received a rude letter from the Lords of Trade, fell into a sulk, awarded himself home leave, and took ship for England in November, never to return to the colonies. You may imagine the warmth of the sentiments

we expressed at Johnson Hall over bumpers of flip and
madeira when this glad news traveled up the river.

The happy messenger was Black George Croghan, who
cut a rum figure at our party in a kilt he had borrowed
from one of the Highlanders on Johnson's advice, because
he was suffering from a nasty complication with his
plumbing that left him dripping from a hole at the bottom
of his belly. I have no doubt how he earned this affliction.
I told him he might take comfort from the thought that
brave men are always wounded in front. Chicha's native
herbs worked their magic and George was dandified in a
fine new pair of velvet breeches within a few days.

At our bumpering in honor of Sir Jeffrey's removal,
Black George offered the following poetical tribute. He
declared it to be his own composition, which I believe, because I think no one but the author would lay claim to it:

> From every generous noble passion free
> As proud and ignorant as man can be
> Revengeful, avaricious, obstinate is he
> Malicious, stupid and obdurate will ever be
> A fleeting consequence he's dully grave
> Rest here my pen enough—the man's a knave.

You will observe that Croghan was ever slow to forgive a
man who questioned his accounts, which, alas, were always highly questionable, as you shall see. Croghan was
on his way to England and spent a good deal of time clos-
eted with Sir William preparing memorials to men of influence in our government. Johnson was determined to use
the native revolt to oblige our ministry to endorse his
schemes to strengthen the Indian Department and set its fi-
nances on a permanent footing, independent of the whims
of military commanders or fickle colonial assemblies. He
was also lobbying relentlessly for his Boundary Line.

About that time we learned from despatches that King
George had issued a royal proclamation, dated October 7,
setting a limit to white settlement. The box-wallahs in
London did not know much American geography; they
settled on the notion that the boundary should run along

the tips of the Alleghenies. Everything to the west of the
heads of the rivers draining the Atlantic seaboard was to
be reserved for the Indians, "for the present and until our
future pleasure be known." We drank the king's health as
prodigiously as we had toasted Sir Jeffrey's backside. The
proclamation was grand as a statement of good intentions,
and Sir William quoted it to good effect at his council with
the Indian nations at Niagara the following summer. But
we all knew it would stand or fall on the fine print, and
there was a multitude of practical difficulties—for a start,
a fair number of English colonists had staked a claim to
the Ohio lands, and the French had a busy settlement in
the rich lands of the Illinois, hundreds of miles west of the
Alleghenies.

For the moment, however, ending the war consumed
most of Sir William's energies. I do not say "winning the
war," because we did not win it. In truth, I believe that
neither Britain nor France ever conquered the great nations
of woodland Indians; most certainly, the Mohawks and
their cousins are undefeated to this day. The army went
looking for a decisive military victory over Pontiac's
hosts. They never found it. Bradstreet went west with one
expedition. He encountered a bunch of Delaware spies on
Lake Erie who persuaded him they were lofty ambassadors
empowered to conclude a general treaty of peace. He gave
them some rum, they gave him their worthless marks and
he sailed on to Detroit in a haze of self-congratulation and
insulted some other tribes by describing them as "subjects" of Britain and chopping up a wampum belt with an
axe. On his return voyage, he chose a stupidly exposed an-
chorage for his flatboats on Lake Erie, lost half his bateaux when a storm whipped up at night, and abandoned
his provincials and his Indian scouts, who included some
Mohawk friends of mine, without provisions while he hied
back to Niagara with his regulars. Bouquet, of the infected
blankets, did a little better on a second expedition down
the Ohio. He met Shawnees and Delawares on the Scioto
and impressed them sufficiently to put their hands to a
ceasefire agreement that meant something. But it was
Johnson, jawing, cajoling and threatening night and day in

private sessions and public councils with the native sachems, who bound the tribes, one by one, to his covenant chain. He did not insist on atonement for every crime committed along the border. He did insist on the return of our captives—Croghan alone took delivery of more than two hundred—on guarantees of safe passage for our soldiers and traders and, in the case of the Senecas, of the formal cession to the Crown of the lands about the Niagara carry. In dealing with the chiefs who stood against him, Johnson showed a ruthlessness that, unlike Amherst's, was practical and specific. I saw him promise blood money to a party of Indian rangers led by Montour, Croghan's half-breed interpreter. He wanted them to kill two Delaware chiefs who had murdered some of our settlers.

Like one of his Celtic forebears, he told them, "The scalp is not sufficient. You will bring me their whole heads."

He did not get those heads, but a war-party in which Joseph served did bring him the notorious Delaware renegade Captain Bull, bound and trussed.

Seventeen hundred Indians came to Niagara for Sir William's peace council in the summer of 1764. They included all the nations that had laid siege to Detroit, but they did not include Pontiac. He was said to be ranging the backlands between the mouth of the Maumee River and the Illinois territory. Croghan's spies reported that he was in contact with the French officers at Fort Chartres and with Governor d'Abbadie at New Orleans, and that the French had renewed their incitement to pursue the revolt. It was unclear whether Saint Ange and his kind were acting on their own initiative or had received new instructions from their government.

In the early spring of 1765, Sir William told me that Black George Croghan was to embark on a mission to the Illinois to make peace with Pontiac.

"I want you to go with him, Shane. George Croghan is the most valuable man we have westward of this Valley. But he is not to be trusted with a cash-box, a land map, or a woman under the age of sixty. I want you to keep an eye on him for me. Your personal connection with Pontiac and his womenfolk may be of special service to our cause."

I wished, of course, that I had not confided the episode with Pontiac's daughter to Sir William.

I had no great appetite for a tedious journey over half a continent, to a dubious rendezvous with the very savages who had promised to grill me alive. But I confess that I saw the chance of a considerable fortune in a scheme Black George had been talking of concerning the Illinois country, and I had another personal reason for wishing to make myself as scarce as possible in the province of New York that spring. As usual, this involved a woman. On a visit to Manhattan, I had contracted a whirlwind marriage with a Suky Van Horn who melted into my arms at the stirring account of two strong lovers contesting the savages. The family maintained its objections, and once the biological interest began to dim, I was bound to agree with them that Suky and I had little enough in common. Not knowing quite how to resolve the affair, I determined to put some distance between myself and the lady.

I told Johnson I would join Black George in his search for Pontiac if he would give me leave to return to England for at least a year.

"I'll not let go of you, Shane Hardacre," Sir William warned me. "And if you let go of me, the Mohawks will bring you back."

I thought this was merely a pleasantry. But even after death, William Johnson kept his pledge.

Dearest Shane,

I had not realized to what degree William Johnson
remained an Irishman, until I read your account of how
he upended an English commander-in-chief and defended
the natives against the general's contempt. I had
feared Billy Johnson was only another West Briton,
who honors his roots by drinking too deep on Saint
Paddy's Day. I find we must be proud of Billy after all.

Does Smithstown House still stand? I would like to
know you under the weeping beeches. Or in the loft
in the stableyard, perfumed by ripening apples.

Your

Valerie

17

Black George

CROGHAN, I SUPPOSE, WAS a poor man's Sir William. He never forgot it, and supercilious snobs in the king's livery found a thousand cruel ways to remind him of it. He consumed whatever money he laid hands on trying to prove he was as grand a gentleman as any blue-blooded brat from the Home Counties or the Pale, quite as grand as Sir William himself. When I caught up with him at Fort Pitt, he was living in a house he called Croghan Hall. The chamber-pots were of pewter, which suggested that the quantities of shrub and sangree that flowed into the master issued without diminution of quality. The lord of Croghan Hall received me in a new suit of crimson plush and a fine embroidered waistcoat with pearl-studded buttons that would have made Dandy Cuillerier stare, and a flashy diamond on his finger the size of two or three deer pellets.

The neighborhood of Fort Pitt—the Fort at the Crotch, we called it—was a deal more lax than the Mohawk Valley in those days, and thus provided a suitable backdrop for its dominating spirit. The man who read the Sunday prayers lived with a whore. The fort doctor had knocked up the blacksmith's daughter and fought a duel over his rights with a subaltern of the Royal Americans. Black George Croghan and Captain Ecuyer of the garrison held Saturday night routs where they pushed the glass about among the ladies so briskly that before half the night was over, they were as proper as a clutch of white-stockinged doxies from the Strand.

Like Sir William, Black George had a native consort, a half-breed Seneca woman who had borne him a daughter with the haunting name of Trembling Earth, one of the prettiest Indian girls I have seen, and one of the few fixtures in Croghan's world that he did not share with all comers.

Croghan aped Sir William's style and his manners, but he could never quite carry it off. In those silks and velvets, his short, ball-bellied, stoop-shouldered frame and pug-nosed, primitive features reminded me powerfully of an organ-grinder's monkey. Black George never learned to spell, and he never got rid of that brogue that marked him, as my Galway nanny used to say, as a child among the ashes; it carried the breath of pig-steam and damp woollen breeches, in a stinking lime-white cotter's hut beside a peat fire. You may think me prejudiced. I deny the charge. I believe that Croghan was as exceptional in his way as Johnson. He was probably the best intelligencer in all of the colonies, and when his blood was up, he was willing to wager his life at odds that would have made Robert Rogers blanch. But Croghan was deeply flawed. Great men, I believe, recognize their native failings and turn them into their strengths, as old Demosthenes worked on his speech defect with pebbles in his mouth and made himself, by his own force of will, the foremost orator in a nation of blowhards. In this sense, Croghan lacked greatness. He allowed himself to stew in resentment over the accident of birth. He was consumed by jealousy of those favored with nobler features and handsomer pedigrees. His constant terror was of being hurled back into the poverty of his childhood. He cheated and connived to hold this fear at bay, and died a pauper at Philadelphia nonetheless, with the ruins of his showy coach rotting outside the door, and no money to put a nag in the traces. But that was a long while later. At Fort Pitt, and on our journey to Pontiac, I saw Black George in his glory days. But I also saw signs of that fatal flaw that led to his rift with Sir William, after Croghan jogged and wheedled Johnson into betraying his own high purpose.

I found Croghan mightily changed by his visit to England the year before. From his account, I gathered that he had set out to play the nabob of the New World, trotting about in a coach with liveried footmen, throwing banquets at his rooms at the Golden Cross, preening himself in the evenings in his splendid new clothes at the Globe Tavern or the Piazzas. London is not easily impressed. Black George failed with the ladies, and he failed with their lordships at the Board of Trade, to whom he applied for payment of various bills for Indian truck that Sir Jeffrey had refused to approve. Over his bottle, Black George grumbled about our distant masters.

"Their talk is mere froth. They know less of the colonies than of the Great Turk, and they look down their noses at anything and anyone that is American. The chief study of the men in power at present is how to lay new taxes on the backs of our settlers. There is no health in it, Shane, and that is the truth of it."

It was plain that George had been royally snubbed at London, and he came home more than half a rebel. It was odd to hear him reviling the Stamp Act, since one of the principal reasons the government brought in this tax was to provide permanent funding for the Indian Department. In the Valley, we took a pretty dim view of the rioters in Boston and the Liberty boys. Sir William would not stand for any of that nonsense, and of course the Mohawks and his Scottish clansmen, who had fought for a different king but thought any kind of king was better than none, were with him to a man. We never heard of a Liberty Tree or a tea-party without cucumber sandwiches in Johnson country until after Sir William's death in the summer of 1774.

"It takes money to wipe out the blot, my bucko," thus Croghan, with two pints of rum inside him, "pots and pots of it! And I know how to get it! Stay by George, my dear, and we'll both be richer than the Duke of Westminster. I've walked a fair portion of the earth's crust, and I tell you there is no land that is fairer nor fatter than the country about the Illinois. The beaver trade alone is worth a hundred thousand pounds a year. The earth is rich and deep and loamy, and there isn't a stone in sight that would turn a plow. You have only to cast your eye on it, and the wheat springs up tall in front of you. The Lords of Trade can't say agin us, because the frogs are there already, and if we let 'em sit easy, they'll steal the whole fur trade from behind our backs and pack it down the yellow Mississippi to Noo Orleens. Gage is in—he knows a deal when he sees one—and Sir William, God love him, is in to the hilt. I'll see you get your proper portion if you serve George right."

In short, Black George was planning to plant a new English colony along the Illinois, five hundred miles west of our famous Boundary Line. It is no mystery why General Gage, our new commander-in-chief, had given this venture his blessing. Gage was slow in his parts, as he demonstrated to the rebels at Bunker Hill, but he had an instinct for a profit and a prevailing wind. You may ask why Sir William approved a scheme that appeared to make nonsense of the line between whites and Indians. In all frankness, I do not know whether cupidity or grand strategy played the deeper role in his calculations. I never met a man in the American colonies who drew a hard and fast boundary between the public interest and private gain, and Sir William, for all his greatness, was no exception. He had taken a one-eighth share in the land company Croghan was forming to take possession of the Illinois territory, using the names of tenants and dependents to mask his own involvement. But there were larger issues at stake. So long as we left Frenchmen, under any flag, in command of the Illinois, they would not only encroach on our fur trade, they would threaten our hold over the Indians and supply new incitements to revolt. We had intelligence that Saint Ange was in charge at Fort Chartres on our side of the Mississippi, that Pontiac was his frequent guest, and that both of them were conspiring with the frenchies at New

Orleans at the mouth of the river to strike a new blow against our colonies. Then, too, Sir William may have hoped that the Illinois venture would draw the press of new settlers far to the west of the country of the Six Nations, the Indians who held his special affection. I do not say that such calculations absolve Johnson from the charge of inconsistency or private greed, only that he was never, by my observation, moved solely by love of money. Ne needed money to work his will in defiance of niggardly Crown officers and Indian-hating provincials, and to pay for the needs of the Indian Department when they refused to honor his bills. I cannot say the same for Black George Croghan.

Croghan had summoned an Indian council at Fort Pitt, to bolt the door behind us, as he put it, before we set off down the Ohio. Shawnees, Delawares and Senecas were still straggling in when a sorry figure rolled off a wagon and hobbled up to the door of Croghan Hall. His clothes were bloodied rags. His skin was blackened and blistered as if he had been badly burned. A few chicken feathers adhered to the clotted blood at the back of his neck. His nether garment was a breechclout, soiled and bundled tight between the legs, as a tourniquet.

"God in heaven!" cried Croghan. "It's Callender! What's happened, man? Where is the convoy?"

"Drink," croaked Callender. I learned that he was one of Black George's business partners, tasked with escorting a cargo of Indian goods from Philadelphia.

Croghan dosed him with shrub and demanded, "Which of the beasts was it? Are the Delawares on the rampage again?"

"Wasn't injuns," Callender gasped, when he had wetted his throttle. "White men. Paxton Boys. Damn the buggers to hell!"

"What of the convoy?" Croghan's eyes bulged from his head.

"All. The bastards got it all. Killed the packhorses. Rode me on a rail."

Little by little, we extracted the whole story, and it will tell you more of Black George Croghan and his business practices than of the manners of our border ruffians. He and his associates had arranged credit to the tune of twenty thousand pounds, no less, with the Philadelphia firm of Baynton, Wharton, of which you shall hear something more in this narrative. Indian goods to the value of half this amount had been loaded in a packtrain and sent to Fort Pitt. Crossing the Scotch-Irish settlements near Paxton, one of the drivers had lost a barrel. It burst open in the plain view of some of the men who had burned out the Conestoga Indians, and they did not like what they saw. The barrel contained steel knives, and any knife destined for Indians makes frontiersmen think of scalping. The Paxton gang staged an ambush. They blackened themselves like savages, dressed their hair with feathers, and descended on Croghan's packtrain with war whoops and scalp yells. They stole, or spoiled, everything, and gave Croghan's men the scare of their lives. I do not know what it feels like to be ridden on a rail, but the thought of a rough-hewn plank sawing between my posteriors, gives me a most unpleasant twinge. Callender took to his bed and Black George took to writing furious letters to Sir William and anyone else whose help he thought he could invoke. The episode not only left Black George drowning in debt, which goes a long way towards explaining his later deceptions; it supplied his enemies with evidence that he was a crook of the first water. You see, Indian agents were strictly forbidden to engage in the fur trade on their own account, and Croghan had been counting on this packtrain not only to sprinkle presents among the sachems of the Ohio and the Illinois, but to engross the peltries of the west while the market was soft.

Sir William stood by him when the public inquisition began later on, because he knew that Croghan was irreplaceable in his territory. But I think that even Johnson's influence would not have saved Black George from being kicked out of the Department and consigned to a debtor's jail had it not been for what we managed to pull off along the Illinois.

Our council at Fort Pitt commenced under the shadow of this disaster on the Pennsylvania border. The Indians delivered up some white captives, and it was curious to observe how sorrowfully some of these men and women parted company with their adoptive families; I have never seen native prisoners shed tears at being returned to their own people. I have shown you something of native cruelty. I may have failed to stress the tenderness with which the Indians regard a white man who is adopted as one of their own. I will not detain you with the speech-making at Fort Pitt. The tribes that were formerly sworn to drive the red dogs into the sea now offered their pledge to respect the treaty with Great Britain as long as sun and moon will shine, or something along those lines.

Black George persuaded some of the Shawnees to accompany us on our expedition. I was a little nervous of these sinewy, painted warriors with the blood of our soldiers and settlers on their hands. I know now that I owe my life to them.

But the most remarkable delegate at our council was a Delaware, and you may believe that I paid him very close attention because he was introduced as the Prophet.

There was nothing exceptional in his appearance. He was of less than middling height, clad in an old matchcoat and a filthy beaded breechclout and deerskin leggings. His lank gray hair swished against his shoulders like a horse's tail.

When the shadows were long, he got up and made a speech. He shook like a souse in powerful need of a drink. He chuffed and he whimpered. The tears made shiny rivulets down his cheeks, cracked and chapped like old leather left out in the sun. He said, so Croghan told me, that he had made a long journey to the realms of the Great Spirit and that the Master of Life had a bellyache because of all the blood that had been spilled in his name. He had commanded his red children to dig up the Tree of Life and bury the hatchet far below its roots, in the underground waters where it would never be found or remembered. The alleged Prophet held up the peace pipe to the sky and the four quarters, shaking so violently I thought he would drop it. Then he passed it around for Croghan and the chiefs to

smoke. An unfortunate hummingbird was suspended next
to the bowl.

All this seemed to have a salutary effect on the natives,
who greeted every statement from the Prophet with approving yells. It left me to wonder whether this shaking lu-
minary was the being Robert Davers had gone questing
for. Only Davers could answer that, and he is not here to
speak to you on the matter. But as I write these words, I
seem to hear his voice.

"And if the Prophet came among you, which of you
would recognize him?"

More airy delusions, of course. Davers always had that
effect.

On the fifteenth of May, we boarded our little flotilla of
flatboats, pirogues and bark canoes, and set off down the
Ohio. It was a lazy, luxurious voyage, drenched in sun and
rum-shrub, colored by wild dreams of the fortune awaiting
us along the Illinois. A rash young officer, Lieutenant Alexander Fraser of the 78th, had gone on ahead to round up
the Indians for a powwow, and Croghan had sent out belts
with Shawnee runners. Black George did not think much
of the martial abilities of the Illinois tribes. He told me he
could lock up all of their sachems in a three-gallon keg of
rum, and that the great panjandrum of the Ouitanons—the
Crane People—was an old comrade of his and a tippler of
note. Between these reassuring words and my long, boozy
naps in the sun, I soon stopped worrying about scalping-
parties and French intrigues. When we made camp under
a blood-red sky, I went stalking with Big Hole, the Shawnee chief, and his son, and came back with a few fat beavers. At night, by the fire, I listened to Croghan's war
stories and his plots to even the score with his riotous
Pennsylvania neighbors, or gave myself over to musing on
what I might do with my share of the Illinois claim. I
could buy a townhouse in London and keep three fancy
mistresses, or fit out a ship and have fun in the sugar islands while making a packet. Yet I could never quite lose
myself in these roving fancies. Something kept pricking at
me—an attachment to Johnson and his Valley, a fear of

what might be lying ahead in the lairs of Pontiac and Saint Ange.

We drifted along with the river, snaking around its loops and bends to the mouth of the Scioto where a large party of Shawnees hailed us from the bank. They were friendly; it seemed that Croghan's charm and his promises of powder and rum had worked their spell. The Shawnees had even brought down six or seven frenchies who had been living in their territory. They were a shifty, disagreeable crew. They smelled as high as the natives and were dressed rather worse, and we could get precious little information out of them. Croghan told off a couple of soldiers to take them back to Fort Pitt.

After three weeks on the river, we came to the mouth of the Wabash where we were supposed to turn north and start poling upstream. But I noticed a rough breastwork of branches and felled logs among the trees—it blended nicely into the greens and browns of the forest—and the sharp-eyed Shawnees quickly detected the spoor of a big party of warriors among the sedge.

"Kickapoos," Big Hole pronounced.

I should explain that the Kickapoos are one of the principal nations in the Illinois Confederacy. Our Shawnees called them the Slug-Abeds. There is a Shawnee legend that once they and the Kickapoos formed a single nation. In a hungry season, one half of the tribe went hunting at night and came back loaded with game. The hunters were disgusted to find their comrades still sleeping soundly, so they went off by themselves towards the rising sun and founded the Shawnee nation. The Kickapoos were too dozy to pick up the trail, so they wandered off in the other direction to settle the Illinois.

Slug-Abeds or no, they were capable of setting an ambush, so we floated six miles further downstream. That was where we lost Ned Connor who served the offices of cook and barber. He went into the woods to see if he could bring down a deer and did not come back. We waited a whole day for him—he was not much of a cook, but was handy with a straight-edge razor—and brought on ourselves the very event we had gone out of our way to avoid.

I was relieving myself under a maple when my ear was offended by a nasty whining sound, like a deerfly thrumming in for blood. I put up my hand, and found the shaft of an arrow, quivering in the tree an inch from my head. At the instant I dropped down, clawing up my breeches, musketry crackled from the woods all along the bank and howling savages fell on us with knives and tomahawks. I saw Black George fall under a hideous blow from a tomahawk wielded by a square-built brute sporting a fur turban hung with feathers and silver brooches. Big Hole was down, and Nemwhoa, another of the Shawnee chiefs, was rocking on his backside gripping his thighs. Blood spurted through his fingers.

I did not see much more of this uneven contest because one of our attackers fell on me from behind. He grabbed me by the hair and I felt the point of his scalping-knife against my skull. I twisted and rolled and struck out with my heel at the part that counts. I missed my aim, but I gave my assailant sufficient pause for me to lay hands on the loaded fowling-piece I had rested against a stump. In my eagerness I pulled on the cock too forcefully and it snapped off in my hand. I need not tell you what a man with no cock is worth.

I believe the savage would have had me but for the barking and braying that issued from his war chief, Fur Turbain. It seemed he had enough scalps to serve his appetite. He wanted live meat as well. After what I had witnessed as a guest of the Chippewas, my reprieve, with a cord about my wrists, did not fill me with optimism.

Two white men had been fatally holed and three of the Shawnees, including Big Hole. Nemwhoa had been shot through both his thighs. Big Hole's son and one of our men had to carry him. I noticed that only the white men had been scalped. Our attackers, who proved to be mostly Kickapoos with a few Mascoulins, did not dare to mutilate Shawnees. Perhaps there was something in the legend of the Slug-Abeds after all.

To my great surprise and relief, I saw Black George on his feet.

He was jabbering away at Fur Turbain and fretting the

roof of his head. Nemwhoa, our wounded Shawnee, added
his powerful lungs to the chorus. Despite his condition, he
seemed to be striking fear into Fur Turbain. The Kickapoo
contemplated his toenails.

"George!" I cried out to him. "Will you tell me what is
to become of us?"

"Nemwhoa is telling 'em that if they don't treat us right
and make up for the ones they've holed, the whole Shawnee nation will come and take their revenge. I think they
believe him. The war chief claims the frenchies told them
we were coming with Cherokees to burn them out and
take their land. It could be a lie, but I think we've got
them on the run."

This seemed rather a sunny view of our situation. I was
unable to share it, swaying there between two painted savages with my arms tied behind my back and my breeches
about my knees.

"Do you think you have enough influence to induce
them to permit me to cover my arsè?" I demanded.

Black George chuckled and strolled over to perform the
office in person. They had not seen fit to bind him.

"You must be the very devil," I told him. "I saw you
take a hatchet blow that should have broken your skull
like a melon."

"My skull is pretty thick," he laughed, rubbing it again.
"You may observe, Mr Hardacre, that a thick skull is of
service on some occasions."

After some more jawing, the Kickapoo chief, who
called himself the Wolf, announced that they would take
us to Ouitanon, about forty miles up the Wabash, for a
council with the allied sachems of the Illinois tribes. It was
a tedious slog, but they loosed my hands and treated me as
gingerly as a spinster walking a lap-dog.

When we came to Ouitanon with its deserted fort and its
straggles of dome-roofed native huts, I found that Black
George had not overstated his popularity with some of the
Illinois nations. The head chief of the Crane People, whom
Croghan addressed as the Count, and was quite the beau in
his lace ruffles, read the riot act to the Kickapoos for

knocking his brothers on the head. The Wolf made whingeing excuses.

"We are your younger brothers and we never had much sense. We broke the peace pipe, but we have sent for a new one. When we struck our Shawnee brethren and our brother the Buck, the hatchet turned in our hands and bit into our own flesh."

There was a good deal more along the same lines. Belts and calumets were sent to the Shawnees with promises that the Kickapoos would atone for their crime. But though we were treated as honored guests and plied with the best food and drink the natives had on hand, there was no indication that they meant to set us at liberty. On the contrary, they sent runners to Fort Chartres to ask the French for instructions. This seemed to me definite proof that Saint Ange was behind the ambush.

We lay in the ruins of the commandant's house or baked in the courtyard of the fort, waiting for something to turn up. The man who turned up was that hell-hound Mini Chêne who went through the Indian settlement with a vicious report that a great chief of the Shawnees living on the Illinois had sent word that the Englishmen must be burned alive. Our Shawnees spoke up for us and so did the Count, but the Kickapoos got quite excited and I do not know what might have transpired if an honest Frenchman named Maisonville had not arrived with a message from Saint Ange—the commandant at Fort Chartres was ready to receive us and he would allow the Indians in his region to listen to what we had to say.

I must say this encouraged me to entertain kindlier thoughts about Saint Ange, who had shown himself to be an officer and a gentleman after all—unless he was scheming to bring us beyond the reach of any friendly Indians. But I had an account to settle with Mini Chêne. I saw him shambling away from the native village like a grizzly stuffed on summer fruit. In the absence of a better weapon, I prized a stone free from the fireplace in the officer's house, and ran after him. I got in one good blow behind his ear before some of the Indians pulled me away.

Mini Chêne staggered a few steps before he fell. When

he got up, his shirt was a new color. We exchanged some interesting promises about what we would do to each other if our paths crossed again.

In the third week of July, we decamped for the Illinois. We were treated as honored guests, but were left in no doubt that we were still captives. A dozen pairs of black eyes kept watch over us night and day.

We had traveled for only a few days down humid forest trails where the treetrunks seemed to sweat and the deer-flies struck deep as poniards, when we encountered a new band of Indians. My heart stopped when I recognized their leader. He was unmistakable, even at a distance, with those bandit-circles daubed about his eyes. He was Pontiac.

I believe that this was the only occasion when I have considered taking my own life. The memory of the fate the Ottawas had prepared for me before Pontiac's daughter helped me to escape brought out a cold fever and loosened my bowels. I do not think I disgraced myself, but an Indian can smell fear in subtler signs as surely as a wolf.

But this was not the Pontiac I remembered.

He greeted us with all courtesy. He took me by the upper arm and embraced me as his brother. He told us he had put down the hatchet and was ready to talk of peace with envoys who came from Johnson, whom he called our Chief of Men.

We made our way back to Ouitanon in his company and the calumet was once more passed around the fire.

"I will no longer stand in the path of the Nations," Pontiac declared. "We will sit with you in council at Detroit. We ask only for your promise that you do not come to take our lands."

This struck a damper on Black George's Illinois project, but it was hardly the moment to air this issue.

Pontiac convinced me of his sincerity when he said, "I have stopped up the rum-keg for many moons. Now I am thirsty. You must open the keg for us, that we may drink."

As I have told you, when Indians take to tippling, a wise man battens down the hatches. But this man of war had made his reputation by forgoing liquor in pursuit of his cause; his eagerness for a convivial drink was thus a very promising sign.

But there was one thing more. Pontiac was ready to follow our party to Detroit and to send runners to Minavanana, the chief of the Chippewas, to tell him to come too. But because there were English soldiers about Detroit who might bear him a grudge, he wanted one of our number to go to Fort Chartres as a surety for his safety.

While he explained this, he was staring at me.

"This is my father's wish also," he added. His "father," in this connection, was Captain Saint Ange.

"It seems that I am elected," I said to Croghan.

Black George did not like the sound of it, but I assured him that I found myself quite keen to go. He scowled. I think he was probably suspicious that I would start marking out some choice acreage along the river. In fact, I had already foreseen the ruin of Croghan's Illinois speculation. I had more personal reasons for wishing to go to Fort Chartres. I was curious to take the measure of Saint Ange, my old antagonist, in these changing times. Then, too, there was the chance of a reunion with Magid, Pontiac's daughter, and it has always been my policy to return a lady's favor.

Fort Chartres stands behind eighteen-foot walls a mile and a half back from the river, facing south—or at least it did then; I am told that in recent years the Mississippi burst its banks in the spring floods and carried away two of the bastions, and that the redoubt is now a picturesque ruin on a grassy knoll, a pleasuring spot for travelers who have never heard of Black George Croghan and his Illinois Company.

Saint Ange received me with all civility. The war seemed to have aged him. The white of his hair was not the work of powder. The skin of his face had shrunk back over the skull, making cavernous hollows under the cheekbones.

He asked me when British regulars were coming to take possession of the fort, which belonged to us, together with everything east of the Mississippi, under the Treaty of

Paris. I told him, quite honestly, that I did not know. I learned later that Captain Thomas Stirling and a hundred kilted Highlanders of the 42nd had already set off from Fort Pitt at Croghan's urgent request; Black George must have believed I needed support.

I asked Saint Ange straight out why he had turned so mannerly.

"Sir William has a good deal of evidence that, only lately, you were spiriting up the Indians to a new revolt. We had marked you as an enemy who would never admit defeat. For two years, you refused to accept the treaty between our two kings. Why now?"

Saint Ange striped his linen tablecloth with the tines of his fork.

He said quietly, "Because my king has betrayed me."

I thought he was talking about the Treaty of Paris, and started to give him a boiled-down version of one of Johnson's lectures on that topic.

He silenced me by saying, "Then you truly don't know?"

"I am afraid your meaning eludes me."

"About the Louisiana!" He shouted so loud that the glasses tinkled against the decanter. "It is bad enough to have to surrender this post to your countrymen! But to be ruled by Spanish dons! *Coquin! Ingrat!* What has been done behind our backs is insupportable!"

I was still pretty much in the dark, but I perceived a faint glimmer. We had heard rumors, traveling circuitously from our secret agents in Paris and Madrid via the American Department in London, that a deal had been composed on the sly between the Bourbon kings, by which France was to give possession of the province of Louisiana—which included all the territories lying west of the Mississippi—to Spain. But these were only rumors, and it seemed incredible to us that the frogs would abandon these rich lands, settled and planted by Frenchmen, to the country of the Santa Hermandad.

Saint Ange put me right. He showed me letters from New Orleans containing news of sealed orders despatched to a dying governor at New Orleans by the decayed rake

at Versailles. In the fall of 1762, months before we signed
our treaty with France, King Louis had ceded Louisiana to
his Spanish kinsman. He had waited almost two years before deigning to inform his proconsul in New Orleans of
this fact, and then on condition that he must conceal it
from the French colonists until the slow-moving Spaniards
sent one of their dons to take his place. This astonishing
bargain—and this scandalous deception—were the seeds
of the first rebellion in arms of white colonists in North
America against a European power, and you will see
shortly how it affected my own fortunes. In Saint Ange's
quivering fury, I saw the first symptoms of this eruption,
though I could never have guessed at its magnitude.

"You see to what I am reduced," he said to me. "I may
stay on your side of the river, and live as a renegade. Or
cross over, to make curtseys to atrophied caballeros."

It was not hard to see why he had lost his passion for
King Louis, and for stirring up the natives to wage war in
his name.

"Why don't you go home?" I asked him.

"Home?" He gave me a blank stare. "Perhaps you will
tell me where that is. I have no home outside these colonies, and the service of an unfaithful king. Like a ship's
captain, I must go down with my wreckage."

We drank pretty deep after this. I wondered if Saint
Ange was having second thoughts, when he said, "And
yet, except for the Indians—"

He did not finish this statement, and he did not need to.
I knew what he meant. There was a reason why the
French, despite the fewness of their numbers, the poor
quality of their manufactures and the poverty of their colonial treasuries, commanded the loyalty of vastly more of
the natives than the British, even after the war. The soldiers and missionaries of New France—not to mention the
raucous, red-capped *voyageurs* and *coureurs des bois*,
squaw-men as wild as any natives—established a rapport
with the Indians that was totally uncharacteristic of their
English counterparts. I will say it again: the English have
a talent for *not* going native. Johnson, of course, was the
sovereign exception. But, of course, Sir William was not

English. It was that O'Neill blood that won the Indians to his side. But for that King's Irishman, I believe we might have lost all the natives to the French, even the Six Nations. But I will preach no more.

Saint Ange did not want to leave "his" Indians any more than Johnson would have been willing to leave "his" Mohawks.

I admire the depth of their commitment, though I never entirely shared it. Now, if I had been permitted to set up house with Christina Brant, Chicha's sister, it might have been a different story.

Pontiac's daughter was no substitute. She had an infant with blue eyes and suspiciously reddish hair. She also had a surly brute of an Ottawa for a husband, with fifty pounds of sinew and packed muscle over me. I thought it prudent to divert my intended gallantries into a safer channel. I resolved to take Sir William up on his promise to allow me home leave in Europe as soon as Pontiac and Saint Ange let me off the leash.

Dearest Shane,

You and Johnson sowed revolution in the woods of
America, as prolifically, as heedlessly, as you scattered
your seed. Even now, you seem to be in a fog about the
consequences of the actions you recount. It is clearer to
me, perhaps because my family lost more than you can
imagine when the mob seized Paris and their black imper-
sonators put an end to our charmed lives in Ste
Domingue. I see more clearly than before how much
of the blame lies with you and your idol Sir William.

I know the charge will startle and offend, but I must
speak my mind. You and Sir William counted yourselves
king's men, even though the two of you were Irishmen to the backbone, as Irish as my grandfather, who
flew off with the Wild Geese. You fought and won battles for a king you did not love.

While you played king's men in your frontier wars,
you were preparing the ruin of two empires. By helping to drive the French out of North America, you opened
the way for the American Revolution. The American colonists would surely never have dared to mount their rebellion so long as they needed redcoat soldiers to
defend them against French armies and French Indian
scalping-parties in Canada. In banging the French—as you
insist on describing your activities in the Seven Years'
War—you and Sir William helped to sink the British
Empire in the most populous part of North America.

This great event whiplashed, as we know, against
those in France who had done most to bring it about.
The wind from America brought us pestilential fevers, fatal to anyone of birth or manners.

Will you admit it now, my irresistible fool?

Toujours,

Valerie

18

The Lost Kingdom

I BOARDED A BRIG at Philadelphia in the spring, bound for Southampton. I did not delay to discover the fate of Croghan's Illinois project, and I am glad of it. All the backwoodsmen of Pennsylvania and a dozen merchants of the town had their knives out for Black George and, despite his success in bringing Pontiac to the peace council at Detroit, no sober official would dare to put his seal on any transaction in which Croghan was the prime mover. Sir William also went cold on the scheme after he powwowed with Pontiac at Oswego. The two of them took quite a liking for each other. Johnson told me later that he would forgo ten thousand a year to maintain Pontiac's friendship in our interest.

I banged about Europe for two full years, with little to show for it save a brush with Signor Gonorrhea. I shall pass over this intermezzo briskly, since it was largely occupied in whoring, tippling and gaming. Peg Walsingham sought to steady me down and even tried to arrange a marriage for me with a budding young heiress. I felt obliged to confess to her that I had acquired a wife in the colonies—she did not yet know about Mirabel—in a fit of absent-mindedness.

Peg sniffed. "Can't be much of a woman if she takes her hooks out of you and lets you go gadding about the globe. You must have another."

I agreed with her, naturally, but I thought that a public wedding in London with a debutante would be too much for Lady Luck's sense of humor.

There was more to it. I could not seem to settle. I fancied I would take London by storm when I finally cranked out my drama about Pontiac, but the playhouse owners— even Mossop at Smock Alley in Dublin—told me that American Indians were a drug on the market, since Robert Rogers had glorified himself in several productions, ghosted in whole or in part by a bibulous archbishop's nephew. I found myself less and less able to abide the pompous conceit of polite society in England who wrinkled their noses at anyone from the colonies as if he had walked in with cowdung on his boots.

I collected my hundred guineas from Gaius since I believe that I won our wager on the square. Whether or not Robert Davers killed himself in the end, and I still cannot agree with myself on the answer to that, he did not die in the time appointed by Gaius. Peg's husband paid up with remarkable nonchalance. I think he had done well in the last year of the war by fitting out privateers. Yet I had the odd sensation that the money was not mine to spend. It made me uneasy. I havered for a bit, and finally sent a banknote for the whole amount to Johnson with a letter requesting that he should apply the money to the new school at Canajoharie at the Upper Castle of the Mohawks.

I rode across the better part of France and explored the domains of the King of Sardinia. I journeyed as far north as Muscovy and watched the performances of a Lapland witch who would have made more than a match for Hole in the Day. I investigated the bagnios of Venice, the brothels of Antwerp and the bordellos of Marseilles. When I ran short of money, I contracted a salutary arrangement with a shady marquise, the very queen of rooks, and we fleeced the unwary at Paris over bezique and picquet.

I dribbled away two good years. Do you think I was happy?

I was obliged to admit to myself I was homesick, not for County Meath, but for the New World, where men seemed to breathe a larger air. I felt that history was being made over there and I wanted to be part of it. All the same, I doubt that I would have gone back, except for Johnson's promise.

"Let go of me," he had said, "and the Mohawks will bring you back."

Twice in my life he was proved right. This was the first occasion, and I know that I will risk you incredulity in telling you what came to pass. The letter is the easy part. It was signed by Chicha, but the orthography and the language were so good that I know she must have had help from Joseph or one of the Johnsons.

Her message was dreadfully plain.

She wrote, "Our great tree is falling. You must come quickly to help us. You are the one that he needs in this trembling world."

On the heels of this missive came a more informative letter from Johnson himself. Sir William complained of intriguers all about him, and the noxious Uri Klock, and the budget-cutting of his new political master, Lord Hillsborough, who seemed to have it in for the Indian Department.

"I cannot offer you much, dear boy," the letter proceeded, "but I will undertake to buy your captaincy in the Royal Americans or another regiment if that is not of your liking. The business is fixed up with Gage who, as you know, is much of our persuasion, though I cannot say as much for others. Our company of ball-drivers is sadly wanting in your absence. Guy attempted to service the innkeeper's wife at the Flats but missed his mark so wide he fell out the window."

The letters, yes, I can share those with you. But how can I share the dreams?

Go looking for the spirit world of the Indians, Sir William warned Davers, and you will find you are already inside it. I will add something to this statement. A man who lives among natives and shares their world, even for a short time, will not dream the same way as he did before. And he will lose the ability to shrug off the content of his night wanderings with the airy phrase: "It was only a dream." Before I received the letter from Chicha, I had received her call. I remember the scene vividly. The colors were intense. The firelight sparkled on the many-row belt, on the shells of life. Chicha and Joseph talked to me for a long time, calmly and rhythmically, the long periods lapping over each other. They spoke of treachery and creeping sickness, of a world that will end when the maples die, and the fish float belly up, and the strawberry plant, which lines the Path of Souls, no longer yields fruit. When they released me, I saw my shadow, skimming salt water like an arrowhead.

You see? I told you I could not explain it. But I returned to America, because Johnson needed me, and because the Mohawks came to bring me back.

Peacocks strutted the lawns at Johnson Hall. I have always thought the peacock an unlucky bird. One of them screamed by the banks of forsythia beyond the eastern blockhouse, where the gardens fall away to the wild hollow where the Cayadutta babbles towards the Mohawk.

"Stop that din," thus Johnson to the peacock, "or the natives will have you for a headdress."

On the rise behind Chicha's herb garden, Sir William asked me to stop. I stood over him, resting my elbows on the top of the wheelchair while he gestured into the distance towards the sun-baked furrow of the road he had hewn through the forest to his new manor. His surveyors had laid out building areas, and the features of a busy market hamlet were beginning to emerge from the brush. There was a blacksmith, a gunsmith, a tailor and a German ironmonger who turned the sleighloads of ashes Sir William's tenants brought him in winter time into potash for the export trade. Robert Adams, Johnson's sharp Dublin bookkeeper, was to open a dry goods store. Gilbert Tice, an officer in our Provincials during the French wars, had already opened his tavern. A jail and a courthouse were already framed on plots that belonged to Sir William, since

there was no nonsense about separation of powers in Johnson country. Johnson talked of his plans to put up a fine
stone church, as fine as St George's at Schenectady, built
under Sir William's patronage, where Mr Stuart would
read to the natives from the Mohawk gospels he had translated with Joseph's aid, and to the rest of us in the salty,
lip-smacking version of King James.

Out of what had been primal wilderness twelve miles
back from the river, Johnson was making a town—not a
brawling, two-fisted, grog-sellers' town, like the traders'
settlements out west—but the capital of an orderly princi-
pality, with a farmers' market on Fridays and a yearly fair
and musical concerts and militia drills.

"I had a mind to make all this," his sensitive hand made
a sweep of the horizon, "a manor. But Colden told me I
was old-fashioned. Can you credit it, Shane! That grizzled
old royalist calling *me* old-fashioned! He said the temper
of the times will not tolerate lords of the manor."

I told him I believed that Colden was right. This was
before the Battle of Golden Hill, when our regulars
chopped down a Liberty Tree and King Sears and his Liberty boys turned out to do battle with clubs and cutlasses.
But passing through Manhattan, I had heard wild talk of
sedition and witnessed rude demonstrations against our
troops, and seen the British lion on an alehouse sign
adorned with a ball and chain by some graffito vandal.
The mood of the times did not favor king's men, nor
manor lords, nor the Indians they protected, though I believe there was far less appetite for rebellion in the Province of New York than at Massachusetts Bay, or among
the gentlemen tobacconists of Virginia.

"So I shall not have a manor," Johnson pursued. "Not in
title, or legal privilege. But I believe I shall have a county,
if I am patient with the governor and allow it to bear his
name. The town, now. Shane, you are a literary fellow."

"To a degree."

"What shall I call it?"

I looked down the road to the half-framed courthouse,
the neat row of artisans' shops, the twist of smoke from
the smithy, the female slave toting a great basket of laun-

dry on her head as if she were walking the bank of the Niger River.

I said, "You'll call it Johnstown, of course."

The suggestion was not original. Guy and Daniel Claus, who had come down from Montreal and married Nancy, Sir William's clever daughter, had told me something of it.

"You don't think it excessive?" Sir William swiveled his head to look at me, but the movement pained him and his hands tightened on the armrests of his invalid's chair. I was alarmed at how sickness had used him. He was pale and puffy and, even in the warmth of the day, his skin was cold and damp to the touch. He had kept his hair—I never knew him to wear a wig—but it had turned completely gray.

"You don't think it is tempting the gods?" he went on. "Fort Johnson, Johnson Hall—Johnstown?"

"It is your world," I said quietly. "You made it. It should have your name."

Sir William rumbled and changed the subject. "Let us go that way, Shane, beyond the slave quarters. I want to show you the crannog I made."

I may have embarrassed him a little. Sir William did not require flattery, though he demanded respect. He did not need reassurance at that time. He was fifty-three years of age. Not so old, you may say. But many of those years had weighed heavier than the whole lifetime of an ordinary man in a peaceful country, and Sir William had been living on borrowed time since he took that poisoned ball in his thigh in the Lake George fight in 1755. He had not had two consecutive months of fair health since. He believed, as I do, that it was Chicha and her native medicine that had kept body and soul together. The constant pain, the insomnia and fatigue, the consciousness of failing powers—these made him desperately vulnerable.

"I am lashed to a dying animal," he told me in one of his insomniac nights soon after my return. "The spirit rebels. My truest counselors flee from me. I am betrayed by inconstant friends and by mine own self."

You may see, from the strangeness of these words, to

what despair Sir William—in other times the jolly master
of Fish House—was reduced. I believe he saw far into the
future and the catastrophes that it contained. I am not
thinking principally of the Great American Mutiny; few of
us foresaw that, or could have believed it would ever pros-
per. I mean the destruction of the Indians and of the
bridges Johnson had sought to build between our world
and theirs.

Native doctors make out that disease is never merely
physical, that the physical manifestations are only symptoms of something happening in the unseen, that we get
sick for a reason.

The big treaty powwow at Fort Stanwix, and other land
fiddles that were going on, in my belief, were the reason
Sir William was so ill that spring that a trivial fall, climbing out of a canoe, had confined him to his bed and his
wheelchair. He was sick with him*self*, because he believed
he had let Black George Croghan bully him into approving
a scheme that drove wagons and ox-carts through his
Boundary Line; and because, at the same time, for all his
power and influence, he had been unable to break Uri
Klock and another bunch of swindlers who had the Mohawks hot and bothered with their underhand deeds. I'll
tell you something more of Klock in a moment. It must be
a puzzle to you, as it was to me, that Sir William and the
Mohawks permitted that hippo-toothed villain to breathe
the same air in the Valley. But first I must say something
of the Stanwix treaty and the conniving that went on
around it.

A grand Indian powwow was summoned to Fort Stanwix
at the eastern end of the portage road from Wood Creek,
in the fall of 1768, to settle all outstanding questions about
the Boundary Line. You may imagine that everyone with
an axe to grind was there. Agents for New England land
companies homed in like shovel-nosed sharks. Even the
Bible-bashers were represented, in the person of a New
Light zealot named Jacob Johnson, sent up by Wheelock
from Connecticut, and most certainly no relative of *our*
Johnsons. This original wore a hair shirt in imitation of

John the Baptist, and heard angelic voices which instructed him that the Seneca envoys were really popish priests in disguise come to murder all Protestants. He had some pull among the Oneidas, and when Sir William declined to reserve a fat chunk of land for this illuminato's purposes, he told them that the King's Superintendent of Indians was the Antichrist. He might have effected some damage had he not been so imprudent as to stave in a keg of rum, whereon the Oneidas offered to do the same to his skull.

Black George got his oar in well in advance of the council. He was up to his hairy earholes in debt to Moses Frank and Messrs Baynton and Wharton, and no doubt he was still smarting over the stillbirth of his Illinois venture. Black George developed a keen interest in Sir William's health. He escorted him to a rough spot in the Berkshires, near the Massachusetts line, where they sat together inside a mud-caulked shelter over a hot spring the Indians swear by, bubbling away like a kettle of toddy. When this failed to produce any single improvement in Sir William's condition, Croghan told him he needed sea air.

"Let's get away to the coast," thus Croghan, "where we can reason like white men."

There you have the clue to what is coming, for Black George, as I have related, was as much of a squaw-man as William Johnson. He knew that to get Johnson's approval for what he was plotting, he needed to detach him from Chicha and the Brants and the rest of his native counselors. In a tavern on the harbor at New London, Connecticut, and around the punchbowl on Fisher's Island, Black George and his business partners, Wharton and Trent, worked on Johnson. This, I contend, is why the Boundary Line that was drawn at Fort Stanwix makes such curious twists and bends.

I was not at the council and it would be tedious to linger over all of the details now that Johnson and his Boundary Line have both gone the long trail. I shall mention only one or two highlights to give you the general idea. The Six Nations were the key to the proceedings. It was Sir William's contention, which they joyously approved, that they were the lords and masters by right of conquest or occupa-

tion, not only of the whole Ohio country but of vast territories southward as far as the country of the Cherokees.
This meant that only the consent of the Six Nations was
required for the colossal land transfers that took place.
Other natives living in the territories involved, like the
Shawnees and the Delawares, were obliged to like it or
lump it.

For ten thousand dollars in Spanish silver and three
thousand more in rum and trinkets, Sir William secured
the greatest land bargain since the native inhabitants sold
Manhattan Island for a fistful of beads. His Majesty's government had issued instructions that the Boundary Line in
the southlands was to follow the course of the Kanawha
River, which I believe is now known as the Tennessee.
Prompted by Johnson, who was prompted in turn by Black
George, the speakers for the Six Nations protested that
their property rights extended much farther west, and that
since they had no present use for these hunting grounds,
they had no objection to seeing them included on the white
side of the line. By a stroke of the pen, the Boundary Line
was pushed seven hundred miles to the west.

Now Johnson was far more attached to the Six Nations
than to the natives in general, and I dare say he hoped that
by this stroke he would channel the tide of white settlers
that was threatening their borders far away from them to
the south and west. But you can imagine the effect this
transaction was likely to have on the western tribes that
had risen with Pontiac.

The northern end of the Boundary Line was no less con-
tentious and it struck deep into the heartlands of the Confederacy. After much haggling with the Oneidas, it was
stopped at the Mohawk River opposite the place where
Canada Creek flows into the larger stream. No one was
happy about this.

But Black George and his partners were delighted by
the side-deals that were cut. They must have been in a
feeding frenzy, snapping up Indian deeds in the days before the Crown obtained the title to the lands in question.
I know that Croghan acquired one hundred and twenty-
seven thousand acres in the Ohio country alone, on the

strength of worthless bonds and promises, under various cover-names, and successfully petitioned the governor of New York to confirm a deed to a hundred thousand acres more about Otsego Lake. I know that his partners obtained the modest grant of two and a half million acres of Ohio lands, which was actually written into the treaty. I cannot begin to calculate the value or compass of Sir William's personal acquisitions. I have heard the figure of two hundred square miles.

And this, you complain, is the man I have offered you as a hero!

I will not try to vindicate him. As I have said, Johnson was literally sick about what he had countenanced at Fort Stanwix. His morals were no more and no less impeachable than those of the other leading men in our colonies. Sir William once said he had never met a Crown agent who could not be wrapped up in a beaver blanket, and I think this was no exaggeration. Johnson, of course, had larger opportunities than others, which raises the notorious question of whether a lady who will bed with a man for a country house and a thousand a year is more or less of a whore than a five-shilling doxy in Covent Garden.

I will let Johnson say this one thing in his own cause, in the words he used to me: "Our people, at home and in the colonies, are poorly equipped to maintain friendship with the Indians. In time of peace, they despise and abuse those whom they fear in war." You see, the very survival of the Indian Department was imperiled by Lord Hillsborough in London, who had cut Johnson's budget in half, and permitted the forts to go to ruin on the grounds that it was no longer necessary to bother about the natives. The colonists, for the most part, regarded the Indians with loathing and dread, or as a nuisance to be hacked away like a stand of timber, to open up the frontier for farming and profit. Between the upper and the nether grindstone, Johnson needed money and land, which came to the same thing, to preserve the Indian Department and all that it stood for. You may jibe that in order to preserve his cause he destroyed it. That would not be fair, and I think it untrue.

A French professor has lately advanced the theory that
the westward motion of our people is a natural force, that
man, like the squirrel in a cage, is irresistibly impelled to
step westward by reason of the earth's rotation in the opposite direction. Ben Franklin told me this is an imposture
of science, and I suppose he would know. But I think that
like the lightning he has taught us so much about, migration across the North American continent is a force that
cannot be suppressed; the trick is to guide it into a safe
course. Sir William came to understand this deeply. The
Stanwix treaty was to be his rod and conductor. Though
the execution was spoiled by cupidity and deceit, the intent must be honored.

"He needs you," Joseph told me, "because there is no
strong man about him he can trust. He has no successor."
     "I can hardly be that."
     The Mohawk stared at me.
     Chicha was with us. She had recently borne Sir William
a fifth child, another daughter. We were out in the woods
sitting under a stand of virgin oaks.
     She said to me, "He is happy when you are here. He is
younger. You requicken his youth."
     I had no words to answer this.
     Chicha turned severely practical. She described to me
the continuing disputes over the Mohawk lands that could
not be resolved at Fort Stanwix nor in the governor's
council either, because the Livingstons and the mynheers
of Albany would not forgo their claims and they had deep
enough pockets to buy the officials who should have torn
them up years before. Uri Klock had sent out rent collec-
tors again to white farmers on the lands of the Upper Castle who were engrossed in the Canajoharie Patent. The
Mohawks at Fort Hunter were protesting a still more spectacular swindling. By jugglery with a compass needle, an
ancient deed to three small farms in the triangle between
the Sacandaga and the Hudson had been magnified into a
claim to all the Mohawk hunting-grounds on the west side
of Hudson's River.
     "You are Mohawks," I said to Chicha and her brother.

"Mohawks have a certain reputation. Why don't you drive Uri Klock out of the Valley? Why doesn't Sir William do it? God's breeches! After all that villain has done to you!"

Joseph smiled a little wanly. "There are so many things you don't yet see, my brother. Sir William is sworn to uphold the law—your law and our law—and he has made us promise to play by the same rules. We are bound even more tightly than your people. If one of you commits a crime, your countrymen say he is a bad apple. If one of us commits the same offense, then our whole nation is abused as a race of wild beasts to be chastised or killed off."

I felt the force of his emotion though his voice was soft and even. I was distinctly uncomfortable.

It was Joseph who shifted the subject.

"Nicholas came back from the Wabash. The far tribes are restless again because of rumors about the treaty. I think Warragiyaguey means to ask you to go west again."

I protested that Croghan was out at the Fort at the Crotch and that no man in our service knew the western tribes as well as he.

Joseph shook his head.

"I do not think he will use Anagurunda." This was Croghan's Indian name. "He must mend what has been broken. For this, he will trust only himself or one who is of his own spirit. You see how he is. He cannot travel. There is only you. He will look to one man to find one man."

"You mean—"

"He must make his heart known to Pontiac. It must speak through your mouth."

I suppose I looked sorry for myself, which is certainly how I felt.

Joseph put his hand on my shoulder.

"We will take this trail together. You always get in trouble when you go among strange Indians without a Mohawk to watch over you."

Eaton Square

April 20th

Dearest Shane,

It was a bad business, this cheating over the line.
You do your best to uphold Sir William's cause. You
even attribute a guilty conscience to him. I should be
glad to believe he had one, because I cannot accept
that a man of his force and standing would ever have
allowed himself to be led against his own instincts by a
vulgar sharper like Black George Croghan. Johnson
knew what he was doing.

Your

Valerie

May 1st

Dearest Valerie,

It may be so. But William Johnson was an adopted war
chief of the Mohawk Nation before ever he held a
commission of the Crown, and I do believe that in
his heart, he was as much an Indian as a white man and
sought to guard their interests as well as his own. That
he was never able to draw a line between public interest and private gain puts him in company with every great and powerful man I have ever known.

I will hear no ill of him. We shall not see his like
again.

Your

Shane

19

Escape to New Orleans

THREE WEEKS TO DETROIT, avoiding Croghan country, by canoe and on foot along the forest trails to Oswego, by army whaleboat to Niagara, under the billowing canvas of the packet boat to the fort on the narrows. We made better time than Sir William on his journey nearly eight years before. But we had no Indian councils to sit through, and we traveled light. Our little party consisted of ten men including Joseph and Conrad The Song, two of Sir William's Irish servants and a negro slave named Cato and four Royal Americans. In addition to our own provisions, our cargo consisted of a bag of pieces of eight, a few kegs of rum and powder, the usual Indian trinkets and a fine set of clothes with a sword and a laced hat for Pontiac. In my own oilskin pouch, I carried the two great peace belts with figures of old adversaries holding hands, one from Johnson, the other from the Mohawk Nation, the Keepers of the Eastern Door of the Indian world.

The military posts that we passed were disheveled or abandoned, except for Niagara. They had rigged up machines called cradles powered by a windlass which moved

our goods up the slippery gully above the Bottoms a damn
sight more comfortably than bearers sweating on all fours.
Along the shore of Lake Erie, especially about the mouth
of the Cuyahoga, I saw new log cabins and shanties.
White traders and settlers were flocking to the northern
side of the Ohio in defiance of Sir William's regulations
and his Boundary Line. They would make fat pickings for
the western tribes if they rose again. Viewing the weakness and disarray of our little garrisons, I had the uneasy
sensation that I had seen all this before.

Detroit was buzzing with rumors about Pontiac. With
the spring thaw, he had left the island on the Maumee,
where the river makes a sluggish bend on its way to the
lake, and moved south with a body of old faithfuls; their
number was said to be anywhere between thirty and three
hundred. Fur traders who knew the back country told me
that Pontiac was taking his winter peltries and his plans,
whatever those might be, to the Illinois country and to
Captain Saint Ange who now commanded at the new post
of St Louis below the junction of the Missouri and the
Mississippi. I was not surprised that Saint Ange had stayed
on in Indian country. But I was astonished that the Spaniards had not yet come up the river from New Orleans to
hang their ensign from his flagpole. I suppose it was a
comfort to discover that there are empire-builders even
slower-footed than our masters at Whitehall and Admiralty
House.

I did not linger at Detroit to renew old acquaintants.
We set off again after two days' rest, with the useful Maisonville for a guide, in the tracks of Pontiac. It was a tedious slog, up the Maumee and over mushy trails to Fort
St Joseph and around the rim of Lake Michigan to the Illinois before we could rest our aching arms—apart from
the occasional struggle with snags and sawyers, fallen
trees whose projecting limbs waggled like arthritic fingers
above the water—and let the current bear us down to the
Mississippi.

I had plenty of time on this long journey for reflection
over the message I was carrying to Pontiac. Sir William
had made me rehearse it over and over until my delivery

met his satisfaction. It was laden with flowery compliments and the promise of presents and assurances that the King's Superintendent would not permit Pontiac's people and their allies to be dispossessed, and that a distant sovereign held them all deep in his heart. But the edge of the steel showed through the velvet. "We are as many as the stars in the sky or the leaves of the forest. You cannot hope to fight us and win and there is no power across the great water that will come to your aid. If Frenchmen tell you otherwise, you should not listen to them. Their voices are only the twitterings of evil birds that will lead you to perdition." Don't ask me how to say "perdition" in Pontiac's language. There must be a word for it, though. As you have seen, the Ottawas are professors of that applied science.

Where the Illinois comes out into the Mississippi we made camp for a day and tracked the buffalo to the wallows on the edge of a grassy plain. I brought down a good-sized bull and took the hide. I thought a buffalo blanket would make a glorious present for Peg. I enjoyed the thought of how her snub nose would wrinkle up with the irruption of that rank black hide among the lavender and orange-flower water scents of her boudoir.

The sky out there is bigger than in the Old World. The plains stretch out below it into near-infinity. There are no boulders here to break a farmer's back, no forests that will defeat Sheffield steel. For a moment, I saw waving acres of wheat, herds of grazing cattle and sheep, wagons and pack trains rolling steadily westward. Croghan's dream of a new colony whipped by me like a dust-devil.

No, by George. I had not come here for that. I had come to renew a peace with the one Indian, apart, perhaps, from a nameless Prophet, whose name could raise the tribes from the jaw of the Gaspe to the buffalo prairies of the Sioux.

I found him at Cahokia, a rough traders' town on our side of the river, across from Saint Ange's little wooden fort of St Louis where the lilies of France drooped like wet laundry from the flagstaff. I wonder if Cahokia is still there. I know Pontiac's friends made an effort to burn it down after what happened. If I had still been there, I would not have stood in their path.

If the tippling-shops and traders' shanties along the Bottoms at Niagara were a branch of hell on earth, the Cahokia was a head depot. The big truck house of the Philadelphia firm of Baynton, Wharton—Croghan's partners, and his nemesis—was the very furnace. It stood among willows and weeping beeches near the river, and the painted shingle told you much of the story. It depicted a monstrous keg flanked by feathered Indians holding beavers and buckskins. The head clerk watched over his merchandise with two horse-pistols in his belt and a blunderbuss ready to hand on a rack behind the wooden cage erected over the long counter. Indians straggled in from all of the four quarters—Kaskaskias and Piankashaws, Kickapoos and Peorias, Ottawas and Chippewas and a few proud, straight-backed Sioux on horseback, sporting painted buffalo robes. They brought in their winter furs. The Baynton, Wharton men whisked them away into back rooms in twos and threes and plied them with liquor and weighed their peltries on crooked scales—or did not trouble to weigh them at all—and told them that their furs were worth only half of what they fetched the season before because there was a surfeit of beaver on the market, and kicked them out with a keg or two of watered rum and a scrap of calico the moths had been at. I saw some of those Indians go in on two legs and come out on four, rolling drunk with a Baynton, Wharton man shining his boot on their backsides.

They were treated no better downriver at Chartres, where dull-witted John Wilkins, now a half-colonel in the Royal Irish, commanded at the fort. I remembered him from Niagara; I am told he distinguished himself at the head of a relief party to Detroit, after I got out of the place, by getting seasick on Lake Erie and losing half his boats and scurrying back to home port before he had traveled as far as Sandusky. This Wilkins was our head man in the Illinois country, but he did nothing to regulate the trade so far as I observed, except to bully the frenchies among the merchants so hard as to confirm them as our resolute enemies, and to flog any native who made a commotion about his post. I suspect he was making a shilling or two selling His Majesty's stores at the back door of the fort. But I shall return to Colonel Wilkins in good time.

I did not say there were no honest traders along that bend in the Mississippi; I say only that they were as rare as a nun in a brothel.

I have seldom seen Joseph so angry as he became when we visited the Baynton, Wharton establishment. Sharpers in the trade were no novelty to him, of course. What stuck in his craw was the spectacle of all those enervated natives begging for a drink.

"Have you forgotten you are men?" he barked at a couple of Peorias. The Mohawk had particular contempt for this tribe. He said that liquor had turned them into rabid dogs that would thieve and murder for a spoonful of rum.

The Peorias did not understand him, but they gave him plenty of legroom. Mohawks, as I have said, have a reputation.

To make his point, Joseph scooped up an empty keg and set it up near the door of the trading-post.

In plain view of twenty or thirty Indians and a few of our border riffraff, he slipped his jumper out from under his breechclout and squirted a prodigious quantity of piss, the color of a light canary wine, into the keg.

"*Kats kanaka!*" he invited the rabble. "Come here! Let us trade! Mine is stronger than theirs, and healthier!"

The natives thought this was a pretty good jest, and a Kickapoo who believed he had been cheated by the traders indicated that he was of a mind to pour Joseph's product over one of their heads.

One of the Baynton crew came out to see the cause of the disturbance.

"Get away wi' you, you dog!" he bawled at Joseph.

Joseph gave him a hard look and the trader's hand twitched after his pistol.

"I would not advise any precipitate action," I said daintily, resting my hand on the pommel of my sword. "We are traveling on the business of the Indian Department."

The fellow gave me the evil eye.

There was something familiar about the bulging Adam's apple, that long, loose-jointed frame, ill-covered by a coarse check shirt and a butcher's apron.

"I believe we have met before," I said to him.

When he swore at me, the burr in his speech became more pronounced, and that is what gave me the clue.

"By God! You're McDonner!"

"You're barking," said he. "My name is Williamson, and I'll thank you to leave honest men to go about their business."

I hesitated. The resemblance to the brute who had fitted a noose to my throat along the Cuyahoga was extraordinary.

"I could have sworn you were McDonner—"

"Will ye no leave off?"

I was sure of it now. This creature was no Englishman. Burrs like that do not grow south of Hadrian's Wall.

"I'll have the truth out of you," I told him. "By God, I'll have it out of your bones."

His mouth twisted up to the side in a curious nervous tic, and he hurried back inside the store.

I ran after him. The place stank like a tannery. The head clerk peered at me like a squirrel inside a cage through the muddy light. McDonner had vanished, presumably into a back room.

"That man in the apron," I demanded. "What is his name?"

"That's Alec Williamson."

"How long has he worked here?"

"Oh, they comes and goes. He came down from Post Vincent after the thaw. Mr Wharton sent him up from Philly with a cargo last fall."

I was quivering with excitement and poorly concealed anger. I forget an injury quickly enough—we cannot go forward through life with our heads swiveled backwards— but I rarely forgive one. The memory of what McDonner's crew had done to Pontiac's daughter and what they attempted to do to me had me boiling for revenge.

"That man is an impostor," I told the head clerk. "I am taking him to Fort Chartres for interrogation."

I showed the fellow my warrant from Sir William. I regretted that I had left my soldiers at the fort and that I was wearing buckskins instead of my regimentals. Sir William was right—if you are going into a tricky situation, never dress as if you might be about to jump into a ditch.

The man behind the cage hummed and hawed, and I told him I would close him down faster than he could rob a drunken native unless he obliged me instanto.

He let me into a back room and, with Joseph following close behind, I made a rapid inspection of the house. McDonner was gone.

We went out the back, on the river side, and hunted him through the willows and among the log cabins and bark shanties that were clustered near the trading post.

Joseph grabbed my arm. "There!"

I looked out across the river. It hurled back the sunlight like beaten copper. I found the canoe and McDonner churning his paddle. He was heading for the far shore, to the Frenchmen at St Louis.

"You men, there!" I shouted at a pack of river rats milling about the landing. "Which of you will take us over?"

Their chief bully-boy swaggered over. He wore a red turkey feather in his cap to prove that he had broken the heads of a few of his own kind. He spat black tobacco-juice into the dust, and grunted, "I don't carry niggers."

I might have enjoyed this pleasantry under less pressing circumstances since this brute was three shades darker than Joseph.

But I had no leisure for banter. I was bent on settling accounts with McDonner. I pulled out my purse and showed them the color of my money.

"Two dollars to take us across! *Now!*" I held up the silver coins.

"Five!" said the bully.

We settled for three. I whispered to Joseph to keep an eye on our boatmen. There was a better than fair chance they would try to get the rest of my money while we made the crossing.

But we came to the French side without mishap.

Soldiers in blue coats trimmed with scarlet formed a reception committee. They jabbered at me, wanting to know my business. I looked over their shoulders, and saw two figures in white dress uniforms.

I hailed Saint Ange, and he came down to greet me with apparent warmth.

"This is unexpected. I had not hoped to see you again, Mr Hardacre."

"Nor I you. I had thought to find St Louis in the keeping of the dons."

"They move as slowly and decorously as a slug in a cabbage-patch. What brings you here? Are you still Sir William's man? I thought you were finished with the colonies."

I mumbled something about the wanderbug and the fact that they had made me a captain in lieu of giving me a wage I could live on.

I stopped short, because I had recognized the second figure in white. It was Pontiac in the plumage of an officer of France. My heart sank to my boots. It was evident to me that all the rumors were true. Pontiac and Saint Ange were on the warpath again, raising the hatchet in the name of a Bourbon king who had entirely forgotten them.

"So it's true," I said softly. "Don't you think it is cruel to deceive them?"

Saint Ange looked genuinely puzzled.

Then he took my meaning and a smile illuminated his lean, sallow features.

"*Chansons!* You are looking at two old men reliving their memories. Come! Our friend will be glad to see you, I think."

"Wait." I told him about McDonner.

The name meant nothing to Saint Ange, but when I described the man and recalled the episode with Pontiac's daughter, the Frenchman scowled.

"Say nothing of this to Pontiac," he said quickly. "There are renegades here—your countrymen and mine. You remember Mini Chêne?"

"I could hardly forget that hell-hound."

"They are trying to foment another Indian war. Yours, to have a pretext to kill the natives and steal their lands. You should ask Mr Croghan about that. Ours, to take back the fur trade. They have corrupted the Peorias and some of the Illinois tribes. These are a feeble, dissipated people, easily led astray. They have no encouragement from me, Shane. You have my word on it. I will not lead the natives to their destruction."

"And Pontiac?"

"He stands against the agitators. You must ask him about them. His battles are over. He knows the state of this country." He glanced at Joseph. "He sees—as they say it—many looks away. He will tell you."

We sat by the commandant's fire inside his wooden house and a deeper friendship grew among men who had once been sworn enemies.

Pontiac's conversation, half in pidgin French, half filtered by Saint Ange, had a dreamy, gusting quality.

His people had read a vision in the face of the last full moon. They saw two great stallions contending. The warhorse that came from the east trampled the horse from the west under its powerful hooves. Then a host of little men marched from the direction of the sunrise, darkening the face of the night sun the natives call their grandmother.

His people were afraid. They were undecided whether to fight or flee. They were starved of powder by the traders and the garrisons. They brought fewer furs back from the winter hunt, and then the swindlers at Cahokia and Chartres paid them a third of what they had earned.

Pontiac was drinking again—a good sign for reasons I have already explained, except that it brought an open show of anger which no Indian will countenance when sober. He and his Ottawas had been cheated at Cahokia, and he swore that he would make an issue of it. He meant to go across the river to Baynton, Wharton and oblige them to return his peltries. He would carry them all the way down the Mississippi to New Orleans in his own canoes rather than suffer the abuse of the English traders.

I begged him to make no demonstration at Cahokia that

might spark the border war our wild men, and Black George Croghan too if Saint Ange was to be trusted, were promoting. I promised Pontiac that I would make a narrow inspection of the dealings of Baynton, Wharton, and that Johnson would drive them from the Illinois country if his charges were substantiated.

Joseph and I drank too deep to trust ourselves on a night crossing in a native canoe, so we bunked on the straw paillasses of Saint Ange's soldiers. I looked forward to a longer council with Pontiac in the morning, and to news of McDonner from the scouts my host had sent out.

I slept late. When Joseph shook me awake, the sun was halfway up the sky.

"We must go now," the Mohawk told me.

"What's up? Have they word of McDonner?"

"Pontiac has gone across the river with blood in his eye for the traders."

Saint Ange loaned us one of his pirogues. We battled the current, but it bore us down, so that we landed a few hundred yards below the traders' town and had to walk back along the bank.

I heard the screeching and shouting before we came in view of the clearing in front of the truck house. It did not prepare me for the sight of the man who gave his name to the last Indian war that the natives of this continent could have won being hurled bodily off the steps of the trading-post like a spoiled side of beef. He was still in his Frenchman's finery, but his coat was bloodied and torn. His lip was split, his eyes wandered like a shaved billiard ball. He was not himself. The liquor was in him. Perhaps he had been up drinking all night.

There was only one Ottawa with him, in no better condition, and the rabble of grog-shop Indians about the post seemed content to play spectators.

"I'll make you eat your license for this," I promised Coleman, the swag-bellied manager of the post, who was observing the entertainment with his thumbs in his belt and his pipe in his teeth.

"Jumped-up varmint tried to rob me," said Coleman.

"There's no reg'lations say a white man has to step aside for thieves."

I had to admit there was truth in this, and the irony in an officer of the Indian Department sticking up for the most notorious rebel in the colonies against one our best-known merchant companies did not wholly escape me.

Joseph hissed.

I turned in time to see a tiger-striped Peoria run howling from a pack of his fellows. The sunlight honed the edge of his hatchet as he brought it down in a sweeping arc on Pontiac's neck where he lay in the dirt trying to raise himself up on palms and knees.

"God's triggers!"

The Peoria raised the scalp-yell. I had my firelock to my shoulder, but remembered myself in time. I drove the Peoria away with the butt instead, and crouched over Pontiac.

A Frenchman who knew some doctoring came to help. When he saw the size of the hole in the back of Pontiac's head, he grunted, *"C'est fini."*

He told me the meaning of the last words that issued from Pontiac's throat.

> I fall, but my soul will live,
> A name for the brave to tell.
> The spirits shall sing it on high
> And young men grow bold at the sound.

At the gate of death, Pontiac remembered who he was.

"Why?" I roared at the Peorias. "Why?"

They scattered and fled at my approach. A craven, corrupted bunch, as Joseph and Saint Ange had said, good only for killing a man when his back is turned.

Coleman was smirking.

"Damn you!" I yelled at him. "Damn you all to hell!"

I am told that the Peoria who split Pontiac's skull was called Ghost Otter and that he was the nephew of a chief of his tribe who had got into a private feud with the Otta-was. I heard the Chippewas killed him later when their great chief Minavanana led them down from the north to avenge the death of his friend.

But you will never persuade me that Ghost Otter was not hired to do it. I think McDonner paid him his shekels, but my instinct tells me there were bigger men behind it. I believe that Black George Croghan and Messrs Baynton, Wharton have a good deal to answer for, though I could never prove this in a court of law. Black George, I heard later, was pushing another of his projects for a new colony about that time. He wanted to call it Vandalia in honor of our Royals' gothic ancestors; the name was apt for other reasons. If the men behind Pontiac's murder ever hear their own consciences through the haze of spirits, I imagine they tell themselves that the Ottawa had it coming. After all, his followers had subjected hundreds of our countrymen to the most exquisite forms of death. Then again, it could be argued that if a new revolt was brewing, Pontiac could not fail to answer the call of the war drums, and he had proved himself already to be the most formidable of all our native adversaries. I think there were finer calculations involved as well. Our Empire lives by the principle of *divide et impera*, as Sir William had taught me well. To arrange the murder of a powerful chief by another Indian nation was bound to spark a bloody feud between the tribes that might prevent a new native alliance from forming. Behind all this was the fact that some of our frontiersmen and speculators were actively fomenting a war that would supply the pretext to erase the Boundary Line and sweep the natives back to the Mississippi and beyond.

You may think I am gone soft in the head to lavish all this thought and emotion on a savage who once appeared to me as the most sadistic butcher this side of the Inferno. But I believed that Pontiac had changed, and that if we kept our word, he would keep his.

We took Pontiac's body across the river to be buried where the Peorias would not be able to dig it up and mutilate it, just behind the walls of St Louis. Saint Ange lined up his soldiers and they fired off a salute. A native witchdoctor came and shook his rattle. Pontiac rejoined the earth flexed like an infant inside the womb with his calumet and his war club and his medals from King Louis at his side.

Joseph said quietly, "Now we wrap you in the mantle of Mother Earth."

Pontiac's widow tore her hair and covered her face with ashes and ripped at her clothes until they hung in shreds.

When the earth was flung into the grave, she raised up and said. "Now I die this life."

Magid was there. She thanked me for what I had done, but told me that I must leave as swiftly as possible because Pontiac's friends were up in arms and any Britisher would be fair game. Saint Ange said the same thing. What a curious gaggle we must have made—a French commandant waiting on the pleasure of the dons, an Irishman in the king's service on the wrong side of the river, an Anglican Apple mouthing formulas from the Longhouse, and a bunch of Ottawas who were getting ready to carve up anyone who talked English!

The throb of the war drums carried from both sides of the river as Joseph and I paddled downstream to alert Wilkins at Fort Chartres. If my warning sank in faster than I might have expected, I have McDonner to thank for it.

I found him on the right bank, a mile or so above the fort.

I did not recognize him straight off because he was half-buried, head downwards. His bare legs spread upwards like the divided trunk of a white birch. From what I could see, they had flayed a good part of the skin off his whole carcass. I confess I did not linger to make closer inspection, or to award him the same burial rites I had secured for Pontiac.

I spent a couple of days at Fort Chartres with Wilkins, and I got a very bad feeling about our proconsul and his post. The soldiers had to go out in parties of six or more to bring in firewood and fresh meat because the fort was ringed by hostile Indians who killed and scalped smaller groups of Englishmen. The traders were running scared. Several had already decamped downriver to New Orleans or to Pensacola which was now our property.

Fort Chartres was low on rations and Colonel Wilkins could think of nothing better to do than double the guard on the liquor store and upbraid me for burying Pontiac on French soil.

"Spanish," I corrected him.

He gave me his pale stare, and muttered something about how all wogs and papists are the same. I decided on the spot that I did not intend to share whatever luck Wilkins had coming to him.

I said to Joseph, "You remember Detroit, don't you?"

He waited, the way Indians do.

"The mind needs air," I said. "I think it will be damned close in here very shortly with men cooped up like flies in a bottle. I have a mind to try the air of New Orleans. Will you risk the passage with me?"

"I wondered how long it would take you to ask," said Joseph.

Firelocks snapped at us as we nosed out onto the river. We lay low among the thwarts letting the current bring us down until the firing and the war drums were far behind.

I will spare you the details of our voyage. It took about a week with the flow as our ally; rivermen have told me it has taken them three months to battle the Mississippi against it. In the light canoe we made easy work of mud-banks and sandbars, though the snags and sawyers were a constant and potentially fatal hazard.

We came down at last into the moss-draped swamps and funereal wilds of bayou country. Herons rose on wide wings from the wood-stained waters. We traveled with alligators between curtains of live-oak and the ghostly arms of the cypresses. The air was heavy and humid. As we neared New Orleans, it carried the sweet smoke of the bargasse-burner and the sweeter promise of female companionship. God's breeches! How long had it been since I had pleasured a lady!

We entered the yellow channel with the crescent city of New Orleans at our right hand and the floating truck stores of English merchants on our left. There was a choice to be made, and I made it without hesitation. I pointed towards the creole shore.

Joseph exchanged a few words in Mohawk with Conrad The Song, the third member of our party.

He said to me, "We'll leave you here."

"You mean, you're not coming?"

"Mohawks don't like Frenchmen."

This was half true and half not, since a lot of Joseph's kinsmen had chosen, generations before either of us was born, to live with the blackrobes in Canada when it still belonged to the frogs.

I reminded him that New Orleans was now under Spanish rule.

He said, "We'll rest for a bit," indicating the trade-boats and the prospect of liquid refreshment, "and go down the coast to Pensacola. We'll wait for you there. If you're coming."

"Don't wait for me."

Joseph gave me one of his penetrating looks. He had told me once in an unguarded moment that he thought I viewed the world through the flap of my breeches. I am sure that he knew the shape of my thoughts at that moment. They were angled firmly towards the satinbacks of New Orleans.

I do not know that I had any larger view of my future when they brought the canoe up against the levee than to put it to the first likely mademoiselle or señorita who presented herself. As I have told you, native men take a somewhat austere view of the sexual act; the charioteer holds the horse on a tight rein in this respect if not in others.

Joseph's stare conveyed neither pity nor contempt but rather sadness.

He said, "We will be waiting for you in the Valley. You will come back to us."

I was kind to him, I hope, because I had made up my mind at that time to be free of Indian affairs for good. The Pontiac affair had sickened me, and though I still felt a strong bonding with Sir William, even stronger perhaps because of his demonstrated failings, I thought that his life, and my life in his service, were as easy as trying to walk a hundred feet underwater. I did not know what New Orleans held for me but I hoped that it was the beginning of my road back to civilization.

What I encountered was the firing squad and the Santa Hermandad—the hooded brotherhood of the Spanish Inquisition.

It was shooting season in New Orleans. In the Place d'Armes—I suppose I should call it the Plaza de Armas since the flag of Spain flapped over the cabildo—olive-dark soldiers led five men along the diagonal path between clumps of unmown grass and offered them the blindfold. Pierre Marquis, Joseph Milhet, La Frenière, Noyan, Pierre Caresse—do their names mean anything today? They were among the leaders of the first rebellion in arms by white men against European rule in North America. I am told that the aims of these creole rebels were not entirely progressive, that they protested, among other things, against a Spanish regulation that it was no longer permissible to whip negro slaves in public within the confines of the town.

But the dons thought their ideas subversive enough to light up a bonfire in the square while the men of the firing squad charged their muskets. A diminutive old man in a rusty black robe circled the flames, throwing papers into the fire and crying:

"This, the memorial of the planters of Louisiana, is publicly burned by order of His Excellency Don Alexandro O'Reilly for containing the following rebellious and pernicious doctrines: that Liberty is the mother of commerce and population. Without Liberty there are but few virtues."

The prisoners refused the blindfolds. Would Sam Adams have faced the sleepmaker with equal scorn?

The town crier announced that the captain-general, in the charity of his Catholic heart, had pardoned the youngest of the rebels, Noyan, because of his years.

"I fought with my comrades!" Noyan yelled. "I will die with them!"

The Spanish soldiers wheeled and fired from the shoulder, and I saw the five Frenchmen fold like empty potato-sacks.

What was all this about? Well, if you must know, and I think you should, there had been a revolt in New Orleans the year before. The frenchies of the town had determined that King Louis had no right to hand them over, body and land, to the rule of his Spanish cousin. They got a cabal together, drove the Spanish governor to seek refuge on his frigate in the harbor and then cut its moorings and applauded as he sailed gently down the stream. I am told that some of them took to parading about with white cockades in their hats to show they were republicans committed to the foundation of an independent state of Louisiana. The Spaniards had to despatch an army of near three thousand men from Havana to take the colony back. It had arrived shortly before I reached New Orleans.

I relate all this because it had a certain bearing on my fortunes, and also to put paid to some of the blatherings of the Sons of Liberty in our erstwhile American colonies. The victors write the history books. Yet it deserves to be recalled that it was the haughty creoles of Louisiana and not the New England mutineers who first raised firelocks against their masters in Europe. They lost and the rebels in the northern colonies won, to the loss, such is my prejudice, of the Indians and of Johnson's cause and the English-speaking peoples. Yet does not a lost cause always harbor a certain magic? I know I wept unfeigned tears among the ghouls who watched the destruction of those five gallant frenchies in the shadow of the caboose and the cathedral.

I thought when I first arrived that New Orleans and I would take to each other. It may be the hottest, dampest, most insect-plagued corner of North America, but the liz-ard side of me, if you take my meaning, found this perfectly agreeable once I had oiled my way into a household where they served a heady blend of brandy and absinthe and the mistress was more than willing. I lost my sole pair of shoes to mildew by leaving them on the floor and was alarmed by waterbugs the size of my fist that offered to

share my mattress, but I learned the ropes soon enough. If
I had only stuck to Genevieve, whose husband was in hiding out in alligator country because he had sported a white
cockade, I might have enjoyed an easy life, even though
the Spaniards had declared that the penalty for adultery
was that the lady in question and her lover were to be
handed over to the wronged husband to be used as he saw
fit.

I blame it on the environment—on those warm fogs full
of love-sweat, on the fluid bubbling in the soil underfoot.
Nothing is constant in New Orleans, not even the grave.
To bury a man in the earth, they have to fill his coffin full
of holes and bring a pair of negro slaves to stand on it until it fills with water down in the hole.

In short, I became infatuated, or as the creoles say,
entiché. This is really another story, so I must give you
only the hint of it.

Her name was Soledad. Who but a don would give his
daughter a name like that? Her father was a sugar baron in
the islands. I suppose he had come to Louisiana to see
whether slaves would work as well in the miasma of the
bayous. I first set eyes on her in the papist church which
I attended because, as you know, there is no better place
to make a survey of fashionable ladies. She was draped in
black with a mantilla, as if we were attending a funeral.
But her elegant weeds drew attention to the boldness of
her figure and the jet-black rhapsody of her hair rather
than detracted from these allurements.

I made her my study. I followed her to her father's
house, a red-roofed palazzo with broad verandahs raised
up on pillars, shaded by magnolias and live-oaks.

I planned my way to a private rendezvous. I found that
she haunted the cemetery. I presumed that she had a relation buried there decomposing in swampy water or baking
in a brick oven above ground, but perhaps it was only her
whimsy that led her to this place. Spaniards, by my observation, have a morbid fascination with death.

She always traveled about in the company of a duenna.
I chose my moment when this porridge-faced chaperone
had gone to avail herself of some shade.

"Oh lady," I gushed, "you are a saint! You are my salvation! I have fallen from the way, but you will bring me back! Say you will do it, or else I must drown myself in the river!"

Do you need to follow the whole encounter? I think not. As I say, it is another story. It is my experience that young ladies raised under the strict rule and rod of family and church, once persuaded that God is on the side of experiment, release themselves with volcanic force. I was not disappointed in Soledad.

Unhappily, her father discovered us banging away in a hammock under the magnolias. I expected a flogging or perhaps a duel. I was badly disappointed. He had me delivered to the crypt-like chambers of the Santa Hermandad behind the cathedral. I found myself charged by the Inquisition, not merely as a fornicator and adulterer, but as a heretic and blasphemer.

A chinless, hairless friar giggled as he showed me an array of glistening devices that would have drawn the envy of a Chippewa bonfire party.

God knows where this might have ended but for a summons from higher authority.

A liveried flunkey materialized in those dank cellars and announced that *Su Excelencia* desired my immediate presence. The chinless friar protested, but was obliged to comply.

I was escorted along underground passages and brought out into an airy pavilion where a gingery fellow in ruffles with a mouth that turned down as if he were trying to suppress a smile inspected me from top to toe.

"Hardacre, is it?" he addressed me at last and in English. "Now, what kind of a name would that be for one of my own countrymen?"

"Who? What—"

"Don Alexandro O'Reilly, Captain-General of Louisiana, in the service of His Most Catholic Majesty." He put his hand to his heart and took a little bow. "You may call me Your Excellency. But I'd rather you call me Alex as long as none of them hidalgos is listening."

I had heard his name, of course, when the town crier

was reading his proclamation over the creoles about to be shot. But to put it mildly, and it had not sunk home that the chief of all the dons was as Irish as I was, if not more so.

We had a drink or three and exchanged memories of the native sod. I found Don Alexandro keenly interested in my knowledge of the Indians. He knew he would never be popular with the Frenchmen of Louisiana, but thought he might hold their attention if he brought the sachems of the neighboring Indian nations into town for a big powwow. I gave him a few tips on how it ought to be done and I must say O'Reilly's performance was worthy of Smock Alley, if not Drury Lane. He rounded up some fierce-looking savages, dubbed them knights with his sword, hung them with medals on scarlet ribbons, made occult signs over their scalp locks and kissed them on the cheeks.

In return for my advice on this and one or two more delicate matters I have no mind to confide at this time, O'Reilly undertook to get me free of the Inquisition and Soledad's irate papa. This was good news. The bad news, as he informed me soon enough, was this.

"You'll have to marry the imp, Shane. The dough is rising, as we say."

I shall draw a curtain over the remainder of this section of my narrative, except to relate that when O'Reilly left New Orleans, I left with him, with a new wife and a new child. You may have kept count of how many I had. I could not afford to.

But life does have a way of getting hold of us.

I got rid of O'Reilly, and Soledad, and New Spain in the end. I went back to London, confident that I had put all my wives behind me, and the Americas, and Johnson, and the Indians. But they came after me. And for the second time Sir William and the Mohawks kept their promise.

Dearest Shane,

From what you say it seems you came as close to real marriage as a canny wolf to the bait in a trap, sensing—behind the succulent tang of ripe meat—something sharpened to a killing point.

I do not blame you for refusing to be snared in a narrow life.

But where is the soul? And where are the children?

Toujours,

Valerie

20

The Wax Sybil

YOU MUST KNOW SOMETHING of Patience Wright, the celebrated Wax Sybil, and her under-the-apron performances. All the best people sat for her. When I last saw her,
she was living in an elegant apartment at Chudleigh Court
on a leafy byway between the Palace Gardens and Pall
Mall. Her raree show was one of the sights of London no
well-bred provincial dared to miss since the king and
queen, no less, had modeled for her at the palace the summer before. Her wax *busto* of plump George, with his
pulpy red lips, his bulging glass eyes and blond eyebrows
was astonishingly *alive*; you expected him to lean over and
ask Queen Charlotte, who sat up prim and dainty as a
Meissen figurine, what they were having for dinner. Ominously close to the royal portraits, Mrs Wright displayed
her famous tableau of the beheading of Charles I. She was
an American, of Quaker stock and openly sympathetic to
the rebels in our colonies.

Peg Walsingham took me round to Chudleigh Court.
She thought I was in need of cheering up and, as usual,
Peg was right.

I had just turned thirty-five, which is an itchy age for a man of my temperament; I saw my glory days slipping away from me. I was nursing a black hangover, well-earned at the masquerade ball at the Pantheon, where I had seen Guy Johnson and Joseph Brant and other members of my old gang from the Indian Department for the first time in more than seven years. Joseph cut a mighty fine figure in that Motley assembly in his ruffled shirt and feathers and warpaint. A masked ball at the Pantheon is a pretty mixed affair, as you probably know—they let anyone in who has a costume and a guinea for the subscription. I came as a monk and rubbed shoulders and noses with a crew of gondoliers, Turks, ballad-singers, matchwomen, Indian chiefs, both make-believe and real, and a formidable lady attired as a fortress with popguns projecting from her highly pregnable bosom. It was hard to get much sense out of Guy and Joseph amid all that din of dancing, gobbling, drinking and fondling. But we got out of the Pantheon in smart order after a drunken Turk in baggy breeches swayed up to Joseph, croaked "Bloody good mask, what? *Bloody* fine face!" and proceeded to give the Mohawk's hatchet-edged nose an almighty tug in the belief that it was made of papier-mâché. Joseph had been tippling and, though he could hold his grog better than any Indian I ever came across, it is never good policy to tweak the nose of a Mohawk when he is in liquor. Joseph whipped out his war club, screamed "Ayyeeeee-OOOH!" and chased the misbegotten Turk from one end of the hall to the other.

When we got Joseph under control, we all repaired— Guy and me, and young Walter Butler, and another Mohawk, one of the muscular Hill brothers—to the Swan with Two Necks in Lad Lane where the Mohawks were staying. We recruited our spirits with flip and negus and I got some news from them about the colonists' revolt and the state of affairs in the Valley. The news did not seem good to me, though Guy chirruped about how General Howe was going to break the back of the rebellion in no time. He was especially proud of the fact that they had brought some ruffian called Ethan Allen over on the *Ada-*

mant with them, manacled in a box in the hold, crawling
with body lice. This fellow had apparently made off with
our guns from Ticonderoga when the guards were asleep
or drunk. The bit that interested me was that the man who
had taken him captive near Montreal was a sixteen-year-
old ensign called Peter Johnson.

"Not Chicha's son?"

"The very same."

It seemed that a spark of the old Johnson fire was still
alive, at least among his Mohawk family.

They told me something of Sir William's death two
summers before. I could picture him vividly, presiding
over one of his interminable powwows, with the Indians
complaining of the usual villains, land-sharks and licentious soldiery and the frontier boors who had holed some
natives in the back country of Virginia. About six in the
afternoon on that stifling July day, so they said, Sir William got on his hind legs, bade the company a courteous
good-day and walked up the stairs unassisted. He paused
in the doorway of his bedroom at Johnson Hall. Then he
dropped forward, straight as a white pine under the axe.
He was dead by the time his people got to him.

The rest of the news made me feel equally wretched.
The Mohawks had sided with Great Britain against the
rebels as I knew they would. Sir William's influence lived
after him, and he was ever a king's man. The upshot was
that the Mohawks had been forced to flee their Valley.
Chicha and her younger children had fled by night across
four feet of snow through the Cayuga country and on to
Fort Niagara, where the Butlers were organizing raiding
parties to shoot up the Liberty boys.

Joseph put his hand on my arm.

"Come back with me, Shane. The Mohawks need you."

I didn't know how to respond. I had had more than my
fill of Indian fighting and I did not much relish the prospect of watching people of both races who had once been
friends and neighbors in Johnson's lost kingdom, scalping
and slaughtering each other. But it is painful to say no to
an old friend that is in need. And I sensed the immensity
of that need. Sir William had left no successor; it is hard

for a sturdy tree to grow in the shade of a great white oak. There was still an Indian Department, of course, and still Johnsons to run it, at least in name, along with the Butlers and a Scot called John Campbell, of whom I knew nothing except that Guy had it in for him. But Guy and John Johnson were not fighters. Worse than that, they lacked Sir William's stamina, his presence and his cunning—and of course the natives knew it. In this terrible upheaval in their world, in which they risked losing, finally and irretrievably, the lands they had farmed and hunted and the burial-grounds of their ancestors, the Mohawks needed Sir William Johnson—the man himself, not his impersonator.

Joseph was relentless. His fingers tightened on my upper arm.

He said, "Come back with me, Shane. You belong to us as well as your own kind."

"I can't give you what you need. I am not Sir William. I am not Warragiyaguey."

Joseph stared into me. I cannot communicate the intensity of that gaze. It seemed to numb my bones.

He said, "You will requicken Warragiyaguey's name."

He began there in the tavern, with the noisy hubbub of travelers and bumperers and painted jilts all about us, to recite the solemn words of a Mohawk condolence in his native tongue.

I trembled. My eyes watered. I could not hold back the tears that came streaming down my cheeks.

"I'm sorry, Joseph, I'm sorry—"

I stood up. I swayed. I steadied myself briefly against the table. I blundered away without farewells, heedless of the curses of men whose drinking arms I disturbed.

I did not want to return to America, to pursue the wraith of a lost kingdom. Yet Joseph's appeal stirred a deep well of humanity that I have too often sought to deny. When he spoke to me in Mohawk, he called up ghosts. I saw Sir William, standing up in the thwarts of a whaleboat in the black night across Lake Erie, willing me to understand his mission to bridge two worlds.

I did not sleep very much that night.

In the morning, Guy Johnson came round to see me at my lodgings.

He said, "It's a serious proposal. We'll find a place for you all right in the Indian Department. Lord Germain says we'll have all the money we want. Joseph has persuaded him that he has only to raise his arm and five thousand Indians will come running."

I said I would think it over.

Guy then dropped a small bombshell. I do not know if he calculated which way it would make me jump, but I most certainly did jump.

He said, "Suky's in London. I met her at Brook Watson's. She came to Newmarket with us."

Now I will not detain you for long with my matrimonial affairs. Suffice it to say that I was at that time a trigamist which is an estate that is tenable only in a Moslem country or so long as the ladies in question have no intelligence of each other. A sensible man will seek to put a good wide stretch of water between them, as I had sought to do.

I have said something of Suky and a little of Soledad, who was at a safe remove, I hoped, among the sugar islands. I have told you almost nothing of Mirabel, the Earl of Eastmeath's daughter who had staked an earlier claim than either of them if she chose to make something of it. I was only a boy when we eloped by night with the aid of ropes and subterranean passages and tied the knot under the nervous eye of a priest among the ruins of Monasterboice. The earl made the devil of a fuss. He sent armed men after us, whisked Mirabel off to England, threatened to have me jailed and promised money if I would hush up the affair and pretend no marriage had taken place. I finally yielded to the pressure from my own family, which took the earl's side, and heard later that Mirabel had had a society wedding with one of our debutante's delights. That ought to have been the end of the story. But I had been imprudent enough to pen a flippant sketch of my American escapades for the *Gentleman's Magazine*, and who should it bring to my door but Mirabel, newly widowed, larger than life—and a damn sight larger than I remembered her—and bent on pressing her connubial claims on the supposed hero of the Indian wars.

You can see that an encounter with Suky threatened to hurl my tangled affairs into the wildest disarray. I tried not to betray my inward agitation to Guy and had the maid show him out as soon as it could be done without discourtesy. I racked my brains for a way to ensure that Suky and Mirabel did not form a feminine scalping-party.

One option, of course, was to return to the colonies and the Mohawks. I resisted it. I had earned a soft life and God's breeches!—I was thirty-five!

There was also the possibility of a job with William Eden, a clever, underhand sort of fellow who ran a confidential office at what they now called the Northern Department. The Earl of Sandwich had sent me round to see him on the grounds that I ought to do something useful with a war on. Eden seemed more interested in my experiences with Alexandro O'Reilly and the dons than my knowledge of the Indians. He told me he might have something for me if I was willing to do a little rogering at Crown expense, which sounded a damn sight more tempting than skulking behind bushes with Joseph and his hairdressers.

I was all afidget when Peg Walsingham arrived at the door, radiant in apple-green silk striped with rose.

"I have come to revive you!" she cried. "Poor Shane! I know how you must feel!"

"How can you? You don't look a day over thirty."

This was gallantry, of course, but Peg was remarkable. I was about to say remarkably well *preserved*, but that would do her gross injustice. She had not only preserved her beauty, she had kept her vitality. You felt the strength of the life-force that was in her, as the color rose beneath her skin. It touched anyone who was near her. Peg's mere presence made me feel more strongly alive. •

Peg announced that she was going to treat me. I suggested the most pleasurable method and she told me I was far too old to be doing that in the mornings. I rose to the challenge, of course, and it was almost noon when we arrived at Mrs Wright's waxworks in Peg's carriage.

We had planned nothing more than a drive in the park. It was pure hazard, I insist, that brought us to the door of the Wax Sybil. To be quite specific about the matter, Peg spied Dr William Dodd, the king's chaplain, sauntering among the beeches with a well-timbered young private from the Foot Guards. She made a remark about Dr Dodd's personal habits that I choose not to repeat, then added, with a trill, "Ah, Mrs Wright has his head too!"

"What in blazes does that mean?"

"She did his *busto*, sweet. Do let's go and see."

There. Pure chance, don't you agree? If I seem to belabor the point, it is because as soon as I walked into Mrs Wright's chambers, I had an obscure sensation of fatality. The sights and sounds of the place were all fresh to me, yet they were thoroughly familiar. I had no sooner entered that raree show than I *knew* that my fortune had shifted as suddenly and as thoroughly as it had one boozy evening at White's.

Do you know what Patience Wright called her wax dummies? She called them her soul-catchers. She said she could bring back the dead. You must judge for yourself.

The housemaid let us in. The first room was bathed in a damp penumbra. Among all those pale, bloodless figures, I felt I was moving through a village of the drowned. I do not remember all the *bustos* that were on display. I recall that Mrs Wright made a special show of her political heroes—Chatham in his red parliamentary robes, lined with silk, trimmed with rabbit; John Wilkes, with his leering, twisted phiz and saurian lips; plump-cheeked Ben Franklin, whom Mrs Wright called her "guardian angel" and wanted to lead a revolution in England, if you can credit it.

The next chamber was more brightly illuminated, but the figures were distinctly more sinister. There was a Cassandra portrayed as a weird pythoness with serpents coiled about her wrists. There were allegorical tableaux drawn from the scriptures. The evil counselor Ahasuerus, scheming to destroy the Chosen People, toyed with a dagger behind the back of a raven-haired Queen Esther.

We came to another room where the faces were half-formed or merely blind spheres awaiting the touch of life. It took a moment before I realized that the large, straight person seated by the window was not one of the exhibits. She wore a plain dark dress and a plain white cap and apron. A white fichu was draped carelessly about her shoulders as if a visitor had dropped it in passing. The eyes came alive first when she saw that I had perceived the deception. They were greenish-olive in color, very bright and intent.

She said to me, "You wouldn't be an American."

"No indeed."

"But you come from there. Come from God's own country, don't you? Something to do with Indians, was it? Mixed with some conniving, belly-cod scamps as well, didn't you? You don't need to tell me, lovey. You just stand there. Yes, that's it. Stay in the light. I'll tell you all about it."

She babbled on like this, talking quite fast and loud.

Mrs Wright was reputed to be something of a clairvoyant, though I did not know this at the time. The gift runs in families, so they say. The father was a bearded vegetarian who dressed his family all in white and fed them beans and cabbage and theories of visions and guardian angels watching over the affairs of men and nations.

All the while she was talking, her hands were working away under her lap-apron. She never once looked down, and the apron concealed what she was doing between those wide haunches. To be perfectly frank, I wondered if my presence had inspired her to exercise some moist fantasy of sex. I wanted to nudge Peg and say, "I think she likes me."

The sculptress rattled on, "Going back, is it? Mustn't, lovey. The Lord of Hosts and of Gideon stands against Pharaoh and will smite all his armies."

She cackled. I began to think her seriously deranged.

"Oh yes, yes, yes," she crowed, and whipped her hands out from under the apron.

I gasped. I stepped back a pace or two. I was looking at Davers's head. The hair had been lifted. It was raised up by the ears in the fists of a savage with boiling eyes, daubed black as slaughter.

Mrs Wright cackled.

"What do you see, lovey? What's past is what's coming. The way forward is the way back."

I looked again, Of course, it wasn't Davers. That was only a freak of the light or of memory. I was looking at myself without eyes or hair.

It was an extraordinary likeness. I could not imagine how she had contrived it without once looking down to inspect her progress.

"How did you do that?"

She dandled my head on her lap. She flexed her thumb and a dimple appeared on the tableland of the chin. It had never occurred to me that I looked quite so much like Sir William Johnson.

"See it all now, don't we, lovey?" she creaked in that maddening singsong.

"It *is* remarkable," said Peg, stooping over to inspect my eyeless *busto* more closely. "Won't you say how you do it?"

"Angel hair." Mrs Wright reached up and stroked Peg's hair. "Shall I do you too?"

"Oh, would you?" But Peg quickly made some excuse about the time.

I was still curious to know how Patience Wright could catch the living spirit of a man without turning her eyes from his face.

"Wants to know it all, doesn't he?" she went on in that irritating fashion, as if I were a tomcat to be mocked in the third person. "I don't catch the likeness, dearie. Oh no. I catch the soul."

This strange interview was making me quite feverish. I ran hot and cold. My bones ached. My knees felt rubbery.

I said too quickly, "Let me buy the *busto*."

"Wants it back, does he?" That cackle again.

I struggled to get a curb on my senses. I was behaving like some ignorant savage who thinks that by making an image of a man you can claim some part of his spirit.

Yet I said, "I really must have it."

"Course you must, lovey. But it's not finished."

"It doesn't matter."

"But this is only a sketch. Give us a week and we'll do it proper."

"You must let me have it."

"Shane, dear," Peg took my arm. "Are you feeling quite well?"

I realized I was acting the complete fool. With some embarrassment, I made my arrangement with Mrs Wright. Her craft was highly complex. In her finished *bustos*—she *never* called them busts, that was far too common—she even introduced the mimicry of veins and capillaries under the wax skin. She paid barber shops to send her human hair of all colors. Her glass eyes were adorned with lids, and lashes, and brows.

I did not go round to collect my head in person. As a matter of fact, I was lying pretty low at that time, having narrowly escaped an encounter with Suky at a rout at the Haberdashers' Hall that I was reckless enough to attend with Mirabel. Aside from my domestic dramas, since that visit to Chudleigh Court, I had been suffering at nights, in the hours when sleep is welcome, from a gusting delirium. I lay between sleep and waking and fancied I heard voices and saw dead men walk. I wondered if I was becoming as crazy as Robert Davers, since, as Mr Tryon writes in his *Treatise of Dreams*, "every madman dreameth waking."

One of these troubled nights I sat up in bed with a start with a fading memory of a dream in which I was in a forest clearing. The treetrunks rose up like the columns around an ancient amphitheater. Many speakers came and went, in togas or Indian blankets, I cannot say which. The last was Sir William. I woke with his voice in my ears. He was speaking in blank verse or something like it; the long, stately periods rolled over each other.

> I am from such as those
> by whom the worlds are shaken.

I opened my eyes with these words rolling like surf in my ears. The voice was so distinct and so familiar that I looked around the room for the speaker. For a moment, I did not know where I was, or whom I was with.

Make of this what you will. I felt I was being called. Hard as I tried to shake this nonsense out of my skull, I could not do it.

Then Peg's negro footman came back from Chudleigh Court with my head sheathed in a velvet sack, which Mrs Wright could well afford to use, given the price she had charged me.

Gingerly, I slipped the velvet away from the wax. The color of the hair was perfect. The skin-tone seemed a little pallid, for I am pretty high in color on an average day; I may have looked whiter at Mrs Wright's. The eyes.

I dropped the head. It would no doubt have shattered on the floor had I not caught it between my thighs, where the Wax Sybil gripped her newborn *bustos*, to keep their substance warm and pliable.

She had got the eyes wrong. They were hazel, green and gray all at once—no, shifting from one to the other. No. She couldn't do that with baubles of glass. A trick of the light. My mind was momentarily dis-eased.

Shall I tell you what I did with my head?

I buried it, together with a fine suit of wine-red silk, hung on a wooden frame, after a most stylish funeral at St George's Church.

Peg was my chief lieutenant in these obsequies and she loved every minute of it. She even thanked me for allowing her, as she put it, her greatest role.

You see, I had hit upon a solution for my excess of wives and creditors and my gathering dis-ease with the part that hazard had written for Shane Hardacre at London.

Captain Hardacre died suddenly, of a capricious hemorrhage that flowered in his brain-pan, or so my widows and money-lenders were informed. Peg picked St George's because she thought that a beau like Hardacre should go out in style. She even persuaded Dr Dodd to give an oration. How she won over the king's own chaplain I will never know, but I have my suspicions of gentle blackmail.

I did not go to the church in person, although Peg and I agreed it would add to the jape if I were present in disguise. I think I might have fooled my widows, but not my

children. I still feel guilty about them, and you may gauge
the depth of this sentiment by how much, or rather how
little, has been said of them in this narrative. A man is allowed some privacy, surely.

What's that? I know, I know. The jolly fellows at
White's said much the same when the truth eventually
slipped out, as truth is apt to do. They voted me Blackguard of the Year, and that is an accolade that is rarer than
the Most Noble Order of the Garter.

Peg gave me a lively account of the funeral. Dr Dodd
had a fit of the sneezes and spent much of his time trying
to avoid blowing the Good Book off the lectern. A prodigious number of my old lady friends turned out, it seems;
Peg said you could have driven a three-master with the
wind off their fans.

And what followed Captain Hardacre's untimely removal from the London scene?

What do you think?

I couldn't help myself. I don't know whether it was Joseph, or my dream of Sir William, or the strangeness that
I experienced at Mrs Wright's.

I went back to the colonies, and the Mohawks, in pursuit of Johnson's cause. What ensued is another story. I am
not yet ready to tell it; perhaps I shall never be ready. I
have a good deal of life in me yet—you may ask several
ladies about that. A man does not complete his autobiography until he is willing to admit he is at the end of his
tether, and 'od rot me, as the Earl of Sandwich would say,
if I ever do that.

Character is fate, or so the Greeks maintained. I was
ever possessed of a roving humor, and like a ranging span-
iel that barks at every bird he sees, leaving his game, I
would have followed all, saving what I should, but for
Johnson.

I know that some of them that chance upon this modest
narrative may criticize the excess of levity in my tale of
madness and of a lost kingdom and of tragedies beyond
the gothic imagination. I say to them with Horace:
ridentum dicere verum quid vestat? Yet may not truth in
laughing guise be dressed?

Dearest Shane,

After deep reflection, I can only counsel you to burn
this manuscript. You must never deliver your memoirs
to the public in this form.

You believe you will shock and titillate, in this
dawning era of bourgeois propriety, when we are required to study morals and manners with shopkeepers.

I think you will only succeed in holding yourself up
to the public view like a stuffed monster from a forgotten epoch. A specimen of some extinct species. A
woolly mammoth, or a saber-toothed tiger. Nothing left
of it except bones and matted hair, shedding in the dust-
grained museum air. Glass eyes. No juice. No longer
able to terrify or arouse. A target for the spitballs of
bad boys on school outings.

They will not know you, Shane. They will not understand you.

Burn your book. Your reputation will fare better
without it, and Sir William Johnson's is beyond redemp-
tion.

Your

Valerie

Dearest Shane,

Since I have no news from you, although several packets have come in, I must assume you have taken mortal offense at my last letter.

I hardly know how I can write to you now. But I feel I must write, because my dream last night was different from the others, more real to me than the shapes and colors of the dressing-room where I am writing this.

I have no idea what this dream means, but I am certain it is putting a question of large moment to me. Since I have no one about me to whom I may speak freely on such matters, except my superstitious Irish maid, I must tell my dream to you. Did you not tell me once that the American Indians believe that unless we honor our dreams, in our waking lives, we will not dream well?

My cat Mamalouke has jumped up on my lap, as if to confirm this advice. He is a spooky blue-gray color, and his pupils are engorged this morning as if he has a mouse between his paws.

Here is the dream.

I am not in my own body. I have the shape of a man. This is not unfamiliar to me, neither is it unpleasant. I am with another man, an old friend. He is leaving his family and dependents.

We walk out from his villa, through verdant foliage, into the dark under the stars.

A very old man is climbing the steep carriage road that winds up the hill to the villa. From afar, he looks like a mendicant seller of codfish or olive oil. As he comes closer, I see he has flowing white hair and a long white beard. I cannot see his eyes.

He fills me with dread.

I scramble up to the top of the hill, beside my friend. From the summit, I see that the old man is following us, moving without haste but at a steady, implacable rhythm. Now his face seems masklike, something to be brandished on a pole by the mummers of Carnival.

I know his name is Death.

I am not ready for him. I whirl and turn, looking for a way to escape. Then it comes to me that I am dreaming, and that I am not confined to ordinary forms of locomotion.

I beat my arms. I shoot up into the air. I am flying, awkward at first, then with gathering confidence. I catch an updraft. I leave the hill far behind.

I am lost in the black night. Then I see a lighted window and fly through it. A woman is seated at her embroidery frame, before the fire. She squints at me oddly, as if I am some kind of flying insect. I realize, in this moment, that I have been traveling through the dark in my own light, and have changed shape and size in some astonishing way. Perhaps, in her eyes, I resemble a firefly. The woman is crooning and making signs. She is letting me know I am welcome.

It is warm in this room, but I feel I do not belong here. And I do not want to look at the shapes that are emerging under her deft fingers, on the embroidery frame.

I fly back out the window.

I am drawn to another place. The odors are rank and lush, crushed sugarcane blended with sweat and feces. A young girl with braided hair and skin the color of wild honey smiles at me and claps her hands. A black man whose face and chest are streaked with ash—her father—bends over me, wary and suspicious. He peers into my eyes. I see Mamalouke, my sooty cat, reflected in his pupils.

He nods, as if some decision has been made. He picks up a small knife, or awl, and starts boring into the head of a coconut. He whistles tunelessly, almost soundlessly, puffing wind between his lips.

I do not want to stay with these people. I am afraid of going through the looking glass, and becoming the cat I see in the father's eyes.

I take flight, and the roof of their hut opens for me.

I come to a room in the sky that is all white. The windows have no panes. My male friend—from the first scene—waits for me in this white space. I ply him with questions, about what I have seen and what has happened to him.

"Are you dead?" I demand. "Are we both dead? Is this what death is like?"

He does not answer. He says only, "When I come back, I will be a maker of plays. They will fight to see my plays performed on Drury Lane."

I woke then, utterly confused.

I recognized nobody in my dream, except my cat Mamalouke.

I did not know who I was, or where I was.

The woman at her embroidery might have been my grandmother. I do not remember her distinctly. My mother told me, one unguarded evening, that my Irish grandmother had the Sight and was a weaver of fates.

The black family could have been people from the plantation. I was never permitted to befriend the slaves, after they took Nounou away from me. I seem to remember childhood dreams in which I lived in a different house, a shanty in the woods, where black people danced all night to the heartbeat of their drums and called spirits into their persons.

I did not recognize my male friend. But when I reflected on his words, I thought of you. Is it still your deepest ambition, as you say in your book, to write for the stage?

The man in my dream was leaving his wife and children. I know something of your wives, Shane—more than you have found it prudent, thankfully, to share in these pages—but you have never spoken of children. Perhaps this is because the child in you still rules,

and will not bow to the duties of parenthood. I grieve
for you if you have denied yourself the joy of children, and deprived them of the joy you could give. I
think you would have made a wonderful father, because
of that child in you.

You would not have denied wonder, as many fathers do.

I believe everyone in my dream was dead. I flew
from the old man Death, but stayed within his pre-
cinct.

What can this mean?

Could this dream be a memory of the future?

I fled from Death, but I sense him now, at my left
shoulder.

My dream is surely a warning. Yet I feel that more
than this, it is a teaching, a preparation for going a journey.

Henry says it is pointless to speculate about what
comes after death since we will learn the truth at the
appointed time. If he remembered his dreams, I think
he would amend his opinion. I think the path of the
soul after death is the path of dreams, except that
we cannot wake from death in the body we used before.

Tell me your truth about these things. You profess
to be wedded to the body, but I know your adventures are not confined to it.

Toujours,

Valerie

British Legation
Lisbon

14th July

Lady Valerie D'Arcy
79 Eaton Square
London

Dear Lady D'Arcy,

I beg to inform you, with deep regret, that Colonel Vivian Hardacre succumbed to a fire at his home at Sintra. The cause of the fire is unknown, though it may be related to the severe lightning storms that have plagued this coast in recent days. No personal effects could be recovered. Since the condition of the remains made normal burial inappropriate, we were obliged to confine the obsequies to a memorial service at which Colonel Hardacre was accorded the honors befitting his distinguished military service.

Prior to this tragic event, Colonel Hardacre entrusted me with a locked trunk and a sealed envelope to be opened in the event of his death. His letter instructed me to forward the trunk to you, as his literary executor. It is my sad duty to comply with his wishes.

Your obedient servant

Hon. Oliver Chubb
H.M. Consul-General

Dearest Shane,

I do not know where to direct this letter, but I feel my thoughts must reach you, wherever you are now. Since your box arrived from Portugal, I have felt you were never far from me.

I do not believe in death, not as we are taught to believe in an eternity of torment or bliss. Eternity would be too dull, especially if we were required to endure it in our old bodies, resurrected from the grave, as the priests profess to believe.

Nor do I believe in death as the black hole so many fear, the final snuffing-out of the candle.

I would have liked to have spoken with Robert Davers about these things, or with the native dream prophet he so revered. A man at the Royal Society said there is a tribe in the South Pacific that believes that the Other World is not one place, but an infinite number of places. That the experiences we encounter after death are as various as our imaginations, and as personal as our dreams.

You live on, of course, in the heap of papers at my feet, which I have barely begun to examine. Did you really recruit the notorious Benedict Arnold for the British cause? I thought the credit belonged to poor Major André, who was hanged for it. There is a vicar in Derbyshire who claims he dreamed the whole thing before John André even took ship for America.

I had intended to burn all of your manuscripts, but I now see that this would do a disservice to those in future times who may wish to know the secret springs of our history, in this world turned upside down. However, I will allow nothing more to be published until it has been put into proper form, a form that does justice to women.

One thing we can never blame you for: you never sought to change us. How you reveled in the tilt and lift of women, just as you found them! You never made a tall woman stoop, or a round one bruise her ribs with corsets, or a skinny one try to puff herself into a silly bull-frog. You praised us with hands and eyes for what we are.

Thus you served the Goddess despite yourself. Her time is coming again. The clanmothers of the forest tribes could have told you, if you had listened.

I do not believe in death, except as a swing-door.

My mother said that when Merlin was ready to depart his body, he shut himself up in an *esplumoir*. The *esplumoir* is the place where the falcon goes to molt, whence he comes again, to soar on shining wings.

I shall look for you in the mornings, in the bright, windy spaces.

Yours, ever

Valerie

Note from the Editor

Where it can be checked against other colonial sources, Captain Hardacre's account of the revolt of Pontiac and life in Johnson's Indian Department seems generally accurate. However, there is much that cannot be verified, and the reader must be cautioned that the author is guilty of one or two egregious lapses of memory, and is suspect— not only in his boastful description of his amours—of magnifying his own role in events.

Captain Hardacre appears to have had a serviceable command of Mohawk and other Indian tongues, but his renderings of native words are as erratic as those of the scribes of his Department who compiled the voluminous Indian Records, now in the Public Archives of Canada, at Ottawa, which were of frequent service to the Editor in his efforts to confirm the details of Sir William's frontier diplomacy. Some effort has been made to regularize Mohawk spellings according to modern phonetic principles, following David R. Maracle's pioneering *Iontewenna-weienhstahkwa: Mohawk Language Dictionary*, compiled with the support of the Native Language Center at the University of Western Ontario and the Mohawks of the Bay of Quinte Band (photocopy, 1985). But many expressions and proper names—e.g. "Warragiyaguey," Sir William's Mohawk title, a garble of an expression that literally means, They Chop Down The Forests For Him—have been left as they were found in the original. The author's versions of Chippewa/Ojibwa and Ottawa words have been checked against the early vocabularies appended to Dr Edwin James's edition of the *Narrative of the Captivity and Adventures of John Tanner* (Carvill, New York, 1830). Tanner's account of his long captivity among these nations provides supporting evidence for some of the more bizarre elements in Captain Hardacre's description of native life, including the place of the *agokwa*, or "she man," in early Chippewa society.

The most important primary sources consulted by the Editor in his efforts to check the veracity of Captain Hardacre's account of William Johnson and his world are two massive printed compilations—*The Sir William Johnson Papers*, ed. James Sullivan et al. (State University of New York, Albany, 1921–65; 14 vols.), cited as JP; and *Documents Relative to the Colonial History of the State of New York*, ed. Edmund B. O'Callaghan (Weed, Parsons, Albany 1853–87; 15 vols.), cited as NYCD—together with the Indian Records and the Daniel Claus Papers in the Canadian archives; the Journal of the Reverend John Ogilvie, Anglican Minister at Fort Hunter, in the New York State Library at Albany; and the Journals and Letters of Samuel Kirkland, Presbyterian missionary, in the Library of Hamilton College, New York.

On the Pontiac revolt, the most important materials used by the Editor for fact-checking are the anonymous French *Journal of the Conspiracy of Pontiac*; John Rutherfurd's *Narrative of a Captivity*; Major Alexander Duncan's manuscript account of the battle of Bloody Bridge; Lieutenant Jehu Hay's Diary, in the William L. Clements Library; the James Sterling Letter Book, in the same institution; George Croghan's Journals, in the John Cadwalader Papers of the Historical Society of Pennsylvania; and the John Porteous Journals in the Burton Historical Collection of the Detroit Public Library.

The Editor has not attempted to verify every incident or controversial statement in Captain Hardacre's narrative. The following comments are intended to be of service to the general reader, and to the specialist who may be startled by the bold challenge the Hardacre memoirs pose to the received version of seminal events in early American history.

Shane in England (Chapters 1–2)

The Editor has found no record of Vivian "Shane" Hardacre's birth or baptism in the parish registers of

County Meath or in the Four Courts genealogical records
in Dublin. However, the original family name, MacShane,
is important in the family tree of the author's kinsman, Sir
William Johnson. According to the genealogy drawn up by
Sir William's younger brother, Peter Warren Johnson, and
recognized by the Dublin Office of Arms on February 24,
1774, the birth-name of the Superintendent's grandfather,
on his father's side, was William MacShane. Through this
MacShane, the Johnsons traced their ancestry back to the
O'Neills, the high kings of Ulster. The Editor suspects
from this that Captain Hardacre's blood relationship with
Sir William was even closer than he admits, though doubtless it would have to be traced on the wrong side of the
blanket.

The "Manor of Waryne" is patently one of the author's
inventions and probably camouflage for the Manor of
Killeen with its medieval castle, whose estates border the
Johnson family property at Smithstown. (When the Editor
visited the castle in the spring of 1987, it had been par-
tially gutted by arson.) "Waryne" is the original spelling of
the family name of the Johnsons' powerful neighbors and
in-laws, the Warrens of Warrenstown. Their intermarriages
are charted in *Burke's Genealogical and Heraldic History*,
ed. L.G. Pine (London, 1959), p. 123.

The Editor can find no trace of Peg Walsingham in the
standard authorities on the Georgian theater; it is possible
that Captain Hardacre altered the actress' name to avoid
an action for defamation. Mrs Peg *Woffington*, the
sprightly offspring of a Dublin flower-seller, was of course
one of the greatest thespians of Captain Hardacre's day. In
his *Humble Appeal to the Publick: Containing an Account
of the Rise, Progress and Establishment of the First Regular Theatre in Dublin* (Dublin, 1758) Thomas Sheridan
describes Mrs Woffington's return to the Smock Alley
Theatre in her famous role as Cordelia; a Dublin rake
leaped on stage and attempted to take "indecent liberties."

To judge by other contemporary accounts, such as
Charles Johnstone's picaresque *Chrysal: or the Adventures
of a Guinea* (Watson, Pearce, London, 10th edition, 1785;
4 vols.) Captain Hardacre has not over-colored his descrip-

tion of the diversions of Sir Francis Dashwood, the Earl of Sandwich and their circle. The earl is nicely sketched in Henry Blyth's *The Rakes* (Dial Press, New York, 1971); Louis C. Jones's *The Clubs of the Georgian Rakes* (Columbia University Press, New York, 1942) cities a number of early visitors to Medmenham who support Captain Hardacre's depiction of the erotic statuary, the "haunted" mineshaft and the ball-shaped drinking den atop the church.

The baboon at the Black mass is mentioned in *Chrysal* and by several biographers of John Wilkes; cf. R.W. Postgate, *That Devil Wilkes* (Vanguard Press, New York, 1929). Prior to the discovery of the Hardacre narrative, most historians considered it apocryphal.

Robert Davers's mystifying remarks on Harpocrates and the Secret Doctrine may be compared with the classical source: Iamblichus's fourth-century work *On the Mysteries of the Egyptians, Chaldeans and Assyrians*, trans. Thomas Taylor (1821); there is a 1984 reprint (Wizards, San Diego). Davers appears to anticipate the importance of the Harpocrates Assumption in the magic of the Order of the Golden Dawn. This topic is clouded in deepest obscurity, but some clues may be gleaned from Israel Regardie, *The Golden Dawn* (reprinted by Llewellyn, St Paul, 1971), 3: 231–32.

Of Daniel, "the Wild Man" at a London tavern in 1761, the Editor has found no trace. However, there are complaints in the *Johnson Papers* and the colonial records about the role of Uri Klock and his partners in exporting Canajoharie Mohawks for exhibit at London and Amsterdam, in the early 1760s, and even as late as the winter of 1773–74, when Sir William was close to death. (See, for example, Edmund B. O'Callaghan, ed., *The Documentary History of the State of New York* (Weed, Parsons, Albany, 1849, 4 vols), 2: 1004–7). George R. Hamell of the New York State Museum has unearthed a 1764 Dutch engraving of a Mohawk named "Sychnecta," who was a sideshow attraction in Europe that year; the Editor is grateful to Dr Hamell for his research paper "An Iroquois Abroad" and for advice on other matters. "Daniel" was a common English name amongst Mohawks. The *Johnson Papers* contain references to a Daniel whose Mohawk-name is sometimes rendered as "Oghnour," who served as a courier between Johnson country and Detroit in 1763 (cf. JP10: 812).

On Sir Roberts Davers, see the notes for Chapters 11–12.

New York and Albany (Chapters 3–4)

Captain Hardacre's physical descriptions of New York and the passage to Albany generally match those of other eighteenth-century travelers, such as the Swedish naturalist Peter Kalm (*Travels into North America*, trans. J.R. Forster, Imprint Society, Barre, Mass., 1972), Dr Alexander Hamilton (*A Gentleman's Progress*, ed. Carl Bridenbaugh, U. of North Carolina, Chapel Hill, 1948), Lord Adam Gordon (whose journal is printed in Newston B. Mereness, ed., *Travels in the American Colonies*, Antiquarian Press, New York, 1961) and, for the upper Hudson, Alexander Coventry (a 2,000-page typescript of his journal is in the Albany Institute of History and Art) and Roland Van Zandt, ed., *Chronicles of the Hudson: Three Centuries of Travelers' Accounts* (Rutgers, New Brunswick, 1971).

A vivid contemporary description of the city of New York, with a south-east view of Manhattan Island, appears in the *London Magazine* of August 1761.

The monument to General Wolfe, Manhattan's earliest recorded public monument, is also described in the *New York Mercury*, July 12, 1762.

The military camp on Staten Island is described in the *New York Mercury*, July 27, 1761. The opening of James Rivington's bookstore was announced in the *Mercury* on October 6, 1761. Cart-whippings like the one mentioned by Captain Hardacre were a common sight; on November 6, 1760, the unfortunate Francis Brown was sentenced to this punishment for stealing stockings off a stage-boat (*Minutes of the General Sessions of the Peace*, 1732–62, MSS). The colonial newspapers were full of complaints about robberies and footpads; cf. the *New York Post-Boy* for February 11, 1760, and February 8, 1762.

The views on the Indians that Captain Hardacre attributes to General Amherst conform fairly closely to those expressed in Sir Jeffrey's private and official correspondence; several specific examples are cited later in these notes. Our author's assessment of the general is shamelessly partisan, but does not contradict the facts as recorded in J.C. Long's sympathetic biography, *Lord Jeffrey Amherst: A Soldier of the King* (Macmillan, New York, 1933). Amherst wrote to Pitt, declining his Order of the Bath, but was obliged to accept (*Private Letters*, Packet 26, July 22, 1761).

Captain James Dalyell, a lieutenant in the 60th Foot, was appointed aide-de-camp to the general early in 1761, and promoted captain in the second battalion of the Royals, or First Foot.

As for the delectable Miss Suky Van Horn, there was a young lady of that name in Manhattan at the time of Captain Hardacre's visit. Major Moncrieff wrote of her to Sir William Johnson that "if I was two & twenty, I would not wish for more than her, & six thousand bottles of her father's old wine" (JP7: 1144). She was one of eight sisters, many of whom made important social and political alliances; one of them married James Rivington, the Tory propagandist and American double agent; another married Stephen Moylan, Washington's aide-de-camp. However, the Editor finds it hard to believe that the Suky in Captain Hardacre's story is the Miss Van Horn of contemporary social pages.

The Editor can find no record of the dramatic entertainment Captain Hardacre organized for the Hero of Montreal. The Editor suspects that our narrator may have improved his story by borrowing some elements from the "Mischianza" staged by the notorious Major André to honor the Howeses departure from New York during the Revolution; it seems that Captain Hardacre may also have had a hand in this later entertainment.

From his first arrival in Mohawk country in 1738, William Johnson was locked in bitter rivalry with the dominant Dutch mercantile families of Albany and with their allies and in-laws, the Livingstons of the upper Hudson valley. The depth of the personal animosity that developed may be gleaned from the journal Sir William's brother kept of a visit in 1760–61 (JP13: 180–214). Warren Johnson describes how Albany Dutchmen once set a pack of dogs on William; his life was allegedly saved by fellow-Irishmen who happened by. Our narrator rapidly acquired his kinsman's prejudices, so it is not surprising that he has little good to say about Albany. For the Albanians' side of the story, the reader may consult Thomas Elliot Norton, *The Fur Trade in Colonial New York* (University of Wisconsin Press, Madison, 1974) and the Minutes of the Commissioners of Indian Affairs, in the Canadian Archives. The Editor is grateful to Charles T. Gehring of the New Netherland Project at the New York State Library, for much advice on the Dutch in colonial New York, and for help with frontier pidgin.

There is no McDonner (or McDonough) in the *Johnson Papers*. It is possible that Captain Hardacre forgot, or deliberately misrepresented, the name of this low ruffian.

Johnson Country (Chapter 5)

Sir William Johnson still awaits a biographer worthy of the man. There are seven published biographies of varying degrees of reliability, all of which were consulted by the Editor. The earliest is William L. Stone, *The Life and Times of Sir William Johnson, Bart* (J. Munsell, Albany, 1865; 2 vols.); it contains some important documentary material destroyed in the fire at the State Capitol early in this century. The most fanciful is Augustus C. Buell, *Sir William Johnson* (Appleton, 1903). The most romantic are Arthur Pound (with Richard E. Day), *Johnson of the Mohawks* (Macmillan, New York, 1930), and James Thomas Flexner, *Mohawk Baronet* (Harper, New York, 1959). The most scholarly is Milton W. Hamilton, *Sir William Johnson: Colonial American, 1715–1763* (Kennikat Press, Port Washington, 1976), though it is flawed by the author's evident distaste for Johnson's "Indian dimension" and his personal life style. Hamilton's work is the first volume in a projected two-volume biography left unfinished by the author's death in 1988; the Editor is grateful to the Albany Institute of History and Art for allowing him access to the Milton Hamilton papers. Sir William's business practices and administrative style are analyzed in a number of unpublished dissertations. Among those the Editor found especially valuable are John Christopher Guzzardo, "Sir William Johnson's Official Family: Patron and Clients in an Anglo-American Empire" (Ph.D. dissertation, Syracuse University, 1975); Edith Meade Fox, "William Johnson's Early Career" (M.A. thesis, Cornell University, 1945); Charles Roscoe Canedy III, "An Entrepreneurial History of the New York Frontier, 1739–1776" (Ph.D. dissertation, Case Western Reserve University, 1967), and the first sections of Paul Lawrence Stevens, "His Majesty's 'Savage' Allies: British Policy and the Northern Indians During the Revolutionary War" (Ph.D. dissertation, SUNY Buffalo, 1984).

The best short introduction to Johnson's views on Indian policy is the memorial on the "State of the Nations" that he sent to the Lords of Trade on November 13, 1767 (NYCD 7: 572–81); the opinions that he expresses to Captain Hardacre are generally consistent with this and similar documents that will be found among his voluminous correspondence as detailed below.

Captain Hardacre's description of Fort Johnson is supported by *Fort Johnson: Historic Structure Report*, prepared for the Montgomery County Historical Society by the architectural firm of Mendel, Mesick, Cohen in 1977, and by more recent archaeological findings. There is a reference to "drawbridges," implying a moat, in a 1756 report on Sir William's defenses; see JP1: 85.

"Chicha" is better known to history as Molly Brant. There is confirmation for Captain Hardacre's revelation that this was Johnson's pet name for his Mohawk consort in a letter from Witham Marsh, the colonial secretary (JP11: 72). "Chicha" appears to be a variant spelling of the Mohawk *Ttitsa*, or "Flower," which is in turn a contraction of *Konwatsitsiaenni* ("They Are Sending Her Flowers"), the lady's Longhouse name. The narrator's physical description of Chicha will disappoint devotees of the Princess Tiger Lily school of romance. However, Daniel Claus, in his *Narrative of His Relations with Sir William Johnson and Experiences in the Lake George Fight* (Society of Colonial Wars, New York, 1904) plainly implies that she had suffered from smallpox. As for her abilities as a medicine woman, Mrs Simcoe relates how Chicha treated her husband, then the lieutenant-governor of Canada, with herbal remedies after the Revolution; see *The Diary of Mrs John Graves Simcoe*, ed. J. Ross Robertson (Toronto, 1911).

Apples and Flints (Chapter 6)

Like most white men on the colonial frontier, Captain Hardacre generally refers to Mohawks by English or Dutch nicknames, for which the reader may be thankful, given the difficulties of transliteration from an oral language. Some of the families he describes, rather cheekily, as Anglican Apples had already adopted European first names and surnames. The Brants are the best-known example. The author's description of their house on Nowadaga Creek (the name is a tautology since it is a garble of *okanawatake*, meaning "on the creek") is borne out by recent archaeological finds, as reported in exhaustive detail in David B. Guldenzopf's important thesis, "The Colonial Transformation of Mohawk Iroquois Society" (Ph.D. dissertation, SUNY Albany, 1986). The material prosperity of families like the Brants and the Hills of Fort Hunter is confirmed by the claims they made on the British government for losses in the American Revolution. Mary Hill put in a successful claim for £1,107; her son Captain Isaac Hill (Anoghsoktea) put in for £1,117. These were small fortunes by the standards of early white settlers. (See the Loyalist Claims in the Haldimand Papers, Public Archives of Canada.)

The Six Nations of the Iroquois Confederacy are (from east to west): the Mohawks, or Kanienkehaka (People of the Flint) whose League title is Keepers of the Eastern Door; the Oneidas (People of the Standing Stone); the On-

ondagas (People of the Mountain)—the Firekeepers of the
League; the Cayugas (People of the Mucky Lands); the
Senecas (Hill People), and the Tuscaroras, who moved
north from the Carolinas after 1712 and are not represented among the fifty *rotiyaner* who sit in the grand
council. In Johnson's time, the Confederacy had two acknowledged "council fires:" at Onondaga and at Sir William's home.

More has been written about Molly and Joseph Brant
than about any other Mohawks known to history. Much of
it, unfortunately, is largely fabricated. But honorable mention must be made of Isabel Thompson Kelsay's biography
Joseph Brant: Man of Two Worlds (Syracuse University
Press, 1984), the product of decades of love and learning,
and William L. Stone's dated but still valuable *Life of
Joseph Brant—Thayendanegea* (Alexander Blake, New
York, 1838; 2 vols.). *The Journal of Major John Norton*,
ed. Carl F. Klinck and James J. Talman (Champlain Society, Toronto, 1970), contains first-hand stories about the
Brants that offer further evidence for Shane's testimony
that Sir William's Mohawk consort was regarded in her
time as a powerful medicine woman.

Captain Hardacre offers many novel details. The allega-
tion that Chicha's mother, Margaret Brant, "stole" her
husband—Brant Canagaradunckwa—from another woman
is supported by the Reverend John Ogilvie's account of a
confession of adultery that he obliged the proud Margaret
to make in his church on February 17, 1754, one week before he received her into the Anglican communion. The
Editor is grateful to the staff of the New York State Library at Albany for access to Ogilvie's manuscript journal,
and much other primary material that supports Captain
Hardacre's account of the Mohawks at a time of transition.
The baptism of Chicha's younger sister Christina at Queen
Anne's chapel on January 26, 1742, is recorded in the
Reverend Henry Barclay's *Register*, consulted by the Edi-
tor at the New York Historical Society.

An interesting semi-fictional account of the Brants at an
earlier time, apparently based on Mohawk oral tradition,

will be found in Robert Moss's forthcoming book, *The Interpreter*.

To the Editor's surprise, he came across independent testimony to support Shane's salacious account of Johnson's arrangement with the two Wormwood sisters at the wondrously named Fish House. It will be found in Jephtha R. Simms's *Trappers of New York*, a delightful compendium of Valley gossip, first published in 1850 and recently reprinted—in a complete, unexpurgated edition—by Harmony Hill (Harrison, N.Y., 1980). Wormwood *père* figures in the *Johnson Papers*; he was one of the deponents who supported Sir William's litigation against Uri Klock.

Passage to Detroit and the Pompadour (Chapters 7–8)

Captain Hardacre's narrative of his journey to Detroit parallels Sir William's personal diary of his 1761 visit, preserved in JP13: 215–74. Our author's account of the Indian councils and of the personal role of Nickus Brant—including his efforts to intimidate other tribes on Johnson's behalf—is confirmed in substantial detail by the Indian Records in the Canadian Archives, for this period. See, for example, the August 10, 1761, entry, for an account of Brant's speech to the Senecas at Niagara; and the September 5 entry for the welcome from the Huron women. Typical of Indian supplications to Johnson was this speech by a Chippewa at Niagara: "You may observe the sun burns bright; I should be glad of a hat to defend me from its rays. I have been trying to catch fish in my hands . . . My gun is broke . . . For want of an axe, I have to make a fire at the root of the tree to get firewood" (Indian Records, July 28, 1761).

The Editor has personally traveled over much of Captain Hardacre's route to the west. Naturally, the landscape is vastly altered. Early descriptions of the roads to Oswego may be found in Benson J. Lossing, *The Pictorial Field-Book of the Revolution* (Carrazas reprint, New Rochelle, 1976; 2 vols.), and John J. Vrooman's *Forts and Firesides of the Mohawk Country* (Baronet Litho, Johnstown, 1951). On early Niagara, the Editor found useful material in

Frank H. Severance, *An Old Frontier of France* (Dodd, Mead, New York, 1917; 2 vols.), and in Brian Leigh Dunnigan, *History and Development of Old Fort Niagara* (Old Fort Niagara Association, Youngstown, 1985).

Sunfish, the free mulatto living in Seneca country, is mentioned in JP5: 795; 12: 386–87.

The naughty ballad Shane heard sung by a carpenter at Detroit and recorded in part originated as a *cantique spirituel* to the nurses of Madame Paris's celebrated bordello in the city whose name she bore. Connoisseurs of this genre will find a fuller version in E.J.F. Barbier, *Journal d'un Bourgeois de Paris sous le règne de Louis XV* (Union Générale d'Editions, Paris, 1963), pp. 216–17.

Father Pothier's friendliness towards the English at Detroit may have been related to the fact that Louis XV was in the process of suppressing the Jesuit order in France in 1761–62; the Superior Council in Louisiana issued an order expelling the Jesuits from that colony on July 9, 1763. The accounts and baptismal records of Pothier's mission at Detroit appear in *The Jesuit Relations and Allied Documents*, ed. Reuben Gold Thwaites (Burrows Brothers, Cleveland, 1896–1901; 73 vols.): JR70: 19–77.

The Cuilleriers, for several generations, were merchants of New France, established at Montreal before Angélique's immediate family moved west to Detroit. Antoine Cuillerier, *dit* Beaubien—Shane's "Dandy"—played an ambiguous role in the Conspiracy of Pontiac. In December 1763, a *habitant* named Jadeau told Major Gladwin that Cuillerier was one of a number of local Frenchmen who declined to risk their own necks by fighting with Pontiac, but urged the war chief to address himself to "300 Young men in the Settlement, who had neither Parents, nor much Property to lose" (Indian Records, Canadian Archives).

Sir William described dancing with "Miss Curie" until dawn in his Detroit journals (JP13: 251, 257). Angélique was keen for a return match; early in 1762, she was inquiring, via an English trader, whether Sir William was planning any more "summer councils" at Detroit. Disappointed in Johnson—and in Captain Hardacre?—she married James Sterling in 1765, after the revolt.

The names of the *habitants* Captain Hardacre encountered at Detroit generally conform with the registers in Christian Denissen, *Genealogy of the French Families of the Detroit River Region, 1701–1911*, ed. H.F. Powell (Detroit, 1976; 2 vols.), though some of his spellings—e.g., "Campau" for "Campeau", in chapter 15—may be contested. Like most colonial writers, our narrator tended to spell names the way they sounded to him.

The Editor has checked our narrator's physical descriptions of the fort and settlement at Detroit with various sources. One of the most useful is the *Journal of Chaussegros de Léry*, the French engineer who made a tour of the posts on the eve of the French and Indian War; the Pennsylvania Historical Commission issued roneoed copies of a translation edited by S.K. Stevens and Donald H. Kent (Harrisburg, 1940).

The island of Bois Blanc near the mouth of Lake Erie, where Captain Hardacre found Davers, was also the site of a small Huron settlement and a farm that supplied grain and fresh vegetables to the Jesuit mission; see JR69: 305–6.

The quotation from Molière's *Le Tartuffe* is from Act IV.

The Untamed and the Mohawk Scare (Chapters 9–10)

Joseph Brant returned to the Valley from Wheelock's school (the original Dartmouth College of Lebanon) in Connecticut in November 1762 in the company of Samuel Kirkland, the new Protestant missionary to the Oneidas. The dates correspond to Captain Hardacre's account of the origin of his friendship with the Mohawk who was later infamous across the American frontier as the leader of Tory and Indian war-parties during the Revolution.

Dream hunting—and propitiation of the hunted animal—are traditions of all native peoples whose spirit world is intact. For sensitive modern appreciations, see Barry Lopez, *Of Wolves and Men* (Scribner's, New York, 1978); Hugh Brody, *Maps & Dreams* (Pantheon, New York, 1982); Tom Brown, Jr. *The Tracker* (Berkley, New

York, 1979), and, from a South American culture, F. Bruce Lamb, *Wizard of the Upper Amazon* (Houghton Mifflin, Boston, 1974). There is a treasury of comparative material on this theme in the great Joseph Campbell's *The Way of the Animal Powers* (Alfred van der Maarck editions, Harper & Row, San Francisco, 1983). Elizabeth Marshall Thomas, *Reindeer Moon* (Houghton Mifflin, 1987), is a compelling fictional exploration of shamanism among prehistoric hunters.

Many medicine songs of *Okwari*—the Bear—survive among the Mohawks of the Six Nations (Ohsweken), Akwesasne, Kahnawake and Oka (Lac des Deux Montagnes) Reserves, to whom the Editor is grateful for much information about native culture and language. A hunting song to call the Bear from another native American culture is preserved in Francis LaFlesche, "The Osage Tribe: Rite of Vigil" in the *Annual Report of the Bureau of Ethnology* (Smithsonian, Washington, D.C., 1925), pp. 31–630.

On scent-lures used by woodland Indian deerhunters, see Frances Densmore, *Chippewa Customs* (Smithsonian, Washington, D.C., 1929). Joseph was probably smoking *aster novae angliae*, mixed with tobacco or red willow.

The Editor is grateful to Ray Gonyea, an Onondaga of the Beaver Clan and the native American specialist at the New York State Museum, for showing him the wampum belts formerly in the museum collection, one of which may be the Wolf Clan Mother's credentials mentioned by our narrator.

Captain Hardacre is reticent about his brush with Mohawk witchcraft. So is Sir William, in his vast correspondence, though this subject was evidently no mystery to him. Many other colonial authorities agree that the fear of witchcraft was pervasive among the Mohawks and the Six Nations in general. Writing to the Lords of Trade in 1700, Governor Bellomont reported that the chiefs of the Confederacy were convinced that the son of Aquendero, "chief sachem of the Onondaga Nation," had been struck down by witchcraft (NYCD4: 689). In 1724, Father Lafitau described a duel between a Mohawk shaman and an evil sorcerer (*Customs* 1:247–48). At the end of the century, Joseph Brant regaled his half-Scots, half-Cherokee protégé, John Norton, with tales of witches and ghosts (Norton *Journal*).

Shane evidently acquired some caution in the course of his unbuttoned experiences. Doubtless this explains why he nowhere describes the "false face" masks (*akakonsa*) that are a special feature of Iroquois medicine societies. The definitive treatment is William N. Fenton, *The False Faces of the Iroquois* (University of Oklahoma Press, Norman, 1987). The Editor is grateful to Dr Fenton, the doyen of ethnographers of the Iroquois, for many insights into Longhouse tradition.

"Fort" Klock, a freestone house north of St Johnsville, New York, is still intact. It is operated as a private museum; the owners kindly showed the Editor Klock family scrapbooks that confirm, *inter alia*, Captain Hardacre's version of the family motto.

Our narrator's version of the "Mohawk Scare" of 1762 is generally supported by the *Johnson Papers* and other colonial documents, but it is not clear from these that it began at Klock's; it appears to have been sparked a little farther up the river, at German Flats. Like his patron, Captain Hardacre clearly had it in for Uri (aka George) Klock, Sr, and may have been over-egging his case a little. The letters relating to this wretched episode that Shane attributes to Johnson, Amherst, and Captain Winepress—there truly was an officer of that name in the Albany garrison!—correspond almost exactly to surviving documents; see, for example, Johnson to Amherst (JP10: 477–78); Amherst to Johnson (JP10: 479; 488–89); Winepress to Johnson (JP3: 854–55).

Davers and the Prophet (Chapters 11–12)

Sir Robert Davers is the most curious of Captain Hardacre's "originals," and the source of a mystery the Editor has been unable to penetrate. A popular writer of recent times (Allan W. Eckert, in *The Conquerors*) has pronounced Sir Robert an "impostor," an idea that would undoubtedly have appealed to Davers, who regarded ordinary life as an imposture. But Davers was undoubtedly a real person, and a certified baron-knight. He was the fifth baronet of Rushbrook, the son of Sir Jermyn Davers who died in 1742, leaving him the title when he was only seven years old, and Margaretta Green. His mother was a melancholic, and two of his three brothers took their own lives while still in their twenties. There is a jumbled account of Davers and his family disease in Mrs Anne Grant's *Memoirs of an American Lady*. His genealogy is confirmed by the *Rushbrook Parish Registers, 1567 to 1850, with Jermyn and Davers Annals*, ed. S.H.A. Hervey (Woodbridge, Suffolk, 1903) and by the registers of the Bury St Edmunds and West Suffolk Record Office (MSS 941/63/6). There are several references to Davers in the *Johnson Papers* (JP3: 759; 4: 150 and 13: 271). He was certainly acquainted with Horace Walpole; he carried letters of recommendation from Walpole when he made the Grand Tour. The suggestion that Davers may have helped inspire *The Castle of Otranto*, however, is a novelty to the Editor. Lieutenant John Rutherfurd, who accompanied Davers on his last expedition, has left a vivid account of the ambush near Lake St Clair: "Rutherfurd's Narrative—An Episode in the Pontiac War" printed in the *Transactions* of the Canadian Institute (Toronto), 1891–92, pp. 229–52. However, Rutherfurd did not personally witness the manner of Davers's death. The mystery has to do with dates. In his private journal of his voyage to Detroit in 1761, Sir William Johnson notes an encounter with "Sir Robert Davis" at Three Rivers Rift on Tuesday, October 20, when the Superintendent was only a few days from home (JP13: 271). It is hard to reconcile this with Captain Hardacre's claim that he and Davers stayed at Fort Johnson together, prior to their departure for Detroit. Perhaps our author—who is, by his own confession, a dramatist *manqué*—has rearranged his cast a little, to give us the psychological drama of Sir William's confrontation with that creature of windy yearnings, in whom he may indeed have recognized a rejected aspect of his own self.

On the Prophet, the Editor has found only a handful of

Robert Moss

contemporaneous sources, all of them untrustworthy. The longest account of the "dream of the Prophet" is in the anonymous *Journal of Pontiac's Conspiracy*, written in French and generally (though probably mistakenly) attributed to Robert Navarre, a prominent *habitant* of Detroit. (The *Journal* has been published in a number of editions, including Milo M. Quaife, ed., *The Siege of Detroit in 1763*, Lakeside Press, Chicago, 1958). This version is full of expressions and metaphors that are alien to native American thought. The Moravian pastor John Heckewelder, in his *History, Manners and Customs of the Indian Nations* (Philadelphia, 1876), pp. 291–93, has no doubt that the Prophet was a Delaware living near the mouth of the Cuyahoga; he claims the visionary was prepared to sell copies of his famous dream-map for a buckskin or two apiece. The best description of the dream-map is in the diary of James Kenny, a Quaker merchant, who encountered the personage he describes as the "Delaware Impostor" in 1762. (Kenny's diary is printed in the *Pennsylvania Magazine of History and Biography*, Vol. 37, 1913, pp. 170–75). However, in Ottawa oral tradition, the Prophet is remembered as a "stranger from the east;" Pontiac's widow, who survived until 1803, believed he came from Canada. There are reports of an Abenaki "prophet," and a Seneca, and as Captain Hardacre recalls, the Onondaga spokesman annoyed Sir William at a council at Fort Johnson by quoting a member of his own nation who had visions. (Captain Hardacre's account closely corresponds to the exchange between Teyawirunte and Sir William at the council of September 8–10, 1762, as recorded in JP10: 505–56, 511.) No doubt several native revivalists were active at the same time. Every upheaval in Indian society has produced its great dream-hunters.

The Editor cannot pass judgement on the veracity of Captain Hardacre's version of the role of the Prophet and various magical practitioners in the revolt, let alone that of Davers, except to note that the *externals* of native shamanism, as recounted, generally conform with the reports of modern ethnographers, with other contemporary narratives of captivity, including Alexander Henry's *Travels and Ad-*

ventures, and with the wealth of information on shamans and sorcerers that may be gleaned from the treasury of material bequeathed by the blackrobes of New France. The *Jesuit Relations* have been the Editor's favorite reading during the years he has been engaged in this project, together with Father Joseph-François Lafitau's more concise *Moeurs des sauvages amériquains, comparées aux moeurs des premiers temps* (Saugrain aîné, Paris, 1724; there is an excellent two-volume English-language version, edited by William N. Fenton and Elizabeth L. Moore, published by the Champlain Society at Toronto in 1974). Those familiar with the Jesuit accounts will detect some curious resonances in Captain Hardacre's descriptions of native conjurers. When Father Pothier tells the author about his discussion of soul-flight with an unidentified shaman, his description strongly resembles the report of an earlier missionary, Father Buteux, who had a similar interview with a sorcerer at Tadoussac near the mouth of the St Lawrence (JR26: 125–27). This must be ascribed to coincidence, or that element of "hazard" in our lives that the narrator purports to value so highly.

Davers's sketch of the "lightning path" of the shaman agrees with shaman dream-maps of the Chippewas preserved in a remarkable nineteenth-century monograph by W.J. Hoffman: "The Midewiwin or Grand Medicine Society of the Ojibwa" in the *Seventh Annual Report of the Bureau of Ethnology* (Smithsonian, Washington, D.C. 1891), pp. 149–300.

As for the preliminaries to the Pontiac revolt, intelligence from Lieutenant Gorrell similar to that received by Captain Hardacre may be found in JP10: 698, 708, 711–12. James Sterling, in a June 1763 deposition, provides damning testimony on the complicity of Mini Chêne with the rebels (JP10: 692–94). The precise origin of the warning to Major Gladwin of an impending attack on the fort remains an open question with historians. There were other purveyors of intelligence not mentioned by Captain Hardacre. Thus a trader called Caesar Cormick (or McCormick) billed Gladwin on May 13, 1763, for £6.17.6 "to be paid a person for privet intelligence" (Amherst Papers,

Vol. 7, Clements Library). On a visit to Detroit in 1845, Parkman (in his *Conspiracy of Pontiac*) recalled a local tradition of "a Pawnee slave"—Davers's Pani?—who conveyed the intelligence. The legend of a "Chippewa squaw"—Sergeant Toole's mistress?—has remained popular with romancers. Yet Captain Hardacre's observation that one does not need second sight to realize that Indians do not file down muskets without a reason (a detail confirmed in the anonymous *Journal*) is surely telling.

The narrator's allusion to Marivaux, in connection with his stratagems of seduction, may recall Scene I of the French playwright's subtly metaphysical *La Dispute*.

Eating Fire and Pontiac's Daughter (Chapters 13–14)

Captain Hardacre's account of fire-torture and cannibalism in the Pontiac revolt is supported by other contemporary witnesses, most notably Lieutenant John Rutherfurd. The Rutherfurd narrative confirms many details in our author's account, including his description of how, following the murder of his nephew, Wasson, the chief of the Saginaw Bay Ojibwa, murdered Captain Donald Campbell and ate his heart. There is a brief entry on Wasson (c. 1730–76) in the invaluable *Dictionary of Canadian Biography, Vol. IV, 1771 to 1800* (University of Toronto Press, 1979), pp. 761–62.

The Jesuit Father Roubaud supplies a terrifying account of Ottawa cannibalism in the previous war (JR70: 125–27) that is supported by the diaries of Montcalm's aide; see *Adventures in the Wilderness: The American Journals of Louis Antoine de Bougainville*, trans. and ed. Edward P. Hamilton (University of Oklahoma Press, Norman, 1964), pp. 143–44.

Our narrator tries to put Indian cruelties in a larger perspective. Readers interested in pursuing his line of thought will find provocative material in Frederick Drimmer, ed., *Captured by the Indians: Fifteen Firsthand Accounts, 1750–1870* (Dover, New York, 1985); Nathaniel Knowles, "The Torture of Captives by the Indians of Eastern North America" in the *Proceedings of the American*

Philosophical Society, Vol. 82, No. 2 (1940), pp. 35–225, and in Georg Friederici, "Scalping in America" in the *Annual Report of the Bureau of Ethnology* (Smithsonian Institution, 1906), pp. 423–38.

The Editor has generally preserved Captain Hardacre's renderings of tribal names. The words "Chippewa" and "Ojibwa" are alternative spellings of a word with the root meaning "puckered up"—apparently a reference to the type of moccasins worn by this nation, but perhaps also to their treatment of captives! See William H. Keating, *Narrative of an Expedition to the Source of St Peter's River* (Carey & Lea, Philadelphia, 1824; 2 vols.), 2: 151. Today, the name Chippewa is generally applied to members of this large woodland nation living in the United States; Ojibwa to their kinsmen in Canada. Ojibwa speakers call themselves Anishinabe, which means roughly the same as the Mohawk Onkwehonwe—the Real (or Original) People.

The word "Ottawa" means "trader," a reference to the middle man role the tribe played in the fur trade, along the river road that bears its name in the seventeenth and early eighteenth centuries, after the Hurons were defeated and scattered by the Iroquois. Colonial French names for the Ottawas included Standing Hairs and *Courtes Oreilles*—Short Ears (Michigan Pioneer and Historical Society *Collections and Researches*, Lansing, 1877–1883; 40 vols.; see 8: 466; 10: 435; 11: 607).

The Editor has found no other documentary evidence that Pontiac had a daughter named Magid. However, this was a familiar Ottawa (and Ojibwa) version of Margaret. An Ottawa oral tradition—as reported to agents of Lewis Cass, whose Indian treaty at Maumee Rapids in 1817 was signed by an Ottawa who called himself "Pontiac"—maintained that Pontiac's widow, Kan-tuck-ee-gun, had borne him a daughter as well as one or more sons. In the 1940s, Howard Peckham interviewed a woman from Hessel, Michigan, who claimed descent from Pontiac. She told him that Pontiac had a son named Njikwisena, and a daughter whose name was not recalled. She also stated that Pontiac's "real name" was Tcimjikwis; see Howard H.

Peckham, *Pontiac and the Indian Uprising* (Princeton University Press, 1947), p. 317.

Bloody Bridge (Chapter 15)

The state of Detroit during the siege is well conveyed by the anonymous French *Journal*, Lieutenant Jehu Hay's manuscript diary and the varied primary accounts collected in Franklin B. Hough, ed., *Diary of the Siege of Detroit* (Albany, 1860). Alexander Henry's *Travels and Adventures in the Years 1760–1776*, ed. Milo M. Quaife (Lakeside Press, Chicago, 1921), provides a gripping narrative of what was going on simultaneously at Michilmackinac and on the northern front. The role of individual *habitants* of Detroit can be gleaned from the depositions collected by Major Gladwin and Captain Grant at the end of 1763—many of which are printed in the *Johnson Papers*—in the course of an investigation that resulted in the arrest of a number of Detroit traders (though not, it seems, Dandy Cuillerier) on charges of treason.

The Treaty of Paris, which ended the Seven Years' War, was concluded between Britain, France and Spain on February 10, 1763. Under its provisions, the French ceded Canada and all the territory east of the Mississippi, excepting New Orleans, to the British Crown; the Spaniards gave up their Florida territory, then known as West Florida. As always, news traveled slowly to the colonies. In the Province of New York, the first information about the treaty appeared in print in the *New York Mercury* on May 16, with a more detailed follow-up report on May 23. Thus it is not surprising that word did not reach the beleaguered frontier post of Detroit until July.

Our narrator's extraordinary tale of a Jewish trader's escape from torture-death is confirmed by a similar account in Heckewelder's *Customs and Manners*; Heckewelder thought his captors were Chippewas. Major Roberts's journal, printed in the *Diary of the Siege of Detroit*, confirms Shane's clear implication that they were Hurons. David E. Heineman in "The Startling Experience of a Jewish Trader During Pontiac's Siege of Detroit" (*Publications* of the

American Jewish Historical Society, No. 23, 1915), suggests that Chapman's first name was Nathan. There was at least one other Jewish trader—whose surname was Levy—in the region of Detroit at that time.

Captain Hardacre's account of Robert Rogers's strange passivity on the eve of the massacre at Bloody Bridge on July 31, 1763, will disappoint Major Rogers's many admirers. Some of them may conclude that Captain Hardacre was jealous of Rogers's military renown; they may be right. However, the author's account closely corresponds to that of a professional soldier, Major Alexander Duncan of the 55th, who sent a detailed report to Sir William that survives among his papers (JP10: 762–66).

Amherst's War (Chapter 16)

With this chapter, Captain Hardacre makes an excursus from his personal narrative, to pursue the famous feud between his patron Johnson and Sir Jeffrey Amherst. With some misgivings, the Editor has allowed passages to stand that may give offense to Sir Jeffrey's admirers, because they set the stage so clearly for the later development of Indian-white relations in North America and because—incredible though it may seem—the views attributed by Captain Hardacre to Amherst conform almost exactly with those expressed by the general in his official correspondence.

Thus Sir Jeffrey wrote of the need "to stop the very being" of the Indians in a letter to Johnson dated August 27, 1763 (NYCD7: 545). A number of other quotations, including the notorious exchange with Colonel Bouquet on infecting the natives with smallpox, have been checked in *The Papers of Col. Henry Bouquet*, ed. Sylvester K. Stevens and Donald H. Kent (Pennsylvania Historical Commission, Harrisburg, 1940–43; 17 vols.).

Sadly, Francis Parkman, the greatest historian of the revolt, idolized Amherst and shared his prejudices on the subject of Indians, of whom he wrote that "their intractable, unchanging character leaves no other alternative than their gradual extinction, or the abandonment of the Western world to eternal barbarism" (*Conspiracy* 2: 170).

Amherst denounced Johnson's plan to send Canada Indians against the rebels as "a dangerous expedient" (NYCD7: 566) and suggested in the same letter that the expenses of the Indian Department should be drastically cut, since so many Indians had turned against Britain.

Both Johnson and Croghan clearly foresaw the revolt Amherst dismissed as "mere bugbears" until it was upon him. A year before the uprising at Detroit, Sir William wrote to Croghan that the general's policy would end in disaster "but it is not in my power to convince the general thereof" (JP10: 652). In December 1762, Croghan warned Sir William that an Indian war was imminent, in his idiosyncratic English: "How itt may end the Lord knows, but I ashure you I am of opinion itt will nott be long before we shall have some croyles with them" (JP3: 964–66).

Croghan's kilt and the embarrassing leak in his belly are also mentioned in JP3: 987 and 4: 63. His doggerel tribute to Amherst is preserved in the Bouquet Papers and quoted in Nicholas B. Wainwright's excellent *George Croghan, Wilderness Diplomat* (University of North Carolina Press, Chapel Hill, 1959), p. 193.

The Mohawk pledge to stand with Johnson to the last man—against all comers—which Captain Hardacre views as the turning-point in the revolt is detailed in the Indian Records and in NYCD7: 534.

After his cursory farewell to Angélique Cuillerier, the author becomes strangely reticent about his private amours. This may have to do with the legal and other problems—including an attempt on his life—that arose from marital entanglements that he describes in the last pages as amounting to "trigamy."

The Editor suspects that one of Captain Hardacre's widows or relations has excised a number of sexual interludes from the later part of the narrative, no doubt because of their grossly explicit nature. The reader will surely require to know more in these free-spirited times. The Editor undertakes to bring the missing episodes to light if and when the manuscript sheets are located.

Black George and the Illinois (Chapter 17)

Croghan's embarrassment over the "Black Boys' " attack on his illicit convoy is the subject of lengthy correspondence in the *Johnson Papers*; see, for example, JP4: 717–18 and 11: 704.

Captain Hardacre's account of his journey to the Illinois, including the ambush on the Wabash and the correspondence with Saint Ange, conforms closely with George Croghan's 1765 manuscript journal, an excerpt from which is printed in NYCD7: 779–88. Differing views of Pontiac's role at this time are supplied by Lieutenant Alexander Fraser of the 78th (JP11: 743) and Colonel John Campbell of the 17th, commanding at Detroit (JP11: 744–45); Campbell used a Mohawk named Nicholas as a spy. In his journals, Colonel John Montresor claims that Saint Ange sent two war belts to the Illinois nations to foment the attack on Croghan's party (New York Historical Society *Collections*, New York, 1881, p. 332). Croghan reported the names of the slain Shawnees to his assistant, Alexander McKee (JP11: 846), and stressed the fact that they were not scalped (JP11: 855).

Croghan comments that "a thick Scull is of service on some Occasions" in a letter to William Murray in the *Illinois Historical Collections* 11: 58.

The etymology of Illinois tribal names is particularly obscure. James Mooney and William Jones in their essay in the *Handbook of American Indians* (Washington, D.C., 1907) suggest that "Kickapoo" derives from a term meaning "people who stand about in different places," although this is disputed by the contributors to the article on the Kickapoo in the 1978 *Handbook of North American Indians*, Vol. 15, *Northeast* (Smithsonian, Washington, D.C.). French colonial officials and missionaries referred to the Ouitanons, or Wea, as the *nation de la grue*, or Crane People.

The legend of the Shawnees and the Slug-Abeds is also recounted in Henry R. Schoolcraft, *Historical Information Respecting the Indian Tribes of the United States* (Lippincott, Grambo, Philadelphia, 1851–57; 6 vols.), 4: 253.

In the original of the Hardacre manuscript, as in the contemporary Indian Records, the name Shawnee is given as "Shawano;" the Editor has made the alteration for ease of recognition by modern readers. Both forms are a corruption of Shawanwa, meaning "Person of the South," according to Charles F. Voegelin, *Shawnee Stems and the Jacob P. Dunn Dictionary* (Indiana Historical Society, Indianapolis, 1938–40), 8: 381.

A minute of the surrender of Fort Chartres (in the neighborhood of La Prairie du Rocher, in Randolph County, Indiana) on October 14, 1765, appears in NYCD10: 161–65; it contains a detailed description of the buildings and fortifications which were so badly damaged when the Mississippi subsequently flooded its banks that the fort was abandoned in 1772.

The enigmatic Saint Ange, who plays a notable part in Captain Hardacre's narrative was a veteran officer of New France. Louis Saint Ange de Bellerive accompanied the famous traveler Father Charlevoix in his 1721 expedition, which suggests that he was not as youthful as our author makes him appear—or was remarkably well-preserved. He was an officer in Louisiana in the 1730s. He was commandant at Vincennes, on the Wabash, before 1764 (JR70: 317). His role in the French and Indian War is obscure, apart from Hardacre's account. Saint Ange succeeded Nyon de Villiers (the correct rendition of the name our author gives as "Neyon") at Fort Chartres in June 1764. He was still active on the Mississippi as late as 1772; cf. NYCD10: 1160 and John Francis McDermott, ed., *The Spanish in the Mississippi Valley, 1762–1804* (University of Illinois Press, 1974). He died at St Louis on December 26, 1774 (JR70: 316–17).

The secret treaty by which France transferred ownership of Louisiana to Spain—with results that color our narrator's fortunes so vividly in the penultimate chapter—was signed on November 5, 1762. The French inhabitants were not informed of this treaty until September 10, 1764, when Governor Jean-Jacques Baptiste d'Abbadie received sealed orders from Paris. He died before the first Spanish governor of Louisiana, Don Antonio de Ulloa, arrived to take up his post on March 5, 1766.

The Lost Kingdom (Chapter 18)

Captain Hardacre's account of Sir William Johnson's medical condition in 1769 possibly understates the seriousness of his disorders. In his letters, Johnson frequently complains of the leg injury he received climbing from a boat near Onondaga (cf. JP7: 94–95, 118–19, 120–21). He was one of the first white men to visit the hot springs later fashionable as Lebanon Springs (cf. JP5: 685, 840–41, 12: 545). There are many references to Johnson's visit to New London and Block Island with Croghan in the spring of 1768, which our author holds to have done such damage (cf. JP6: 205, 221). Sir William offered the following description of the general state of his health to Samuel Johnson in December 1767: "The Ball which was Lodged in my thigh at the Battle of Lake George becomes daily more troublesome to me, insomuch that I can very rarely attempt to Sit on a Horse or take my usual Exercise, and [I suffer from] a Disorder which is much more Dangerous & troublesome to describe, as the Doctors are at a Loss what to call it. It first attacked me in 1761, put me to the most Excruciating torture, during which I became delirious, its duration was about 4 or 5 days, since which Time I have had Several returns of the Like, sometimes thrice in a Year but a Very irregular and uncertain periods. It seems seated near the stomach, which swells much during the Paroxysm of the Disorder attended with a Jaundiced Countenance, the Eyes being particularly discoloured."

Given his physical condition, it is not only less surprising that Sir William allowed himself to be imposed on by Croghan, who presumably assumed part of his workload; it is impressive that Johnson was able to carry on at all in his immensely exacting office.

Johnson got his county, though not his manor. (On Cadwallader Colden's advice to him to be more "modern," see JP12: 699). It was organized in 1772 as Tryon County (in honor of the new governor). It did not survive the Revolution.

The "crannog" referred to was an artificial island in the grounds of Johnson Hall, one of the best-maintained historical sites in the State of New York.

The minutes of the Fort Stanwix treaty conference, in the Indian Records in the Canadian Archives, generally confirm Captain Hardacre's summary. Wainwright's biography of Croghan contains a shrewd discussion of the shady side-deals. Johnson's personal apologia (to General Gage) for his dealings at Stanwix will be found in JP7: 81–84.

A hard-nosed analysis of the Kayderosseras swindle and related land-grabs, offering many details that Captain Hardacre glosses over, is Georgiana C. Nammack, *Fraud, Politics and the Dispossession of the Indians: The Iroquois Land Frontier in the Colonial Period* (University of Oklahoma Press, Norman, 1969). Sir William never succeeded in squashing Uri (George) Klock's claims.

Johnson's correspondence contains numerous intelligence reports of renewed Indian trouble on the western frontier after the Stanwix treaty. He expressed high alarm to General Gage about the risk of a new uprising on May 26, 1769, about the time that Captain Hardacre apparently returned to the Valley (JP6: 776–77).

Sir William's quoted opinions on how the Indians were despised in peace may be compared with a letter from him that appears in NYCD7: 836.

Captain Hardacre appears to be the sole authority for the statement that Joseph Brant accompanied him to the Mississippi in 1769. Who is the Editor to quibble with a man who was there?

Escape to New Orleans (Chapter 19)

Pierre Chouteau (1758–1849), a Frenchman who lived on the Illinois, also claimed that Pontiac's Indian murderer was suborned by a British trader. Differing accounts of his version of the event appear in Parkman's *Conspiracy* and in an earlier nineteenth-century essay by J.N. Nicollet, *Report Intended to Illustrate a Map of the Hydrographical*

Basin of the Upper Mississippi River (Washington, D.C., 1841). Chouteau gave this Englishman's name as Williamson. An Alexander Williamson was engaged by Baynton, Wharton—Croghan's partners and creditors—to take a cargo to Post Vincent (Vincennes) on the Wabash in 1768; he was expected to winter at the post. Howard Peckham, in his generally admirable *Pontiac and the Indian Uprising* (Princeton University Press, 1947), p. 310, judges the Chouteau report to have been "propaganda started by the Peorias and spread by the French." Captain Hardacre's account may open a new perspective.

It is interesting to note that a *premature* report of Pontiac's death, sent by General Gage to Johnson in the summer of 1768, asserted that he had been killed by an Illinois Indian "excited by the English" (JP12: 54). After the genuine murder, Gage stated that Pontiac was slain by "one of our friendly Indians" (JP7: 76).

The most detailed independent account of Pontiac's murder is the manuscript "Memoire" of Daniel Blouin, a French merchant at Kaskaskia. It contains a devastating indictment of Lieutenant-Colonel John Wilkins, the British commandant at Fort Chartres; it is in the General Thomas Gage Papers at the William L. Clements Library.

Cahokia, the scene of the murder, is now East St Louis.

Wilkins's instructions for Pontiac's burial are in his manuscript "Journal of Indian Transactions," also in the Gage Papers. Local tradition in St Louis has long held that the French were permitted to carry Pontiac's body across the river for burial. Captain Hardacre confirms this, as did Lieutenant Jehu Hay, in an August 1769 letter in which he reported to Sir William that he had met a Frenchman who was "an inhabitant of St Louis and the person that buried Pontiac, who was (interred?) at his house" (JP7: 94). The exact place of Pontiac's burial is still contested. The Missouri Historical Society once maintained that the exact site is twenty feet east of Broadway and fifty feet south of Market, which would have placed it behind the settlement as it was laid out in 1769; see Walter B. Stevens, *St Louis the Fourth City* (St Louis, 1909).

The panic among English soldiers and traders at Fort

Chartres after Pontiac's murder is vividly conveyed by a
merchant named Edward Cole, who escaped downriver in
a style similar to that of our narrator; see JP7: 15–16.

Captain Hardacre's description of the execution of the
creole rebels in the Place d'Armes (now Jackson Square) at
New Orleans agrees with the vivid accounts in George W.
Cable, *The Creoles of Louisiana* (Scribner's, New York,
1884)—which contains a portrait of Captain-General
O'Reilly—in Herbert Asbury's delightful book *The French
Quarter* (Garden City, New York, 1938) and in Lyle Saxon,
Fabulous New Orleans (Appleton, New York, 1937).

Captain Hardacre's good fortune in hitting it off with the
remarkable Don Alexandro O'Reilly may be connected not
only with the fact that they were fellow-Irishmen, but with
the captain-general's eagerness to come to an understanding
with the Indians. In October 1769, O'Reilly entertained the
chiefs of nine tribes at New Orleans with a sense of theater
that must have delighted our narrator, who may have helped
inspire the ceremonials. O'Reilly festooned the sachems
with medals on scarlet ribbons, knighted them with his bare
sword, made occult signs over their heads, and gave them
copious embraces; cf. Lawrence Kinnaird, ed., *Spain in the
Mississippi Valley, 1765–1794* (Washington, D.C., 1946–49;
3 vols.), 1: 101–2.

The Wax Sybil (Chapter 20)

Captain Hardacre's account of Joseph Brant's visit to London in 1776 in supported by Boswell, who met the Mohawk war chief at a ball at the Haberdashers' Hall and
interviewed him over tea two days later for an article that
he published in the *London Magazine* (July 1776). There
is a gossipy account of the Mohawk's reception at St
James's Court in the *London Chronicle* of March 1 of the
same year. Ethan Allen, so ungraciously depicted by Captain Hardacre, describes his confinement on the *Adamant*
and his maltreatment by Guy Johnson in *Allen's Captivity,
Being a Narrative of Colonel Ethan Allen, Containing His
Voyages, Travels, &c* (Boston, 1845), pp. 42–45. The incident with the raised war club at the Pantheon is described

in Stone's *Life of Brant* 2: 258–60, but is associated by that author with a later visit by Joseph to London. Perhaps Captain Hardacre has conflated two separate episodes in his sometimes erratic memory. A rout at the Pantheon attended by Joseph after the American Revolution is vividly described in the (London) *Gazetteer and New Daily Advertiser*, March 1, 1786.

The remarkable Mrs Patience Wright—the Wax Sybil—is the subject of an excellent scholarly biography, *Patience Wright: American Artist and Spy in George III's London*, by Charles Coleman Sellers (Wesleyan University Press, Middleton, Conn., 1976). It appears that Captain Hardacre does not exaggerate in his description of Mrs Wright's "under-the-apron performances," her politics—she was at the center of a plot to overthrow the king in 1780—or her pretended clairvoyant powers.

Captain Hardacre's quotation from Thomas Tryon is from his *Treatise of Dreams and Visions* (London, 1695), which together with Robert Burton's *Anatomy of Melancholy* (London, 1652)—from which several citations in the book, in English and Latin, are culled without attribution—must have been bedtime reading for Sir Robert Davers; the Editor has used the three-volume New York edition of Burton, published by W.J. Widdleton in 1870.

There is no record of Captain Hardacre's funeral in the registry of St George's Church, Hanover Square, and the Editor cannot rule on the truth of his scurrilous innuendoes about Dr Dodd, sometime chaplain to George III. Dr Dodd was an ecclesiastical dandy who fell into disgrace when it was alleged he attempted to buy himself a handsome living (at St George's) by simony; one account of this scandal is Percy Fitzgerald, *A Famous Forgery, Being the Story of "the Unfortunate Dr Dodd"* (London, 1865).

As for Captain Hardacre's return to his old stamping-grounds, and his adventures during what he offensively terms "the American Mutiny," the Editor harbors a number of suspicions, but will keep them to himself unless another folio of the author's memoirs comes to light.

POSTSCRIPT

Valerie D'Arcy's letters arrived at the Editor's door in a tea-chest, smelling strongly of the Irish Breakfast blend they must have recently displaced. With some misgivings, the Editor has interleaved this correspondence with the chapters of the original Hardacre narrative at the appropriate points, taking every effort to avoid disrupting the flow. Though Lady D'Arcy first met the narrator long after the events described in the book, and can have no first-hand knowledge of those events, her sometimes acerbic commentary on Shane's behavior and attitudes, especially towards women, may be of interest to readers. Her dream experiments and her investigation of the modern founder of hypnosis—in collusion with Benjamin Franklin—reflect an adventurous and well-educated mind.

Of Lady D'Arcy herself, it has been possible to verify few solid facts, though her second husband, Sir Henry D'Arcy, is well-known in the annals of the East India Company. From the internal evidence of her letters, Valerie was of mixed Irish and French descent, and was raised on a planter's estate in the French colony of Ste Domingue before the bloody slave uprising. She was considered something of a beauty in her day, and took special pride in her blazing-red hair. She left Sir Henry without seeking a divorce before the end of 1805, leaving him with three children. All records of her cease at this time. Perhaps more will be discovered if the rest of the papers that were placed in her trust ever come to light.

The presence of several glaring anachronisms in Valerie's epistolary style and her understanding of events may lead perceptive readers to suspect a literary hoax. Unfortunately, the Editor is not at liberty to make inquiries on this front. He is strictly advised that if the record of Shane's further adventures is ever released to the public, it will be through the same channel that supplied Valerie's letters.

It seems that at least one of the women in Shane Hardacre's life has exacted posthumous revenge on our hero.

R.M.